**JAIMIE ADMANS** is a 35-year-old English-sounding Welsh girl with an awkward-to-spell name. She lives in South Wales and enjoys writing, gardening, watching horror movies, and drinking tea, although she's seriously considering marrying her coffee machine. She loves autumn and winter, and singing songs from musicals despite the fact she's got the voice of a dying hyena. She hates spiders, hot weather, and cheese & onion crisps. She spends far too much time on Twitter and owns too many pairs of boots.

She will never have time to read all the books she wants to read.

Find out more on www.jaimieadmans.com or find her on Twitter @be_the_spark

## Also by Jaimie Admans

*The Château of Happily-Ever-Afters*
*The Little Wedding Island*
*It's a Wonderful Night*
*The Little Vintage Carousel by the Sea*
*Snowflakes at the Little Christmas Tree Farm*
*The Little Bookshop of Love Stories*
*The Little Christmas Shop on Nutcracker Lane*

# The Wishing Tree Beside the Shore

## JAIMIE ADMANS

ONE PLACE. MANY STORIES

HQ
An imprint of HarperCollins*Publishers* Ltd
1 London Bridge Street
London SE1 9GF

www.harpercollins.co.uk

HarperCollins*Publishers*
1st Floor, Watermarque Building, Ringsend Road
Dublin 4, Ireland

This paperback edition 2021

1

First published in Great Britain by
HQ, an imprint of HarperCollins*Publishers* Ltd 2021

Copyright © Jaimie Admans 2021

Jaimie Admans asserts the moral right to be
identified as the author of this work.
A catalogue record for this book is
available from the British Library.

ISBN: 9780008466916

MIX
Paper from
responsible sources
FSC
www.fsc.org FSC˚ C007454

This book is produced from independently certified FSC™ paper
to ensure responsible forest management.

For more information visit: www.harpercollins.co.uk/green

Printed and bound in Great Britain by
CPI Group (UK) Ltd, Croydon, CR0 4YY

*For Marie Landry.*
*This book wouldn't exist without you, for so many*
*reasons.*
*Thank you for being a light in the darkness every day.*
*Caru chi!*

# Chapter 1

How can one man have so much dry-cleaning?

I hold the array of garment bags above my head as I step out of the tube train and go in the direction of the escalators. The platform is crammed even in the middle of the day and I can't see where I'm going, so I've got a fair fifty-fifty chance of making it to the escalators or tumbling onto the tracks, which really would be the cherry on top of what was supposed to be my lunch break but has actually been spent arguing with a dry-cleaner who couldn't grasp that a sequinned evening dress was *not* the designer suit my boss made me drop off last week and took half an hour to find the correct dry-cleaning while I leaned against a washing machine and stuffed my sandwich down my throat amid looks dirtier than the laundry from customers and the tonsil-clenching acrid dust cloud from multiple sprinklings of laundry powder.

Even while trying to keep the bottoms of the garment bags off the floor, I tread on one and yank it taut, accidentally tripping over it and stumbling into a grumpy-looking man who turns and growls – actually growls – at me. I mumble an apology and try to fold the bags over my arm as I finally make it to the escalator and grip the side gratefully. The growling man is on the step above me and he turns around to give me another glare and I involuntarily take a step back and accidentally tread on someone's toe. As I turn around to apologise profusely, the garment bags slip and get caught between the moving stairs, causing the entire escalator to let out a loud grinding noise as it hits the zip and judders to a halt with such a jarring screech of metal-on-metal that it's almost as loud as the collective groan that goes up from the other passengers around me. I shrink into the side, trying to protect my boss's trapped dry-cleaning, until the station staff finally close off the escalator and an engineer comes to cut the garment bags loose and repair the escalator while muttering about idiots trying to carry too much.

It feels like hours later when I finally emerge into the afternoon sunshine and hurry down the busy street towards the grey and foreboding office block, managing to keep the garment bags off the floor and only bump into a record number of people. Once I get into the building and through the foyer, I eye the lifts to take me up to the fourteenth floor but quickly think better of it. The way my day is going, there's absolutely no way it *won't* get stuck. The stairs it is.

I regret the decision by the time I've made it up two flights, never mind the next twelve. It's early August and the London heat is stifling. By the time I eventually crawl out of the stairwell, sweat is dripping down my face and there are wet patches under both arms, which makes me *extra* glad I wore a lilac shirt today. I've produced enough moisture that each plastic garment bag is stuck to me like someone's liberally coated them in Pritt Stick.

I daren't look at my watch. I'm going to be so lat—

'Felicity!'

I know that tone in my boss's bellow. I *am* late.

*Conference room three*, I repeat over and over in my head. My boss has got an important meeting this afternoon and being late will be another notch on the ever-increasing list of ways I've annoyed him lately. I keep my head down and pick up my pace as I hurry down the hallway, throw open the door of the conference room, tread on the bottom of a garment bag and trip myself up. I go careening into the room and land with a splat on top of the plastic and skid along like I'm on a home-made water slide.

'Ah, there you are.' My boss, Harrison, appears in the doorway behind me, looking down disdainfully while twirling his curly moustache around a pen. 'I was waiting for you in the office but I see you've decided to barrel straight in. How nice of you to make time for work in your busy schedule.'

Harrison strides into the room, sidestepping me so expertly that it seems like flailing around on the floor is a regular occurrence.

'Sorry, gents.' He addresses the group of business-suited men around the long table, who are looking down at me with sneers on their haughty faces.

At least they can't tell how embarrassed I am because my face is already red with heat and dripping with sweat as I pant to get my breath back and push myself upright.

Harrison uses his pen to point to a chair behind him like he's training a dog to go round an obstacle course. I consider wagging my tail and offering him my paw, but the group of businessmen look like they're in no mood for jokes.

I stumble to my feet and sink gratefully into the hard plastic chair, and after all the effort of keeping the garment bags smooth and straight, I drop them to the floor and kick them underneath, like if I can somehow hide them, all the embarrassment they've caused will go away.

I don't even know why I'm here. It's not like I bring anything to these meetings. Well, apart from the tea and coffee. That's my job – sit at the edge of the room, take notes of anything my boss might need to remember, and also magically divine exactly what sort of things he might need to remember and usually get it wrong. I also refill anyone's water glass when it looks a bit empty, and offer refreshments if there's a lull in conversation or if a

PowerPoint presentation stalls. A monkey could do my job, but a monkey would consider itself better qualified.

There's something intimidating about the office being full of businessmen wearing suits that cost more than my yearly rent, with their smooth, slick hair that's never so much as a breath out of place and the overpowering smell of their eye-wateringly expensive cologne – both eye-watering *and* expensive. I can't tell the difference between the seven men sitting around the table – they could be the same man cloned. They've all got the same beady eyes, like they're constantly looking out for the next money-making opportunity. People like me may as well not exist. As far as they're concerned, despite my unmissable entrance, Harrison is the only person who's walked into the room.

Which is probably a good thing considering I'm still so hot that I must be glowing, and not in a good way. In a sticky way, my face is so red that I feel like a lighthouse with a pulsing light on top, warning ships to stay away.

Despite being told to sit down like a naughty dog that's just rolled in something nasty, I'm grateful to have a chance to rub the sweat out of my eyes and take a few minutes to try to regain some composure. I like that term. "Regain" makes it sound like I ever had any in the first place.

I have no idea what the meeting is about and I've forgotten who it's with, but it's some *very* important client in the property development business, and this meeting is to secure a site that will be the first of many if it goes well. It's one in a long line of meetings that are duller than actual dishwater – a regular occurrence when you work in the property acquisitions department of Landoperty Developments. We source land with development potential for big businesses who want to expand. Businesses come to us saying what they want to open and my boss finds a good area for them; alternatively my boss finds areas with untapped potential – like a busy tourist area that doesn't have a café or a bar – we acquire it and then pitch it to businesses who might be interested in opening there. Usually they snap my boss's hand off in their rush to accept and there's often a bidding war over who gets to buy the space.

Something's gone wrong with this one though. Harrison keeps muttering something about protesters and has groaned every time he's looked at his computer in the last couple of weeks. I don't blame protesters for protesting. We see so many beautiful, natural areas, and it always seems wrong to buy them up and sell them off to the highest bidder. I don't know how I ended up in this job. It's been four years since I started here, and still the only promotion I've ever had is being given a bigger desk.

I was hoping to work my way up from being an assistant – to prove my worth, and maybe one day, get projects of my own and get to travel the UK to scout locations for clients. I'd get to go out to sites in the beautiful Scottish Highlands or the Cornish coast and oversee sales of land and development. I picture myself striding along a beach with a clipboard and a hard hat ... I don't know why I picture either of those things because everyone uses tablets instead of clipboards these days, and our firm is out of the picture long before any construction begins so there'd be no need for a hard hat, but it's a nice fantasy. It makes me feel like I could be important one day, and it's more interesting than listening to my boss drone on about protestors.

There's a little side table beside me, and the intern responsible for filling the drinks has thought to put out a box of tissues, so I surreptitiously reach over to grab one and try to mop my forehead, which is still prickling with sweat. I can feel it sliding down my spine and pooling at the base of my back. I'm going to stick to this chair if I try to get up. I make a squelching noise as I reach across, and the businessman nearest to me looks up. I freeze like a wild rabbit when you put the outside light on, like if I stay still, he somehow won't notice me. It's completely normal for assistants to sit in on meetings while striking a pose with a tissue in their hand as sweat drips casually down their face. He gives me the kind of look he'd give a bluebottle buzzing around the fruit bowl and looks back at the folder on the table in front of him.

Sweat chooses that moment to drip into my eyes, and I suck in a breath as it stings, causing the businessman to frown in my direction again. The bluebottle would probably be less annoying. At least he could squirt a fly with Raid. He can't do that to me. With a bit of luck, anyway. I didn't think this day could get much worse but a quick blast of Raid would certainly finish the job.

They must think I'm so unfit. Despite the smog and oppressive heat in the city today, the two fans at the other end of the room are not plugged in, and the sun is hitting the glass windows and turning everything inside into such a roasting greenhouse that we could grow coconuts and oranges indoors if we were so inclined, but not one of them looks hot or sweaty or uncomfortable in the slightest, and those wool-silk suits are *heavy*.

I mop my forehead yet again and while my boss is still going on about protestors and no one's looking at me, I undo a button that's stretching apart over my boobs and slip my hand inside my shirt, trying to reach across to an armpit to mop those as well.

And then one of the businessmen mentions "Lemmon Cove". The words break through the overheated haze in my brain. Lemmon Cove is a place I try to think about as little as possible. Its name doesn't belong in a London business meeting. One of the main reasons I live here is because it's about as far as you can physically get from Lemmon Cove without crossing the channel.

'That's my hometown.'

Not only have I interrupted a Very Important Businessman, but I've got one arm behind my head and the other through the gap in my shirt, trying to mop up the opposite armpit with a disintegrating tissue. I am clearly the image of professionalism and poise.

Usually when I say something stupid, I know it was stupid before the words have finished leaving my mouth, but this time it takes a good few seconds for my brain to catch up. Seven pairs of smarmy eyes turning sharply in my direction also tips me off.

'You're *from* Lemmon Cove?' One of the businessmen leans forward.

'Er … yes?' I sound decidedly unsure. This seems like something I might need to backpedal on fairly soon.

'That's fantastic.'

'It is?' No one has been this interested in anything I've had to say for years. It doesn't feel fantastic. And from the predatory way one of them has started licking his lips, I think that back-pedalling should start right about now.

I also *really* wish I'd been paying attention and had a clue what I was interrupting *before* I interrupted it. 'Well, not really, I've been living here for as long as I can remember … Lemmon Cove was a long time ago. I almost never go back there at all now …'

I may as well be on mute. I don't think any of them has heard a word since "hometown".

'Well, this changes things.' One of them bangs his hand on the table. 'Why didn't you tell us you had an "inside man", Harrison?' He glances at me. 'Apologies, an inside *woman*.'

'I'm not an in—'

Harrison's head whips round so fast that I'm sure the first thing on my afternoon to-do list will be to make him an appointment with a chiropractor to fix his neck. I know his "shut up, Felicity" look well enough to stop talking. Why couldn't this meeting have been the one I chose to pay attention in? Why didn't I think blurting out that Lemmon Cove was my hometown might be a bad idea? And what on earth is all this about protestors? Protestors in Lemmon Cove? Last time I checked, the population of Lemmon Cove is tiny and they don't admit anyone under the age of ninety. Preferably older.

'This is brilliant, Harrison.' One of the businessmen sips his coffee and raises the cup in a toast.

'Innovative,' another one says.

'Sneaky and underhanded,' another one adds. 'Just the sort of people we like to deal with.'

I think that must be sarcasm, but the look on his face is completely serious.

Brilliant, innovative, sneaky, underhanded … All words that have never been associated with me before. What *is* going on here?

Harrison is trying to give me a conspiratorial wink over his shoulder. Or he needs that chiropractor more urgently than I thought. 'I was about to introduce you to my assistant, Felicity Kerr … when she's finished groping herself.'

As if my cheeks could get any redder. I'd completely forgotten my hand was still under one armpit and I go to yank my arm out of my shirt, but it gets caught and as I pull to free it, a button pings off and skitters across the room, leaving my shirt gaping open, showing my bra. It's not even a good bra. It's a comfortable old bra that had seen better days many moons ago, but it's not easy to find a comfortable bra so I tend to hang on to them until the last thread frays, and this one doesn't have many threads left.

I clear my throat, smooth my hair down and hunch my shoulders, trying to close the bra-level gap in my shirt buttons without overtly holding it closed and drawing more attention. These businessmen do not need any *more* reasons to look at me when their menacing eyes are already making my armpits prickle with more sweat.

I get the feeling Harrison is delaying while he tries to formulate a plan. There's something panicked in his eyes that says my interruption has caught him completely off-guard.

'My secret weapon,' he states eventually.

I am no one's secret weapon.

'When I implied that I could acquire this land for you, gentlemen, I had of course hoped we wouldn't need the assistance of Felicity, but these protestors aren't giving up, so I thought now was the time to bring in our undercover man. Er, woman.'

I've got to give him points for improvisation because until a few minutes ago, he didn't have the foggiest idea where I came from. He could probably have narrowed it down to somewhere in Wales, because even he is observant enough to notice my Welsh accent.

The businessmen clap. For me. The most one of Harrison's businessmen has ever done for me before is condescendingly ask if I'd like to get myself a cup of water when I coughed in a meeting once.

Why didn't I pay attention to this meeting before now? "Undercover man" sounds suspiciously like someone might expect me to go back there. To Lemmon Cove. The only time I go there is to see my father and sister at Christmas and special occasions, and those visits are planned with military accuracy. I get a late-night train down, spend never more than a day with my family, and leave that night, always under the cover of darkness, so there's never a chance of running into *him*.

Ryan Sullivan. The guy I was in love with. The guy who broke my heart. The guy who might not even still live there. Who probably doesn't still live there. The guy I never want to see again to find out.

I'm going to be honest and tell them I don't know what they're on about, but Harrison holds up a preventative hand. 'Felicity, a word outside, please. As you were so late today, we didn't have time to reiterate our plan. Excuse us, gents.' With two swift finger jerks, he indicates for me to follow him into the hallway and the chair makes squelching noises as I unstick my body from it, silently seething at being yet again blamed for causing a gap in some fictional idea he's made up on the spot.

'This is brilliant, Felicity.' The door closes with a click behind him and he ushers me along the corridor, away from any chance of being overheard. 'I wish you'd mentioned it before.'

'Mentioned what? Being from Lemmon Cove? Since when are you interested in where I'm from?'

'I'm not, unless you happen to be from a village where I've promised those chaps the acquisition of a plot of land, and my plans have been scuppered by protestors.'

'What? What village? What protestors? What land?' I can feel myself starting to panic. I can *not* go back there. I haven't been back there, not properly, for fifteen years.

Harrison raises an eyebrow at how much attention I've been paying to this project. I knew he was looking at land for a hotel company in Wales, but Wales is a big place. How was I supposed to know he was looking at land on the South Wales Gower coastline where I grew up?

'This is a real "in" for us. A game changer for that lot in there …' He starts pacing up and down, clicking his fingers as he formulates a plan that I already know I'm not going to like. 'You're exactly what we need. You have family there, don't you?'

'Yes.' I can't deny it, and I'm impressed that he's remembered me mentioning going to visit family on days off. 'My dad and little sister. But I don't see them often. It's a *long* way, and—'

'Then it'll be a wonderful chance to visit, won't it?'

'I'm not going to—'

I'd be fired if I cut people off as much as he does.

'This is exactly what we need,' he continues. 'This protest is getting out of hand. We need someone to go in and pour water on the flames, and who better than you? You're one of *them*. A local. You've got a family connection to the area.'

'I have no connection whatsoever to—'

'You can earn their trust from the inside out. Find out what their plans are. Gently persuade them that their time would be better spent playing bingo and doing jigsaw puzzles while eating prunes and having blue rinses or whatever it is old people like to do.'

'What?' I say again. I really am failing to grasp what he's getting at.

10

'Care home residents, Felicity. Those men in there are all set to buy a big chunk of land in Lemmon Cove, on the clifftops above the beach, but the grounds currently belong to a care home. It's all overgrown and no one's used it for years, but as soon as the owner decided to sell it, the residents took it upon themselves to object and suddenly it's this all-important garden for them even though no one's set a house-slippered foot out there since the days when woolly mammoths were roaming it.'

'Right,' I say slowly. There are a few care homes in Lemmon Cove that overlook the beach. That doesn't narrow it down.

'They're all out there with their placards every day. They're playing the environment card, but they're being stirred up by some youngster who owns a nearby campsite, so there's clearly an ulterior motive because a campsite would be impacted by a state-of-the-art hotel across the road. No more slumming it in tents for all the tourists who visit the area. This youngster is using his adorable team of old biddies to save his own business. It's exploitation.'

Campsite? Since when is there a campsite in Lemmon Cove? And Harrison is not one to lecture on exploitation – he's a cut-throat businessman who will exploit every opportunity he can.

'One of the old biddy protestors has discovered how to use Twitter for their cause … Well, she hasn't really discovered how to use it because she keeps tweeting random things that aren't supposed to be tweets, like that time Ed Balls tried to do a search for his own name and it became known as Ed Balls Day. She keeps posting photos of the bottom of a Zimmer frame and blurry ground where she's accidentally pressed the camera button and tweeting things like "What do you do with a courgette?" and "What IS a courgette?" and "Is a courgette the same as a zucchini?"'

'So it's all very vegetable-based then?'

'You can laugh, but the public are falling in love with this technically challenged old bat. Her tweets are getting more and more likes and retweets, and it's only a matter of time until she

11

goes completely viral and the national news agencies pick up the story, and our clients don't want to be known as the heartless hotel magnates who threw a load of old biddies out of their garden.'

'Why are they doing it then? Some of those care homes don't have much garden space at all. The paths down to the beaches are too steep for the residents, so the garden is the only way they can enjoy the view. You can't plonk a hotel outside their windows.'

'That's for the owner to decide, and the owner's decided that no one's using the land and he wants a chunk of money for it. There's untapped tourist potential because there's nowhere in the area for civilised people to stay – a campsite doesn't count – and now all these old folks are rioting and it's gaining traction. Not the sort of publicity we want getting out, you know?'

'You've dealt with protestors before. You usually just get the police in.'

'Local police are in their pockets, I reckon. They've given an excuse about not having a legal right to turf them out when some of the protestors are chained to trees.'

I snort at the idea of anything so lively happening in Lemmon Cove, but I quickly realise he's not joking. 'They're chained to trees?'

'There's some old tree that they're up in arms about losing.' He waves a dismissive hand.

'It's not on the strawberry patch, is it?'

'How should I know?'

'Is it a sycamore tree? Where wishes are made?' I try to ignore the sinking feeling in my stomach. No one would even contemplate felling *that* tree, but the old strawberry patch *is* right behind a care home on a clifftop …

His brow furrows. 'Why would anyone make wishes on a sycamore tree?'

'It's a local legend. All the kids used to rush there in the autumn for the falling sycamore seeds. It's said that if you make a wish

12

and throw one over the cliff and it makes it to the sea, your wish will come true.'

He looks at me like I'm a few slices short of a full loaf. 'Honestly, Felicity, I sent you out for my laundry, not to have a few gins down the pub. Don't mention wishing trees out loud – we'll be a laughing stock. Now, this protest has been going on for a couple of weeks, and they're showing no signs of giving up. The youngster has got them all stirred up, and that's exactly where you come in. We need to deliver this sale quickly and quietly. You'll go there as one of them. Infiltrate this protest as a local. Pretend to be on their side and earn their trust, and find out what it's going to take to get them to give up. Everyone has a price – we just need to find it.'

Harrison's answer to every problem is to throw money at it, and if that doesn't work, throw larger amounts of money at it. 'I can't do that. I don't want to go back there. I haven't been home in fifteen years.'

'You go to visit your father occasionally, don't you? I distinctly remember you saying that was how you'd spent a holiday once.'

'Yeah, but not … properly.'

'I'm going to level with you, Felicity. This is a *huge* client for us and we couldn't risk them going elsewhere, so I've taken a leap of faith and indicated I have this land for them, but I don't yet have a signed agreement from the owner. It looked straight-forward. I never expected it to go wrong like this. The care home owner has got cold feet with all the protestors and is dillydallying about signing, but if we can stop the protest quickly, he'll soon be back on our side. This is no time for your silly family disputes. You *are* going to Lemmon Cove, you *are* going to go undercover as a protestor, you *are* going to find out what it's going to cost to shut these people up, and this is *not* a request.'

'You can't—' I start, my voice rising with indignation.

He rolls his eyes. 'This is a chance for you to move on from being my assistant and start to head up your own projects. If we deliver on this without problems for the client, they've got their eye on several other spots around the UK and they're going to be coming to us for *all* of them. We're going to be busy, so it'll be time for me to get a new assistant and for you to oversee your own project, have your own office …'

An office would be nice. Right now I have a desk in the corner of his office and if he wants to take a private call, I get sent out into the corridor to twiddle my thumbs until he's finished, and then yelled at for wasting time. A project would be nice. Something of my own. Seeing the potential in different spaces and selling that to a client … It's what I've wanted since I started here. I'd love to show him that I'm capable of more than making tea.

'So you'll do it then?'

I don't know why he phrases it as a question when it's clearly an instruction. He threatens to have me replaced at least once a week. I live in London; I can't afford to be fired for refusing this.

Maybe it won't be that bad. I've got an idea of where the care homes are, and they're a good few miles away from Sullivan's Seeds where I used to work with Ryan Sullivan; also I know the company went into liquidation years ago. The chances of him still living there are slim to none. I always get jittery when I think about going home, but I've gone back for visits and never seen him around, and this could be a much easier job than it sounds. A youngster who owns a campsite could be easy to sway. Harrison hasn't given me a budget yet, but he's usually pretty generous when it comes to removing obstacles. A chunk of money, even the promise of a spot of land elsewhere. It shouldn't be difficult to offer enough to put an end to the protest. I could be in and out within a day; no different from family visits.

Harrison takes my quiet overthinking as an agreement. It wasn't, but I also know I have no options if I want to keep my job, and I haven't been collecting his dry-cleaning and polishing his shoes for the last four years just to give up now. This is an opportunity I thought would never happen – a chance to prove that I can be a reliable and valued member of the team, capable of more than non-work-related errands and wiping down tables and refilling water jugs.

This is what I've always hoped for. I've always wanted to travel for work. I left Lemmon Cove all those years ago for an opportunity in a job that involved travel and when that fell through, I ended up in a series of dead-end admin jobs until I landed here, with promises of training and promotions and working my way up the corporate ladder. So far, none of them have come true, but this could finally be my chance.

'There we go. Now you're all up to speed.' Harrison pats me patronisingly on the shoulder like this was the plan all along. 'I have total faith in you, Felicity. You'll get this sorted in a jiffy.'

He has more faith in me than I have in myself. And he's been exceptionally good at hiding it up until now. Generally he doesn't trust my ability to open a bottle of milk for his morning tea. 'And if I do this, I'll get my own projects? My own office?' I prompt, determined that if I have to face going back to Lemmon Cove, I'm doing it for a good reason.

'If you succeed, this client is a *big* firm with unlimited money and a budget to build several hotels in unspoiled spots around the country.' He gives me a lion-like smile. 'And if you fail, our firm will have lost their biggest client and we'll all hold you personally responsible.'

Nothing like that for a bit of motivation.

'Go on.' He shoos me away. 'No time to lose.'

'But the meeting …' I point towards the room we came out of, a finger hanging limply in mid-air. I might have agreed, but I expected a few days to worry about it first. I mean, to plan, obviously. To prepare. There's *nothing* to worry about, but I didn't think he expected me to go *now*. What does he think I'm going to do? Jump on the train *today*?

'You can claim your train fare back on expenses,' he says, making me sure he has an ability to read minds. He also has a look that says "why are you still here?" 'I'll explain all to the lads in the meeting. They were impressed by our brilliant plan, don't you think? I must give myself a pat on the back for such quick thinking.'

He reaches around and pats the back of his own shoulder. People don't actually do that, do they?

'Have fun, Felicity. Wear some … daffodils or leeks or whatever it is you Welsh people like. Dragons? Sheep? I'll have your office ready by the time you get back.'

An office of my own. A job that feels like a "real" job. Colleagues who see me as an equal. It would be so nice …

And all I have to do is deceive a few old people and offer some youngster a chunk of money. Harrison makes it sound business-like and sensible, but it sounds like underhanded and deceitful bribery when I say it.

It's business, I tell myself as I walk back to my desk. I am a professional. If Harrison really is going to let me head up my own projects, I'm going to have to get used to things like this. Making deals and thwarting protestors and overcoming obstacles. I've got to start somewhere. Maybe this is exactly what I was supposed to do with my life and I just need the opportunity to become a shrewd businesswoman who zips up and down the country for work, carries a briefcase, never has a hair out of place, and always manages to walk in high heels. Maybe she's inside me somewhere and I need the right opportunity to find out. Maybe I was cut out for this shrewd businesswoman lifestyle and this'll turn out to be a piece of cake … A shrewd businesswoman who doesn't get distracted by thoughts of cake, obviously.

What could possibly go wrong?

# Chapter 2

Why does my heart start pounding as the train gets closer to the South Wales coast? There is no way Ryan Sullivan still lives here. There is no way I'm going to accidentally run into him. He was ambitious; he wanted to travel and see the world. His family company is long gone from the area. He wouldn't have stayed here.

I wipe sweaty palms on my jeans as the announcement of reaching the end of the line comes over the tannoy and I gather up my bags. I had no idea what to bring, no idea how long I'm likely to be staying, so I shoved some summery clothes into a holdall bag along with toiletries and overnight essentials.

I don't do well with things I have no time to prepare for ... I don't do particularly well with things I *do* have time to prepare for, but today has been a real flailing around in the deep end moment. At first I was glad that I didn't have time to overthink it, but I've been *exceptionally* grateful for the four-hour train journey that my brain has spent inventing all the hypothetical things that could possibly go wrong, and having one final stalk of Ryan Sullivan on Facebook, but – like all the other times I've checked – he doesn't exist on social media. I thought *everyone* had an account on at least one platform, and while there are millions of Ryan Sullivans online, none of them are *that* one. I know because I've stalked *all* their profiles over the years. But wherever he is now, he clearly doesn't *do* the internet. Which is useful, in a way, because I'm not a regular Facebook stalker and it's only once in a while that I decide to check if he's got a Facebook account yet, but what would I do if he was actually on there? I'd like to say I'd send him a friend request and a bright and breezy message asking if he remembered me, but if I sent him a message, he'd know I'd been stalking him. He'd know I still thought about him often enough to seek him out online, so I'd probably just lurk and follow his every post and never comment or do anything to let him know I was watching.

And then I'd inevitably end up accidentally hitting a "like" button and he'd see it before I could undo it, and then he'd know that even though fifteen years have passed since I last saw him, when I'm lonely, or at the end of yet *another* break-up, I still think of him and wish I'd never kissed him. Maybe we'd still be friends if I hadn't.

And no matter how much I wish I could passive-aggressively follow his every move on Facebook, I never want to see him again. Not after the way things ended. That's why I usually stay as far away from Lemmon Cove as land borders will allow – because running into him would be my worst nightmare.

It's late when the train doors open, and I briefly wonder how thoroughly they check the trains and if I could stay here for the night and go back to London on the return trip tomorrow without anyone noticing. It's a nice thought, but I force myself to get up and hoist my holdall bag up my arm and adjust my T-shirt. My sister texted ten minutes ago to say she's waiting in the car park, and no matter how apprehensive I am about the idea of being in Lemmon Cove again and pretending to be a protestor, it will be nice to see her and Dad. It's nearly four months since I last saw them at Easter.

Outside, the night air is warm but thankfully missing the

humidity of London, and I spot Cheryl's little blue car in the car park, the doors open and the lights on inside it. I go around to the passenger side and duck my head in. 'Hi, Cher.'

She squeals and drops her phone in shock, and then squeals again in excitement and jumps out the car, sending her phone clattering onto the seat as she comes round the side to give me a hug. 'I can't believe you're actually staying and not rushing off in a few hours. Dad's so excited. He's been out and got you a bed today; it's all set up in my room.'

'We're sharing a room?'

'Of course!' She brushes bob-length blonde hair out of her eyes and the summer breeze scatters it across her face again. 'I've got your old room and the spare room's full. You didn't give us enough notice to clear it out.'

'Believe me, no one had enough notice for this,' I mutter. Why am I surprised to be sharing a room with my little sister? I know she moved into my room when I left, and her smaller childhood bedroom became Dad's spare room full of his half-finished craft projects and ill-advised gym equipment. 'He didn't have to go out and buy a bed though; I'd have taken the floor.'

'You haven't seen it yet. You might well prefer the floor.' She laughs and stands back to run her eyes over me, just like Mum used to do to make sure I was wearing suitable clothing when leaving the house to go to the beach. 'I *love* the hair.'

How much she sounds like our late mum makes me smile and step back to shrug out of her grip. She's taller than me now, slim and curvy with bouncy hair and the bright eyes that only a twenty-year-old can have. I was twenty when I left Lemmon Cove. Twenty when I kissed Ryan Sullivan and lost the best thing in my life. Did I look like her? Did I have the enthusiasm and Energizer Bunny relentless energy? I remember feeling like my whole life was ahead of me. Now I'm thirty-five and wondering where it went.

I pull one of the blue ends of my hair over my shoulder and

waggle it around in front of me. So far my attempt to be edgy and youthful by bleaching the ends of my dark hair and then dying them bright blue hasn't even been *noticed* by anyone at work. I wanted to shake things up a bit after my last relationship fizzled out. I don't even have break-ups anymore; I just seem to get into relationships that have no magic, no spark, and no hope of going anywhere beyond a few dates. They end with mutual agreement and pleasant partings and I can barely remember the guy's name after a while.

Everything has felt boring lately. My days are the same; my evenings in front of Netflix are the same. My friends have their own lives, their own families, and I'm the odd one out because I don't have a partner or children. I don't have a significant other, because all my attempts at dating end in … not even disaster, just dull dates, with men who are nice enough but nothing special, none that I feel anything remotely like chemistry with.

'You're so cool. I wish my boss would let me do that.' Cheryl works as a teaching assistant in the local primary school, and it's been a long time since anyone thought I was "cool". Maybe hanging out with my little sister for a few days won't be so bad.

I look over at her as we pull out of the station and leave the city centre behind us. Cheryl was still a child when I left, and my presence in her life has been to send expensive birthday gifts each year and come home with a suitcase full of presents every Christmas and leave on the next train out. We text occasionally, usually when I ask her how Dad's doing because I don't trust him to tell me honestly when I speak to him on the phone, but we're not exactly close. Not like I always imagined I'd be close with my sister. She doesn't turn to me for advice and we don't have girly days out shopping or giggle over hot guys. It's been years since we did anything together.

The city buildings turn into coastal road with a vast expanse of beach on the left and seafront hotels on the right, and we pass a park with a lake and golf courses before we turn up into the green hills and mansion-like houses of the Gower villages. It's dark outside and gardens are lit up with solar-powered strings of lights and paths brightened by stake lights. Most houses are shrouded by tall walls that hide their grandness from passing cars, and the road is lined with leafy trees and wildflower patches full of daisies, buttercups, and poppies.

Lemmon Cove is half an hour away from the city centre, and I can't help looking over towards where Sullivan's Seeds used to be, on the hills behind the village. A tiny little street that boasts a post office and corner shop, pub, bakery, and surf shop – it's the last place of civilisation tourists pass through before reaching the empty dunes and sandy beaches of this stretch of the southern Gower coastline.

'They built on it years ago.'

'What?' I jump as Cheryl speaks in the silence.

'The old greenhouses where you used to work.' She jerks her head in their direction without taking her eyes off the road. 'The firm went into liquidation and the site was sold off years ago. There are houses on it now.'

'Oh. Right.' I knew that. I mean, I'd guessed as much. I've googled enough to know that Sullivan's Seeds doesn't still exist, and it shouldn't make me so sad to hear confirmation of that. Or to think of houses crammed into the wide expanse of land that used to be home to Sullivan's Seeds and Plant Nursery, acres of fields of crops, greenhouses where we grew experimental varieties of fruit and veg and forced flowers whatever the weather so they were always in season. It was far enough away from the sea that the coastal weather wouldn't affect the crops, but near enough to have a sea view from the highest points – the hilltop where Ryan and I used to eat lunch on sunny days, looking out at the sea in front and the fields of crops, greenhouses, and polytunnels behind.

I don't realise I'm smiling at the thought until I feel Cheryl's eyes on me. I shake my head sharply to clear the thoughts away.

It's good that Sullivan's Seeds has gone. It means there's no chance Ryan will still be here, running that huge patch of land, walking around in knee-high welly boots even in the height of summer that he somehow managed to make look sexy, singing some obscure Nineties song that no one but me had ever heard of.

I have to stop thinking about him. Being back here always puts him at the forefront of my mind, because these are the roads we used to walk together. This is where we spent so much time. When I'd accompany him on deliveries in his van for no reason at all, and it would always feel like bunking off work even though he was my boss, or he'd give me a lift home even though it was only ten minutes' walk and in completely the opposite direction from where he lived.

'Where's this protest then?' I ask in an attempt to distract myself. 'I haven't heard anything about it.'

'Why would you hear anything about it? The Easter Bunny visits Lemmon Cove more often than you do and the Easter Bunny doesn't exist.'

Ouch. For the first time, I can hear the sting in her voice. 'I work in London, Cher …' I start pathetically. It's an excuse, I know it, but this is the first time I've ever realised she knows it too.

She doesn't pursue it. She doesn't need to. I've often thought that she and Dad must feel abandoned, but she's so bright and breezy until every so often, the mask slips and a hint of bitterness will sneak out. It makes me feel guilty for how little I come to visit.

'It's the old strawberry patch on the clifftop above the beach. Where the sycamore tree is? You must know the place. Dad says it was more your generation than mine. It closed before I was old enough to remember it.'

A chill goes down my spine.

'Oh, *that* place.' I laugh nonchalantly and wave a hand so

dismissively to show that I'm not bothered *at all* that I nearly smack her in the face. I put my hands guiltily back on my lap. 'Of course I'm not bothered.' An edge of hysteria has crept into my voice.

'I didn't say you were bothered.'

'Oh.' No, she didn't, did she? 'That's all right then. Because I'm not.'

Of all the places to haunt my dreams, it's *that* place. The tree where I kissed him. Where I was certain he felt the same. After all the years of flirting and laughing and spending time together, all the easy touches, lingering hugs, and flirtatious smiles. I was *so* sure we were more than friends ... I can still feel the imprint of his hands on my shoulders, pushing me away. I can hear his voice saying: 'I can't do this now, Fee ...'

My foot getting caught in a strawberry runner and tripping me up as I ran away. Juicy berries squishing under the soles of my boots because I was in such a rush to get away that I couldn't even stick to the paths ... Making sure he wouldn't have a chance to catch up with me and see how much I was dying of embarrassment after throwing myself at him and getting the worst rejection of my life.

I suddenly realise what she means. '*That's* where they're going to build a hotel?'

'I guess.'

'That's a terrible place to put a hotel. What about the sycamore tree? It's hundreds of years old; they can't take it down. What about all the carvings? All the wishes?'

'No one carves trees anymore, and it's been years since anyone made a wish on that thing. The land is all overgrown and prickly now. No wonder they want rid of it.'

We're not far from the old strawberry farm, and even though it's dark and I can only see reflections in the passenger window, I look out to the left as we drive up the hedge-lined narrow lanes that give way to a beach car park, and set back from that, the

23

large driveway of Seaview Heights care home. The rocky footpath down to Lemmon Cove beach starts here, and you pass the strawberry farm on the way down. Even in the dark, I can see the shadow of the huge tree's branches waving in the distance, looming over the horizon.

'Dad said we all used to go strawberry picking there when I was little …' Cheryl says.

'Yeah.' The strawberry patch was one of my favourite places. 'You used to love strawberries. Mum and Dad took us at least once a week in the summer months, and then we'd take the punnets we'd picked and go down to the beach to eat them. It's been years since I thought of that.'

'And now you have to go undercover like some kind of superspy?' Cheryl's clearly changing the subject, and I'm not going to push it because Lemmon Cove is crawling with memories I'd rather forget. I'm absolutely certain that no promotion is worth having to spend any extended amount of time here.

'The name's Kerr. Fliss Kerr.' She dissolves into giggles at her own James Bond impression before I have a chance to answer the question.

'It's not exactly like that. I just have to earn the protesters' trust and pretend to be on their side. As a local.'

She gives me a look that says a stegosaurus is more local to Lemmon Cove than I am. 'You haven't lived here for fifteen years.'

'No, but as far as they're concerned, I'm visiting you and Dad and heard about the protest so I've come to join in because I used to love that strawberry patch and can't bear the thought of a big, ugly hotel being parked there.' I hate the way the lies roll off my tongue. It sounds like something Harrison and his business-suited cronies would say. Deceitful and flippant, without a care or concern for who the protesters are or *why* they're protesting. I rush to make it sound less underhanded. 'And that bit's not a lie – I did genuinely love that place when I was younger. And that tree. They can't seriously be considering destroying the

24

sycamore tree. They *must* be working around it and my boss has got it wrong. No one would actually cut down that beautiful old thing.'

The idea that they might *not* be working around it makes an uncomfortable sting bristle at the back of my neck, and not for the first time, I wonder how on earth I got into this. Not just the Lemmon Cove job, but working for Landoperty Developments in the first place. As the Joni Mitchell song goes, how many "paradises" has Harrison been responsible for seeking out and "paving over"? If I succeed in this, *I'll* be doing the same thing. I think about the girl growing plants at Sullivan's Seeds fifteen years ago. Cross-pollinating plants and flowers by hand to breed new varieties. Creating things, not destroying them. If she could see me now …

I shake my head to clear it. Again. My head has needed a *lot* of clearing since Harrison's bright idea this afternoon. Was that really only a few hours ago? It feels like weeks have passed.

'Do you know who's leading the thing?' I say, thinking the youngster could be around her age. If she knows him and can direct me straight to him, this could be over before it's even begun. Before I've stayed long enough for my conscience to get the better of me.

'Not a clue. People chained to trees and stuff isn't my scene. All I know is from one of the little girls in my class – her grandma lives at the care home and has roped her into helping make their placards and banners. There's a surprising amount of glitter for a protest.'

It makes me laugh and something inside softens at the adorable mental image of a young girl helping her grandma to make sparkly protest signs. 'They're not really chained to trees, are they?'

The car starts climbing the hills up towards our little house. *Our* little house. I tut at myself. Dad and Cheryl's little house. It's been many years since I was part of it.

'It's a peaceful protest, but yeah, as far as I know, they're making sure the site is never unoccupied.'

It makes that coldness expand in my chest again. That was another one of Harrison's instructions. He's given me the number of a local contractor who I'm supposed to call to secure the site the second I've got the last old person cleared out of it, so his sidekicks can muscle in and throw barbed wire around to prevent them getting back in. It wouldn't be the first time. I sigh and chew on my lip.

'Don't look so worried,' she says. 'I'm sure it's not as bad as it sounds.'

I don't say anything. It feels *worse* than it sounds, especially with how well I know the area and what kind of impact a shiny bells-and-whistles hotel is going to have on the landscape here.

Dad is waiting in the doorway with the outside light on when Cheryl pulls into the driveway and turns the engine off. I go to open the car door but her hand shoots out and grabs my wrist. 'He doesn't get out much these days. Maybe you can encourage him to get involved in something. He's … disengaged and isolated. All he does is garden and I'm the only person he ever sees.'

She's out the door and round the back getting my holdall out before I have a chance to question her. I sit in the darkened car and look around for a few moments, taking in the front garden with meticulously trimmed hedges, paving so clean it looks ultra-violet in the darkness, and flower borders full of a rainbow of flowers without a deadhead in sight. A world away from my concrete balcony in London, barely big enough to turn around on, and overlooking a busy main road.

Every year I buy some plant or another as a throwback to my previous life here; every year I imagine going out to pick ripe, red tomatoes or crisp green peppers from the pot on the balcony and coming in to make a homemade and healthy pasta dish for my adoring family. In reality, every plant I've put out there has died from a combination of pollution and me not being home from work often enough to water it; I can't cook to save my life and the last time I had any sort of pasta dish, it was a case of piercing the film and putting it in the microwave for five minutes; and my fantasy adoring family is … well, the neighbours watching TV in the adjoining flat or the children stampeding around like a herd of dinosaurs in the flat above probably don't count, do they?

'Good to see you, Fliss.' Dad steps off the doorstep and comes over to wrap me in a tight hug, and I relish in it for a long moment. I can't remember the last time I hugged someone – probably the last time I visited these two. The nickname makes something in my chest swell, the earlier coldness being replaced by warmth. It was Mum's nickname for me, and no one but my family have ever used it.

'How are you?' I pull back and try to get a good look at him, concerned by Cher's comment just now.

'All the better for seeing you, m'dear. Both my girls home again. I've got your bed all set up in Cheryl's room, and I've cleared out some of my wardrobe so you've got space to put your clothes, and there's a free shelf in the bathroom for your toiletries. You've had a long journey; why don't you go and have a shower and I'll get some supper on?'

Same old Dad. Can never do enough for you. When Mum died, it was like he became both mother and father to us. I don't have the heart to tell him I'm not planning on staying long enough to need bathroom shelf space and anywhere to hang my clothes.

I can't get this protest sorted out and get back to London fast enough.

# Chapter 3

I wake up feeling refreshed and ready to face the day.

Okay, that's a lie. I wake up with my spine bent in ways I didn't know it could bend, having got about two hours of fitful sleep in total, while the "bed" slowly deflated underneath me. It's now half the size it was when I threw a duvet onto it last night, and it's ten o'clock, which is two hours later than the usual time I have to dash out of my flat and face the demoralising crush of rush hour on the tube.

I left my phone on Cheryl's dressing table, and when I pick it up, there's a text from Harrison telling me to do my best, and after I didn't reply to that, there's a voicemail telling me I'd better not be having a lie-in because I've got work to do.

I don't think it counts as a lie-in if you're still trying to get comfortable when the sun comes up. I send him a quick reply saying I'm purposely being late so as not to arouse suspicion, and can't help wondering why he thinks I need reminding to do my best. Don't I do my best every day?

Probably not, actually. Most days are a constant stream of reminding myself that pouring hot coffee down people's necks is considered bad and hoping to get through the day relatively unscathed.

When I've had a shower, I throw on my best casual seaside visitor look of three-quarter-length trousers and a vest with lace roses on the straps. I need to look as un-businesslike as possible. Nothing can tip the protestors off about my real job.

Dad's downstairs and he comes over to give me a hug. 'You don't look like you're eating well enough.'

He forces me to sit at the kitchen table and puts a cup of tea and a slice of his homemade roasted peach pie in front of me.

I take this to mean that I look like I survive on shop-bought sandwiches and cereal for dinner every night, and that's reflected in my wobbly waistline and complexion that would make a teenager cringe. But I'm not in work so I'm not making it worse by putting on make-up if I don't have to. I'm just going to have to hope that the old folks' eyesight is bad enough not to be able to make out every acne scar and red mark that may or may not erupt into a volcano-style spot.

Cheryl's already gone to work. I know because she tripped over my feet where they were sticking over the edge of the "bed" as she got ready this morning, and I try to get Dad talking about what she said last night, but he constantly turns the conversation back to me and how I'm doing, and when I question him on the protest and who's running it, he doesn't know either.

It's a ten-minute walk to the strawberry patch, and I try to persuade Dad to come with me, but he says something about needing to make a loaf of bread. It's weird to step out of my dad's house in the morning sunshine, like I've gone back in time fifteen years and I'm on my way to work at Sullivan's Seeds. I did this every day for four years of my younger life, from the age of sixteen when I started to twenty when I left.

The sea air fills my lungs as I walk down the street, intermittent trees in dark green leaf for summer, birds pecking at red berries in the wild cherry trees that are interspersed with the hedgerows opposite, and I frighten off a flock of sparrows from a bird feeder as I walk past one of the neighbour's gardens and out onto the main road. Even "main road" is a misleading term in these quiet Gower villages, as the cars are few and far between, and mostly full of families enjoying the summer holidays with bikes and colourful surfboards strapped to their roof racks as they head to the beaches further along the Welsh coastline.

The sycamore tree is on the horizon, a beacon visible for miles from its spot on the clifftop, overlooking the Lemmon Cove beach. Seaview Heights care home looms over the car park, and a big metal gate to the left lets me onto a wide cobblestone path that gently slopes towards the sea on the horizon, not giving any hint of the steep and rocky path that lies ahead. Only people with strong ankles and a high level of fitness attempt to reach the beautiful, unspoiled Lemmon Cove beach. The gate clangs as I close it behind me. There's a slice of cardboard tied to it with "Save Our Garden" painted in big red letters, and someone's attempted to draw a flower underneath it but it looks more like a cauliflower in the middle of a murder scene.

Ah ha, the campsite. To my left is a neatly cut hedgerow and I stand on tiptoes to see over the top to fields that stretch out for miles, some with tents pitched here and there, and further over there are campervans parked up on the lush green ground. No wonder the campsite owner is protesting. A luxury hotel across the path from his campsite is going to have a hugely detrimental effect on his business.

On the right-hand side, hidden from the coastal path by a hedge that's so overgrown I can't see over it, is the land that used to be the strawberry patch. I loved strawberries and I loved the seaside – what could be better than a pick-your-own strawberry patch on the way down to the beach? And with the sycamore tree on the edge overlooking the sea as well … I can't imagine the number of hours I must've spent here.

There's vague chatter and noise from behind the hedge so I walk further down the cobblestone path to a gap in the hedgerow that used to be smooth double wooden gates hooked open on summer days, a wide and welcoming entry to the strawberry patch and the sycamore tree, but now the space is filled by haphazard metal fencing, those temporary panels that builders put in place to keep people out of building sites.

A few of the care home residents are milling around in the garden area. There's an old woman sitting on a bench, and one standing in front of her having a natter while she leans on a Zimmer frame. There's a man walking around with a placard that reads "Make peas, not war", but I can't work out what pea puns have got to do with saving a strawberry patch. One old man is on his knees on a kneeling pad, doing something to a pair of garden gnomes, two men are sitting on the wall of what was once a raised flowerbed playing a board game, and one woman is sitting on a rickety-looking bench looking at her phone.

Something lets out an extended "baa".

Another cardboard sign with "No Hotel Here" scrawled on it in brushstrokes of red paint is tied to the metal fencing, and the rusty panels are joined by a loose chain that's hanging open. I shift one aside and squeeze through the gap, wondering what sort of protest this is if they're sitting around playing board games. I'd expected to see them chanting and marching with their billboards and petitioning in the streets. I turn around to push the metal panel back into place, and when I turn back, there's a walking stick pointed at my chest like a bayonet.

I gasp and take a step back in alarm, and every eye in the garden area has turned to me.

'Who are you and what do you want?' The man holding the walking stick brandishes it at me. God knows what he thinks he's going to do with it. The rubber-capped end is coated in mud, so maybe stain me? He's certainly not going to cause much bodily harm with it.

'I'm Fel ...' My voice comes out squeaky and I have to swallow before I try again. 'I'm here to join the protest. I'm Felicity. I'm visiting my dad and heard about what was going on, and I want to help.' I give them the lie I've been practising all night, except in my head, I was self-assured and confident and my voice didn't wobble *at all*.

The white bricks of Seaview Heights reflect the sun arching across the sky from the east. There's a neat hedge surrounding the walkway around the building, and then it opens out onto this couple of acres of land that gently slopes towards the cliff edge and the humungous tree.

'The thought of it being ruined by a hotel is unthinkable.' That part isn't a lie. What is Harrison *thinking* in trying to buy this land? What are the hotel company thinking in wanting to destroy this area? It might not look like it used to when it was a straw-berry patch, but it's got to be the best view in the south of Wales. Uninterrupted panoramic views, the sea stretching all the way along the horizon, endless dunes and craggy cliffs that form the borders between different Gower beaches, soft waves lapping at long stretches of golden sand many metres below us, and in the distance, the weather-beaten wooden remains of a ship's hull, still buried beneath the sand from an eighteenth-century shipwreck.

The walking stick is removed from my chest and the old man leans on it as he takes a step back, and the woman who was sitting on the bench with her phone gets up, a head of baby-pink curls bobbing as she comes across. 'Who's your father? Do we know him?'

'Dennis Kerr.' Everyone in this village knows *everyone*. It's the kind of place where if you're lucky enough to live here, you don't want to leave, so most of the residents have been here for decades.

'Fliss! Dennis's oldest daughter!' A woman with curly greying hair approaches. 'I remember you! Haven't you aged! Oh, and you've grown into your boobies nicely! Congratulations!'

'Ffion!' I finally make the connection while simultaneously trying not to die of embarrassment and dissolve into a fit of giggles at proportionate boobs being something worthy of congratulations now. She used to run the ice cream van that stopped in the car park and I went to every day on my way home from the beach.

'Oh, I am sorry, *bach*. I'm Morys.' The man with the walking stick introduces himself. 'Didn't mean to startle you. We're expecting someone from that awful property developer's London office to come and try to buy us out. With the number of retweets our last message to the world got, Ryan thought it might be this week.'

Ryan. The name makes my blood run cold, but it's a common name. In the fifteen years since I left, twenty-six Ryans could have moved to Lemmon Cove. There's no way it can be the same Ryan.

The sycamore tree is on the lower left side of the garden area, a path to it has been cut through the brambles … or possibly chewed, because that's where the baa-ing was coming from. A sheep is eating the vegetation at the base of the tree, next to a thick silver chain wound around the huge trunk. They weren't joking when they said people were chained to trees. I just never realised it would be *this* tree.

I see a flash of grey T-shirt and dark hair as someone jumps out of the branches and lands on the ground, but I'm distracted by the care home residents coming over to introduce them-selves.

'I'm Tonya,' the pink-haired woman says. Her phone is perma-nently in her hand as she waves her arm around, gesturing to each person and telling me their names. 'That's Cynthia with the Zimmer frame and Mr Barley is the one with the gnomes, and—'

And then it happens. A voice cuts through the air and the whole world stops.

'Fee?'

If my blood ran cold before, now it turns to ice and stops running completely. There is only one person who has *ever* called me that. Back then, people at school and work called me Felicity, I was always Fliss to my family, but Ryan Sullivan called me Fee from the first time we met, and it stuck.

I don't realise my eyes have closed, but when I open them again, he's coming up the path from the tree towards me, and I force myself to blink again to make sure I'm not hallucinating.

It's definitely him. Older and more rugged than he was fifteen years ago, but I'd know his voice from just one word. It's a voice I've barely stopped thinking about for fifteen years.

I feel frozen in time as I turn towards him. I've pictured this moment so many times. What it would be like to see him again. How calm and composed and *non*-awkward I'd be. How we'd laugh about old times, and I'd congratulate him on his undoubtedly high-flying life and he'd tell me he always knew I'd go places and do great things in my career, and I wouldn't be the gawky awkward teenager with too many spots and a blazing crush on him. In my fantasies, I've always lost a couple of stone, got glowy skin, non-frizzy hair, and chic clothes that fit perfectly, not gape at the hips and stretch so much to accommodate my boobs that the stitching is liable to burst apart at any moment.

In reality, my breath immediately leaves my lungs and my knees start shaking.

'Fee, is that really you?' He laughs a disbelieving but not unhappy-sounding laugh, picking up speed as he comes towards me. 'I don't believe it!'

'Are you all right, dearie? You've gone all pale. Shall I fetch some water?'

I mumble something to the well-meaning lady, but Ryan has blazed through every thought and every molecule of my body. Something pulls me to him like a magnet, and I picture myself running down the path and into his arms, a moment of reunion akin to the lift at the end of *Dirty Dancing*.

What actually happens is my foot plunges into a pile of sheep poo, which squelches across my ballet flats, and one of the old ladies screams in horror.

At the exact same moment, the chain that's secured to the tree at one end and around Ryan's waist at the other reaches the end

34

of its tether and yanks him backwards, causing the sheep to baa in annoyance.

'I'm still as undignified as ever,' he says with a bright grin in my direction, and I could be mistaken, but it looks like his hands are shaking as they fumble to undo the chain around his middle.

He couldn't be nervous of seeing me as well, could he?

I don't have time to think about it because I'm suddenly swamped by care home residents.

'Oh dear, such messy animals.' One lady bends down to slip my shoe from my foot, leaving me hopping around on one leg, while one of the men puts a hand on my elbow and guides me to the nearest bench, forcing me down onto a wooden slat covered by what looks suspiciously like bird poo. Honestly, within two minutes here, I've encountered more poo than anyone ever needs to encounter before half past ten in the morning.

The woman who took my shoe rushes back towards Seaview Heights with it held aloft, and another man appears seemingly from the bushes with a Pooper Scooper and comes to collect the offending clump of sheep poo.

'Good for the hydrangeas!' he tells me gleefully, rushing off with it held out in front of him like he's won a prize.

Another man is pacing around in front of the bench on "Sheep poo watch" in case there are any more unspotted clusters lurking in the undergrowth.

I've never known sheep poo to cause so much excitement before.

Is this really happening? This is nothing like my fantasy. I look awful. I'm wishing I'd put on full-length trousers *or* shaved my legs this morning, because the combination of three-quarter-length trousers and my current look is more yeti than sultry. It's the first day in years that I've left the house without make-up on, and the hot morning sun is making me glisten, and *not* in the good way. I can't remember running a brush through my hair, I just scragged it back and tied it in a knot. I was trying to

35

look beachy and casual, not like I was about to see the love of my life for the first time in fifteen years.

I mean, no, he's not the love of my life, obviously. He was just a teenage crush. A flirtatious, fun highlight of my life for nearly four years, but it wasn't love. Can it ever really be love if it isn't reciprocated? And despite all signals to the contrary, it clearly wasn't.

Just thinking about it makes me go even redder than I am anyway. *Why* is he here? What is he doing here? No matter how much I *used* to like him, I'd quite happily have never seen him again after the way I humiliated myself fifteen years ago. And now he's here. Literally chained to a tree in the middle of this protest that I somehow have to infiltrate. It was a bad enough plan *without* Ryan Sullivan smack-bang in the centre of it.

Ryan's untangled himself from the chain and is standing awkwardly at the edge of the people around the bench, shifting from one foot to the other like he used to when he was nervous.

He goes to say something, but the woman with pink hair plonks herself down next to me, not caring about the bird poo in the slightest. 'Ooh, I like your hair.' She reaches out to twirl a bit of the blue hair that's sticking out from the knot at the back of my head. 'Blue always comes out green for me.'

I can't take my eyes off Ryan. The intense sunshine is making his forehead prickle with sweat, and we're just sort of staring at each other in a daze. He used to sweat when he was nervous too. But it's obviously just the sun – it's not like he'd be nervous about seeing me again. He's *gorgeous* and I'm a sheep-poo-ridden disaster. *He* didn't humiliate himself and run away fifteen years ago. *He* hasn't spent fifteen years thinking about me and subconsciously comparing every other relationship to what he had with me.

'People say I'm too old for bright-coloured hair,' Tonya is carrying on without waiting for an answer. 'But I'm not having any of that. Age is nothing but a number, isn't that right? I go into town to get it done every few weeks – the brighter the better to pee off the haters.' She does something with her fingers that's either a peace sign or some kind of gang overlord symbol.

Ryan's chewing his lip and trying not to laugh, his eyes not leaving mine as I blink up at him, the sun stinging my eyes and making them water.

'I can't believe you're here, Fee. I never thought I'd see you again,' he says when Tonya stops talking about the various hair colours she'd had recently.

He takes a step closer, like he's going to bend down to hug me, and I'm all of a dither. Do I get up and risk putting my bare foot down on this sheep-poo-covered ground? What about the bird poo I've probably sat in? I'm going to have to furtively make sure that hasn't left any marks behind.

'No!' The woman returns with my now-clean shoe and a kneeling pad, which she throws onto the ground and kneels on in one swift movement, lifting my leg and slipping the shoe back onto my foot like it's a glass slipper and I'm some sort of poo-ridden Cinderella.

'Do you two know each other?' Tonya looks between me and Ryan.

'We used to work together,' I say.

'She was my greatest friend,' Ryan says at the exact same moment.

'I was?' I say before I can think about it.

'Good as new.' The woman with the shoe declares before Ryan has a chance to answer, sitting back on her knees and looking satisfied with her work.

She gets up and she and Morys get their hands on my elbows and pull me to my feet, and the momentum propels me headfirst into Ryan.

His arms come up to steady me, wrapping tightly around my shoulders and pulling me to him, and I realise it's a hug. He's hugging me. Ryan's hugs were always a force to be reckoned with, and the surrealness of this situation makes my brain sputter to a halt and hug him back, my hands rubbing over the smooth curves of well-defined shoulder muscles and a strong back through his grey T-shirt. I breathe in his still so familiar scent, a mix of sea air and some kind of earthy cologne.

'Oh my God, Fee,' he murmurs in my ear, the sound so low that I'm not sure if I've heard it or felt it. 'You look amazing. I've missed you.'

I have to bite down on my lip to stop tears prickling at my eyes. *He's* missed *me*? At first, I missed him like half of my body had been ripped away. When I moved away, I didn't know what to do with myself without him. I looked at his number in my phone so many times and wondered what it would be like if I pressed dial. But I never did. I couldn't after the kiss.

I croak out something that hopefully bears a resemblance to 'Missed you too.'

It must have been intelligible because his arms tighten around me, squeezing me as tightly as you'd imagine such muscular arms could squeeze and rocking us from one foot to the other, just like he used to.

I lose track of time as we stand there, still lost in the weirdness of this situation, of the chance encounter in exactly the same spot I last saw him. I can't compute that he still lives here or that when I laughed at the idea of protestors chained to trees, it was *him* all along. And I'm still half-certain that this is all a hallucination brought on by heatstroke or overexposure to the tang of prunes that Morys is now funnelling into his mouth.

Ryan's arms get impossibly tighter. 'My Fee,' he murmurs, making my legs feel decidedly weak. 'I don't believe it. I don't *believe* it … And I appear to have accidentally turned into Victor Meldrew.'

It makes me laugh out loud and disentangle myself from him so I can take a step back on knocking knees. I blink up at him as he holds a hand up to shield his face from the sun, grey-blue eyes smarting in the light, a wide nose, and dark stubble covering his jaw. Pale lips that are so full you'd think he'd had something done to them, but they've always been naturally like that, the kind of lips that are impossible to look away from, and even though I'd *never* repeat it, that familiar urge to kiss him tingles again, apparently not deterred by the fact he's undoubtedly married by now.

'Of all the protests in all the world, you walk into mine.' His voice sounds as shaky as I feel, and it buoys my confidence that maybe he *is* a little bit nervous too.

'Yours?'

'Well, ours. I'm just helping these folks out. Can you imagine what kind of heartless, soulless company would want to put a hotel here?'

I gulp, and suddenly remember we're not alone and take a further step backwards to put a bit of space between me and Ryan.

'It's our only outside space,' Tonya says. 'We know it's a tad overgrown, but we still come out here to sit on the benches, and some of us do the flowerbeds ...' She gestures to the knee-height red bricks that form the walls of square flowerbeds, although they're at least seventy-five per cent weeds now. 'A lot of us chose this place solely for the view.'

It's a huge area, big enough for the most luxurious of hotels, but there's nowhere you could put a building without completely cutting off Seaview Heights. The land is overgrown, and it gets worse further away from the care home. Up here, it's trampled and worn down around the row of rickety old benches on either side of the entrance, but the rest of the ground is lost to brambles and gorse bushes creeping in from the surrounding fields. Some of them have reached such heights that I have to look *up* at them, and there are a variety of self-sown wild trees rambling away.

'A hotel would block their view completely,' Ryan says. 'They'd have walls outside their windows. I can't stand by and let that happen.'

'So you … chained yourself to the tree?' I nod towards the solid steel chain, still lying on the path where he discarded it, brambles on either side looking like they've been hacked away and are already making a resurgence.

'For as long as the site's occupied, they can't swoop in and steal it.'

'What about at night?' I remember several incidents where Harrison has sent men in to secure protest sites when the protesters drop their guard and go home at night.

'I'm here all day, every day. Sleeping here, eating here, I go home for showers when one of this lot will cover for me.'

'Sounds uncomfortable.' I try not to show my surprise. When Harrison said people were chained to trees, I didn't think he meant actually *living* in the tree itself.

I look past him to where the sycamore tree sits on the cliff edge, so close to it that from here you'd imagine the roots to be coming out of the rocks themselves, but close up, it's further from the edge than it looks, and surrounded by a sturdy barrier keeping everyone safe from going over.

'We're expecting someone to come and offer us blood money any time now,' Ryan continues. 'Those property developers have no morals. They think money solves everything, and they'll do anything, no matter how morally corrupt, to get what they want without a second thought to the human cost involved.'

I gulp.

'Like that tree could ever have a price.' His face shows every emotion and none of them are good. 'Three hundred years old, visible for miles across the sea, a guiding light that's stood here since times so long ago that we can't even imagine them. Not even Mr Barley, and he's about the same age.'

From across the garden, the man who's finished rearranging his gnomes and is now sitting on his kneeling pad sticks a finger up at Ryan with a grin.

I catch sight of his gnome arrangement and nearly do a double-take. The male gnome is painted to look like Boris Johnson and the female one is reaching across ... Blimey, what is Theresa May's hand doing down *there*? And why does Boris look like he's enjoying it so much?

'Aw,' Tonya sighs. 'He's already done that one but with Margaret Thatcher and Ed Miliband. We need more inventive gnome sex positions! Gnome sex positions, anyone?' She claps her hands to get the attention of the group. 'Suggestions on my Facebook page to get people talking!' She turns back to us. 'Anyhoo, I must go and photograph them. My Twitter followers will be waiting for today's update.' Tonya rushes across to the gnomes, and I can feel Ryan's eyes on me.

'Welcome to the land of fabulous mad old people.' He leans down to whisper in my ear, making me jump with his sudden closeness. 'You'll get used to it. Gnome sex positions are a regular topic of conversation around these parts.'

Gnomes or not, talking about sex positions with Ryan is a bit too much for me and there's a genuine possibility I might be about to spontaneously combust.

'And I'm not sure that was the best choice of words. These people spend far too much time thinking about gnome parts.'

Either I'm delirious or it's the most hilarious thing ever, and I let out a guffaw so loud that every eye in the vicinity swivels towards me, including the sheep's. A guffaw, for God's sake. I *don't* guffaw. I'll be tittering and chortling next at this rate.

Ryan obviously takes pity on the guffawing fool and changes the subject.

'Are your dad and sister okay?'

He's still so nice. He was always the kindest, most caring guy. No matter what he had going on in his own life, he always checked to make sure my dad was okay after my mum died. Always kept boxes of Sullivan's surplus fruit and veg to make sure he was eating well. Cheryl was still young when I knew him, and he'd always buy her toys and have more fun playing with them himself before he gave them to her. He was like an older brother, always looking out for us. I swallow back the lump in my throat. 'They're fine. Just well overdue a visit.'

'Oh my God, Fee. There's so much to talk about. I don't know where to start.' He runs a hand through his hair like he always used to – surprising that someone's little habits don't change over so many years, and surprising me by how natural the instinct is to reach out and grab his hand, like I always used to when he went to do it with compost-covered gardening gloves on.

My nails make crescent shapes in my palm as I force myself not to be so stupid. 'So how are you? I didn't think you'd still be—'

'What's this? What's this?' A lady with long champagne-blonde hair rushes down from the care home waving a phone around. 'I lost the last round, I can't lose this one too!'

She stops to show the phone to Tonya and Mr Barley as she passes them, and then she spots me and Ryan. 'Ooh, young people, you might know!'

No matter what she's talking about, it's quite nice to be considered a young person. Generally that term stops when you creak your way out of bed every morning and feel too decrepit to shop in Primark.

The long-haired woman is out of breath by the time she reaches us and pushes her phone in front of us. 'What is it?'

On the screen is a photograph of some household object, but she whisks the phone out of sight as the two men abandon their board game and come over and Cynthia on the Zimmer frame hobbles this way, and Tonya pulls Mr Barley up from his seat and they all gather round.

The woman must notice my look of bewilderment because she holds out a hand and shakes mine. 'I'm Alys. I play "Guess the Gadget" with my friend in the next county over. We send each other photos of household objects and score points for each one we get right, and she's beating me by nine points at the moment. I'm not letting her outfox me on this one too!'

The phone is passed between all of them and they chatter about what the mystery object onscreen could be. Eventually someone's holding it under my nose again, and Ryan steps closer to see the screen over my shoulder, and his closeness once again makes something inside me sputter to a halt. If I was made of electrics, a circuit board would've definitely just fried.

I'm hyperaware of his presence. His tall frame behind me, six-foot-one of solid muscle, so close that I can feel the brush of the dark hairs covering his tanned arm against mine. It takes all I have to remember how to breathe. Of all the ways I thought this day might go, trying to identify household gadgets with Ryan Sullivan standing so close I can feel his body heat certainly wasn't one of them.

'Isn't it a cherry pitter?' I say, trying to focus *everything* onto the phone screen in front of me and not the warm body behind me.

'Oh, yes, I think you're onto something there.' Tonya nods her head of pink curls.

'Yes! It can't be anything else!' Alys claps her hands together. 'Fantastic! Thanks, Felicity!'

I go red even though the ability to identify a cherry pitter isn't exactly something impressive.

'As I said,' Ryan whispers into my ear. 'The land of fabulous mad old folks.'

It makes me laugh again, especially when he steps back and the distance allows me to take a much-needed breath. I hadn't realised I was so perilously close to passing out from lack of oxygen.

'How long's it been since you two saw each other?' Ffion peers at both of us.

'Fifteen years,' we say in perfect unison, and our eyes meet over the sea of old people between us.

43

'I didn't think you'd ever come back,' he says without dropping my gaze, a smile tilting his lips. 'You must have such a glamorous life. Didn't think I'd ever see a high-flying career girl from the big city back in this little village. What are you doing now?'

'I'm a—' Oh God, I can't tell him. I can't tell any of them. The one thing they *cannot* know is where I work. They've made it quite clear what they think of companies like Landoperty Developments and how open they'd be to the idea of someone turning up and offering them a wodge of money in exchange for giving up the protest. They *cannot* know who I am or why I'm here.

Alys is texting her friend the answer to "Guess the Gadget", but all the others are still surrounding us, and I'm squirming under their expectant gazes. They're going to be suspicious if I don't come up with something soon. It can't feasibly take this long to remember what you supposedly do for a living and I look around desperately for inspiration.

One of the care home staff is making her way down from the building towards us, carrying a tray of cakes and cups of tea.

'A chef!' I say it so suddenly that I make myself jump, and two of the old folks glare at me in fright. One of the board game men takes his hearing aid out and gives it a whack.

A *chef*? What the heck am I thinking? Of all the fake careers I could possibly have chosen, why on earth did I say that one? I can't cook for toffee. I definitely can't *cook* toffee. Does toffee even need cooking? Why have I gone off on a toffee-related tangent when these people are standing around thinking I'm a chef? The most complicated thing I can cook is a Pop Tart. And that usually ends up burnt.

'Oooh, where do you work?' Tonya asks.

'A restaurant. In London.'

She looks at me expectantly, like that's plainly not enough info.

'It's called Riscaldar.' I remember a property my boss sold last

year. 'I'm kind of an assistant, a kitchen manager, a waitress …
I do a bit of everything.'

Why didn't I think this through? I spent so long last night
practising everything I was going to say, but it didn't once cross
my mind that they'd ask about my job.

Ryan quirks an eyebrow up. 'A sous chef?'

What the *heck* is a sous chef? 'Er, yeah, one of them.'

He lowers that eyebrow and raises the other one. '*You?* You
didn't used to be able to make a piece of toast without needing
the fire brigade on hand.'

'That was *one* time! And it wasn't my fault that a passer-by
saw smoke coming out the window and called 999! And the blame
was half yours for distracting me!'

'You'd set the timer knob for ten minutes. A block of ice
would've charcoaled in that time.'

'I'm not sure ice quite works like that when you heat it up.'

He grins. 'Well, you're the chef – you'd know.'

Tonya's looking at her phone and making impressed noises.
'Ooh, it says that rich and famous people eat there. Who's the
most famous person you've ever met?'

Oh God, did she have to google it? 'Oh, I don't really—'

'Holy moly, those prices! It's a good job they display them on
the website or people would be having heart attacks all over the
place when the bill came.' She hands the phone around to show
everyone. 'It looks *so* fancy. Who knew a girl from Lemmon Cove
had done so well?'

They give me a round of applause. They seriously give me a
round of applause for working in a posh restaurant I've never
even been to. All I did was sort out Harrison's paperwork when
he sold it.

It won't be the disaster it seems to be, I tell myself. All I have
to do is find this youngster and all this will be over. It's not like
I'm going to have any reason to prove my occupation. It's a couple
of days and then I'm out of here again, because I can already feel

the need to put as much distance as possible between me and Ryan Sullivan.

'Seriously, how'd you get into that?' he asks.

'I, um ...'

'No wonder you knew the cherry pitter.' Alys finishes her text before I have a chance to think up a response to his question. 'I'm going to come to you for all my "Guess the Gadget" needs.'

Oh no. I'm going to have to start studying up on household appliances. They're going to expect me to know what *everything* is now. Let's hope they don't play "Guess the Gadget" too often.

'Wow.' Ryan runs his hand through his hair yet again. 'Of all the things I imagined you doing now, that was absolutely the *last* one.'

Me too. Trust me on that. Although the thought that he's imagined me doing anything is nice. I thought he'd have tried to erase every memory of me from his mind. 'What about you?'

'Nothing as interesting as cooking for the rich and famous. I do this and that. Odd jobs around the area. And I—'

'There's *nothing* Ryan can't fix,' Ffion interrupts. 'He unblocked my loo last year and it's been working like a charm ever since. Seaview Heights has got him on a retainer to fix all problems.'

'Thanks, Ffion, I really wanted the person I haven't seen for fifteen years to think of me up to my knees in the sewage tank.'

'Glad to be of service.' Ffion salutes him as his sarcasm goes over her head, but I can't help giggling.

'The level of excitement in this village hasn't changed then?'

'What a day *that* one was. I'm not sure I've ever recovered.'

I can't get my head around him still being here. It's the opposite of what Ryan wanted to do with his life. Not that I can talk. Collecting Harrison's dry-cleaning wasn't exactly my greatest ambition either.

The nurse who came out sets the tray down on the flowerbed wall, and the elderly gang start hobbling across for cakes and cuppas, leaving me alone with Ryan.

'And I own that over there,' he carries on like this is not an unusual situation to be in. He lifts a muscular forearm and points across the hedge.

I follow his finger and push myself up on tiptoes because I must be missing something. All I can see is the campsite, fields and fields of static caravans, campervans, and tents, all spread out with little amenities buildings at the edge of each field.

He *cannot* mean the campsite.

I glance back at him. He doesn't appear to be joking.

'*You're* the youngster?' I say without thinking.

He looks confused.

I am *terrible* at this. 'I overheard some village gossip,' I say quickly. Village gossip is a believable excuse for *anything* in this village. 'Said a youngster was running the protest and stirring up all the old 'uns.'

He laughs a gentle rumble of a laugh. 'I'm only a youngster by comparison to that lot. And I assure you, it's *them* stirring *me* up. This was all their idea. I'm just helping out because, well, the youngest of 'em is seventy-seven, they can't be spending hours chained to a tree every day, and if we leave the site unoccupied, those underhanded property developers are going to prevent us getting back in.'

I try to ignore how sick that makes me feel, and pretend that I *haven't* thought about him on every birthday that's passed. I know he's thirty-eight now, three and a bit years older than me, and definitely not a youngster. From Harrison's description, I was expecting a teenager to swagger in wearing a black mask with a skull on it and a can of spray paint in one hand. He is *nothing* like the protest leader I was expecting, and *nothing* like the kind of person who's going to give this up in exchange for the cash Harrison expects me to throw at him. And how can I *now*?

Ryan loved this place, especially that tree. There is nothing of monetary value that could persuade him to let it go. He's made it clear what he thinks of the company I work for, and I've told him I'm a chef. How am I ever going to *un*-lie this lie I've told? And if there's one thing I know about Ryan Sullivan, it's that when he commits to something, he *never* gives up.

'Occupy the sycamore tree!' He shouts and punches a fist in the air, and the group of old 'uns return the cry with mouthfuls of cake being spat everywhere and tea being dribbled out. Alys wallops Mr Barley for spilling crumbs on her skirt.

He grins and starts back down the path towards the tree. 'C'mon, let me show you my humble abode.'

I hesitate. Is going to the tree with Ryan a good idea? After all, it is the *exact* spot where I kissed him. The very place I last saw him. Do I really want to stand under those branches with him again? I glance at the care home residents. Someone's produced a packet of biscuits and now they're having an argument about which biscuits the Queen would prefer if she eats biscuits. She's British – it would be a crime if she *didn't* eat biscuits. Judging by the heated arguments about the merits of Rich Tea versus Arrowroots, they're going to be occupied for a while.

I need to make an excuse and get out of here. Go and phone Harrison and tell him I'm on the next train back to London, no matter what. This can't continue now, not with Ryan here.

# Chapter 4

Ryan must take my hesitation as wariness of the brambles because once he's picked the chain up and reattached it around his waist, he turns back and holds his hand out to me. 'It's not as bad as it looks, honest.'

It takes me a moment to realise he's talking about the narrow path towards the tree. My brain has a conniption again because something possesses me to slip my hand into his.

His fingers squeeze around mine as he tugs me with him. Brambles scrape my legs at either side, and the ground underneath my feet is stony and green with a mixture of moss and grass, but nothing registers except for his hand in mine. His skin is warm and his hands are somehow bigger and even more solid than they used to be. The kind of hands that make you feel everything's going to be all right whenever they're near you.

The sheep baas as we approach the tree, not sounding very happy at having her grass-munching interrupted again. 'Do you know there's a sheep tied to your tree?'

'Yeah, she's my sheep.'

'You have a pet sheep?' I give the white fluffy thing a wide berth as she takes an inquisitive step towards me. She's wearing

49

one of those hefty dog harnesses with "SECURITY" embroidered in capital letters across either side, and attached to a dog lead that's tied onto the chain that criss-crosses the tree trunk.

Ryan looks back at me with a shrug, like this too is not at all unusual.

'Aren't they herd animals that live in fields? Generally quite a lot of them?'

'Well, I did have two sheep that lived in a field and kept each other company, but one sadly died. They came with the campsite land. The guy who sold it to me couldn't take them with him, so I offered to rehome them for him, but no one wanted two extra sheep so I kept them.'

'Does she have a name?'

'Baaabra Streisand.'

I let out such a loud bark of laughter at the name that it makes Ryan, myself, *and* the sheep jump.

'You can't have sheep and not give them funny names,' he says incredulously. 'The other one was called Dolly Baa-ton. And I have a long list of sheep puns in case any more come along. I nearly got two more just so I could call them Meryl Sheep and Lady BaaBaa. And yes, I *am* very proud of my sheep-naming skills.'

I howl with laughter again and it eases some of the awkwardness between us. I've forgotten how funny he is. I've forgotten his poker face that I used to recognise in an instant, even though it drove others up the wall because they could never tell if he was serious or not.

'She's a comedic sheep – you'll see.'

I'm so distracted by the hand-holding and trying to avoid the sheep that I haven't realised how close to the sycamore tree we've got, and I have to duck sharply as a low branch threatens to decapitate me.

Ryan looks around at the sudden movement and then glances at our still-joined hands. 'I'm so sorry. I have no right to hold your hand. You must have a husband who'll want to punch me for that.'

'I'm not married,' I say, my words coming out at a pitch that only mice can hear. Maybe I should go the whole hog on the lies front and tell him I am. I'm a successful chef who *hasn't* had a string of failed relationships because she wants just one man to make her feel even a fraction of how you did. Happily married, thank you very much, just like you undoubtedly are.

'Good.' He coughs. 'I mean, me neither. At least we're old spinsters together. Er, can men be spinsters?'

My hand falls out of his in surprise. There is *no* way he can be single. *Look* at him. The sheep would probably marry him given half a chance, never mind the rest of the female population of South Wales. I've imagined running into him again hundreds of times, and in every single impossible, ridiculous, unlikely scenario, he's happily married. It doesn't make sense that he wouldn't be in real life.

'I've just realised I've called you old too.' He smacks his forehead. 'What a *great* first impression I'm making. Well, second impression. Well, we saw each other every day for more than three years, so I suppose nine-hundredth-and-something impression. To clarify, I meant that *I'm* old; you're not. You're young, beautiful, and strapping. Oh good God, now I've made it worse by calling you strapping. *Not* strapping. Just as perfect as you always were. I'm going to shut up now.'

I can't stop giggling. Ryan's nervous rambling really hasn't changed. He's just as adorably awkward as he always was, and I clearly remember the time we went for a meeting with suppliers and he tried to tell one of the farmers that her cows were a credit to her but accidentally rambled that she was just as lovely as her cows before realising it had *not* come out as the compliment he'd intended.

I try to concentrate on the tree instead. There's a blue and white striped deckchair secured to the chain around the trunk too, undoubtedly a seat for whoever takes over because I doubt they're up to scaling the branches like Ryan does.

The towering tree's huge trunk is covered with the carvings of thousands of visitors over the years. You'd probably need seven or eight people to put their arms around its circumference. It's a tree full of nooks and crannies and foot-holds, probably easy to climb if you're as fit as Ryan obviously is. The trunk goes up and then splits off into several directions, leaving a big space in the middle that every child in Lemmon Cove has climbed up to at some point in their lives.

There's a canopy of blue tarpaulin to keep the rain off, held taut where it's tied to the branches above, and I can see a rucksack and sleeping bag rolled up to one side. It's the sort of magical treehouse den that any child would love, but I can't believe he's really *living* here.

It's shady under the branches and the wind has picked up the closer we've got to the sea, giving a welcome break from the blazing August sun. I avoid Baaabra Streisand when she doubles back and appears from the opposite side of the tree and trots over to me. I've never known a sheep that didn't run away from humans before.

I let my hand trail across the etched bark, my fingers crossing the dips of carving after carving, not a space left anywhere after so many years. There is so much history in this tree. This big old thing has seen everything happen beneath its branches, from first kisses to marriage proposals to weddings and ashes being scattered, and everything in between.

I glance at Ryan, who's now leaning on the sturdy metal barrier looking out at the sea. Does he remember the "Ry + Fee" he carved in a love heart to commemorate my leaving day? Does he know that heart was what made me kiss him?

Local legend has it that when a couple carve their names into the tree, it cements their relationship and if a carving stays strong then the relationship will too, but if a carving fades then so will the relationship, so it's safe to say that Ryan's carving of *our* names is long gone by now.

He's leaning on the metal fence, a strong and secure barrier between the land above and the sand below, and I go to stand next to him. I've stood here so many times and watched sycamore seeds twirl down to the sea. When I was growing up, another local belief was that in the autumn when the sycamore seeds were falling, if you threw one over the cliff when the tide was high and made a wish before it twizzled into the sea below, it would come true. Kids flocked here in October when the helicopter seeds turned brown and started to fall.

'It's been a long time, huh?' He shifts closer until his warm arm presses against mine. 'It's good to see you.'

'Good to see you too,' I stutter, feeling like I need a drink of water. It sounds like I'm lying. It *is* good to see him in a way, but it's also absolutely horrendous to see him.

I look out at the sun-bleached ruins of an old stone castle on the hills in the distance, while simultaneously trying to sneak glances at Ryan. He looks exactly the same. A little older, a little more rough-around-the-edges, like he's spent the past few years outdoors, but like there might be a Dorian Gray-style painting in his attic that we should be concerned about. His dark hair is short at the back and soft and wavy on top, at just the length that it'll start to curl if it grows any longer.

'Are you staying?' he asks quietly, facing the sea instead of looking my way.

I should leave; I know that. Abandon plan. I can't stay here with Ryan Sullivan running the place. But at the same time, the idea that he's still single makes something flitter through me that has no right to be flittering anywhere near me, and it feels a little bit like fate has had a hand in us meeting again, and in this exact spot too.

And aside from Ryan, I get the feeling there's something going on with Dad, something Cheryl hasn't said in as many words, and it feels wrong to walk away. And now I know where the hotel's going, I can't just stand back and let them destroy this place.

'For a while.' Those are the words I hear come out of my mouth, but I'm pretty sure I didn't really say them, because I'm not, am I? I can't stay here and infiltrate this protest with *him* leading it.

He's smiling when he looks at me. 'I was hoping you were going to say that.'

A smile that does a stellar job of taking my breath away. It's the first one that hasn't seemed hesitant so far today, and it makes me feel better – like he could be genuinely happy to see me.

'I want to help. The prospect of a hotel going here is *unthinkable*.' I'm not lying as I say that. He's right – they're *all* right. How could anyone want to ruin this place by plonking a hotel here? This tree is visible for miles across the ocean, guiding sailors home. No one wants to be guided home by a hotel on a cliff, do they? Well, Sat Nav and Google Maps probably do a better job these days, but still. 'Do people still come to visit the tree?'

'They used to, but … Look at how overgrown it is. Until a couple of weeks ago, this tree hadn't been accessible for years. The weeds and brambles had taken over. *Have* taken over. All I did was cut a path through. The rest of it is …' He sighs and glances behind him.

He doesn't need to say anything. The land is a disaster zone. Between the thorny brambles and spiky gorse, there are clumps of stinging nettles and other unsavoury-looking weeds that seem like they're about to burst forth and attack you at any given moment. It doesn't look like anyone's set foot here for at least a decade.

'What happened? Why did people stop coming here?'

'The tree ran out of space for carving.' He takes a step back and reaches across to pat the big old trunk. 'You couldn't fit another thing on here if you tried. The care home lost their gardener. I think the residents agreed to do it between them, but it only takes a few months for weeds to take over, and it was too much for them. And as for visitors, well, one look at this place is enough to make anyone turn back.'

He leans his elbows on the barrier again and rests his chin in his hands. 'Sycamores only live for four hundred years, and this one has had three hundred already. Can you imagine standing somewhere for that long to be cut down in the last quarter of your life? For someone to see you as being "in the way" instead of for the magic you bring to the area?'

I look up into the boughs high above our heads as huge five-lobed leaves rustle in the sea breeze.

'I think the residents have an affinity with it. They look happy now, but when they go back to their rooms at night, they're on their own. Some of them have no family to visit. They look out at this tree, standing here by itself, and they feel less alone. That sort of significance can't be understood by property developers. See that man on the bench?' He ducks his head closer to mine and points to a man drinking a cup of tea, but sitting alone, away from the rest of the group. 'That's Godfrey. His wife of seventy years has got severe dementia and lives in a nursing home forty miles away. Visits are few and far between because it's slim-to-impossible to arrange the ambulance for transportation, and he has no idea if she's going to recognise him when he goes there. Nine times out of ten, she doesn't.'

I bite down on my lip to stop it wobbling.

'They have no children and no other family. Most of their friends have passed away or moved away. He's alone.'

'Wait … Godfrey … I know that name.' I also know the wobble in my voice is audible.

'His great-great-grandfather started the strawberry patch in the late 1800s. It was just a farm then. The care home hadn't been built, but pick-your-own was big in Victorian times. It passed down through the family for generations. There are strawberries carved into the tree trunk with the names and dates of each couple taking over. He and his wife were the last ones in the 1960s. They ran it together for over forty years. Before that, they got married under this tree in 1951. All they wanted was to grow old together here, looking out over it every day while future generations ran it. They were unable to have children and she needs more specialist care than they can provide here, so they've been split up at the very end of their lives.'

'Flipping 'eck, Ry.' I can't hide the fact I'm crying. Stories like this have always got to me. When I was younger, I used to love coming here and running my hands over the bark of the tree and imagining what stories were behind each carving.

He inches nearer and drops an arm around my shoulder and tugs me closer to him like fifteen years haven't passed between us.

Instead of saying anything disparaging like some men would, he squeezes my shoulders tighter. 'I was a mess when he first talked to me. We're talking, like, snot everywhere and serious consideration of buying a shareholder stake in Kleenex.'

It makes me snort amidst the tears, which doesn't end well, and I have to turn away to hide the snot bubble and surreptitiously swipe my hands over my face.

'Look.' He uses the arm around my shoulder to turn me towards the tree, and his arm falls away as he gives me a bit of privacy to compose myself. 'I know where it is because he puts his palm over it when he wants to feel close to his wife.'

I follow his finger as he points out a carving of a heart with the names Godfrey and Henrietta in it and the date 21st September 1951. Right above it is a carved strawberry and a faded date in May 1962, the day he and his wife took over.

'For some of these residents, that view is the only reason to get out of bed in the mornings. The social aspect of the garden is important for them. It might not look like much to an outsider, but it's a *lot* to them. For some people here, this is the only thing they've got left.'

No sooner have I stopped crying, than a lump forms in my throat again.

'Think of the amount of life that's gone past under this tree. This sycamore has seen *everything*. In a few years' time, future generations aren't even going to *know* it once stood here. Can you imagine what growing up in Lemmon Cove would've been like if this tree hadn't been here? If the strawberry patch wasn't a part of our lives? Our summers would've been different. Our autumns would've been void of the magic of sycamore wishes. We can't stand by and let that be erased.'

'We?'

'You said you wanted to help, didn't you?'

Oh, God. I *do* want to help, but genuinely. *Not* because I'm supposed to be infiltrating the protest for Landoperty Developments. He's right – the thought of anyone destroying this tree is unimaginable. Being here again has unfurled the permanent tightness that sits on my chest as I rush through London on whatever wild goose chase Harrison has sent me on – occasionally for something even more impossible than actual wild geese – and I don't want to walk away. 'Er, yes. Yes I did.'

The sunlight hits his face, dappled through the branches, and it seems to make him physically brighten up. 'Good, because you always made me believe in the impossible, Fee, and I feel like we can succeed with you here.'

'I'm in.' I try not to show my uneasiness through my smile.

This is a recipe for disaster. And *that* is the *only* thing I'm adept at cooking.

# Chapter 5

'I can't do this. I'm coming back to the office.' I'm in Dad's garden that evening, pacing up and down the neat lawn, while Harrison rabbits on about the hotel in my ear. I've got my sensible head back on – the one without Ryan Sullivan's cologne and hot muscular body dulling its senses and making it say stupid things like I'm staying and I'd be happy to help. I mean, I *do* want to help, but it's the opposite of what my job is supposed to be.

'Are you indeed?' Harrison sounds as overjoyed by my plan as he would be at the prospect of a dental check-up.

'I know the area too well,' I say into the phone, pinching the bridge of my nose with my other hand. 'I know the guy leading it.'

I also know I shouldn't have said that.

'Oh, that's fantastic. An "in". A way to get your foot in the door. I told you this was a good plan. Have you had a chance to find out what he wants yet? I'm prepared to be generous with the budget.'

I barely contain a snort at the idea. 'He would *not* be receptive to that plan.'

'Well, as you know him, you'll have an easy way of wheedling out what he really wants. Enough money for a nice car, bit of extra land for his business, et cetera. No man would turn down that sort of prize in exchange for staying chained to a tree. We men are practical creatures and no tree is worth a substantial amount of money, especially to small village folk like that, who've probably never even seen a Lamborghini before, never mind had a chance to own one ...'

I prickle at the insinuation that someone's worth is based on what car they drive or that people in little villages are somehow different or lesser than Harrison's millionaire cronies.

'Don't even *think* of coming back yet, Felicity. If this chap won't give up, start on the old folks. Offer 'em all new mobility scooters or something. If they give up and the Tree Idiot is on his own, he'll soon walk away with his tail between his legs.'

I want to tell him about Ryan Sullivan, the man who *never* understood the meaning of the words "give up". The man who would never be convinced that a plant was dead, even when it was shrivelled up, brown, and crisp in front of him. You could see the sycamore tree from the top of the hill where Sullivan's Seeds and Plant Nursery was. Birds could be heard chirruping for miles, and as the leaves turned from green to yellow, we'd watch it together, mapping the arrival of autumn as the tips of each leaf changed and autumnal colours gradually crept along each branch. It was inconceivable that someday the tree might not be there. It's as much a part of Lemmon Cove as the beaches or the cliffs themselves.

'Some things are worth more than money,' I say eventually, hoping I sound more confident than my stuttery voice suggests.

'Everyone has a price, Felicity. It's up to you to find it. Or you'll *find* yourself in the queue for the job centre next week.'

'That's not fair. My whole career isn't based on this one job,' I say. 'I've been working hard for ages. You can't fire me if one little thing doesn't go my way.'

He's hung up. I pull the phone away from my ear and the dark screen comes back on. Before I even dialled his number, I knew how that conversation was going to go.

Great. Now what?

The idea of staying gives me a little fizzle of excitement, the thought of spending time with Ryan is a thrill I didn't think I'd ever feel again. I thought he'd hate me for misreading his signals and mistaking his friendship for flirting all those years ago, but he seemed genuinely pleased to see me. And it felt good, I think. But it's marred by the idea that my job is to put an end to their protest and at some point in the *very* near future, I'm going to have to admit where I work and try to persuade Ryan that he'd prefer a new Ferrari than trying to save the wishing tree, which is never going to be the case.

'Everything okay, Fliss?' Dad asks when I go back in.

He and Cheryl are still sitting at the table in the living room. He's made a mixed pepper and lemon pasta salad and we'd just sat down to eat and of *course* Harrison chose that moment to ring.

'Fine,' I say breezily, because this only gets worse if it causes Dad to worry too. 'Just my boss checking in.'

'It's half past seven!' Cher looks up at the clock on the wall in horror.

'He works late. A lot.'

'Don't tell me you usually work this late too?' Dad looks worried.

I gulp as I sit back down. 'Not often, no.' Lying is becoming a far-too-easy habit lately.

'Good. I wouldn't like to think of you having no time for a life outside of work. There must be so many fun things to do in a big city like that. You wanted to live there from the first time you saw the New Year's Eve fireworks when you were little. It must be a dream come true. The life you always wanted.'

I don't realise I haven't answered until they're both staring at me expectantly. 'Oh, er, yeah. Great. It's great.'

I can't even remember the last time I saw New Year's Eve in at midnight, never mind bothered with fireworks. I'm usually asleep by then. I don't know what they think my life is like, but I drag myself home on the tube at somewhere between eight and nine every night, pick up something to eat on the way, do whatever studying up there is for the next day, and then crawl into bed with a book and usually manage a paragraph or two before falling asleep on top of it.

'Speaking of work, if anyone asks, I'm a chef.'

'A chef?' Dad says.

'A *chef?*' Cheryl asks. '*You?*'

'Why does everyone keep saying that?' I quickly explain why I can't tell anyone where I really work, and why they have to back me up if they get asked because my whole story will fall apart otherwise.

It all feels so wrong, but the lie is out there now I've told it. I can't go back and change it, and I can't come clean because the protestors will throw me out, and Ryan will despise me for lying to him.

'Fliss ... *why?*' Dad asks, sounding more confused than a giraffe with a knot in its neck.

'The guy running it ... It's Ryan Sullivan.' I say his name like it explains everything.

'Oh, your ex-boyfriend!' Dad exclaims.

I choke on the pasta salad. 'He's *not* my ex.'

'Of course he is. I always thought he'd be my son-in-law someday. Loved that lad. All I heard for years was "Ryan this and Ryan that".'

I can feel how red my cheeks have gone at the idea that even my dad knew the extent of my crush. And I'd thought I was so good at hiding it. 'I talked about him because we worked together every single day, and you always made a point of asking me what we'd been doing that day.'

'It was a bit more than just work though, wasn't it? All those field trips you went on together ...'

'That was just Ryan being protective. The old farmers spent too much time ogling my boobs and he knew I was uncomfortable being alone with them, so he asked me to go along for the ride when he went to meet suppliers or collect stuff. It was all perfectly innocent.' I can see that now, but at the time, I thought he wanted an excuse to spend time with me. 'He was being friendly. Because that's what we were – friends.'

'Never could understand why you two had that falling-out.' Dad shakes his head, continuing like I haven't spoken.

I remember the lie I told back then too – on the morning I was leaving and Dad asked when Ryan was coming to say goodbye, and I'd muttered something about us having a row. I was too embarrassed to tell anyone the truth.

'It's a shame neither of you thought to tell me he was still here. I could've done without the heart attack this morning.'

'Didn't know he was,' Dad mutters.

'I didn't think you'd want to know,' Cheryl adds. 'You fell out with him, remember? The one time Dad mentioned him to tell you about his company closing down, you snapped his head off and said you didn't want to know.'

'I *didn't* want to know; that doesn't mean I didn't *want* to know.' I sigh. Nothing I've said tonight has made sense. Was Ryan Sullivan always this confusing?

'He's the one trying to save the tree, is he?' Dad asks, and continues when I nod. 'Good. I always loved that tree. Did you girls know that your mum and I carved our names onto the trunk many moons ago?'

'What?' Cheryl and I say in unison.

'On the night we got married. We were both a bit tipsy after the reception and wandered home to clear our heads, and back then it was impossible to walk past the sycamore tree and *not* add a slice of your own life to it. Your mum checked our carving hadn't faded every time we went there after that. I used to joke that she'd trust the tree and chuck me out pre-emptively if it ever did.'

I never knew that. Of all the time I've spent looking at the names on that trunk, I never knew Mum and Dad's were on there somewhere.

'I remember scattering her ashes on the beach and feeling like she was watching over us. The tree was a reassuring presence in the background, like she was somehow there with us.'

Dad swallows hard. 'It's a good thing that you and Ryan are going to save it then, isn't it?'

I put on a bright smile for him even though I'm not sure doing anything with Ryan is a good idea … but saving that tree *definitely* is. No matter what Harrison says, no matter what my job is supposed to be, I can't be responsible for destroying the wishing tree, especially now I know that. Maybe there's a happy medium. Maybe I can genuinely help with the protest by pretending to be undercover but not really pretending to be … I give my head a shake to clear it. I've even confused myself.

# Chapter 6

'Will you stop tossing and turning? The hiss of you deflating is invading my dreams!' Cheryl throws a cushion at me.

The idea of me deflating makes me giggle, and I turn over again, which causes the inflatable bed to squeak with friction against the carpet and let out a nails-on-blackboard screech, and I hear the unmistakable unsticking of the repair patch I stuck on earlier.

If I'm going to stay, I need to get something better than this to sleep on. I'm listing to the side, the bed threatening to tip me out altogether and I take it as a sign.

'I'm going for a walk.' I roll out and land on my knees on the bedroom carpet.

'And would this walk happen to take you past the strawberry patch?'

'No.' I sigh. 'Maybe. I can't stop thinking about him being out there at night, Cher. He must be freezing.'

'It's August.'

'It still gets cold at night.'

'It's twenty-something degrees! It's warmer tonight than most of spring!'

'Well, he might be hungry. Ryan was always a night owl and

it's barely midnight. I doubt he'll be asleep. And there are a ton of leftovers – I could take some and walk past, and if he is asleep then I'll leave them so he's got something to wake up to.'

'You keep telling yourself that,' she mutters. 'Just do it quietly because I've got to get up for work in the morning.'

I change my pyjamas for a pair of joggers and a T-shirt and creep down to the kitchen. I load some leftover pasta salad into a Tupperware container and clip the lid on, and cut a slice of the chocolate cake Dad had made when I got back earlier and then rethink it and cut another slice, put them both in a tin, throw in two forks and make a flask of tea, put the whole lot into a backpack and hoist it over my shoulder. There's a torch on the table in the hallway and I grab it as I sneak out the door.

It's sensible to get up and do something when you can't sleep, I tell myself. Fresh air is good for you. And if I *happen* to stroll past the strawberry patch …

I do, of course, head straight there, at such a pace that I'm out of breath by the time I reach the beach car park and let myself in the gate to the footpath. There's the glow of what looks like a lantern from the direction of the tree, but I don't want to shout out and wake everyone up, including the care home residents and Ryan if he *is* asleep, so I undo the metal chain and push a steel fence panel aside, wincing at every clang in the silence of the night.

'Who's there? Don't come in! I'm armed!' Ryan's voice from the tree makes me jump.

'It's me, Ry,' I answer. 'Are you really armed?'

'Fee?' He sounds confused. 'And no, of course not, but you never know who's going to walk in here and throw their weight around. There's *nothing* I wouldn't put past those heartless companies. Stay there, I'll come and get you. It's hazardous in the dark. Well, it's hazardous in daylight; it's even worse in the dark.'

I hear the rustle of branches and the thunk as he jumps down from the tree, and there's the murmur of his voice reassuring

Baaabra Streisand, and I shine my torch down the path to see him coming towards me, the chain rattling as he moves, carrying a glowing lantern.

'Hey.' He lifts his hand to his eyes to block the beam of my torch. 'What are you doing here so late?'

'Couldn't sleep,' I say honestly. 'Kept thinking about you on your own out here.'

'I'm not on my own.'

My heart jumps into my throat. He said he wasn't married and something about spinsters. He didn't actually say he didn't have a girlfriend. I've probably interrupted a romantic cosy summer night sleepover in a tree. 'Oh, I'll go. I didn't—'

I've already started backing away when he interrupts me. 'Baaabra Streisand's here too.'

'Oh, right!' The relief makes me start laughing. 'Of course she is. I, er, just thought I'd wander past, see if you needed anything. Thought you might be cold. I brought tea.' If in doubt, always fall back on tea – the Great British answer for everything. 'Have you eaten?'

'Not since earlier, but I *love* the sound of a chef asking me that. Makes me wonder what's in that bag.' He nods to the backpack over my shoulder, and I cringe at the idea of him thinking I'm a chef. 'C'mon, come and sit with me. Catch up. It's been too long.'

Has he forgotten that I saw him a few hours ago? I think he means more than that though and it makes my heart pound faster. His voice is deep and he's speaking quietly given the time of night. Without realising it, I've drifted closer to him and he holds his hand out.

I automatically slip mine into his as he turns and leads us back towards the tree, holding his lantern up to light the way, and I turn the beam of my torch towards the uneven ground in front of my feet to be extra sure of no more sheep poo incidents.

When we reach the clear area surrounding the tree, my torchlight falls onto the sheep, who is now lying on one of those huge dog bed cushions. She looks up uninterestedly and puts her head back down.

Ryan tugs me around the tree to a spot between branches on the lower left side. 'It's taken a bit of trial and error and bumps on the head, but this is the access point.' He lets go of my hand and holds the lantern to the trunk so I can see where he taps the bark. 'See this dent? Put your right foot here and use it as a foothold to push yourself up, and then you can use this branch to pull yourself the rest of the way.' He reaches a long arm up and pats a branch above his head, seemingly forgetting that not all of us are six-foot-one.

He hands me the lantern and, within seconds, he's on his knees in the big dip of the tree trunk and leaning over the side, holding his hand out. I pass him up the lantern and then my backpack, and hold the torch between my teeth.

Clambering up here has the potential to go horribly wrong and end with me flailing about in the water metres below. I do what Ryan said and position my foot in the dented part of the bark and use the foothold to launch myself upwards, and he grabs my hand and hauls me into the tree.

It's a huge, almost-flat space where the trunk splits off in different directions, leaving a wide dip in the middle. The wood is smooth and silky; the bark worn away from so many years of children climbing it. Ryan hangs his lantern from a branch above, giving us just enough light to see.

He's got a real little den up here. The canopy of tarpaulin to one side is like a tent to keep his stuff dry, and a sleeping bag is opened out across the middle of the trunk, and a couple of fleece blankets, one mussed up like it was pushed off in a hurry, along with a book open face-down. 'Were you trying to get to sleep?'

'Nah.' He stops rifling through my backpack long enough to glance at me. 'You know me, I never could sleep at this time of night.' He holds up the Tupperware container he's got out. 'Did you make these?'

'No.' I decide to be honest. For a change. 'My dad did.'

'Aww, Dennis always was an incredible cook. I used to love him sending lunch in for me. When Mum and Dad were at the hospital, it was often the only real food I ate all day. How is he? I never see him around these days.'

'No. He's …' I don't know. What have I become that I don't even know how my own father is? 'I don't think he goes out much. Cher said something the other night and I haven't got to the bottom of it yet.'

'You should bring him down here. Get him involved in the protest. Cynthia was asking about him after you left this afternoon. Apparently they used to work together? She has *fond* memories of him.'

'Does she now?' I waggle my eyebrows and he laughs. 'Imagine having *fond* memories of someone you used to work with.' I don't know what it is about the dark that makes me braver, but the intensity in his eyes is dulled by the night and I feel less uptight than I did earlier.

'No, I can't imagine that at all,' he says, deadpan, with his mouth full as he shovels pasta into it. 'Seriously, Fee. I'm glad you came back.'

I'm not sure if he means to Lemmon Cove or tonight.

'Sorry if I was weird earlier,' he carries on. 'Seeing you again was like being hit by a low-flying spaceship. The shock did something to me. Most of this afternoon is a blur. I can't remember what I said, but I probably embarrassed myself.'

'I feel exactly the same.'

'But it's a good spaceship, right? I mean, I'm ecstatic to see you again.'

It makes me go hot and red all over. Only Ryan could sort spaceships into good and bad categories.

'The whole of today feels like some fuzzy dream. Ever since

you went home, I've been going over everything I said and trying to remember what I said and *shouldn't* have, and what I didn't say and *should* have.'

I feel exactly the same about that too. It's kind of good that we're on the same page, and I feel better if he feels even half as awkward and shocked as I felt when I saw him this morning.

'And I'm glad you came back tonight too,' he says, unintentionally clarifying my earlier question. 'We couldn't talk properly earlier, not with everyone milling about, waiting to snaffle up crumbs of gossip. And just so you know, I was grilled *mercilessly* after you left.'

I giggle. 'They're certainly an interesting bunch.'

'That's one way to put it.' He laughs but the fondness in his voice is unmistakable.

'I saw what Tonya's been posting on Twitter,' I say. 'I didn't know you'd be here. I wouldn't have come if I had.'

He stops with the fork halfway to his mouth in mid-air. 'Why on earth not?'

Does he really not know?

'Because of the …' I rethink and realise that reminding him of the way things ended is *not* a good idea. 'Because it's been so long, I guess.'

'I know. I thought you were going to come back and visit me *all* the time. I missed you.'

Again, I can't help wondering if he *really* doesn't know why I didn't. Yes, we'd promised to keep in touch, but then I kissed him and he made it clear he wasn't interested. I didn't think he'd ever want to hear from me again.

The new job had been stressful and I was out of my depth. I'd known it was a mistake from the first day, and most nights there was nothing I wanted more than to hear Ryan's low Welsh accent and reassuring words, but how *could* I breezily pick up the phone and pretend nothing had happened?

'You knew where I lived.' My voice comes out tetchy, but it's almost like he's forgotten an event that changed my life, and *not* for the better. 'You had my number. You didn't keep in touch either.'

'I didn't think you'd want to see me again.'

I didn't think *he'd* want to see *me* again. Silence hangs in the air between us, until the sheep starts snoring and makes us both burst into laughter.

'You did say she was a comedic sheep.' I'm grateful to Baaabra Streisand for her flawless timing, a perfect cue to change the subject. 'I can't believe you're sleeping here.'

'Too uncomfy for your refined tastes these days? Used to sleeping on posh beds from Harrods? The Fee I knew would've loved this. A hideaway in a tree, being part of nature …'

'Midges, spiders, woodlice, snoring sheep, rude garden gnomes … although it can't be worse than what I'm sleeping on.'

He looks at me curiously.

'One of those inflatable sofas that were retro in the Nineties. God knows where my dad even managed to find one in this day and age. I've already used two puncture repair patches, and it only came with three. I keep waking Cheryl up by deflating.'

'Oh, the mental image.' His eyes crinkle up as he laughs and finishes the pasta salad in the container.

'Where do you live now?'

'Same place I always used to. The old family house. It's mine now.'

I loved his house, but if he's alone there, it can only mean one thing.

Like he can tell what I'm thinking, he ducks his head. 'My father died the year before last. He and my mum divorced years ago – she lives in Spain with a toy boy now.'

'I'm so sorry, Ry.' I go to reach out and touch his hand but force myself not to.

Ryan's father ran Sullivan's Seeds and gave me a job when I was sixteen. I didn't have any experience, but he knew my mum

70

had died and took pity on me. It was only as a picker at first, but the fresh sea air and the hard, outdoor work saved my sanity that summer. The monotony of harvesting their wide range of plants kept my mind welcomely blank and my brain occupied. The exhaustion at the end of every day meant I slept at night. It was only meant to be a summer job, but he kept me on through the autumn and winter months packing mail orders and wrapping plants bought as Christmas gifts, and when the spring came, he encouraged me to start growing new varieties in their greenhouses.

That year, he had a heart attack and although he survived, he could no longer work, and Ryan took over. Three years older than me, gorgeous, funny, kind, and lovely. As lost as I was. We'd connected from the first day.

'He'd been ill for a long time. He spent the last few years of his life living here.' He indicates over his shoulder towards the care home. 'That's how I got to know the residents. It's also why I'm not going to sit back and let them put a hotel here.'

This time he points to a window on the edge of the big white building, despite the fact it's dark, and no lights on inside make it difficult to tell one room from another. 'That was my dad's room. He spent the last few months of his life bed-bound, and this view and the smell of the sea breeze coming in the open windows were the only things he had to keep him going. If they put a hotel here, the residents are going to lose their view, and the only scents coming in the window are going to be from the hotel kitchens and rubbish bins. *No one* has given a second thought to the people who live here.'

'So you chained yourself to a tree?'

'For as long as someone's chained to this tree, the police are not going to chuck us out.' He winks at me. 'I've got a buddy on the force. The police are on our side. The tree can be considered a residential property while I'm here.'

'Right …' I know he can hear how sceptical I sound, but I

keep thinking about what Harrison said about the police in their pocket.

'What?' Ryan gets out the two pieces of cake I wrapped in kitchen towel and hands me the spare fork.

'You own the campsite next door. A hotel popping up here would have a negative impact on your business.'

'No it wouldn't. We cater to a completely different clientele. This would be a luxury hotel with *luxury* prices. People who can afford to stay in places like this are never going to come to a campsite, and vice versa.'

He's got a point, but I've still got Harrison's words ringing in my ears. And it doesn't matter what Ryan thinks – I'm going to lose my job if I don't find a way of stopping this protest.

'First you're checking up on me at night and now you're questioning my morals? Anyone would think you didn't trust me anymore ...'

'Oh God, no, nothing like that,' I say in a rush. I can't be honest with him. I can't tell him I work in an office full of hard-nosed businessmen who'd stab you in the back soon as look at you and would do just about anything off the moral scale to get their hands on a piece of land they could make a profit from.

His serious face breaks into a smile. 'I'm kidding, Fee. Don't worry, it always takes people a while to adjust to my weird sense of humour.'

He was always self-deprecating, but he never tried to change. I liked that about him. I never fitted in, and I tried to change myself so I would – he was proud of being himself and didn't care whether people liked him or not. I also feel guilty because it doesn't even cross his mind not to trust me. *I'm* the one whose motives we should be questioning.

I'm impressed at how quickly he scoffs his slice of the cake and then takes the two cups from the top of the flask and hands me one. He pours steaming hot tea into each of them and screws the top back on.

'To old friends.' He clinks his plastic cup against mine and then raises his in the direction of the care home. 'And, y'know, *old* friends.'

I can't help laughing. 'To being old in all senses of the word.'

He takes a sip of tea and sighs, and I do the same, letting it warm me. It's not cold tonight, but there's something about being outside late at night that makes a warm drink welcome, even in August.

'I know how it looks, but this genuinely isn't about business,' he says without being prompted. He puts the cup down on the smooth wood in front of him and pushes himself up until he can get his hand around a branch and tug it down carefully. He holds it with a hand outstretched above his head. 'Look at the size of these leaves. Trees don't get any bigger or more special than this. It's got to be one of the oldest trees in Wales – definitely the oldest sycamore. It would be criminal to cut this down for any reason, let alone for profit.'

He holds the branch by the tips of his fingers, being careful not to pull it down too far and not to damage a single leaf. The bright green leaves are huge, bigger than Ryan's palm when he opens his hand to compare the two. Some are the size of small dinner plates. It's a pretty spectacular sight.

'They're not even sure it's all one tree. People think it might've combined with other smaller sycamores – probably the ones around it that grew from its own seeds in the first few years of its life, and they melded together as one and that's why the trunk splits off like this. Three hundred years ago, it might've been seven or eight different trees.' He's looking up at the huge leaves in admiration as he speaks. 'And where else in the world are you going to find a view like that?'

I shift around to face out to sea because I've been so focused on Ryan that I've forgotten about the view. The branches are high enough above us that the view is unobstructed and the Bristol Channel is spread out in front of me. So clear and for so many miles that I'm surprised I can't see Devon on the horizon. The water is purple under the night sky, reflecting the twinkling of a million stars from above, and it's absolutely motionless. There isn't a breath of wind to disturb the water's surface.

I hear the rustle behind me as Ryan lets the branch go and the thud of his boots against the wood as he sits and pulls the blanket around.

It's so peaceful. Even the sheep has stopped snoring so the only sound is the gentle lap of the waves below. The tide has reached its highest point and is retreating down the beach, leaving darkened damp sand behind.

'Bit different to your usual views, huh?'

Views. I remember them. I remember being really taken with the view across the Thames when I started my job, but now … I can't remember the last time I had a chance to look out a window. I'm always rushing from one thing to the next. I never have time to stop and stare for a few moments.

I turn around to see he's settled back. He's still holding his plastic cup of tea, but he's reclining half-upright against the junction where one of the trunks splits away and the blanket is pulled over his legs. He pats the spot next to him and smiles when he catches my eyes.

It's a nice idea, and it's so serene up here that it would be easy to crawl across and forget everything that's happened between us and snuggle up beside Ryan, but I shake my head and cross my legs under me.

He throws me the other end of the furry fleece blanket and I drape it over my crossed legs and lean forward with my elbows on my knees and both hands wrapped around the plastic cup.

'I guess we could say you're in bed with me.'

'My teenage self can die happy,' I say, feeling braver than I could ever have been all those years ago.

He looks like he's about to say something, and I wonder if my inadvertent reminder of the teenager who had a crush on him is going to prompt him to say something about the kiss. Even though I'd like to never think about it again, I can't work out if he's genuinely forgotten it or if he's just being polite by not mentioning it, and it's got to the point where I want to know one way or the other. He couldn't have forgotten it, could he? You don't *forget* your friend throwing herself at you underneath the branches of this very tree.

He smiles at me. Or maybe you do.

'I heard the company you moved to went under ...' he says, and I can feel his eyes burning into mine.

'Yeah. About a year later. But you knew that was going to happen, didn't you?'

Ryan had told me not to go. When I left Sullivan's Seeds, it was for one of those "too good to be true" opportunities that did, indeed, turn out to be exactly that. A London-based plant and seed company who'd heard about my success at Sullivan's Seeds and wanted me to work for them as a plant finder. A job that would involve moving to London and travelling – my two biggest dreams in life. I was going to be responsible for finding new and unusual plants from across Europe, testing them for UK suitability, and working with a team of scientists to crossbreed them into hybrid versions that would suit the UK climate. Ryan tried to talk me out of it. He thought there was something dodgy about the company, and it turned out he was right. But I knew I'd never forgive myself if I didn't take the opportunity. I reasoned that even if it fell through, I'd have got out of Lemmon Cove – and staying here, never managing to escape this tiny coastal village, was my greatest fear.

He gives me a sad smile. 'I nearly phoned to say your old job was waiting for you a hundred times, but then I thought it might look like an "I told you so" and it wasn't intended like that. I thought about you all the time.'

What would've happened if he *had* offered me my old job back? Would I have taken it? I'd been homesick as all hell. I hated

London. It was nothing like the dream city I'd always imagined. It was crowded, stinky, noisy, and expensive. The world was *not* at my feet while I sang songs from musicals and lots of friendly strangers joined in as I skipped along golden-paved streets. Instead I huddled into myself while I dodged crowds and felt guilty for not helping homeless people because I didn't have enough to get by myself.

'But it's a good job I didn't because you clearly found your calling as a chef.'

I'm so lost in the past that it takes my brain a few moments to catch up to what he means. 'Oh! Yes, right. That.'

'Did you go to culinary school or something?'

Oh God, am I supposed to have gone to culinary school? 'No. Er, just learnt as I went. Like an apprenticeship!'

'Because you didn't used to be able to cook a Pot Noodle, it must've been quite a discovery to realise you could cook. Like Harry Potter getting his Hogwarts letter and discovering he'd been a wizard all along.'

'Oh yeah, there were owls delivering letters and everything.'

We smile at each other, and I have an overwhelming feeling that he knows something's going on. I was the worst cook in the universe. I *am* the worst. Baaabra Streisand could cook a better meal than I can. And I *had* to mention the fancy restaurant that caters for celebrities, didn't I? Only the most dis-believable place in the country for me to work.

'What happened to Sullivan's Seeds, Ry?' I ask, mainly to stop him thinking about my cooking ability.

'In a word – cucurbit poisoning.' He thinks for a moment. 'Technically two words.'

'Is that when the level of cucurbitacin is too high and makes squashes inedible?'

He drops his head into his hand and nods. 'Yep. And you don't know there's anything wrong with the produce until you've eaten it.'

My face screws up in sympathy. 'You poisoned people?'

'A couple of families up in the Midlands. Not seriously – I mean, a couple of days of nausea and diarrhoea, not death or anything. They'd bought my courgette seeds, grown the plants, eaten the courgettes, thought they tasted bitter, and then ... yeah. I had to get in touch with everyone who'd bought any of the gourd seeds, and I didn't have customer details for anyone who'd bought in person so had to put up big notices and issue product recalls and all that fun stuff. Then there was the compensation claims I had to settle ...'

I nod because lines have creased his forehead and his voice is quiet anyway, but it's dropped even lower.

'It's to do with cross-contamination from other plants, right?'

He nods. 'I had no way of telling how it happened and no way of testing for it, so no guarantee that it wouldn't happen again. The following year, I had no way of safeguarding against it so I pulled all of our squash products from sale. A big chunk of our income, and a big chunk of our growers' time and effort, but word gets around and mud sticks, you know? The year after, we only sold thirty per cent of our usual income. It seemed like everyone in the UK had heard of Sullivan's Seeds causing toxic squash syndrome and no one would touch us with a bargepole. I haemorrhaged customers *and* the wholesale firms I was supplying.'

The hand not holding his cup is twisting in the blanket and I want to squeeze it, but force myself not to be so daft.

'The year after, I met a Chinese wholesaler at a grower's conference and he offered to invest. Wanted to take our products to China where no one would've heard of the poisonous squash incident ... for a small fee ...' He looks up at me. 'You already know where this is going, don't you?'

I nod. Nothing good ever comes of businessmen who want a small fee.

'If I'm honest with myself, I knew it was a scam before I did

77

it. The company was on the edge and it was a last-ditch effort to save it when I already knew it was unsaveable. That investment tipped us over the edge, and unsurprisingly, there *was* no Chinese firm waiting to buy up all our stock. But at least when it failed, I could somehow blame that instead of my own inability to run a business.'

'I knew my job would fall through before I went.'

He meets my eyes and his mouth tips into a half-smile. 'I've never admitted that out loud before. And I'm guessing you haven't either?'

My smile matches his as I shake my head.

'Turns out, even fifteen years later, we still can't lie to each other.'

The thought makes my stomach turn over. *Can't we, Ry?* I swallow hard. 'So now you've got the campsite?'

'Yeah, after Sullivan's Seeds went, I had to sell the land and most of the money went to paying off the company's debts, but I had a little bit left over, and the farmer who owned that patch was an old friend of my dad's, and he did me a deal. There were always people turning up and illegally pitching tents in fields around here, and I had this idea of offering somewhere cheap and legal for them to stay, and it grew summer by summer. I earned enough to buy extra land and expanded from tents to on-site caravans, and then to a camping ground for campervans and motorhomes.'

I want to ask him why he never left Lemmon Cove. All Ryan ever wanted to do was travel, but I can't think of a way to word it that doesn't sound demeaning.

'Things don't often work out for me, but the campsite turned out to be just the thing Lemmon Cove needed at exactly the right time. Now I want to expand into proper holiday lets – a more luxurious experience. I want to put up little chalets with electricity, running water, kitchens and bathrooms. The highest level of glamping. It'll appeal to people who like the idea of camping but not the aspect of sleeping on the ground with insects crawling through their hair. I've got my eye on a patch of land that would be just the ticket, but I don't know if I'm going to get it yet.'

No wonder he doesn't want a hotel popping up here. If he's wanting to expand into luxury holiday lets, the *last* thing he needs is a hotel across the way. It totally contradicts what he said earlier about appealing to a different kind of clientele.

'I've not told anyone that before. Sorry, Fee, I never could stop myself talking to you.'

It makes me feel warm inside. We always shared everything and never tried to hide things between us, but something niggles at me. Even though it's dark, I look over at the campsite and the farmer's fields spread across the hillsides into the distance, too dark to see anything but indistinct mountainsides. 'Where's this patch of land?'

'Oh, it's near. Really near. I don't want to say too much in case I jinx it.'

Really near. What if it's literally *here*? Ryan's a businessman. What if he's seen an opportunity to put up his holiday lets on *this* patch of land? I have no idea how much more of the land surrounding the campsite he owns, but it can't be much or it would be in use because the campsite looks pretty full.

I narrow my eyes at him and he doesn't flinch, but his involvement in this protest is suddenly muddied, and I can't get the thought out of my head. It's a conflict of interests to be planning to expand into luxury holiday lets and also be involved in the protest against a luxury hotel being built right next door.

Maybe he thinks he can buy this bit of land if the hotel pulls out. Leave the tree intact, and only block the view with a few chalets. It's all a bit too convenient.

Maybe I'm not the only one being dishonest here.

# Chapter 7

Somehow, the idea of Ryan not being entirely honest makes me feel better about my job. I have to infiltrate this protest and discover what's got Landoperty Developments so spooked. It can't be personal. I can't let my feelings about the ex-strawberry patch cloud my judgement. I was sent here to do a job and that's what I have to do.

I have to admit I'm wondering what Harrison is so worried about as I push the gate open the next morning and look at the wilting cardboard sign with "Save Our Garden" written on it. It must've rained overnight because it's starting to disintegrate. I did some research last night and found an article on the local newspaper website about the residents protesting the sale of their garden area, but it only had one spam comment offering free penis enlargements, so I don't think it's getting much attention. The garden or the penises, clearly. The residents have been at this for two weeks now, and while I agree with Harrison that it *could* go viral, it's got all the potential of a damp squib at the moment.

The sign flops limply against the gate as I clang it shut behind me.

'Good morning!' It's Ryan's cheerful Welsh accent that greets me. 'I was hoping you'd be back today.'

I look up and meet his grey-blue eyes as he lifts aside the metal fencing to let me into the strawberry patch, and my resolve to remain professionally aloof wavers.

Ryan's lengthened the chain tethering him to the tree so he's up this end of the overgrown land, and he's wearing black three-quarter-length cargo trousers, solid-looking hiking boots, and a tank top, which is *really* unfair because his biceps are on show for all the world to see, and they're tanned and so huge that he must live on a Popeye-style diet. He's so distracting that I don't realise Tonya has come over to say good morning and has got an eye on exactly where my gaze is directed.

I swallow, trying to remember my own name. Those arms are enough to make you forget *everything*.

Everyone else calls over a greeting too, and I wave to them all, trying to concentrate on *anything* other than Ryan's presence behind me.

'What's this?' Alys comes over holding her phone out.

I really should have swotted up on household gadgets and things chefs might know … for example, how to cook … last night, but I didn't have a chance. However, the picture on the phone she shoves under my nose isn't a household gadget. 'Only Ryan got it so far. None of this lot did.' She tuts.

My face screws up in confusion. 'It's someone holding up a … tool in a bookshop?'

'It's a spanner in The Works!' She announces gleefully.

I don't know if I'm delirious, or if she is, or if Ryan's biceps are responsible for people losing their minds, but it's quite possibly the funniest thing I've ever heard and I burst out laughing.

'My friend and I compete to see who can do the best puns too,' Alys says by way of explanation.

'It's tree-lly funny,' Ryan adds.

'Oh, don't you start.' I point at him and he grins. He was always the king of bad jokes.

The site is abuzz with activity this morning, and not just with the bees zipping around the white bramble flowers in search of nectar. Cynthia is hobbling up and down with her walking frame and giving said bees words of encouragement. Mr Barley is sitting on the wall of a flowerbed with a set of paints and a gnome in hand.

'Boris Johnson!' He calls over when he sees me looking.

At first I think he might be insulting me and I put a hand on my head in case I forgot to brush my hair this morning, but Tonya quickly clarifies. 'He makes his own gnomes out of clay and paints them to look like people he hates. He's already done Donald Trump. Gnome Boris and Gnome Trump are going to do a photoshoot for Twitter later.'

'Gnomes sound like better options for world leaders than the current ones,' Ffion calls out. 'Can we vote for them at the next election?'

The two blokes are sitting on one of the other brick flowerbeds and playing chess, and Godfrey is on the same bench as yesterday reading a newspaper. There's another man painting another cardboard sign, this one reading "Give peas a chance" with a picture of a green pea with a peace symbol drawn over it. Baaabra Streisand is down by the sycamore tree, happily scraping through blackberry bushes and eating whatever she uncovers.

Chaos is the word that springs to mind. As Harrison's assistant for the past four years, I've dealt with a few protests, and none of them have been like this. If it weren't for Ryan chained to the tree, it would be like a regular day in the care home garden. No one looking in would even know there was a protest going on.

Up at the care home, a middle-aged man in a baggy salmon-pink polo shirt emerges and struts past the hedge, but doesn't come through the gateway that joins the care home to the garden. After a few paces up and down, he turns and walks away.

'See that guy?' Ryan's voice is in my ear again, so close that his chin is millimetres away from my shoulder and his arm comes up to point around me.

I nod, following the direction he's pointing in even though the man in question has long since disappeared around the front of the building.

'That's Steffan, the owner who's planning to sell this land. Checking up on us again.'

'He does that every day,' Ffion says.

'He expects us to give up,' Cynthia says.

'We're not giving up,' Tonya reassures her.

'We're *never* giving up,' Ryan says. 'Not while I'm still breathing.'

Ryan's stood back up to his full height now, but he's barely stepped away, and I'm wondering how much longer I'll be breathing for, never mind this lot.

'He never comes down here. Just skulks around and looks over several times a day – hoping to catch it unoccupied so he can put his fences up and call his morally compromised property developers. They're all lying in wait, you know.' Ffion uses a walking stick to point towards the unkempt hedgerows like property developers might be lurking in the undergrowth.

'But he hasn't actually sold it yet, right?'

'He was all set to sign on the dotted line, but I faked a heart attack to distract him,' Tonya says.

'And I stole the papers from his desk!' Mr Barley shouts. 'It really put the willies up him! I put willies on my gnomes that day in celebration!'

All the talk of willies and property developers is making me uncomfortable and reminding me that I have a job to do.

'Right, so what are we doing today?' I clap my hands together and try to get a combined attention span of longer than 2.5 seconds before gnomes and willies take over again.

'We?' Ryan says in my ear, mimicking what I said yesterday.

'Well, I'm here, aren't I?' I turn around to face him. 'I want to help.'

He smiles at me and I get lost in his light eyes for a moment.

'Well, we've got the chess, Monopoly, and Scrabble out,' Tonya is saying when I come back to myself.

'Yahtzee!' One of the old blokes cries, accidentally upending the chessboard and sending the pieces scattering in his excitement. The other bloke takes his cap off and thwacks him with it.

'Guess Who!' Mr Barley says.

The two chess players start setting out their pieces again, resigning themselves to starting the match over.

'I meant in non-board-game-related terms,' I say carefully, wringing my hands together. They can't really think a protest is just sitting here playing board games … can they? 'For the protest? To get people talking about it?'

'We've all relocated our lives to spend as much time as possible outside, so it's occupied. And *he's* chained to a tree!' Ffion points to Ryan.

'Well, yeah, but …' I look between them all, wondering what right I have to barge in and tell them they're doing this wrong. For my job, they're *supposed* to be doing it wrong. Board games are Harrison's best-case scenario. But for my heart, I want to say, *For God's sake, this is a protest and you may as well be churning butter. Three more games of Buckaroo and the builders will be along to dig the hotel's foundations.*

'I know that look.' Ryan smiles at me. 'Your "I want to say something but you're not going to like it" face hasn't changed in fifteen years. Go on – we're all ears.'

Somewhere, a hearing aid squeals with perfect timing.

'You're campaigning but you're not campaigning *for* anything,' I say in a rush. 'You're just … here. As far as anyone outside is concerned, you're sitting in your garden on a summer's day. And you.' I turn to Ryan. 'You're a guy chained to a tree. With a sheep. You're vaguely making a nuisance of yourself, but you have no case. No alternative. Nothing to fight them *with*.'

'Steffan inherited Seaview Heights from a business partner who died. He's not interested in it – but he doesn't want any trouble. We just have to make it so difficult for them that they don't *want* to build here.'

'But someone else will. If it's not *this* hotel, *this* developer, there will be others. There are plenty of property developers out there who will see the potential in a patch of land like this. This protest is attracting attention in the industry. Even if you win this time, Steffan is going to get bigger and better offers, and next time they're going to be for a high enough price that he won't hesitate to turf you all out. He might not want trouble now, and I'm guessing he's umm-ing and ahh-ing because of some loyalty to whoever he got the building from, but that might be a different story when he gets a high bid he can't refuse. You don't just have to see this particular developer off – you have to *save* the land.'

'How do we do that?' Mr Barley asks.

I glance at Ryan again. I hadn't thought that far ahead. Motivational speeches are not my strong point.

'There's nothing to make anyone take notice,' I start. 'Take the gate sign. It's visible from the road, and this is one of the main routes through the Gower area, and it's the middle of the summer holidays – there are a *lot* of extra people driving past to the various beaches along the coast. But it doesn't *say* anything. There's no call to arms. No explanation. Nothing to make people care. It should be lit up in red with a banner to explain what's going on. There—'

'We've got a petition! My son set it up online for us! There are thirteen signatures so far!' Tonya says.

I count them. 'And nine of them are yours, right?'

'The rest are our families' and some of the staff have signed too, but some were a bit worried about putting their names down to go against their boss.'

Yeah, imagine doing that. I shudder to think of Harrison if he could see me now. 'A petition is … it's something, but what's it going to do? If you get 100,000 signatures, they're not going to debate it in parliament. This is what I mean about not having a goal.'

'We're going to send it to the hotel company.'

I think about those men in business suits sitting in Harrison's meeting rooms. 'They won't care. You aren't the people who'll be staying in their hotel. A list with a few hundred names on it won't make a jot of difference.'

'You think we can get a few *hundred* signatures?' Cynthia asks, sounding awestruck.

I look at Ryan again and he grins. 'Yes, they do always miss the point this much.'

The fact that he doesn't think I'm mad buoys my confidence. 'I think you could get a few hundred *thousand* if this is run the right way.'

Shock waves go through the group and they shuffle closer like I somehow hold the secret. I involuntarily take a step backwards and crash into Ryan and his hand closes around my arm to steady me.

'We're online.' Tonya waves her phone in the air. 'I'm @BeachBattleaxe on Twitter. We've all been learning to use it. I got nine retweets the other day.'

'I thought retweets sounded like something you'd need a swift course of Imodium for.' One of the chess-playing men steals the other one's bishop and thrusts it in the air even though it wasn't his turn.

It makes me laugh. 'Yes, and your Twitter account is getting a bit of attention, but it's not done right. Your bio reads "I don't know what to put. Is this the right place? What does it want me to write?" and your profile photo is of the veins on the back of your hand.'

Ryan nudges me. 'You've been doing your homework.'

'I want this place saved.' The shake in my voice is un-hideable. I sound like I'm lying even though I'm not. 'You're posting photos of your naughty gnomes, and people are enjoying little old ladies getting to grips with technology, but you've barely mentioned the campaign, and there's nowhere people can go for more information.'

'I posted the link to the petition,' Ffion says. 'Two people retweeted it. One of them was an escort looking for men so I blocked that one.'

I meet Ryan's eyes again and we both start giggling.

'I think what Fee's trying to say is that we need a website,' he says. 'I've been intending to find someone to design one for us, but I'm not into social media and stuff like that, so I haven't got around to it yet.'

Maybe that explains why he's unstalkable on Facebook. And I have to be *very* careful not to say that out loud.

'I'll do it,' I say. 'Website repairs are part of my job. I know my way around the free hosting sites.'

'As a chef?' Lines crinkle around his eyes as they screw up in confusion.

Oh, for God's sake. Think before you speak, Fliss. 'You have to be a multi-tasker these days!' If my tone was any breezier, I'd gust them all over the cliff's edge.

Something's missing here. This place has got all the potential to go viral, but no one's tapping into it. I look around for inspiration and my eyes fall on Godfrey. A few wisps of white hair are blowing on his otherwise bald head. He's still sitting on the bench with his newspaper spread across his lap, but he hasn't turned over a page since I got here, and I get the impression he's listening in without getting involved. I think about what Ryan told me yesterday, how much this place must mean to him, how heartbroken he would be to see it destroyed, to watch someone cut down the tree where he goes to feel closer to his wife.

I was in tears when Ryan told me Godfrey's story. Other people would be too.

'My mum died when I was a teenager,' I say. 'We scattered her ashes on the beach, and I looked up at the tree from the sand below and felt like she was watching over us. As we walked back up, a robin was sitting in the branches singing. You know how they say robins appear when departed loved ones are near?' I don't realise I'm getting choked up until Ryan's hand squeezes my shoulder and I have to stop myself and take a few deep breaths. 'I always felt closer to her when I came here afterwards. You know like Cinderella with the hazel tree but no one ever turned my dress and shoes to gold. There was always, always a robin sitting in the branches.'

'I had my first kiss with my late husband under that tree,' Ffion says.

'My wife and I carved our names on our first anniversary. Even though we moved away, we came back to visit the tree every year around our anniversary to make sure our carving hadn't faded ... She died a few years back, and I couldn't think of anywhere I'd rather spend my final years than right here,' Mr Barley says.

I have no idea where that old legend came from, but local people of their generation believed it wholeheartedly. The tradition of happy couples carving their names into the bark and then coming back to visit it every year to make sure their relationship wasn't doomed ... It gets the cogs in my brain working.

'Ry told me about your carving, Godfrey,' I call across to the elderly man on the bench.

He looks up at me, gives me a smile and a nod, but makes no other move to get involved.

'This is it,' I say. 'This is the key. The trunk is *covered* in carvings from across the centuries. How many other stories are connected to it? How many other people would be devastated by the thought of it being cut down? *This* is how we save the land – by saving the tree.'

'How do we do that?' Tonya asks.

'We, er ...' I really need to start finishing thoughts before I say them out loud. 'We have to share its stories. Trees this old are magical, ethereal, otherworldly things. It could be *The Magic Faraway Tree* with different lands coming to the top of it. Moon-Face and Silky could be living in those branches. Looking up at something like this makes you feel like a child again. Look at all those bunches of helicopter seeds ripening ahead of autumn. When I was young, I'd look up at them and feel like magic was just around the corner.' I dodge past Ryan and walk a little further down the path between blackberry bushes, gesturing towards the towering branches as I step over the long chain attaching him to the trunk. 'There is no one alive today who can remember it ever *not* being there. Landoperty Developments cannot be allowed to take something like this. It doesn't belong to anyone. It belongs to the earth itself and cutting it down would change the landscape forever.'

'Hear, hear.' Ryan claps and I'm blushing when I look over and meet his eyes.

Tonya has tottered along the path behind me, and she's reaching her hand out in my direction. I take hold of it because I think she might need assistance, but instead of gripping it like I expected, she pumps it up and down like a business deal. 'All those in favour of Felicity being our new campaign manager?' she yells, making me jump at the sudden volume.

A chorus of "ayes" goes through the group.

Tonya beams a toothy beam at me. 'Congratulations, you're officially our new campaign manager.'

'I can't do that,' I say instantly. 'I have a job to get back to.'

'Well, for as long as you're here, and then you can hand over to Ryan when you leave. He can be your deputy.'

Ryan meets my eyes with two raised eyebrows. 'Oh, how the roles have reversed. I used to be Fee's boss, you know.'

I smile at the mocking indignation in his voice and the playfulness in his eyes as he waggles his eyebrows at me.

'A million per cent the best boss I've ever had,' I tell Tonya.

'You were the best employee I've ever had,' he says quietly and then hesitates. 'And the best friend.'

I momentarily forget how to breathe. Ryan was never like a boss to me, but to hear him say it too …

'Wait, wait, wait.' I snap back to reality. 'This has all gone too far. I said I wanted to help, not be your—'

'Well, you can help by being our campaign manager, can't you?' Tonya claps me on the arm. 'There, that's all settled.'

Harrison's angry face appears in my head. When he said "infiltrate the protest and gain their trust" I don't think he meant take over the running of it.

'What's our first task, boss?' Cynthia shouts.

Oh God.

'Want me to show you the ropes on your first day?' Ryan gives me a wink that has no right to make me feel as fluttery as it does.

I remember showing *him* the ropes on *his* first day at Sullivan's Seeds. He'd bumbled in on a typically dripping summer day, late and panting for breath from rushing, wearing welly boots he'd clearly bought that morning because they still had a tag in the back of them and he was limping from blisters within an hour, and realised he'd left the keys to the office in the car and had to go back to get them, while four drenched gruff farmers swore at him and told him his father would never make mistakes like that. I liked him from the moment I walked in on him singing "Sunshine After the Rain" to a bed of bedraggled plants that afternoon. I'm not sure random Nineties music has ever been responsible for an instant connection before, but it was one of my favourite songs and no one else thought Nineties music was cool.

Like he can tell what I'm thinking, he's come closer again and I find myself comforted by him being nearby, stepping back into his space while I try to think of something to say to the waiting residents.

'People will care about this tree,' I say eventually. 'There must be hundreds of people who are responsible for some of those carvings on the trunk. Does anyone know of anyone else who used to come here regularly, or carved something into the bark? Any of the other residents? Any of your friends?'

They all start chattering amongst themselves, and I look up at the tree. It must have so many stories to share, and there must be so many people who'd want to know them. I feel myself pulled towards it like it's a magnet.

'Morning, Baaabra Streisand,' I say as the sheep gives me an annoyed look for interrupting her grass munching. She takes an inquisitive step towards me, and I stand still to see if she's going to attack. Her furry white nose starts twitching towards my pockets, like she might be expecting food, and when I turn one out to show her only my phone, she gives an annoyed baa and goes back to the munching.

When it seems safe to turn my back, I walk around the tree, glad of the shade from the branches even this early in the morning. I reach my fingers out and run them over the trunk. The pinkish-grey bark would be as smooth as it is on the higher branches if it wasn't for the thousands of carvings wallpapering the trunk. They cover every inch – from the tips of the lowest branches to the points where the roots spider out and burrow into the earth.

I had no idea until last night that my mum and dad's names were on here somewhere. As my fingers trail along each dip in the bark, it's not really their names I'm searching for. Somewhere on here is the "Ry + Fee" he carved in a love heart. It *has* to still be here. For as much as I've tried to put that day out of my mind, I can remember every second of it. How he gave me a lift home from Sullivan's Seeds and stopped here because it was my last day and he said he didn't want it to end. How we walked down to the tree hand in hand. It was early autumn, the beginning of September, too early for the seeds to be falling, but the very tips of the leaves on the higher branches had started to yellow. He'd jumped up into the tree and grabbed two helicopter seeds and insisted we throw them off the cliff and make a wish. We'd closed our eyes and on Ryan's low count of three, thrown our sycamore seeds off the edge, made a wish, and opened our eyes to watch them plummet directly to the sand below, far too wet and heavy to spin that early in the season. We'd laughed. He'd pulled me closer, and I'd been sure he was about to kiss me.

I was twenty, far too old to believe in sycamore wishes, but the wish I'd made on that seed was that he'd like me in *that* way.

And I was so sure he did. But instead of kissing me, he'd bypassed me and started running a hand over the trunk until he found an empty space, pulled out the Swiss Army Knife that always hung on his keyring, and crouched down to carve our names, encasing them in a heart shape. I took it as a sign, and when he stood back up, I had that now-or-never feeling. I was leaving the next morning. I had to know if the years of flirtation, jokes, excuses to spend time together, and the looks he kept giving me had meant something to him like they had to me.

While he was putting the keyring back into his pocket, I'd slipped my hand around the back of his neck and pulled his head down, using the grip to push myself up too, until our lips had smashed together.

At first, he didn't respond. He didn't kiss me back. And then his hands were on my shoulders, pushing me away. 'I can't do this now, Fee ...' He'd spoken to the ground, too horrified to look me in the eyes. Cold realisation slowly dawned on me and I stumbled away from him. I'd gone from now-or-never to fight-or-flight. I had to get away. He'd called after me. A kind of hoarse 'Fee ...' but I hadn't stuck around. I didn't want to hear his polite reasoning that we were just friends and he didn't feel like *that* about me. I'd gathered that much.

Despite the sun, goose bumps prickle my skin at the memory of that day. Unequivocally the most embarrassing moment of my life. The stupidest thing I've ever done. And I've done many stupid things since. Had so many embarrassing moments that you could say I was on a one-woman mission to somehow embarrass myself so much that it erases the memory of that one awful moment with Ryan Sullivan, but nothing has. Yet.

'You always did have a way with words,' Ryan says softly, and I wonder how I can have been so distracted that I didn't even hear the clang of the chain as he moved or the crunch of his footsteps over the sun-roasted ground.

He smiles when I look up and meet his eyes. There's always been something about his smile and the way it makes dimples appear right at the corners of his mouth, which have some kind of hypnotic effect, I'm sure.

And then I realise I'm bent double looking for the spot where he carved our names. I can't remember where it is – not exactly. It was around this side, the left of the tree, and it must be near the bottom because he'd crouched to carve it. But the trunk is so wide and there are *so* many carvings that it's impossible to pick out just one.

'Looking for your mum and dad's name?' He says like he can read my mind.

'Yeah.' It's a lie that's not entirely untrue. 'It'd be nice to find it, but there are so many. It might be impossible.'

My mum and dad's name being on here is a good enough excuse to carry on looking. Maybe he's completely forgotten about *our* carving. If it's even still here. Maybe the "Ry + Fee" is gone. Faded, like local legend says it will if the relationship isn't meant to be, and it's safe to say that Ryan and I definitely weren't.

His arms are folded across his chest as he stands back and looks up at the tree. The tarpaulin to keep the rain off is flapping in the sea breeze, and I'm struggling to tear my eyes away from him. He's got a wide and flat nose, and stubble that's scruffier than it was yesterday. Up close, I can see the first odd grey hairs at the edges of his jaw. I force myself to look away and continue rubbing my hand over so many indentations in the bark.

'Makes you feel small, doesn't it?' Ryan's voice is quiet. His strong Welsh accent gives the words a soft lilt and he drops the middle letters of "doesn't" so it sounds more like "dun't". His voice always did something to me.

I walk around the trunk to put some distance between us because standing here ogling Ryan's arms and daydreaming about his accent is guaranteed not to end well. 'I can't believe the hotel company wouldn't want to keep the tree. It's an attraction in itself.'

'Companies like that only care about one thing, and no one's going to *pay* to come and see the tree, so it doesn't fit into their agenda. Besides, even if they could somehow be persuaded to save it, it would lose its beauty with a multi-storey modern architecture building plonked beside it.'

I'm so distracted by Ryan that I let out a yelp when Baaabra Streisand headbutts my leg. She looks morally offended by my yelp, and I apologise profusely, going to ruffle her head like you would a dog, but I stop with my hand hovering mid-air. Do sheep even like being petted?

She answers the question for me by jolting herself up to head-butt my hand, and I stroke her woolly white head for a moment, and then she gives an annoyed huff and trots away, clearly unimpressed by my sheep-petting abilities.

When I risk a glance at her, she's staring at me and grinding her teeth. She may be plotting to kill me. Or has got trapped wind and could do with a Rennie.

'I *hate* their entire industry,' Ryan continues. 'They don't care about *people*. It's all about money. They hoover up every spare inch of greenery and pave it with concrete. We all know the planet is dying as we stand and watch, and people like Landoperty Developments are making it worse.' He sighs and pushes a hand through his hair. 'Sorry, I must sound like a real hippy-dippy tree hugger to someone who lives in a paved paradise city.' He waves around a hand like he's trying to draw skyscrapers in the air.

'Plenty worse things you could be.' Like a property developer.

Someone intending to screw over their friends to get a promotion. I'm so ashamed of working for a company who destroys places like this. It makes me start wondering how many other trees Harrison has been responsible for cutting down. How many other beautiful areas he's annihilated. How many other people has he made to feel inconsequential, like their feelings and opinions don't matter because of their age? How many other care homes and vulnerable people have lost special areas because they didn't have someone as dynamic as Ryan to fight for them?

'I don't think enough people in the area know what's happening,' I say. 'The land hasn't been sold yet, so no planning application has gone in, so there's been no public notices or chances for the public to object. I've seen a lot of protests and they only work if the whole community gets involved.'

'Are there a lot of protests in the food industry then?' He asks with a raised eyebrow.

*Oh God.* 'Oh, yeah, loads. Over, er, salmon prices mainly. They add astronomical import duties.'

He looks confused. 'Aren't salmon British? I thought most were caught in our rivers.'

He's probably right. Trust me to choose import duties on a fish that, if it was any more British, would be queuing in the rain with a cup of tea and biscuits and complaining about the weather. 'These are special salmon. From, er, Japan. Sushi, y'know? The Japanese are good at fish and add the price to prove it.' Oh God, Fliss, *shut up*. I sound like I've never even eaten in a restaurant, never mind work in one.

'Is Riscaldar not Italian then?'

Oh God, *is* it? 'Nooo, it's a bit of everything. Whatever customers fancy.'

'Right … Sorry, I'm clearly a simple Welshman who doesn't understand gourmet food. You seriously have to protest about salmon prices?'

'Well, people will protest about anything these days, won't

they? Even fish.' I'm a vegetarian. I don't even *eat* fish – how did we get into this conversation and how quickly can we get out of it? 'What I mean is, we need to make this protest *big*. This tree is forgotten about. To everyone in the area, it's just *here*. It's always been here – it *will* always be here, but what happens when people realise it won't be if the hotel company get their way? Can you imagine all of these carvings – all of these stories – being lost forever? We need to find some of the people behind these markings and share their stories – locally and online with the wider world in general.'

He grins. 'I should've known if anyone would know how to save this tree, it would be Fee Kerr. You always did make the unlikeliest of things seem possible.'

If I develop sunstroke later, it will be nothing to do with the burning orb in the sky and everything to do with Ryan Sullivan's easy compliments. I never knew he thought that. To me, *he* always made the impossible seem reasonable. At the plant nursery, he always had complete faith in me. I liked experimenting with different varieties, cross-pollinating, cross-breeding, playing around with different ideas, and he never once doubted that they would go well, despite the various disasters I was responsible for.

'This is brilliant.' He sounds as young and excitable as he used to when seedlings we'd given up on popped through the compost. '*You're* brilliant. Fee ...'

I've somehow drifted closer to him and he goes to hug me, but the chain hooks over his foot and pulls taut and he stumbles against the tree instead.

I sidestep like it was an intentional accident. Hugging Ryan Sullivan is better avoided when I can still feel the imaginary imprint of his arms around me from where the old 'uns pushed me into him yesterday. It's not something that needs repeating anytime soon.

'As you can see, I've retained my elegance and decorum through the years.' He pushes himself up, rubbing his bare shoulder where it hit the bark.

'How can you be comfortable in that thing?' I ask, to distract from the idea of him *wanting* to hug me.

'What, this?' Both his hands settle on the heavy chain clipped at his waist, drawing my eyes to what is undoubtedly a washboard stomach underneath his vest top, like anyone needed any extra reasons to focus on Ryan's body today, given what that blue tank top is doing for his arms. 'It's fine. I need to be able to move around freely, but from a legal point of view, someone has to be chained to the tree at all times. If any authority figures show up, I'll jump back in to be on the safe side.' He pats the bark near where my hand is resting on the tree trunk, so close that the tips of his fingers graze the tips of mine.

I expect him to yank his hand back like he's touched a stinging nettle, but he doesn't move. The warmth of the tips of his fingers where they're pressing against the side of mine are like burning hotspots, making my fingers seem cold in comparison.

He stares at them too. 'Do you believe things happen for a reason? You coming back here after so many years, right at the exact moment we need you? I always thought I'd see you again when the time was right. And I guess the universe has decided the time is right.'

I melt. If I was a snowman, I'd be a puddle by now. He always knew exactly what to say to make me feel valued.

And I can't be feeling things like that around Ryan Sullivan.

'We should …' I yank my hand away and gesture vaguely towards the group of residents. I start back up the path through the brambles and go to sit on the bench occupied by Godfrey.

'Hi.' I hold my hand out and he takes it between both of his liver-spotted ones and gives it a shake. 'I'm Fliss. I used to come to your strawberry patch all the time. It was my favourite place in the world when I was growing up.'

97

'I remember. And your mother before you. I've never forgotten watching her pass the magic on to you as well.'

I bite my lip to stop myself tearing up. 'I'm sorry to hear about your wife. Ryan told me your story. I think we could use it to save the land.'

I tell him everything I've just said to Ry and he thinks about it for so long that I'm almost certain he's going to say no. He keeps to himself, and although he's out here, he's staying away from the board games and "Guess the Gadget" players. 'I'd like that. I think Henrietta would like that too. Anything we can do to stop this being built on. I blame myself ...'

'Why?'

'It was mine, wasn't it? When Henrietta first went downhill, I tried to carry on alone, but every day got harder. She had always been the heart behind our business, and without her ...' He trails off and shakes his head, unable to finish the sentence. 'She had to move because this is an assisted living facility. The residents here have nothing more serious than regular pensioner niggles, but none of them require round-the-clock care. At first I'd vowed to keep the strawberry patch going in her honour, but my broken heart was no longer in it. The weeds crept in and my back gave out. The chap who owned Seaview Heights before Steffan was a good sort. He could see I was struggling and he offered to buy it as a garden area for the residents. A good price that allowed me to pay for Henrietta's long-term care. It was good, in a way. Saying goodbye to the past to pay for the future she needed.'

I'm captivated as he talks. 'Maybe everything happens for a reason ...'

'You're just like Ryan.' He pats my hand. 'Always looking on the bright side and saying things like that.'

Why does that make me smile so much?

'You two young folks just let me know what you need me to do.'

'We need to get this online. We need to get people talking

98

about it. A petition is one thing, but petitions are outdated now. We need a social media campaign – people from all around the world seeing our sycamore tree and sharing it and caring about it.'

We sit there in silence for a moment as he thinks about it. I've not seen anyone else sit by him, and I'm not sure if he's glad of the company or surprised by my intrusion.

'It was always flyers when we were running the strawberry patch ... Every summer in the weeks before we opened, we'd get thousands printed out and pop one through every letterbox in Lemmon Cove and the surrounding areas. And the local shops all displayed them in their windows. Kids used to take a handful with a punnet of strawberries and distribute them.'

I go to tell him flyers are a bit outdated now, but I think about it for a moment. Flyers could be a good idea. Everything in this tiny village is outdated, and to find people connected to the tree, it's the locals we need to target.

I thank him as I get up and walk back down to the group. 'Godfrey's suggested flyers, and I think that's a brilliant idea. Sending something out into the community. Something tangible. No one carves trees anymore because we know it can introduce pathogens and kill them, so I'm guessing the people we need to target will be closer to your generation than ours.' I gesture between the residents and me and Ryan. 'They might not be up on technology and social media, so flyers might be a good way to go. Through every door around the area. If nothing else, it will let people know what's going on. And we need to create social media accounts for the tree with a memorable username and a profile photo.'

'Gno—' Mr Barley starts to say.

'No depraved gnomes,' I add quickly.

I glance at the one he's painting ... Who knew gnomes could do *that* with a seed dibber? And who knew Boris Johnson could bend like that?

'Just a nice photo of the tree, maybe with you lot standing underneath it. The tree can tweet about each carving and cross-post to its other accounts on Facebook and Instagram and wherever else young people are posting these days.'

'Myspace!' Mr Barley shouts. 'Tinder!'

Tonya, clearly the only one of the group who knows what Tinder is, tries to muffle her giggles.

'Er, Fee …' Ryan says. 'It might be alive, but I don't think the tree is *quite* sentient enough to run its own social media accounts.'

I roll my eyes at him but I can't help laughing. 'We tweet on its behalf, obviously. One carving a day. We could take pictures and ask people to make up the stories behind them. Don't you ever find messages written inside second-hand books and think about who wrote them and who they were intended for? I used to love coming here and imagining who all these people were and what the carvings meant. This is the sort of thing people would love if we shared it. Actually, imagination might be an even more important part. Something as big and old as this has had an unfathomable life. It's living history. It bears traces of lives gone by. Tattoos of the thousands of moments it's witnessed.'

'This place was a hotbed for smugglers back in the eighteenth and nineteenth centuries. Some of those marks could've been carved by pirates or bandits amidst all sorts of maritime mayhem. I remember learning about that in school and coming here on the way home and imagining all the people over the years who could've left a mark. Tweeting about stuff like this could get kids' imaginations running wild.' Ryan always had a way of making my ideas seem better than they are, and I'm grinning at him and he's grinning back at me, and no one's said anything for a good few minutes.

'You've already got the right idea.' I tear my eyes away from Ryan and turn back to the residents. 'You're sharing daily photos and trying to entertain people and get people interacting on your Facebook page, but we need to shift the focus to the tree and away from handmade gnomes doing surprisingly supple and mildly concerning acts of nature.'

They all look forlorn, so I quickly add, 'You can keep the gnomes as well, but maybe you could take photographs of them beside the tree to keep that at the forefront and not just showcase Mr Barley's impressive talent with a paintbrush and the Kama Sutra of garden ornaments.'

'Ooh, maybe I can expand my horizons into other garden decorations. We've got some concrete snails somewhere that would make excellent—'

'Let's turn this into capturing the imagination of local children and move away from where Mr Barley wants to put his snails,' Ryan says.

The idea of children's imagination sets me off thinking again. 'Hey, you can draw.'

'I haven't for a long while.'

I cock my head to the side. Ryan was always creative and artistic. He loved working the soil of Sullivan's Seeds, digging and growing and experimenting with new and unusual plants, and hated the bookkeeping and financial side of the job. 'You could draw a sycamore leaf and we could print loads out …'

'We could give them to children to colour in,' Alys suggests.

'Exactly!' I feel buoyant by how much they're embracing the idea. 'The possibilities are endless. We could laminate them and get thousands of sycamore leaves circulating with our website address printed on the back. We could ask locals to display them in windows so everyone visiting the area will see them and wonder what's going on. We could ask kids to draw their own sycamore trees and display them somewhere. Kids love getting involved with things like this.'

'Children are our future,' Tonya cries and starts warbling "Greatest Love of All" popularised by Whitney Houston.

'Can we carve "HELP" in the ground so anyone flying over can see it? I've always wanted to do that,' Morys muses.

'I don't think that's … Actually, that's not a bad idea. One of us could run down to the beach every morning …' I glance at Ryan because, honestly, there's only one person capable of tackling that hike and it's not me. 'We could write something in the sand so anyone walking along the coastal path would see it. Does anyone have a drone?'

'My grandson does!' Tonya stops singing. 'He's always making a nuisance of himself with it.'

'It could be a great campaign video if we wrote "save our sycamore" in the sand and filmed the tide gradually washing it away with the tree in the background. It would make a great video clip to upload to our new YouTube channel.'

I look up at Ryan and his eyes are warm and smiley. The group's chatter fades away and something hovers in the air between us, so tangible that I think I'd feel it if I swiped my hand towards him.

He blinks and takes a step backwards. 'I'll take some photographs.'

'I'll make a start on the website and social media accounts.'

That look again. It's like once my eyes lock on to his, it's impossible to tear my gaze away, like a thread is pulling me to him.

'Fee …' His tongue wets his lips, which shifts my gaze from his eyes to his mouth, and memories of Ryan's mouth are *not* a good thing.

I shake myself and spin around so I'm facing the residents again. 'Let's do this! Let's save this tree!'

I punch a fist into the air and they all do the same and then clutch at their shoulders with grunts of pain.

I wonder if Harrison would let me claim muscle ache gel on expenses?

# Chapter 8

'Domain name, anyone?' I ask loudly.

'Gno—'

'Not gnomesdonaughtythings.com, Mr Barley,' I say quickly.

'Beach Battle-axes and, er, Battle-gents,' Tonya suggests, her voice trailing off before she's finished the sentence. 'What's the male equivalent of a battle-axe? I'll ask online and see if anyone knows.'

'Seaside Sycamore Tree?' Alys suggests.

'Ooh, that's good.' I do a quick google on my phone. 'It's available.'

'I like it,' Ryan calls up from where he's taking photos of various parts of the trunk.

'Seaside-sycamore-tree.com. All in favour?' I ask, and I'm greeted with a chorus of "ayes".

A few clicks and I've paid a year's fee for the website and set up a blog. I defiantly ignore Harrison's angry face in my head. He is going to be *thrilled* when he discovers this protest has now got a website that it didn't have before I came here.

'Do you want to borrow my laptop?' Ryan calls over without looking up. He's still taking photographs by the tree, and Baaabra Streisand has unravelled a bit of her lead and mooched into the brambles for some fresh shoots to munch.

'I'm going to ring my dad and ask him to bring mine down here,' I say, watching as Cynthia edges closer with interest. 'He doesn't seem to get out much nowadays and it'll be a good excuse to get him here. He can't refuse a request from his second favourite daughter.'

'Aww, you couldn't be *anyone's* second favourite anything, Fee,' Ryan says without looking up.

The sun gets inexplicably hotter. Well, something does. If I moved, there would probably be singed patches of grass underneath my feet.

Baaabra Streisand is rustling around in the bushes when I get off the phone to my dad, who reluctantly agreed, and the residents have started drafting out slogans and campaign mottos, and Mr Barley's got a gnome who's baring its bum and is painting "seaside-sycamore-tree.com" on its bare bum cheeks, and no one has the heart to tell him that that is *not* child-friendly advertising.

I yelp in surprise again when Baaabra Streisand jumps out at me.

'I think your sheep has finally murdered someone,' I call out to Ryan while backing away slowly in case I'm her next intended victim.

'Side-splittingly hilarious,' he calls back without looking up.

'Seriously, Ry, she's got red all round her mouth. You should see this in case it's something to worry about.' Rabies? Eating rodents from the bushes? I shudder at the idea of what might be lurking in those brambles.

He puts his phone down and walks up the path towards me.

'Hello, *ewe*.' He rubs her head and gets the sheep between his legs and bends over to look at her face, quite happy to stick his fingers into her mouth to examine her. 'What have *ewe* been up to?'

'You kept the sheep solely for the ewe puns, didn't you?'

'It may have been a deciding factor.' He laughs while poking around in her mouth. 'Well, it's not blood. It's ...' He eventually removes a bit of greenery from between her teeth and holds it up.

'Is that the …'

'… Munched hull and stem of a strawberry?' His lip curls up as he looks at it, and quickly throws it into the bushes and bends to wipe his hand on the grass.

'All right, who's been feeding strawberries to the sheep?' He addresses the group of residents. 'Fruit messes with her digestion – you know that. If this is because you want more fertiliser for the hydrangeas …'

No one owns up. There's a longer chorus of *it wasn't me*'s than that song by Shaggy.

Baaabra chooses that moment to slip away from between Ryan's knees and tangle herself back into the bramble bush she came out of.

'So where did she get a …' He meets my eyes and realisation dawns on us both at the same moment and we turn in the direction of the sheep's snuffling.

'We're standing on a strawberry patch.' His eyes light up and his whole face follows. 'Fee! We're standing on a strawberry patch!'

'And strawberries grow in the shade of other plants.' I feel his excitement spreading to me too. 'Does this mean …'

'It *has* to! Some of the plants must still be living! Morys?' He dodges around me as he runs up and takes the walking stick from the old man, currently sitting on the flowerbed wall and painting a cardboard sign that says "May peas be with you." 'All right if I borrow this a minute?'

He comes back with the walking stick, shoos Baaabra back towards the tree, and starts whacking at the brambles.

'Here, let me.' My arm presses against his as I get close to him and my fingers cover his hand and take the walking stick out of his grasp. Instead of whacking at the spiky bushes, I insert the walking stick at roughly the spot where Baaabra emerged and use it to gently prise apart the thorny branches until there's a gap and we can see a bit of the ground.

'Look at the serrated edge of that leaf. That's a strawberry leaf.'

He shuffles closer and ducks his head until it's practically leaning against mine so he can see what I'm seeing. I don't think standing at this proximity to Ryan is doing my cardiac health any good, so I pull the walking stick out and ram it in a couple of inches over, using the leverage to gently part the bush so we can see what's living underneath it.

Or uncovering a nest of adders, knowing my luck.

'Look,' I say as the walking stick pushes the thorns aside and a ray of sunlight shines down into the bush. 'That is unmistakably a strawberry.'

Once again, Ryan ducks so near that his head is almost on my shoulder. He's so close that his breath makes the hairs on the back of my neck stand up as we both look down at the crown of green leaves with a red berry standing tall above them, a little white at the edges where it isn't ripe yet.

'And look, it's got runners coming from it …' he whispers, like speaking at normal volume will break the spell and frighten it away.

'… Which means there are probably more.' I finish the sentence for him.

'And that's nowhere near where Baaabra was just now …'

The possibility hangs in the air. Could there really be a lot *more* strawberry plants still alive in the undergrowth?

Tonya, Alys, and Ffion have come down to see what we're doing, and Ryan takes the walking stick out of my hand and the three women stand with me and watch as he walks a few paces down the pathway, chooses a spot in the bushes and jabs the walking stick in and carefully wriggles open a gap in the brambles.

'There's another one. And I might be able to …' He crouches down and slinks a hand into the bush, wincing as thorns catch his skin, before returning with a strawberry held between his fingers. 'Look at this!'

There's a lot of green-to-white skin on the unripe fruit, obviously struggling to ripen with the lack of sunlight under the bramble bushes, but the possibility of them simply existing under all these weeds is phenomenal.

Ryan throws the walking stick to me, and I squeeze past the ladies and use it to part yet another area of thick-knitted brambles. 'They're here too!'

Ryan looks up and our eyes meet, his looking bright with excitement and I know the same look is reflected on my face. I've drifted down to stand next to him again, and his green and herby cologne like a mix of bamboo and eucalyptus is swirling around me, blending with the unripe berry scent as he rolls it in his fingers.

'Ooh, I love strawberries,' Alys says, jolting me out of the mind-swimming closeness to Ryan. 'That reminds me, I've got an apple corer that I must take a photo of for "Guess the Gadget".'

The randomness makes me giggle and I'm momentarily distracted from Ryan's closeness until his arms slide around my waist and I freeze. At first I think he's giving me a hug and my fingers twitch with the urge to slide them over his sun-warmed arms and squeeze, but thankfully I feel the heavy metal of the chain resting around my middle before I do anything stupid.

His hands are at my front, hooking the silver clasp onto one of the chain links. 'Will you stay here while I run across to the campsite and get some tools? We'll cut down these bushes and see what's happening under there.'

'Of course,' I rasp, my mouth so dry that it feels like I've taken a mouthful of the sandy beach below.

His arms are gone from around me as quickly as they appeared, and the chain left in their place is weighty and cold through my T-shirt.

'Back in a sec.' He trips on the chain and I have to plant my feet wide apart to stay upright. He mumbles an apology and rights himself, nearly crashing headfirst into Godfrey, who's hobbling down the path to see what's going on.

He takes the strawberry as Ryan rushes off and holds it up, examining it like a cashier might examine a twenty-pound note for being a forgery.

'He's single, you know,' Tonya sidles up to me.

'Godfrey? He's married to Henrietta, isn't he?'

She smacks my arm lightly. 'You know I meant Ryan.'

I laugh. 'That's very interesting information that is in no way, shape, or form relevant to me in any way whatsoever.'

Tonya's hands shoot to her hips. 'Isn't it now?'

'Isn't nature amazing?' Godfrey interrupts, barging through the middle of the ladies and saving me from what was undoubtedly going to be an awkward conversation about my love life, or lack thereof. 'Look what happens when you leave the earth to get on with it. I never thought I'd see a strawberry growing in these parts again.'

'They must've been there all along,' Ffion says.

'Strawberry plants don't live that long. They pass their best after about five years and you have to replant. We did it several times over the course of running the patch.'

'Yeah, but they send out runners that root into the soil and form new plants,' I say. 'You never dug up the old plants?'

Godfrey shakes his head.

'Then potentially they could have carried on growing and producing young plants, which kept growing and producing more young plants. There could be enough of them to compete with the brambles and that's why they're still going.'

'So this could be from the great-great-grandson of one of my plants.' He bounces the strawberry in a shaky palm. 'This strawberry could be my grandson.'

It seems like a serious moment and I try to bite back the laugh, but Alys lets out a giggle and it starts us all off, and as I stand there laughing with four old people about the possibility of a fruit being a long-lost relative, I feel the tightness that was in my chest loosening, and for just a moment, it feels like I'm exactly where I'm supposed to be.

The idea of strawberry plants still living under all this mess fills me with fizzing joy, and I'm bouncing on the balls of my feet, waiting for Ryan to get back and find out if there really are as many strawberry plants as there has the potential to be.

'Hello? Fliss?' My dad appears at the metal fence and pokes his head round nervously, holding up my laptop bag like it's a shield.

Cynthia bolts up with such speed that you can almost see sparks as the Zimmer frame feet hit the ground. 'Dennis!'

Dad looks taken aback as he stutters out a greeting and asks her how she is and how many years it's been.

I purposely hang back, hiding behind Alys and pretending to be too absorbed in following the trail of strawberry runners to have noticed his arrival. I remember him talking about Cynthia. A friend from work, he'd called her. I remember Cheryl teasing him when I visited a few years ago, before he retired. Since then, he doesn't really talk about anyone. I refuse to rescue him yet.

The three women look at me watching and sense that there's something there *to* watch, because all eyes swivel to where Cynthia has got her hand on my dad's arm and is chattering away, and Dad has gone from looking uneasy to getting involved in the conversation and the sight makes the sun's heat spread to my chest.

'Dennis!' Ryan comes rushing back in and nearly trips over the Zimmer frame.

'Ry!' My dad throws his arms around Ryan like he's a long-lost son.

Cynthia looks miffed at the interruption as Dad and Ryan have a quick catch-up and my heart is warmed by how genuinely pleased they are to see each other. I'd forgotten how much Ryan was like part of the family.

Eventually Ryan excuses himself, holding up the armful of garden tools he's got with him, and Dad makes a move to follow him, but Cynthia yanks him to the bench and forces him to sit down. Dad finally spots me and waves hello. I wave back, but I'm still not going to rescue him. Cynthia asks Mr Barley to fetch them tea and cake and when he goes to object, she bangs her Zimmer frame on the ground and Mr Barley gets up and scuttles back towards Seaview Heights.

'Brambles, prepare for death.' Ryan approaches with his loot of various garden tools – a scythe and machete, a garden fork and spade, a couple of saws, secateurs, and long-handled loppers, and dumps everything in a pile on the ground along with two pairs of gardening gloves.

His arms slide around me from behind and he fumbles to undo the chain clasp. I'm sure he could've done it more easily from the front, but there's something about Ryan's arms around me that makes every other thought in my brain disappear. All I can concentrate on is the feeling of his solid forearms pressing against my sides, under my ribs, as he unclips the chain, standing so close that I can feel his body heat and his breath stirs my hair, and I get the feeling he's lingering. The chain loosens a long few seconds before he unhooks it and pulls away.

When I come back to myself, Tonya, Ffion, and Godfrey are watching us with knowing looks. Alys has picked up a scythe and is brandishing it at the brambles.

'Ooh, I could do with getting some aggression out.' She swishes the blade at a thin shoot and squeals in surprise when it slices through and falls away.

Ryan takes the scythe carefully out of her hand. 'How about a cup of tea and some of those cakes Mr Barley's bringing out? Me and Fee will tackle this.' He hands the scythe to me and locks the chain back around his own waist.

It's been a long time since I used a garden instrument of any sort, but the handle fits perfectly into my hand and I give it an experimental slash at the brambles in front of me once Tonya and Alys have escorted Godfrey safely back up the path. It slices through easily and I put it down to pull my gloves on.

'Sorry, I kind of volunteered you for this. You don't have to stay; I can manage.'

I test the weight of the scythe in my hand. 'No worries. I'd like to. It's been a long time since I did any outdoor work. It'll be a welcome change.'

'Good to see your dad,' Ryan says. I can hear something unsaid behind his words.

'Yeah. I don't think he gets out much. And he looked unexpectedly glad to see Cynthia.' We both look towards the bench where they're now deep in conversation over tea and homemade butterfly fairy cakes. Dad looks more animated than he has since I arrived. 'Is she single?'

'Yeah, her husband died years ago.' He stops slashing at the brambles and looks over at me with a raised eyebrow. 'That's relevant information then?'

For some unknown reason, I blush. It must be the chat with Tonya just now.

'I don't know.' I glance at my dad and Cynthia. 'It could be.'

We're both slashing at the brambles, chopping the tangled bushes away and watching them fall to the ground. We're almost back to back, Ryan's doing huge sweeping motions and I'm being more careful and cutting the longest parts of the bush away before switching to the secateurs to chop the thicker stems down as far as possible, until I can see the anaemic green of strawberry leaves standing above their crowns, lighter than their usual deep green from the lack of sunlight, but there are berries hanging over from chunky stems.

'Isn't nature wonderful?' I murmur to Ryan as I stand back to look at them.

Under all this debris, strawberry plants are thriving. Even in the shadow of huge bramble bushes, they're still there, going about their lives like nature intended.

I crouch down and start untangling the brambles from around the plants. They've only rooted in sporadic places and the rest of the tangled mess of spiky branches can be easily pulled away and gathered up.

'You're going to get scratched.' Ryan crouches down beside me. 'Let me help.'

'I have more sleeve than you do!' I nod towards the line of his blue vest over his shoulders, and yep, I really shouldn't have drawn attention to his biceps again *or* done anything that would get his eyes on me, because I feel him looking up and down my arms too.

Between us, we pull out clumps of scratchy blackberry that snags on everything and take armful after armful across to an ever-growing pile behind the hedge. It's a while since I did proper physical work, and it feels good. We regularly dug over patches of land when I worked with him, just the two of us, usually with one of his Nineties playlists playing as we sang along to Steps and the Spice Girls, complete with dance moves at any opportunity. Spending time with Ryan was always a conundrum – I was so afraid of making a fool of myself in front of him, and yet I felt totally at ease with him. At ease enough to sing at the top of my voice – always dangerous lest it set off car alarms and send small rodents running for cover – and risk dance moves to Gina G's "Ooh Aah … Just A Little Bit" in the middle of a muddy field.

He crouches down beside me. 'Who knew strawberry plants could survive against the odds like that? Do you really think the rest of the land will be the same?'

'Well, there are plants over here, there, and over there too.' I wave a hand behind me, towards the part he started cutting down and the general direction of Baaabra Streisand who has disappeared into the bushes again. 'When the strawberry patch was here, the plants stretched right the way across to that crumbling wall ...' I point to the farmer's fields that join the patch of land to the right in the distance.

'We'll be overrun with strawberries,' Tonya says, making us both jump. I'd been so focused on Ryan's proximity that I hadn't noticed she'd returned.

I reach out and touch a reddening berry, still white on the underside. They should be ripe by this time of year, but the lack of sunlight has set them back. Now they're uncovered, a bit of sun on them will soon turn them red, and the mass of plants we've found are covered in small green berries, which need time to grow, and plenty of dainty white flowers with yellow middles waiting to be pollinated. On cue, a bumblebee buzzes across to visit one and I pull my hand away to give it space.

There's a rustling in the bushes behind us and we both go to turn around, but before we get even halfway, Baaabra Streisand appears through the brambles and runs at us, headbutting neatly into the space between our knees and I squeal as the impact sends both of us sprawling. Ryan lands on his back and I topple forwards to land smack against his chest.

The sheep backs away with a self-satisfied look on her face.

Ryan's arms automatically snap around me and hold tight to prevent me rolling off onto the ground that's covered with leaves and thorns. I'm half frozen in surprise and half warm from being pressed against his body. My initial instinct is to scramble away, but it's not an entirely undesirable position to be in.

I lift my head and meet his eyes, and although I'm trying not to laugh, one look at him trying so valiantly to hold back laughter finishes me off, and we're just lying there giggling.

Baaabra comes forward again and bumps her head against Ryan's arm and bounces backwards. She looks at us with the sheep equivalent to a smirk, hoovers an unripe strawberry straight off one of the exposed plants, and runs away again.

'And people wonder why sheep aren't more traditional pets,' I say. 'Who'd have a dog when you can have that?'

He laughs, and I go to push myself up, but his arms tighten at the movement.

'Don't move for a second. I've got fifteen years' worth of hugs to catch up on.'

I'd say I go hot all over, but I was already hot from the weed pulling and lying on top of Ryan is doing *nothing* to improve the situation.

I tell myself to relax. To be honest, I could do with the lie-down because it's been a *long* time since I did that sort of physical exercise, which he can undoubtedly tell with my podgy bits pressed all over him, and I'm hyperaware of being sticky and sweaty after a couple of hours of beating down bramble bushes, and there are probably thorns in my hair.

He thunks his head back against the ground, his body shaking with laughter that reverberates through me too. I can honestly say that if there's one place I never thought I'd be, it would be lying on top of Ryan Sullivan on the strawberry patch in Lemmon Cove again.

'Oh dear, are you okay? Are you hurt?' Alys starts tottering towards us to help, and I quickly hold up a hand and reassure her we're fine. Ryan's arms release me and I stagger to my feet, bracing my knees to get my balance, unexpectedly out of breath.

Dignity, I have it in *spades*.

He folds his arms behind his head. 'Think I might stay here for a bit.'

I hold my hand out to pull him up, and he slips his fingers around mine, and for one second I think I'm going to lose my balance and go careening into his lap again, but my feet find their bearing and I drag him back upright.

We stand there and look over the patch of ground we've cleared between us. There are still stray bramble branches and chopped leaves from what we've taken away, but the ground underneath is green, mossy in places, and there are tall strawberry plants with their neat clover-shaped leaves popping up all over, a mass of runner tendrils tangling each plant with the others near it.

It takes me a few moments to realise he hasn't let go of my hand.

He peers down at our joined hands, and his fingers tighten instead of letting go. 'We still make a good team.'

'We always did,' I whisper, like speaking in a normal voice will make him wrench his hand away.

I even manage to momentarily forget how sweaty my palms are. And how there are undoubtedly pieces of bramble stuck to my clothes, just to reinforce how much grace and finesse I have.

'This was fun, right?' He looks down at me and quirks an eyebrow. 'It's been too long. In *all* senses of the word.'

That fluttering takes off in my chest again, but I force it down, imagining myself stomping on the beating butterfly wings. Misinterpreting Ryan's friendly flirtation was where I went wrong last time. I can't make that mistake again. He doesn't mean anything by it, just like he didn't before.

'We've got a lot more to do.' I jerk my head over my shoulder, indicating the rest of the bramble-covered land.

'Same time tomorrow?' he says with a grin.

I look up at the sky. It's late and dark clouds have rolled across the sun and the residents are starting to rub their arms and make noises about it being nearly teatime. 'I'm in if you are.'

He grins. 'It's a date.'

Ryan Sullivan *cannot* say things like that to me. 'Yes. The eleventh of August. That's a date, right?'

'That is, quite literally, a date,' he says with a laugh and then ducks his head nearer to me. 'But that's not what I meant.'

My stomach rolls with an unease I haven't felt for fifteen years. This is what he does – he's just being friendly, but it's easy to misinterpret. I extract my hand quickly, and remember we're not the only people here.

115

Cynthia and my dad are admiring the flowerbeds now, Tonya is on her phone, and Ffion and Alys are deep in conversation about what gadgets the kitchen in Seaview Heights might have that would be impossible to guess.

No matter what I tell myself, I'm looking forward to coming back tomorrow. Working with Ryan again. Spending time with Ryan again.

I do know one thing though – I can't remember the last time I thought about getting anyone to give up this protest.

# Chapter 9

It's raining the next morning, which is much more like the Welsh weather I've come to expect over the years. I throw my laptop into a backpack and put it on my shoulders, which are a bit sore from yesterday's scythe wielding, and head down to the strawberry patch anyway. Even if clearing weeds is out in this weather, at least Ryan will be there. There's plenty to be getting on with for the website, and Tonya sent me three phone numbers of people who might have stories connected to the tree, so it's not like there's nothing to do.

'Say hello to Cynthia for me,' Dad calls as I open the door.

'Oh, I *will*,' I say, sad he can't see the raised eyebrows.

'And don't violate Ryan too much, I think we all saw enough of that yesterday.'

'You're hilarious,' I call back as I put my umbrella up and step outside.

Dad sticks his head out of the upstairs window and calls down to me. 'If it helps, it didn't look like he minded too much.'

'Neither did I,' I mutter to the sparrows eating from the neighbour's bird feeder once I'm well out of Dad's earshot.

The rain hammers down on the umbrella as I walk down the residential street and turn onto the coastal road that leads to

Seaview Heights. On the gate to the coastal path, the cardboard sign is now hanging limply by one corner and looks like it might drop down with a wet plop at any moment. The campsite is busy though, and most of the tents and caravans have lights glowing from inside, brightening up the dull greyness of the morning, along with people in neon anoraks trying to save campfires in the foggy fields.

The gate to the strawberry patch is undone and I let myself in, not expecting to find any residents out in this weather. Ryan's got a camping lantern glowing beside him in the tree and he lifts a hand in greeting. I wave back, unable to stop the smile that spreads across my face.

The only other person here is Godfrey, who's still sitting on the same bench with an umbrella open above him, held by an attachment clipped onto the back of the bench leaving his hands free to read the newspaper that's spread across his lap.

'Good morning, Fliss,' he calls when he sees me. He doesn't particularly look like he wants company, and even the gnomes aren't doing anything dodgy today. Instead, there's a gnome painted like Prince Charles holding up a sign that reads "Free beer this way" along with an arrow pointing to a row of slug traps buried in the soil and filled with beer. At the end of the row of traps, there's a sheet of cardboard that Mr Barley has drawn a maze on in permanent marker and covered the lines with walls of salt, and written, *"Drunken Slug Maze: may the odds be in your slimy favour."*

It makes me laugh out loud.

'Those slithering slime-goblins aren't having our strawberries,' Godfrey says. 'Mr Barley is taking up my vendetta against them. They were always our biggest pest when Henrietta and I worked here.'

Just when you think you've heard it all, you have an octogenarian referring to slugs as slime-goblins.

I ask Godfrey if he needs anything before I head down towards the tree. The path is wider now after all the brambles we've taken down in the past few days, and the uncovered strawberry plants are hanging their heads under the onslaught of rain as water drips from their pale berries.

Baaabra Streisand is under the cover of the sycamore's branches, dense enough to keep her dry as she stands looking out at the rain, giving it a displeased glare. 'Good morning, Baaabra.' I go to give her a stroke, but she looks like she might want to eat me so my hand shrinks back before she decides for definite.

Ryan grins down at me from where he's sitting cross-legged in the tree, kept dry by the canopy of tarpaulin spread above him. 'You're early.'

I hadn't even looked at the time until now, but it's before nine. I *am* early. I can't remember the last time I voluntarily got anywhere before nine a.m.

Everything feels different here though. Like I'm doing something good. Something healthy. Something that benefits the community. And it makes me think way too much about the other projects I've been involved with. The other land where I've done admin on Harrison's acquisitions and sales, and I start thinking about the communities behind those too, and if Landoperty Developments were always as welcome as Harrison would have people believe.

'Come up, it's nice and dry here.' He pats the wood beside him.

I flap my umbrella a few times to shake the water off and leave it leaning against the tree. Baaabra will probably eat it before the morning's out.

I go around to the side of the tree where he showed me the other night, pass my backpack up to him, fit my foot against the dip in the trunk and hoist myself up. His hand closes around my forearm and he hauls me into the branches.

'Thanks, I could've managed,' I say, breathless from the

119

exertion, or possibly from Ryan's hand around my arm. His hands are big and warm and make me realise how cold I am. I'm only wearing a T-shirt – my usual summer attire because it's always so hot in London, even when it rains.

'Hi.' He's smiling as he shuffles backwards, giving me space to sort myself out.

'Hi.' I stop in the middle of moving when his bright eyes meet mine and I'm smiling almost as widely as he is.

He's wearing trainers and short trousers today, and a charcoal grey T-shirt underneath a cobalt blue hoodie with the sleeves rolled up, showing off forearms that I really want to lick.

Where did *that* come from? I do *not* want to *lick* his arms. That's just wrong. And would be really, really weird. Thank God I didn't say that out loud.

The chain around his waist jangles as he moves, going back to sitting with his legs crossed and pulling sketchbooks into his lap to make room for me to sit down beside him.

'Did I ever tell you I love your hair?'

I freeze mid-movement and my stomach turns over and twists itself into a pretzel. 'You did.'

He nods. 'Okay, well, it bears repeating. I love it. I wouldn't have thought they'd let you have bright hair in a fancy restaurant like that. It looked very upmarket from what Tonya showed me.'

'Oh, it's … freethinking.' I grasp onto a word at random. I'm not even a hundred per cent sure what freethinking means. 'And it's not like it's too obvious. It's kind of hidden.' I wave a hand vaguely towards my hair. It's not much lighter than black anyway and the blue ends sort of melt into it. It does nothing to ease the guilt about him thinking I work somewhere I don't though.

He reaches out like he's going to stroke it and then pulls back quickly. 'Sorry. There was a llama.'

'A llama?'

'Yeah. Because that looked suspiciously like I was going to touch your hair, and I wasn't. I was batting away a llama.'

120

'Right.' I push my laptop bag safely to one side and sit cross-legged beside him, my knee pressing against his.

'Good morning.' He meets my eyes with a smile.

'You've already said that,' I say, even though every time I look into his eyes, I'm not sure if it's morning or three Thursdays ago in the Mayan calendar.

We're both silent for a while. Sitting in this tree feels magical. The rain patters down on the tarpaulin above our heads, a thick protective canopy, and the drips that land bounce off the taut waterproof material. The tree protects us from the worst of the elements and makes it feel like sitting in a cave high above the ground but without the shut-in feeling. The wind on the edge of a sea cliff is strong, but in this little nook of the huge tree, it's almost non-existent, apart from the occasional gusts that dodge the branches and blow through.

'Can I say something that's going to sound really stupid but you have to promise not to laugh at me?' I blurt out before I have a chance to rethink it. Ryan was always someone who would listen to anything without prejudice or judgement.

'Anything.'

'Do you think the tree knows we're trying to help it?'

I think he's going to laugh at me for being so daft, but he reaches out a hand and runs it over the line where the smooth worn-away wood meets the cracked bark creeping up the trunk. 'I've said that from the very beginning. As soon as I got here, I felt like it was welcoming me, inviting me, protecting me.'

The wind whispers through the branches and the leaves above us rustle, sending a flood of raindrops bouncing against the tarpaulin, almost like it's answering the question too.

'And yes, you *are* the first person I've said that to, and no, I *won't* ever forgive you if you repeat it.'

I laugh. 'You can trust me with your tree-hugging secrets, Ry.'

His knee presses harder against my knee and he leans over to nudge his shoulder against mine. 'I know. Could always trust you with anything.'

The cold shiver that goes down my spine has nothing to do with the drizzly dampness of the day and everything to do with the deceit of why I'm here. 'You too.' I swallow hard. 'Most bosses don't treat employees like you did.'

'You were never an employee, Fee. You were my right-hand man. Woman. Oh God, I've just called you a man.' He drops his head into his hands and shakes it.

It makes me giggle. His rambling is still just as charming.

'Sorry. I just meant you were the heart and soul of Sullivan's Seeds. It fell apart without you.'

It makes my breath catch in my throat. I don't think anyone's ever considered me the heart and soul of anything before, and it melts my heart to think that Ryan ever thought that, and makes me feel about two seconds away from tears. This feels too raw, too serious. 'Without me, it started poisoning people with toxic squashes, didn't it?'

'Not intentionally, I assure you.' He lets out a peal of laughter. 'Oh, speaking of unintentional things, when Baaabra attacked us yesterday, Tonya was recording video and she's put it online. So now about three thousand people have seen us being knocked over by a sheep. If there's anything more stereotypically Welsh than that, I don't know what it is. Aren't you glad you came back?'

Actually I am. Kind of. I think. 'See, that's what we need to harness. If she can get those kind of views with a daft video, think of how many we could get to know about the tree.' I steadfastly ignore the idea of a few thousand people seeing me flailing about on top of Ryan. Concentrate on the positive, not the negative.

I reach over and flick at the pages of the sketchbooks in his lap. 'What are these?'

'I've been playing with your ideas about the sycamore leaves. Look, I thought we could hand these out to kids to colour in and hang in their windows, and then these ones, we could laminate and tie onto trees and bushes right across the Gower area.' He hands me a sheet full of sketches of sycamore leaves. 'Which ones do you think are best?'

'All of them,' I say. Ryan always had a talent for doodling. He drew the Sullivan's Seeds logo that appeared on all our seed packages and plant labels, and was always doodling little swashes on price tickets and signboards.

There are seven variations of a sycamore leaf sketched onto the scrap bit of paper, and I point at one in the upper left corner. 'This one would be best for colouring in with all the lines and veins, and then this one would be simpler for tying onto trees and spreading across Gower because there's more space to put the website address.' I let my finger drift across the page. 'These are amazing.'

If I didn't know better, I'd say he's blushing when I glance up at him, and I have to shake myself from the urge to reach over and touch his face. The old 'uns are rubbing off on me – I'll be pinching his cheeks like a doting granny next. 'I was talking to Cheryl last night. Her class are going on a nature walk next week and they'll put a flyer through the door of every house they pass. I bet they'd love to get involved with tying laminated leaves onto bushes too …'

'That's not child labour, is it?'

His deadpan tone makes me burst out laughing. 'Probably, but she seemed quite happy about it. She loved the suggestion that the kids could draw the tree, and offered to ask the headmistress if they could get every class in the infant school involved – a project to draw a picture of the tree and write a paragraph about what it means to them and how the village would be different without it. There could be a class trip here too. And I thought about how young kids these days don't even know about the wishing aspect that our generation grew up with, so we were thinking another aspect of the project could be the kids thinking about what wish they'd make – what they'd ask the tree for if it's still here in autumn when the seeds fall. And if you get that many kids talking about the tree, they're going to talk to parents and grandparents who might know something about the carvings.'

He shivers, but I get the feeling it's nothing to do with the weather. 'Can you believe we live in a reality where we've even got to think that? *If* it's still here in a couple of months' time …'

I nudge my knee into his. 'It's stood here for three hundred years – it's not being cut down on our watch.'

He gives me a soft smile. 'You were always a force to be reckoned with.'

Me? Does he really think that? I don't feel like I'm anything to be reckoned with these days. I work so much that I don't have time to feel anything. My life is a constant rush, from my flat to the office and back again. This is the longest I've sat still other than waiting for Harrison's lunch of choice to be prepared at the deli down the road from work, which he's too busy and important to go and get himself.

'How things change,' I mutter. I've forgotten what it's like to work with someone who treats you as an equal and makes you feel valued and important to the company.

Ryan cocks his head to the side, looking like he wants to prod for more information, but I speak again before he has a chance. 'How about the flyers you were going to design?'

He shoves his pile of papers at me and jumps up to retrieve his laptop from a bag under the canopy and sits back down, somehow closer this time. He rests the open laptop on both our knees where they're pressed together and leans across me to use the mouse pad. 'What do you think of this?'

There's a photo of the tree taken from the beach below, and a call to arms mentioning the hotel and Seaview Heights, the social media accounts and website, and how we want to hear from anyone who's carved something into the tree and wants the world to know how special it is.

On the back, there's an illustration he's drawn of the sycamore tree, and a paragraph about Godfrey and Henrietta. It ends with the line ~ *When Henrietta was lucid a couple of years ago, we returned here, and she threw a sycamore seed from the cliff and made a wish to see this place as it was one last time.*

I'm blinking back tears again and have to turn away, and Ryan switches to his left arm supporting the laptop and drops his right one around my shoulders.

'I've done nothing but cry since I came here.'

His arm tightens. 'Proof of how much we need to share this story.'

'These are perfect.' I sniffle. '*You're* the force to be reckoned with, Ry.'

'You inspired the idea.' He squeezes me tighter and then lets his arm drop away. 'Do you think it's going to do any good?'

'What the property developers want is no one to make a fuss. They sought out Steffan because they thought it would be an easy buy, another bit of land they could spirit away when no one was watching. None of them banked on this little protest.'

'How do you know that?'

Oh, bollocks. 'I, er, ran into him yesterday,' I mumble, feeling like the worst person in existence. This is getting worse with every passing second. I can't even keep track of things I'm supposed to know and not know. 'This looks bad for the hotel company. The heartless hotel magnates who want to take joy from care home residents and destroy this gorgeous monument to times gone by and all the people who have left their mark on it over the years ... It's bad press, and the more people who are talking about it, the worse it's going to be.' I lean my elbows on my knees and rest my chin in my hands, looking out across the vast expanse of land, now mostly cut brambles dotted with sprays of tangled strawberry plants, the hanging red berries creating spots of colour in the otherwise green landscape.

'The residents want strawberry recipes to use them up.' Ryan nods towards the plants, which will soon start ripening. 'I was given strict instructions to ask my favourite chef what the best ones were.'

'I didn't realise you knew James Martin …'

He laughs. 'Go on, Fee, what's your best strawberry recipe? The residents are worried they'll all ripen at once and we'll have a glut of them. I'm more concerned that Baaabra Streisand will eat the lot and then we'll have a glut of something far less pleasant.'

I think I've had enough close encounters of the sheep poo kind to last a lifetime, but strawberry recipes? Come *on*. 'I think classic is best when it comes to strawberries. With cream and sugar and a glass of Pimm's when the tennis is on. Did you know there are 28,000 kilograms of strawberries consumed at Wimbledon every year?' I attempt to distract him with random facts rather than admit that when it comes to strawberry recipes, there is nothing but a tumbleweed blowing around my brain.

'Nah, most of the folks here only find fruit acceptable if it's disguised by cake. You must have something better than that. What strawberry-based dishes do you do at Riscaldar? They'd get such a kick out of having a dish prepared for them by a world-class chef.'

'I'm *not* a world-class chef, Ry.' Never has a truer word been spoken. A world-class chef would have me in prison for the kitchen-based crimes I've been known to commit.

'You always were too modest, but you forget how well I know you, Fee. You're world-class at *everything* you do.'

That faith in me. No one has *ever* believed in me the way he did, and guilt prickles at the back of my neck. I'm the worst person to believe in.

He's still looking at me expectantly, and I can't even *think* of a cake that contains strawberries. My mind is blank when it comes to recipes anyway, but now it's as blank as a question on *Blankety Blank*.

'Strawberry crumble?' I suggest. I've never actually heard of a strawberry crumble, but my mum used to make apple crumbles, so surely the same principle could apply to our heart-shaped red friends?

He wrinkles his nose. 'That's a bit basic, isn't it? Even I could make a strawberry crumble and the most complicated thing I do in a kitchen is chuck vegetables into the soup maker – a present from Alys after it had come up on "Guess the Gadget". You must have something fancier than that.'

Oh God. 'Okay, my favourite strawberry recipes are …' I look around for divine inspiration. A cow moos in the distance. Quite fitting. I'd appear more chef-like if I sat here mooing.

Suddenly, inspiration strikes, and it has nothing to do with strawberry recipes.

Goose bumps break out across my entire body and I shiver at the possibility. I don't want to move or even speak too loudly in case it scares the idea away. 'Ry, I know how to save the tree.'

The thought snowballs through my brain, picking up speed and getting bigger as it moves. Like he always used to, he knows exactly what I need, and without saying a word, he holds his hand out and my fingers automatically curl around his, scrunching them as I think it through. 'This is a wishing tree. It has to grant a wish.'

'Any wish? I mean, I wish to save the tree – there you go, job done.'

'No. Henrietta's wish, the one you wrote about in the flyer. She wished to see this place as it was again. And Godfrey was telling me yesterday that when she came here, the tree was inaccessible but she so desperately wanted to see it that one of the wardens put down boards to make a pathway for her wheelchair, so I wouldn't mind betting that was the last ever wish made on this tree. Wouldn't it be incredible if the tree granted the last ever wish made on one its seeds? We could do that – you and me. We could make this place like it was again.'

'Go on …' The tone in his voice is instantly recognisable – barely contained excitement.

'We're already halfway there with the strawberries,' I say eagerly, not sure if it's the idea or the inhalation of Ryan's cologne that's making me feel so giddy. He smells like sea salt and herbs today. 'All we'd have to do is clear the rest of the brambles away ...'

'Are you talking about reopening the strawberry patch?'

'Yes!' Somehow, he still hasn't let go of my hand and I squeeze his fingers again. 'Look at all these plants. There are *so* many of them, more than when it was open before, and they're *smothered* in fruit that's still to ripen and flowers that are still to form berries. Strawberry season is going to run for another couple of months yet. They're not in the neat rows they used to be, but if we clean up the ground around them and get rid of the last of the brambles, why *couldn't* we let the public come in to pick their own again?'

'It doesn't belong to us. It's not Godfrey's land anymore – it belongs to the care home.'

'So any money that's earned goes there. Even Steffan isn't going to complain about that. He hasn't sold the land yet – he wanted to because it's just dead space sitting here. If we could use it for its intended purpose *and* bring in a little bit of money, maybe he could be persuaded to keep it.'

'I don't know what the hotel have offered him, but it's going to be *slightly* more than a couple of £2.50 punnets of strawberries.'

I don't know how much they're offering either, but he's surely got a point. 'Yeah, but how incredible would it be to see families strawberry picking here again? Even if it's one last time. Even if it doesn't work and he still sells it. The tree will still have granted that wish. For just this summer, we could make this place like it used to be.'

'Are you staying for the summer then?'

I look over and meet his bright eyes. Why does he look so hopeful? He looks eager, like he's anticipating my answer, and it makes that fluttering come again. 'Guess I'll have to, won't I?'

The words are out there before I've thought them through. I can't stay for the summer. I can't stay for the rest of the *week*, never mind the summer. As soon as Harrison knows this protest isn't going away, I'll be back in the office in London. Which is where I should've gone the moment I realised there was a conflict of interests and the only man I've ever loved was running the show.

I mean, no, that's wrong. He's not the *only* man I've ever been in love with. I think. Probably. There was the guy I dated for a few years in my twenties that I kind of convinced myself I'd end up marrying, until he realised there was no passion between us and left, which was fair enough because I had a more exciting relationship with the microwave.

'There's something else. Tree of the Year competition.'

He snorts. 'There's no way that's a thing.'

'It is.' I can't tell him I know because my life is so empty that I spend my free time watching obscure documentaries on channels no one's ever heard of about weird things like tree competitions. 'It's saved trees before. Every year, people submit nominations, a panel of judges do a shortlist and that goes to a public vote. If we tell the story of Godfrey and Henrietta's last wish, and of the tree granting it ... There's no other tree like that in Britain.'

'Call me sceptical, but I *think* people are going to realise it's us and not the tree. I doubt they'll think it uproots itself at night and moseys about digging up blackberry bushes.'

The mental image makes me giggle. 'It's not about that. It's about making people believe in hope. This tree has always felt magical and otherworldly. We grew up thinking it could make our dreams come true. All we need is for people to know about it. Even being shortlisted would garner attention that no hotel company is going to want heaped on them with the stigma of cutting it down. People will boycott them. Environmental protestors will go for their jugular. And if it wins Tree of the Year, there's bound to be something we can do about getting it protected status.' I suddenly realise I'm clasping his hand with both of mine and my nails have left indents in his skin, and I release him quickly and pull away, shuffling back to sit up straighter.

He goes to say something, but there's a rustle above us, and we both look up to see a sycamore leaf floating down towards us. Neither of us breathes as it sways back and forth on the wind while it falls, eventually drifting underneath the canopy and coming to rest on the bark between us.

I look at the leaf and then up at Ryan's eyes, and I can see the same thought reflected back at me.

I reach over and pick it up carefully. 'Do you think that might be the tree's way of letting us know it approves?'

'I think it might,' he murmurs.

The whole world has gone silent as I turn the sycamore leaf over in my fingers. It doesn't have any signs of anything wrong with it, and it's way too early in the summer for the leaves to start falling.

Ryan reaches out and touches a fingertip to the toothed edge of the leaf as I spin it between thumb and forefinger. 'Do you really think we can do this?'

'Yes.' For the first time in a really long time, I have no doubts about what I'm doing.

'Then so do I.' He looks up and meets my eyes again. 'You always made me feel like *we* could do anything.' He shakes himself and pulls his hand away. 'You're unbe-leaf-able, Fee.'

In the midst of all the seriousness, it makes me cackle with laughter. 'Oh God, don't you start. We've got enough problems with "Guess the Gadget" and naughty political gnomes.'

To distract myself from how much Ryan makes me laugh, I nod towards the elderly man sitting on the bench under his umbrella. 'I can't believe he still sits there in the rain.'

'That was "their" bench,' Ryan whispers. 'Apparently they used to sit there every night after everyone had left and watch the sun go down with a glass of wine and some strawberries.'

'Do you think he'll approve of our idea? From what you've said, Henrietta may not ever be able to come here and see it.'

'No, but he would. He'd know. He'd be able to tell her. Take photos. And you never know, she has good days, we could ask her nurses to see if she was up to the journey one day. It's a long shot, but there's always hope.' He sighs. 'He was supposed to go and visit her today, but they needed the ambulance for something else. He's worried because the staff told Henrietta he was coming and now he can't get there. Routines and following through is important to someone in the advanced stages of dementia.'

'Can you take him?'

'I'm a little tied up.' He rattles the chain, sounding like Jacob Marley's ghost clomping around Scrooge's bedroom.

'I'll stay here.'

'Seriously?' He raises an eyebrow.

'I don't have a car so I'm pretty useless for the driving part, but I can sit in a tree for a while.'

'It's forty miles each way. It'll be a *long* while.'

'That's okay. I'll have Baaabra Streisand for company.' I glance down at the sheep, who is indeed now taste-testing my umbrella. 'And I need to work on the website. I've got my laptop and can jump on the care home's Wi-Fi. It makes no difference if I'm sat here or at my dad's kitchen table.'

'You know you can't leave *at all*, right? Not even for the loo unless one of the residents comes down to cover for you, and that's unlikely in this weather. Alys thinks the rain will make her wrinkles develop wrinkles of their own, and Tonya thinks they'll all go pruney and they might never unscrew at their age.'

It makes me laugh out loud again, as he opens his laptop and transfers the flyer design onto a USB stick. 'And I'll drop these at the printer's on the way out.'

Ryan unlocks the chain from around his waist and does what he did yesterday – crouches behind me and slips it around my middle from behind, his arms sliding around me as he blindly locks the chain into place at my front. And this time, I am *definitely* not imagining the lingering hug.

'He'll be overjoyed,' he murmurs. 'Thanks, Fee. You're a star.'

His lips brush against the shell of my ear and his arms tighten momentarily. It would be easy to snuggle back against him, but every nerve ending is on alert and there are flashing red lights in my head, screaming warnings about getting too close to Ryan Sullivan, and the thought makes a shiver go down my spine.

He must feel it too, because he pulls away, and I force myself not to watch as he moves around, the branches above us more than high enough to be able to stand at full height in the tree. He tucks his laptop away and unzips his blue hoodie. As I look away, he leans down again and drapes his hoodie over my shoulders. 'In case you get cold.' His soft Welsh accent is low in my ear and makes me shiver much more than the weather does.

His hands stay on my shoulders as he holds the jacket in place. 'Be back as soon we can.'

Our hands brush when I reach up to take it from him and his fingers linger as they cross mine and I'm sure I imagine the little squeeze.

The material is warm from his body heat and the fresh greenery scent of his cologne fills my senses while I watch him grab his wallet and keys and climb out of the tree.

It's impossible not to smile as he ruffles Baaabra's head and says goodbye to her, covertly removing the shredded canvas of my umbrella from her teeth. He turns around and his eyes don't leave mine as he walks backwards up the path, his grey T-shirt getting soaked with rain, and isn't *that* a thought for another day. He salutes me with a seductive grin that suggests he knows exactly what I'm thinking, before turning again and jogging up to the bench.

He ducks under Godfrey's large umbrella and talks to him, and then the old man turns in my direction and gives me a wave and a nod of thanks too, and Ryan helps him to his feet, lifts the umbrella, and holds it over both of them as he escorts him up to Seaview Heights to get ready.

I let out a sigh as I watch them disappear, and suddenly realise how alone I am out here. With the weather, there's not even a brave dog walker on the beach. The waves are lashing at the cliff edges around the coast, and the wind is howling around the outside of the tree, although there's still a microclimate in here and the worst of it is missing me, protected by the big trunks of wood that rise around me.

Baaabra doesn't seem bothered either. She's looking around for what she can eat next, and eventually settles on boring old grass at the base of the tree. No sheep has ever been more disappointed.

I crack open my laptop and start the website developer app. It's up with a holding page, but it needs a real design, and soon. Tonya's @BeachBattleaxe account is already linking to it, and there's no time to waste in getting our story out there.

I have a good idea of what I want the website to look like. Ryan's already drawn a picture of the sycamore to use as a background image, and we're going to use each branch to link to different areas of the website – a page for news and updates, a page to share the tree's plight and talk about why we need to save it, one that links to however many stories we can find out, a form where people can share their own stories and upload their photos, and a "how you can help" page. I thought of asking the residents to write a blog too, even though it will probably be filled with pictures of naughty gnomes and photos of Zimmer frames and courgettes and household gadgets. Why shouldn't people get to know the residents, warts and all?

Oh God, warts. You can guarantee that *those* will be the subject of at least one blog post.

I'm writing copy for Godfrey's story when my phone rings. When I get it out of my pocket and see the name on the screen, I groan so loudly that even Baaabra Streisand looks up worriedly from her grass munching and I have to reassure her there's nothing wrong.

'Harrison!' I overestimate the level of excitability needed in answering a call from your boss and overshoot it by at least six exclamation points. He's going to know I've been dreading this phone call because of how falsely happy I sound to hear from him.

'Felicity. You're still alive then – quite a surprise given how long it's been since our last debrief.'

I rub my fingers over my forehead while I try to think of how long it *has* been. The days here have sort of melted away in a fuzzy haze of brambles and sea air and Ryan's aftershave. 'I thought I was meant to be undercover ...'

'Yes, from *them*. Not from me. You're still working for me, are you not?'

Am I? Even though it's pretty impossible to forget, it hasn't felt like it for the past few days. 'Just trying to gain their trust!' I chortle. What even *is* chortling? Why do I suddenly sound like a distressed bird with its head up a drainpipe?

'Only I thought you might've checked in. I *am* paying you to visit your family, after all. Usually you'd have had to use holiday time for that. Two birds, one stone, et cetera.'

Oh, how I *love* his habit of speaking words you'd only ever expect to find in text. 'You told me to infiltrate the protest as a local and earn their trust. They're not going to let me in if I'm on the phone to my property developer boss at every given opportunity, are they?' I glance down at Baaabra again. She's watching me with a judgemental look on her sheepy face, but I'm almost certain she'll have no way of passing on this information.

I feel guilty for talking about it in front of her, like she's bearing witness to my horrible secret, and she can't tell anyone because she's a sheep. I'm exploiting her judgy sheep status and putting her in an awkward position. An ewe-kward position. Oh God,

Ryan is rubbing off on me. I let out a hysterical giggle, and can easily imagine Harrison's mildly disturbed face on the other end of the phone.

'So where are we with the protest, Felicity? Only from my end, it doesn't seem to be dying down at all, and that *is* what I sent you there to do, isn't it? Why aren't I seeing results yet?'

'Well, they're very ... er ... determined. And distrustful. And dedicated to their cause.'

'A few grand for a nice new mobility scooter would be something to be dedicated to. Have you tried gin?'

I snort at the unexpected comment. I could do with a bottle of gin to get through this conversation. 'I prefer wine.'

'I meant ply *them* with gin, obviously. Get them tiddly and tottering off to bed, and then you've just got to bribe the trousers off this Tree Idiot and we'll be away.'

'They're care home residents!' I exclaim, wondering if he'd *really* expect me to ply them with alcohol. Are there *no* lows he won't stoop to? 'They're probably on God knows how many medications that would interact with gin. And I'm not going to ask them what because, believe me, when they get onto the topic of prescriptions, they *never* stop.' I steadfastly ignore the comment about Ryan. Seeing him sans-pants would be *hazardous* for anyone's health.

'Have you not got *anywhere* with persuading them to give up?'

'People *love* this tree,' I say. 'It means a lot to this village. To everyone. It's stood here for three hundred years and they reckon it's only got another hundred to live naturally. It would break people's hearts to cut it down. It's proving more difficult than you anticipated.'

'Hmm.' I can envision his narrowed eyes and hear the click of a pen as he presses the end of it up and down again and again. He's shrewd and can always tell when a businessman is trying to pull a fast one – there's no way he'll believe my lies. That was a pitiful attempt to appeal to his better nature and make him realise how special the tree is. He doesn't care. He's exactly the type of corporate city man who thinks only in money, not about nature.

'Start peppering conversations with info about fines, Felicity. Make sure they know the law is on our side and they'll be fined for being there. And pretend you care about them and don't want them to have to lose so much of their paltry pensions. Old people don't like fines.'

*No one* likes fines. 'It's still their garden.'

'But not for much longer. I was speaking to Steffan yesterday and he's wavering. I told him I'd got someone onsite and he was pleased at having the backup. It boosted his determination to sell.'

Backup. Someone onsite. I briefly look around for this person before I realise it's me. I'm still the undercover man. That feeling of being the worst person in the world washes over me again.

I'm doing exactly what he sent me here to do. I'm gaining people's trust. The gang of residents have accepted me as one of their own unquestioningly. They trust me. And then there's Ryan. He trusts me like he trusted me fifteen years ago, like no time has passed at all. This lie is going to come out eventually. They'll feel like *he* betrayed them too when this is over and they find out the truth.

I'm not sure which thought makes me feel more ill – the thought of them finding out or the thought of this being over.

'You are still on my team then?'

Team. I barely conceal the scoff. Harrison's team consists of him and whichever of his millionaire buddies he can gain the most out of.

'Of course.' I swallow hard. I cannot lose my job. The reality of this situation is that I live in London and have bills to pay and an unforgiving landlord. Sitting in a magical tree with my "one that got away" is nice but it's only temporary. When this is over, I have to go back to London and still be able to afford my rent and bills.

'Only you're not meant to be designing a website for them.'

A shiver goes through me and not the good kind this time. I pull the phone away from my ear and peer at it suspiciously. Has he installed some sort of spyware? A remote secret webcam?

Like he knows I've pulled the phone away, he shouts after me. 'I saw your name on the domain name registry, Felicity.'

Oh. I hadn't thought of that. I reluctantly put the phone to my ear again, wishing I could accidentally drop it in the sea.

'I'm monitoring their activity scrupulously.' He pauses. 'I haven't had much choice since my informant has given up on informing me of *anything.*'

Informant. That makes me sound like I belong in a gangster movie as some sort of criminal overlord with minions. It also makes me sound like a horrible person who doesn't deserve the trust of the good people she's deceiving.

'Since when is "end this protest" translatable to "create a website to further push this protest"?' Harrison is saying.

He really doesn't seem to get the concept of going undercover. 'They're old. They didn't know how websites worked. You *told* me to pretend to be on their side. They have to think I'm part of their protest.' The words sting as they come out of my mouth. I *am* part of their protest, but if I admit that, I'll lose my job, and if I admit the truth to the residents, they'll never believe I was ever genuine.

'Hmm.' Harrison is clicking the pen again. 'It sounds windy so I assume you're there actually doing your job and not wasting this *paid* holiday time in some other frivolous way. None of them are listening to this, are they?'

'Yes, I'm here.' If he knows I'm alone, he's going to send the builders in to secure the site within a matter of minutes, and if I'm not alone, he's going to question how I can have this conversation without being overheard. 'They're all deaf,' I say quickly. 'The wind has played havoc with their hearing aids.'

I've clearly taken to being underhanded and deceitful far too

137

easily. I don't know whether to be concerned or impressed that I even thought of that.

'How many of them are there?'

'Right now?' I look out at the empty strawberry patch. 'Oh, plenty. It's very crowded.'

'And what are their plans?'

'Plans?'

'For the protest. What are they going to do next?'

'I don't know.' I brace myself for the yelling that will inevitably follow, but I can't tell him anything. It's not for him to know.

'You don't know?' He doesn't sound as surprised as I expected. 'I expect you were too busy being headbutted by a sheep to find out?'

I glance down at Baaabra, who's still watching me judgementally.

'I'm following @BeachBattleaxe,' Harrison explains before I have time to question it. 'Since you got there, the protest now has a website, and you're its mascot being headbutted by a sheep. Being headbutted by a sheep was *not* on your agenda, Felicity!'

'I didn't *ask* to be headbutted by a flipping sheep,' I snap. 'Is being headbutted by a sheep on *anyone's* agenda?'

'You're a gif on Twitter!'

'I'm trying, okay? You told me to go undercover and I *am*. What more do you want?'

He's quiet for a moment, probably surprised into silence by me snapping at him. There's a first time for everything – both his silence and me saying boo to a curly-moustachioed goose. 'I want results.'

'And you'll get them, but I need a bit longer.'

'You've had a week and a half! This is not a free holiday, Felicity. Don't think I'm paying you to have fun with a sheep.'

The line goes dead and I blink at the blank screen in my hand. That went about as well as I expected.

How the heck am I going to get out of this? There are only

two options – walk away and go back to London, tell Harrison I couldn't do it, and hope he lets me keep my job, or ... Actually that's it. That is the *only* option.

But it *isn't* an option. Running away, never stopping to look back, leaving this place and these people behind. Losing touch with Ryan again, knowing he's going to find out this terrible secret about me. Just like last time when he realised in the most embarrassing way possible that I'd been harbouring a gigantic crush on him for all the years we'd worked together. I ran away then, but I don't want history to repeat itself. And I don't want to leave. I don't want this tree to be cut down, or the strawberry patch to be destroyed after it's somehow survived all these years, or the quirky bunch of residents to lose their garden space and have a soulless hotel plonked in front of their windows. I don't want this beautiful landscape to be defined by a modern archi-tecture-style building sticking out like a strawberry in a bowl of sweetcorn. I want to help. Not because Harrison wants me to, but because I can't bear the thought of *not* helping.

Baaabra Streisand is still watching me like she's understood every word of this conversation and is severely condemning me.

'I'm sorry, okay?' I say to her. 'I didn't mean for this to happen.'

And then I realise I'm talking to a sheep. A sheep who intensely dislikes me.

She does the sheep version of a snort and walks around, hunting out the remains of my umbrella and starts shredding what's left of the fabric, spitting out pieces of it with revulsion, like it somehow demonstrates how much she disapproves of me.

The conversation with Harrison makes me double my efforts with the website, and I hunker down, adding pages and hammering out descriptions so quickly that the laptop rocks under my fingers.

Harrison is *not* having this tree if it's the last thing I do.

I get the website into a reasonable state with all forms and contact info working correctly, and even though it needs prettying up a bit, it will do. I open the emails Tonya sent last night with some names and details of the people behind some carvings, and dial the first number.

'Hello, is that Edie?' I introduce myself when she picks up and say Tonya passed on her name and thought she might be able to help.

'Cutting it down?' She squeals in horror when I explain what's happening with the tree. 'Good grief, I'm not having that! I'm mostly retired now, but I was a florist for forty years and I wouldn't have even considered the industry if it wasn't for that tree.'

Goose bumps break out across my skin again. 'How come?'

'When I was little, like all children in Lemmon Cove, I waited for the autumn to come so I could pick up the falling sycamore seeds and shout my wishes to the shore, and every year, I'd pick up broken branches of autumnal leaves to make flower displays for my mother. I liked watching my displays make people smile. When I was fired from my retail job unexpectedly, I was at a loss. I was twenty-nine, my husband had just left me, and I went back to stay with my elderly mum in Lemmon Cove. I visited the sycamore tree, picked up a seed and watched it spin off the cliff edge, and my wish was that I'd somehow know where to go with my life.'

What is it about this tree? My eyes are filling up as I listen to her talk, and I've already got a sixth sense about what she's going to say.

'While I was there, I picked up some autumn leaves and branches and as I stood in my mum's kitchen arranging that autumn vase, I started wondering if there'd be any demand for a florist in the area. There were always lots of weddings in the summer and I mentioned the idea of setting up my own shop to my mum, and she realised there was an empty unit in town, and wrote me a cheque then and there for the deposit and first few months' rent. I'm sure the tree had a hand in it. Well, a branch. Tree's don't really have hands, do they?'

I let out a wholly embarrassing sob and cover it by pretending to cough.

'It's all right – it always gets to me too. That tree has a way of touching people. It's the unknown magic of it. We're adults, we *know* it doesn't really grant wishes and it's not really magical, but it *could* be, couldn't it? I never lose the sense of childhood wonder when I look up at it. There's always a possibility that magic twinkles through its leaves.'

She puts into words what I've always thought. It was a fairy tale when I was young, and I loved it, but now, even though I know that magic and wish-granting trees don't exist in the world, whenever I look up into its branches, I still get the fairy-tale feeling, and for a fleeting moment, I wonder … *do they*?

'And nearly forty years later, I've had the best career I could ever have wished for,' Edie continues. 'I met my second husband through the shop. He was an event organiser for floral art competitions, and we were married for twenty glorious years before he passed away. I've supplied the Chelsea Flower Show and done arrangements for Buckingham Palace and fulfilled every dream I could never even have imagined all those years ago when I stood under that tree. My daughter runs the shop now, and my granddaughter helps out after school. She can't wait to take over one day.'

'That's incredible,' I murmur into the phone. The wind rustles the leaves again and I look up into the tree, convinced it can somehow hear me.

'The day I opened, after a roaring first day, my mum and I went to visit the tree. We had a glass of champagne to toast the new beginning and I added my own carving – a little flower and the date 27/06/1983.'

'I know where that is!' I scramble to my feet and jump down from the tree while holding the phone between my ear and shoulder. Maybe I'm getting better at this because I'm quite impressed when neither me nor the phone end up in the sea, but then I instantly disprove the theory by falling over Baaabra and sending the phone sprawling onto the grass.

I grab it before she can eat it and shove it back against my ear.

'It's on the side facing the beach,' Edie says.

'I remember it. A little daisy. I always loved daisies and wondered what it meant.'

'That's rather wonderful. To know other people saw it. Somehow, a little part of me will always be in the world.'

The unspoken dread of the tree being cut down crackles over the line, and I swallow hard as I run my fingers across the trunk once more, having looked at that particular carving many times before. 'Found it!'

'Is it really still there?' She sighs with what sounds like happiness. 'I always wondered. I was going to show my granddaughter a couple of years ago, but the land was so overgrown that we turned back.'

'Bring her,' I say instantly. 'We're clearing it. We *have* to share these stories and what this tree means to people in the area.'

'I did the flowers for a wedding that took place there once.'

'A wedding *under* the tree?'

She makes a noise of agreement. 'I always kept in touch with the couple afterwards. I've got their phone number somewhere, shall I give them a ring?'

'Oh, wow. Yes, please. That's *so* romantic. That's *exactly* the sort of thing we need.'

'I'll do anything I can to help. I might sound like a mad old bat, but I've always said that tree changed my life. I'll call everyone I know. What was your website again?'

I give her the seaside-sycamore-tree.com address and tell her about the petition and the page where people can put in their own stories and upload photos, and she says she's going to bring her granddaughter here as soon as she can.

It's still raining by the time I hang up, and the chain rattles around behind me as I move, clinking with every step, but it's surprisingly easy to forget after a while. The metal warms with body heat and the weight around my waist becomes like a well-worn belt.

Baaabra Streisand is following me as I walk around, and I'm glad there's a strong barrier at the cliff edge, because she's definitely waiting for her chance to off me. Or hoping I might have food in my pockets. I try to be brave and offer her my hand, but she turns her head away, like she knows exactly how much of a traitor I am now.

While I'm still alone out here, I take the opportunity to have another look for the carving Ryan did, because I'm half-convinced it never happened and want to prove it to myself. He hasn't given any indication that he even remembers what happened under this tree, and if I could find that "Ry + Fee" in a heart shape, it might prove something.

I never believed the old legend that if a carving fades, the relationship is doomed, but it feels like a sign that I can't find it. Maybe it faded or got carved over by someone else. Maybe he stood there and scrubbed it out as I ran away.

I glance up at the tree and the leaves shake, splattering me with raindrops. Maybe a sign that I'm wasting my time. What difference would it make if I found it? Do I want it to somehow prove I was right to kiss him? To explain what it was that made me think he *wanted* to be kissed? If Ryan *has* forgotten, I certainly don't want to jog his memory. It's better to let it be lost to time and the weather that batters the clifftop.

Talking to Edie has boosted my confidence and confirmed my feelings that there are many more people who would be up in arms about the hotel – we just have to find them. My fingers trail over the bark as I walk around the vast trunk, like I can somehow *feel* the amount of life this tree has seen. Every name, every date, every symbol is an emblem of a life that's passed under these branches.

I jump back into the tree, leaving Baaabra Streisand looking up me dejectedly. Probably upset that her chances for murdering me are reduced by the fact sheep can't climb trees.

The rain has dulled to a drizzle now as I look out at the empty strawberry patch, but the heavy grey clouds are making it feel much later in the day than it actually is, and I crack open my laptop again.

I lose track of time passing and I'm still tweaking the website hours later. Baaabra has shredded the remains of my umbrella and spat the pieces out all around the base of the tree, like she was trying to trap me in some sort of pentagram, and I had to gather them up and shove the wad of sheep-drool-covered fabric into my bag before they blew away and further polluted the ocean.

I look up when the gate rattles, and instead of saying hello like anyone else would, Ryan starts singing "Here Comes the Hotstepper", the Nineties classic by Ini Kamoze, and I'm kind of impressed that his musical tastes haven't got any more refined after all this time.

I can't help laughing as I join in, effectively murdering the song. It was on one of the playlists he used to make us listen to at Sullivan's Seeds, and we always duetted it, even though neither of us can sing.

We don't stop the duet until he gets close enough for me to see his face in the early evening light.

'Even after so many years, you never forget the pinnacle of Nineties music,' he says, smiling widely.

It's an unmistakable segue into a bout of "Never Forget" by Take That for us both, complete with the dance move of clapping and throwing your arms out on my part.

'I debated going for "Return of the Mack", but I'm not a "mack" whatever one of those is. Did anyone ever find out what a "mack" is and why it needed to return? Mind you, I'm not much of a hotstepper either, but hotstepper sounded better than drawing comparisons to a raincoat favoured by old ladies.'

I burst out laughing. 'I don't know what a hotstepper is either.'

He tilts his head to the side, screwing up one eye as he considers it. 'Me neither, actually. Was all Nineties music about random made-up words that no one understands?'

'Probably. There were songs about Peaches and Scrubs and MmmBop. Maybe the appeal is in no one having a clue what they're about.'

He's grinning a proud grin and holding something behind his back, which he pulls out as he approaches the tree. A paper bag dangles from his index finger. 'I brought sustenance.'

My eyes fall on the logo. 'No way! That place is still open?'

'Same family. Recipe hasn't changed in twenty years. I'm assuming you're still vegetarian?'

I nod. I don't know why it makes me smile so much. Twenty years ago, not eating meat wasn't as popular as it is now, and Ryan and I were always the odd ones out at Sullivan's Seeds. Vegetarian takeaway food wasn't a big thing, but there was this restaurant further round the Gower coastline on the peninsula that did vegetarian fish and chips, and it was even better than the real thing. It was always my favourite place to eat. After I introduced him to their merits, he started getting food from there on special occasions. Birthdays, if something good happened, sometimes just if we were working late.

The bittersweet tang of him bringing in a bag just like that on the lunchtime of my last day – hours before The Kiss That Shall Not Be Mentioned.

The last time I ever ate their food.

He says hello to Baaabra Streisand and steps right up to the trunk, smiling up at me. I'm still a way up in the tree, but he's tall enough that if he leans up and I lean down, I'm only a little bit above him.

'I can't believe you remembered.' I shove my laptop aside and take the bag when he holds it up.

145

'Are you serious? How can you possibly think I'd forget *anything* about you?'

It makes me go warm all over, even though there are *some* things I'd certainly hope he might have disremembered.

He pushes himself up on tiptoe, folds his arms against the curve of the trunk and rests his chin on them. 'It's nice in there, right? Like a treehouse crossed with a childhood den. Makes me feel like a kid again.'

'Yeah. And with a bonus of homicidal sheep not being able to reach you.'

It's his turn to burst out laughing, and I love the way his eyes still crinkle up – more crinkles than there used to be now, but the sight of his crow's feet makes me smile, and I still want to reach across and smooth them out.

His laughing eyes meet mine and he wets his lips slowly with his tongue, making me swallow hard. His eyes are bright, and his stubble is dark and just the right level of tantalisingly prickly to make me imagine the feel of it against my skin.

'God, I missed you.' He pushes himself up and I don't realise I've automatically moved towards him until our foreheads come within a millimetre of crashing, and my balance suddenly goes and I have to grip the tree trunk to avoid falling out.

'It's only been a few hours,' I say quickly to distract from how close that was – both the kiss and ending up face first on the ground.

'I didn't mean today. Fee, I meant always.' He pushes himself away from the tree and drags a hand through his dark hair, and the ends that are starting to curl over catch on his fingers. 'We shouldn't have lost touch, and I know it was my fault, and—'

'Well, these things happen, don't they?' I say, breezier than the gale-force winds that were battering the cliff earlier.

He looks at me for a long moment, waiting, expecting me to say something more.

'Baaabra Streisand hasn't murdered you yet then?' he says

146

when I don't. He makes his way around the tree and I hear his boots scraping against the trunk's natural footrest to hoist himself up.

'Not yet, but I think she wants to. She's been plotting something all day.'

'Probably how to snaffle out more strawberries.' He pulls himself up into the tree easily, unlike the flaily mess I've made of it today with a sheep snapping at my heels.

Inside the bag are two hefty portions of chips and vegetarian fish, and I'm so touched that he remembered, that it's a fight with myself not to well up as I get out the two packages. There's no one in my life who knows what my favourite restaurant is *now*, never mind has remembered it from over a decade ago.

He sits cross-legged beside me and I plonk one of the white paper packages in his lap and start unwrapping my own, the rustling paper attracting Baaabra's attention, who gets up and comes to the trunk, looking up at us with the sheep equivalent of puppy dog eyes, her furry nose sniffing the air with interest.

It smells like real fish and chips, and it's liberally drizzled with vinegar and sea salt, complete with a little wooden fork, and steam rises into the night air as I dive in.

'Thank you,' I say around a mouthful of the most perfect crisp-on-the-outside and fluffy-on-the-inside chips.

He puts a chip between his teeth and grins around it. 'You're welcome.'

He always was the kind of guy who would never leave the office without bringing something back for me. Chocolate, a hot drink, a cream cake from a bakery he'd passed, or any other little thing he'd thought I'd like. The kind of guy who could take one look at me and know there was something wrong, who instinc-tively knew if I needed a hug, a cup of tea, a bar of chocolate, or all three.

He makes a noise of pleasure. 'Oh, this is so good. It's been *years*.'

'Don't you go there often? If I still lived here, I'd go there *all* the time.'

He stops mid-chip and looks up at me. 'I couldn't. Not after you ... It wouldn't have been right. It would've been like a betrayal or something to eat at your favourite restaurant without you. Besides, it was my favourite because it was *your* favourite. I loved getting takeaways from there *with* you. Without you, it would've made me miss you too much.'

I almost swallow my own tongue, never mind the whole mouthful of chips I was stuffing down.

His cheeks redden and he looks away, picking out a chip, testing it for coolness, and throwing it to the waiting sheep below.

I watch the trajectory as it lands, and Baaabra Streisand looks a lot less interested in it than she did moments ago. 'Is there anything she won't eat?'

'She doesn't eat much, really. However, she *loves* chewing things up for the sole purpose of destroying them. Tory leaflets are her favourite. Mr Barley collects them for her at election times.'

Her fussiness is proved when she plods over to the chip, considers it uninterestedly before eventually deigning to pick it up with her teeth and promptly spit it out again. She looks up and gives Ryan what can only be described as such a death glare that it makes me laugh out loud.

We're quiet for a while as we eat and the tree is filled with noises of content. I hadn't realised how hungry I was, and how happy something so simple makes me.

'How'd it go today?' I ask.

'Really well.' He half-stumbles over his words as they fall out in a rush, like he meant to tell me before. 'Henrietta was having a good day. She knew who Godfrey was and cried because she'd missed him so much. It doesn't happen often, but he couldn't stop smiling all the way home. I'm really glad we went. Sorry we've been ages. He wanted to stay with her for as long as possible, then there were roadworks and his back gives him gip if he sits still for too long, so we stopped at the services for a leg stretch. Thanks for staying.'

'It's fine. It's been fun.' I tell him about Edie and the second phone call I made to a number Alys sent over – a man who had scattered his dog's ashes here because his dog had always loved playing with falling sycamore seeds every autumn. He lives far away now, but wanted to sign the petition and pass it on to his friends and family.

By the time we finish, it's late evening and the pink-tinged storm clouds are still hanging over the ocean and the mist is rolling in, making it seem darker than it would usually be at this time.

The chain is back around Ryan's waist and he's settled in for the night. I should be going home, but I can't make myself move. The more time I spend with him, the worse this all gets, but he's here and his leg is warm where it's pressed against mine. My laptop battery ran out, so now we're fiddling with the website on his, and he keeps leaning closer to show me things and I have to tilt my head so close that it could almost be resting on his shoulder, and it's nice somehow. Every part of my brain is screaming at me to keep my distance from him, but every part of my heart is warm and fuzzy because he makes me feel special and important in a way that no one has in many years.

Every boyfriend I've ever had, and admittedly they've been few and far between, has ended up fizzling out like a candle in the rain. Over the years, even if I've liked someone, I've always held back. I know what happens when you throw yourself at a man, and it wasn't a mistake I was going to make twice. I've never plucked up the courage to tell anyone I like them, and even in a relationship, I've always kept boyfriends at arm's length. Never made the first move, never gone in for another kiss, never said an "I love you" first. I'm always terrified of being rejected again. One guy I dated told me I was hard work and closed-off as we broke up, and it's probably accurate. What happened with Ryan made me second-guess every feeling I've ever had from then on, because if I can get it so wrong once, what's to say I won't again?

And then there's the whole chef thing. I'm lying to him and he's never going to forgive me when he finds out. I should get it over with, tell him now, make sure he knows that this has become so much more than my job, but when I glance at him, steeling myself to say something, he catches my eyes and a smile turns his mouth halfway up, and that enormous butterfly starts swishing around inside me, and I don't say anything.

We're both distracted by the noise of a door closing up at the care home, and the beam of torchlight as someone makes their way towards the tree.

'Godfrey?' Ryan calls, clearly possessing better old people recognition skills than me.

The old man stops and shines his torch onto us before angling it back down to illuminate the path in front of him, like headlights on a foggy morning. He's holding something under his arm and tottering towards us, and Ryan shoves his laptop aside and clambers out of the tree, rushing around the trunk to help him.

The movement disturbs Baaabra Streisand from her chip-induced angry slumber and she climbs to her feet and trots after Ryan to see if Godfrey's got anything she can shred.

'I found something for you two young folks.' Godfrey is holding onto Ryan's arm as they approach. 'I knew I had them somewhere. I spent half the journey today wondering where I'd put them.'

He has a stack of what look like documents in his hand, and when he's safe on solid ground, he takes his hand off Ryan's arm, splits the stack of papers in two, and hands one to Ryan and one up to me.

'What are these?' Ryan flicks through them, squinting in the low light.

'Old strawberry plant catalogues,' I say in delight as I leaf through them.

'From my great-great-grandfather's time in the late Victorian era all the way to the last one Henrietta and I ever had printed. Of course, printed flyers were already old-fashioned by then, but it was tradition and, no matter what young and modern folks say, I think the strength of a place like this is *in* tradition. Henrietta and I never wanted to modernise. We wanted it to invoke that sense of nostalgia in everyone who came here. There were always a lot of return visitors. People who grew up coming here would return years later with their own children. We were privileged to run it for long enough to witness that, and we wanted people to feel they were coming to the *same* strawberry patch, not one run by robots or something.'

The idea makes me giggle. Considering it closed in the late Noughties, robots hadn't *quite* taken over the world by then.

I can feel Godfrey watching me as I flip through the pages. They're old newspaper-style print with hand-drawn images of strawberries, and the defining features and benefits of each different variety. On the front is "Lemmon Cove's finest seaside strawberry patch" like there had ever been more than one to compete with, and inside the cover of the stapled pages, is a map showing a layout of the strawberry patch and marking out which varieties grow in which area.

'We used to put one together every spring to showcase what varieties would be available and send them out all along the Gower coast. We had stacks of them in the tourist information office, and gardening magazines used to slip one in with each copy. We used to supply the little shop in Lemmon Cove. Tourists used to come here and pick them fresh, and then get another punnet from the shop as they drove through the village on their way out.'

He pets Baaabra Streisand as he talks, and fishes a Glacier Mint out of his pocket, unwraps it, and holds it out on his fingers for her. Something else I haven't seen since the Nineties. It really is like stepping into some kind of time warp when you come back here.

The sheep takes it greedily and trots away, stopping to give a quick snort to Ryan – as if chastising him for giving her anything as distasteful as a chip. A sheep who turns down the best chips in South Wales but likes hard-boiled sweets. Just when I thought my hometown couldn't have any more surprises in store.

'These are amazing.' I trace the outline of the hand-drawn strawberry on the page. 'Can we hang on to these for a while? I'm sure there's a story here somewhere.'

He reaches up to pat my hand. 'For as long as you want.' His hand-patting turns into a grasp as his fingers curl around mine. 'Thank you, my dear, for letting your prince take me to see my Henrietta today.'

The idea of Ryan being a prince makes me grin, and when I look down at him, he's blushing.

'You're a prince to all of us, lad.' Godfrey lets go of my hand and reaches over to pinch Ryan's left cheek and I have to bite the inside of mine to keep from falling out of the tree with laughter at how uncomfortable he looks.

Ryan's eyes are twinkling when he looks at me again, and I can't hide how much I'm smiling.

'You're welcome,' I say to Godfrey. Ry was always uneasy taking compliments. 'Ryan did the difficult part. I just sat here.'

'It was your idea.' Typical Ryan. Always giving credit to everyone else, unlike every boss I've had ever since.

'Tonya has been showing everyone how busy you've been with the website you've put together. And everyone knows that Edie the florist is coming to visit, and we've had three new signatures from that man's family.' He looks between me up in the tree and Ryan standing next to him. 'You two make a good team.'

'That's what I've always said,' Ryan says. 'She brought out the best in me. And sometimes it needed excavating from great depths.'

I tilt my head to the side at his self-deprecation. He struggled with confidence when he first took over Sullivan's Seeds, because he was young and had no experience, but it grew as time went on. 'It never took any finding. You were always perfect just the way you were.' I cringe as I say it. Who do I think I am – Mark Darcy?

Ryan looks up and meets my eyes, and I blink at the sudden intensity in his. My mouth goes dry. His Adam's apple bobs as he swallows. I should *not* have said that. He didn't need the reminder that I was head over heels for him all those years ago.

He wets his lips and swallows again. 'You were—'

'Henrietta had a good day?' I interrupt him by asking Godfrey. I'm sure he's only trying to be kind, but the last thing I need is an awkward "you were just a friend" speech.

Godfrey doesn't detect the awkwardness between us as his face breaks into a toothy smile. 'Yes. She's lost in time most days. She thinks I'm a resident there and asks when her husband's coming, but for brief snatches today, she knew who I was. She always used to love a cuddle, and most of the time nowadays, she thinks I'm a stranger so I can't go near her, but today we sat on the sofa together and held hands. Every time I go there, I always wonder if it's going to be the last time – if she's ever going to recognise me again. We used to say we were all each other needed, and that everything would be all right as long as we had each other.' He shakes a finger at us in turn. 'You two young folks remember that. You never have as much time as you think.'

I swallow hard, his words making me well up again. 'I wish more days were like today for you.'

'Say it a bit louder, perhaps the wishing tree will hear.' His eyes move up towards the branches and he stares at it for a moment. 'Maybe it hears everything anyway.'

Ryan and I look at each other and glance up at it too.

Godfrey sighs and looks away. 'Look at me getting all sappy. How about you two? You're old friends but nothing *more*?' His wiry eyebrows waggle.

'I was never good enough for Fee,' Ryan says before I can answer.

'What? You were the best thing in my life.' The surprise of hearing him say that makes me speak without thinking first.

'I was?' His head twitches like he's taken aback.

'Of course you were. Ry, I loved …' My breath catches and I cut the sentence off in a *very* inconvenient place when he meets my eyes again.

Everything goes so still that I'm not sure he's breathing, and I'm definitely not. My hand moves automatically like if I reached out, I could touch him, and it would be okay, like he was somehow mine to touch.

His Adam's apple bobs again, and I need to swallow but my mouth has gone too dry to even consider it. Neither of us blinks as we hold each other's gaze for a long, long moment. He wets his lips again and my eyes are drawn to his tongue as it slides across full lips, and …

Baaabra Streisand lets out a long, foghorn-esque fart.

'… Working with you,' I finish, more limply than a wet kipper, glad of the excuse to look away because I have to stop watching his mouth. Between that and my earlier comment, I couldn't make myself sound any more smitten if I'd tried.

'Well, there's a way to ruin the moment,' Godfrey says, thankfully easing the tension and making all three of us laugh.

Baaabra Streisand's perfect comedy timing certainly comes in handy.

'I'd best get back for my unimaginative, boring supper. Porridge, again.' Godfrey makes a noise of distaste. 'Maybe when we've saved the tree, you can put your skills to use in campaigning for a better menu at Seaview Heights. They'd definitely listen to a chef.' He nods to me. 'You know how to stir up a whole generation, Felicity.'

'Fee always did know how to shake up a life.' Ryan's eyes meet mine again and I try a smile. It's so strained that it probably looks like I'm going to bite him.

154

He hands his stack of the old strawberry leaflets up to me and undoes the chain around his waist and passes that up too, before turning to offer his arm to Godfrey. 'I'll walk you back.'

That weird mid-twilight is still hanging over us from the surrounding, almost-purple storm clouds over the ocean, and I watch as Godfrey slots his arm through Ryan's and they make their way slowly back towards Seaview Heights.

What is it about a man who's kind to animals and old people? Ryan was always the most respectful person, and that clearly hasn't changed. He's a real gentleman, something that's seriously missing in my life lately.

# Chapter 10

I have to tell him. It's not right that I'm pretending to do a job that's the opposite of what I actually do, but it's even worse that he trusts me and doesn't have seem to have an inclination of who I really am. What would he say if he knew I'm the person who was sent to bribe him?

I'm still thinking of the best way to broach the subject as he makes his way back towards the tree, covering the ground sure-footedly despite being sans torch, having safely returned Godfrey to his porridge and evening of board games in the living room.

He lifts a hand in greeting as he approaches, giving me a bright smile and a flash of flexing forearms that gives me something else entirely to be distracted by. He pats the trunk as he walks around the tree and pushes himself up again, once more making his bare forearms flex in the most delicious way.

'Are you *always* working?' He takes the couple of steps nearer to me in the space we've got between the branches.

I hadn't bothered to fasten the chain this time and I hand it back to him and watch as he loops it around his waist and does up the catch. 'We have to grab ideas as and when we can. We don't have much time.'

'Why not?' He sits down cross-legged opposite me. 'I'm in this for the long haul. My assistant can run the campsite for as long as needed, and I can do admin remotely. I'm quite happy to stay here indefinitely.'

'It's August, Ryan. Next month, the first frosts will start coming in. Winter comes sharply from September onwards. You can't stay out here forever.' I shake my head. 'It's not about that anyway. This isn't your land ...'

'I know. I can't afford to make an offer on it. I tried.'

'You did?' I can't hide how much that surprises me. I think about his expansion plans for self-contained holiday lets. Maybe I wasn't that far off base if he's already tried to buy this land.

'I thought it might be the only way. It's not about the money or the space. I'd do anything to save this tree and the garden for the residents, but I can't compete with multinational companies.'

'So what are you trying to do with this protest – drive down the price? Keep the tree, but park some tents around it? Free wish with every booking?'

'You really don't like me, do you?' He quirks an eyebrow.

I know he's joking, but the words make me go cold. I *more* than like him, even after so many years. 'I didn't mean it like that. Steffan has already delayed because of the protest, but the longer this goes on the more likely he is to *want* to get rid of it. And the more attention we gain, the more likely he is to get *higher* offers from *more* businesses.'

'Maybe ones who would be on our side. Ones who would reach a compromise and see the value in this land as it is. We need you around to help us vet any offers that come in. You were always good at knowing who to trust when I wasn't. How soon do you need to get back?'

'I, er ...'

'Please don't leave me yet, Fee. I was hoping you'd be back for good.'

It's an open segue into another Take That song, but neither

of us do it. It doesn't feel like the time. Whoever thought there'd be a bad time for a Take That flashback? And it's a good job I'm sitting down because the words make me feel light-headed and everything goes a bit fuzzy.

'I have a job to get back to,' I mumble. I *need* to tell him the truth, and my stomach rolls more than the choppy waves below.

'How much longer can they spare you for? Can it be offset by the lower bill from the fire brigade without you there?' He winks at me, and although he's teasing, it makes me feel unwell again.

'I've got annual leave stacked up,' I mumble. *Come on, Fliss. You* have *to tell him.*

'Just like the Fee I knew. Always working.' His teeth pull his lower lip into his mouth and let it out slowly, and I can feel his eyes burning into me and I squirm under his gaze. 'I'm glad you don't have to go yet.'

He wouldn't be saying that if he knew the truth about where I work. He'd never believe there was anything genuine about my involvement in this campaign, and he'd definitely never trust me again.

I realise that my body language is going to give me away faster than anything else. Unless Baaabra Streisand finds a way of telling him first. She may be a sheep, but she could spell it out in tree branches or chew up enough items to form letters from the remains. I glance down at her, currently asleep half-on and half-off her dog bed cushion, snoring loudly. Maybe I'm giving her too much credit.

I lift my chin defiantly and try to push it out of my head. Ryan's not being entirely honest here either. How convenient that the owner of the campsite next door wants to expand, has tried to buy this land, been refused, and now become the head protestor to prevent someone else buying it. And then I feel horrible, and jaded, and cynical for thinking the worst of him. Ryan isn't like the businessmen I deal with at work.

Like he can sense we've reached an impasse, he reaches out

both hands for some of the old strawberry leaflets that I've been mindlessly flicking through but not taken in a word of since he got back. I hand him half the stack, and shift around so I'm facing the strawberry patch again. I don't even know when I turned around to face Ryan. Or when we drifted so close that our knees are touching again.

'These are a piece of history,' he says.

'Real British heirlooms. We used to grow these ones at Sullivan's Seed's.' I lean across to show him a picture in a leaflet dated 1906. 'We can take pictures of these and put them on the website. This is real history. These are the same plants – their heritage can be traced back through these catalogues. Look at this one: 1892. Victorian strawberry plants.'

'Whoever thought fruit ancestry could be so interesting?'

It could be a plumbing course, and it would be interesting with Ryan. Back in the day, he even made a good time out of mandatory health and safety courses and risk inspection days.

I hold up one of the hand-drawn maps inside a strawberry leaflet from 1987 and try to work out where each variety of strawberry plant is likely to be, and how we'd identify them.

After a few moments, Ryan moves too, and the chain drags against the tree as he stretches out on his stomach beside me, and I quickly put the map down to hide how much my hands are shaking at the sudden closeness.

'This okay?' he murmurs, tipping his head to the side so it knocks against my arm.

'Fine.' I stutter so much, it comes out sounding more like "greebavlchowblhe", but what it's meant to be is: "That feels really nice actually; I like that".

He lifts his head again, but I can feel the space where he was is burning, tingling with the imprint of his skin against mine like when someone with warm hands touches your cold ones and you can tell they're there but you're too numb to really feel them.

His body is warm against the side of mine, his ribs pressing against my thigh, the side of his abdomen against my hip. He pushes himself up on his elbows and spreads Godfrey's papers in front of him. 'You were the best thing in my life too,' he says softly, deliberately not looking up. 'All the overtime I put in was solely because I didn't want to miss a day with you.'

I take in a breath so sharp that cold air hits the back of my throat and chokes me. Ryan shifts until he can snake an arm between us and rubs my back until I've got myself under control. His arm is underneath his hoodie that I'm still wearing, and his fingers are burning hot through my T-shirt.

He pulls his arm back and leans on his elbow again, looking ahead instead of at me or the leaflets now. 'I always thought things would be perfect when I met you again. I'd be mature and sophisticated and not the awkward gawky nerd I was back then, but it turns out, when I do meet you again, I'm chained to a branch with a sheep, trying to save a magical tree. You must think I'm such an idiot.'

'I think you're amazing.' I get the words out before I can second-guess myself. He deserves to know that. Who else would literally move into a tree in an attempt to save it? And not just that – it's the way he treats everyone around him. The respect and banter he has with the residents here, the way he cares about everyone and everything, the way Baaabra Streisand has clearly got everything a sheep could ever wish for in life. 'Besides, I always thought I'd be sophisticated and not an awkward grieving teenager, but when I met you again, I had a foot full of sheep poo.'

I'm not sure reminding him of that was the best idea, but I don't even mind that when he bursts out laughing so hard that it shakes me too, making me giggle even though sheep poo is really no laughing matter.

'Ah well, at least we can be unsophisticated adults together now.' He hesitates. 'I wasn't an adult back then, Fee. If I had the chance again, there are certain things I'd do differently. You should know—'

I get a sixth sense that he's talking about the kiss, and I really, *really* don't want to hear it.

'That makes two of us!' I think even the tree jumps at the high tone in my voice that sounds like an out-of-tune violin.

Instead of saying anything, he drops his head to the side so it rests against my arm again.

'I'm glad you came back,' he whispers. 'Maybe it'll give me a chance to make up for certain things.'

I go to tell him he has nothing to make up for, but the words are either going to choke me or make me start crying, and they stick in my throat. My mouth opens but nothing comes out. He isn't the one who did anything wrong, but being this close to him, surrounded by the scent of his cologne and with the heat of his body filtering into mine, I hadn't realised how lonely I'd been, and it feels nice to just *be* with him again.

He doesn't lift his head, and even though it's by far the strangest position I've ever been in with a guy, it somehow feels right with Ryan, and I let myself enjoy it for a few moments. It's temporary – all this is temporary. What harm can it do?

I put the leaflets down and lean back without moving my left arm and dislodging him. Instead, I move my right hand across and my fingers skate over the muscles of his back, warm through his grey T-shirt.

His hand reaches up blindly to catch my hand and his fingers hold it on his shoulder, and I get the feeling it's his way of letting me know it's okay to touch him. When he lets his hand drop again, his head still heavy against my arm, my fingers rub mindlessly against his shoulder. In my head, I'm shouting at myself to stop touching him and keep a professional distance, because I *am* supposed to be here as a professional and this whole thing is going to come crashing down the moment anyone finds that out, but my hand moves of its own accord, slinking towards the nape of his neck and the dark strands of hair that start to curl there.

It's a natural instinct to touch it and my fingers graze the hair at the back of his neck, and I look down, watching him, expecting him to jump up and put as much space as possible between us, but his dark eyelashes are blinking slower as his eyes drift closed, and his head grows heavier against my arm.

I let my hand play with more of his hair, stroking through it, pulling it back and letting it spring forward again. His hair is straight for the first couple of inches and then starts to curl over, and he always used to keep it short enough not to show the curliness, but now it's more unkempt than it used to be, and if it gets much longer, it's going to turn into a mass of waves.

Without opening his eyes, he lifts his head, curls his fingers around my other hand and holds the back of it to his mouth. 'I missed you.' He breathes the words against my skin and presses his lips behind them.

He must be able to feel the way my whole body flushes. Every inch of my skin feels tingly and overheated, and with the prickly burn of his stubble against it, my hand must be so hot it's currently akin to touching an oven that's been on full blast for three hours.

'I missed you too,' I say honestly. My fingers tighten in his hair as he finally lets go of my hand and nestles his head back against my arm, where it's resting uselessly against my leg, held stiff and starting to ache because I don't want to make any movement that's going to destroy the peace of this moment. I let my fingers keep carding through his hair, enjoying the peacefulness and the warmth of his body against mine.

The idea that he didn't think he was good enough for me keeps doing three-point turns in my mind, and the thought that he didn't realise he was the best thing in my life back then prickles at me. Maybe I was so busy not letting him see that I had a ginormous crush on him that I never let him see how much he meant to me as a friend, and I decide here and now that I'm not going to make that mistake again. He deserves to know that he was the highlight of my life for many years.

He starts singing under his breath – another Nineties classic that fits the moment perfectly, "Together Again" by Janet Jackson, and I join in, humming along quietly. There were a lot of times I wouldn't be self-conscious about singing in front of Ryan, but *this* is not one of them.

'Not sure if I'm falling asleep or already dreaming,' he mumbles as he leans even heavier into me. 'Lying in a tree shouldn't be this comfy, should it?'

'I haven't felt my bum for the past two hours.' Great, Fliss. Draw attention to the one part of you doesn't need any extra attention drawn to it, not with the amount of time I spend sitting on it at my desk in the office.

'Ah, you get used to that. Trees don't come with built-in cushions. Well, unless this counts.' He lifts his head to rub his chin against my arm and when he glances up, I meet his eyes, and it's like it unlocks something in the haze we've been in.

He shakes himself and pushes off me, shifting over to put some space between us. 'Sorry, I think I entered a different reality for a minute. I'm forgetting myself. It's been a long day and I think my brain melted there.'

'There's something about this tree,' I say, because his cheeks have gone so red that even the weird evening light can't disguise it.

'It grants wishes,' he says softly. 'I mean … that was mine. That you'd …'

'Sit in a tree and stroke your hair while murdering a decades-old Janet song? That's quite specific for a helicopter seed. Spending so much time in this tree is clearly affecting you. Maybe it's got psychotropic properties or something and that's why everyone thinks it grants wishes but really it just makes people lose their minds when they're near it.'

He looks at me for a long moment, and then drops my gaze and looks away. 'That must be it.'

I get the feeling he wants to say more, and my thigh feels cold without him lying next to me, but it's for the best. Getting close to Ryan is a recipe for disaster in more ways than one.

# Chapter 11

'I'll see you in a bit,' my class is coming to your strawberry patch this morning,' Cheryl calls as she leaves the bedroom the next morning, leaving me half-asleep on my mostly deflated bed, and wondering if I should see about getting something more permanent, but that would be guaranteed to jinx Harrison into calling me back to the office, and I'm not ready to face that yet.

I toss and turn for a while longer before I finally persuade myself to go downstairs, surprised to find Dad feather dusting around the living room with music on in the background.

'You're enthusiastic?'

'Thought I'd get an early start. The sun's shining, the birds are singing … well, technically the birds are pooing all over my laurel hedgerow as they queue up for the neighbour's bird feeder, but we can't win 'em all. Are you off to see Ryan?'

Is it that obvious? 'Well, I thought I might get some breakfast first.' I start heading towards the kitchen and then stop. 'And I'm not going to see Ryan, I'm going to the strawberry patch to help the protest. There's a difference.'

He ignores me. 'Thought I might stop by later myself. Cynthia said she had some old photos to show me from the good ol' days at work.'

'You always did like her ...'

'It's always nice to reconnect with an old *friend*. Isn't it?'

'It's certainly been an eye-opening experience.' I look pointedly at the corner of the curtain rail he's dusting. This is the first time it's had so much as a sniff of a feather duster for months. *That* is not the influence of an old "friend". 'It would be good to see you. We need all the help we can get, and you're brilliant at gardening.' I nod out the window towards his pristine front yard full of fancy planters bearing rainbows of flowers and not a weed in sight.

'It would be nice to know I'm doing something to help the community. I keep our garden nice because your mother always did, but it's only myself and random passers-by who appreciate it. I'm told you're uncovering strawberry plants?'

'And who would've told you that, I wonder ...' I leave nothing out of my voice, my tone clearly telling him I know *exactly* who told him that.

'I may have had a little conversation with Cynthia on the phone last night.' It's really something when even your seventy-year-old dad goes the colour of a Parcelforce van.

'It's okay if you like her, Dad. Mum's been gone for nearly twenty years. She wouldn't want you to spend the rest of your life as alone and unhappy as you've been until now if there's someone out there who you deserve a second chance with.'

'You and your sister are just the same. I've already had this conversation with Cher this morning. I don't know where you're both getting these ideas from.'

'And I guess that big grin you can't get off your face wouldn't have tipped us off at all, would it? Or the matching one Cynthia's wearing around the strawberry patch ...'

I go to the kitchen before he has a chance to respond, throw some cereal down my throat for breakfast, and pack a couple of slices of the lemon meringue pie Dad baked last night for Ryan too. I'm rushing because I can't wait to get there.

I can't wait to see him again.

Chaos. Chaos is what awaits me at the strawberry patch. The gate is open and there are at least forty children hanging around on the coastal path and a couple of the local primary school's minibuses are in the car park with teachers trying to herd children into groups. Some of the children have filtered down towards the strawberry patch where Cheryl and a couple of other teachers are standing inside the gate, talking to Ryan, Tonya, Mr Barley, and Morys.

There are so many people that I seriously consider turning back, but like he's got some kind of radar for my footsteps, Ryan looks up at that exact moment and catches sight of me. Or maybe it's because the lower half of my hair is blue. I thought it blended in, but maybe it makes me impossible to miss.

He beams and waves, and the sight of his smile is enough to make me dodge my way through the groups of kids and teachers on the coastal path.

'Like your hair, Miss,' one of the little boys says, making me grin as I thank him. No matter his age, his simple compliment puts a spring in my step.

Ryan's excused himself from the conversation and is coming over, and Cheryl waves to me, and I don't miss the stealthy gesture as she points to him and then gives me a thumbs up.

Even though the gate's already open, Ryan meets me there like he did the other day and before I realise what's happening, he's hugging me.

'Good morning,' he says in my ear as strong arms tighten around my body, making me feel steady despite the swirling in my head caused by his closeness.

I murmur something that might also be "Morning" as my hand drifts up his back and my fingers curl into his shoulder like a claw, involuntarily pulling him closer. He must've been home to change because he's wearing ripped jeans cut off to mid-calf length, which don't go at all with his usual black and grey hiking boots, and a navy vest tight against ample tanned shoulders that my chin is somehow resting against as I hug him.

His hair is still damp from a shower, and I know drying it in the sunlight will make the curls go mad, and he smells of shampoo and that green, herby cologne again.

This isn't weird. He used to hug me when I got into work at Sullivan's Seeds every day. I repeat it to myself until one of the little boys makes an "oooo-ooooooh" noise and I blush and push myself away rapidly.

Ryan rolls his eyes and looks at me with a grin, and for one second, I think he's going to lean down and kiss my cheek, and that *would* be weird.

I take a step away from his arms, and then because I can't keep my distance no matter who's watching, I reach out and jiggle the soft fabric of his vest. 'No chain today?'

'Alys is on tree duty.' He nods towards the giant sycamore where Alys is sitting in the deckchair underneath it, the chain wound around her, and Baaabra's non-murderous head in her lap, like an overly large dog. 'I thought I'd better handle flyer distribution to this lot.'

He looks around the sea of children. 'Who'd have thought summer camp would be so busy?'

Even though it's the summer holidays, the school stays open as a summer camp for children who have got nowhere else to go. All ages are mixed together, none of them are in uniform, and from what Cheryl says, it's a lot more relaxed and fun than an ordinary school day.

Ryan takes my hand and pulls me along with him. 'Everyone's waiting for you. And when you get a minute, Alys wants your opinion on the latest round of "Guess the Gadget". Her mate is winning and she knows you'll be able to outfox her.'

I appreciate his faith in me, but it makes my stomach sink again. Lying to them all is making me feel worse every day. Ryan's hand tightens around mine as he tugs me over to rejoin the group.

Tonya comes over for a hug and I have to let go of Ryan's hand to hug her back, which is just as well because there is no universe in which I should *ever* be anywhere near his hand, never mind holding it.

I feel welcome and wanted here. It's something I haven't felt in a long time. Every day at work in London is a dread. I'm wanted there an equal amount to how much I want to be there.

Mr Barley hands me a flyer. 'Look, aren't they brilliant? The printer delivered them this morning.'

They're as perfect as the mock-up Ryan showed me a few days ago. It contains the mention of Godfrey's story, and I wave to the elderly man who is sitting on his regular bench and holding court with a small group of children who keep asking him for his autograph on their flyers, and he looks the brightest I've seen him.

'This lot are going for a nature walk,' Morys says. 'They're going to put our flyers through every door they pass. Different age groups are going in different directions, and then they're going to meet back here for their packed lunches and they want a talk about the tree for their summer projects.'

'Which *Ryan* is going to do,' I say quickly before he can volunteer me. I've never been good at talking in front of people.

Tonya is handing out the sycamore leaves to colour in, and Cynthia is sitting on a flowerbed wall talking to a woman with her arms around a little girl who looks ten-ish, older than most of the kids here, and one of the nurses from Seaview Heights has come down to collect a bunch of flowers from her.

'Is that Edie?'

'It is. She's waiting for you,' Ryan says. It makes me feel important again, and like I matter here. I wave to Edie, and both she and her granddaughter give me a bright smile and a wave back.

'If you're looking for stories about your tree, one of the boys in my class says he was made here.' Cheryl points out a little boy on the coastal path, currently using sticks to have a lightsabre fight with a friend.

'Made?' I say in confusion. 'They built him like a robo— Oh! *Oh! That* kind of made!'

I blush because I'm such an idiot, and they all laugh, but it feels like they're laughing with me, not *at* me.

'His parents might've told him the stork who delivered him lived in the tree for all we know,' she says.

'Well, they might not want people knowing about the alfresco naughtiness they get up to, but pass on my email address, will you? If they're happy for their young son to tell people that, maybe they'll be happy to share it with the website.'

'Will do.' Cheryl salutes me.

There are masses of flyers all around, everyone seems to be holding a stack, and it's the first time I realise how many Ryan must've ordered. If there's a chance of getting even half of these distributed, we *must* be able to find more connections to the tree.

Mr Barley has gone to chat to Edie, and a couple of other teachers have taken flyers and are trying to direct restless children back towards the car park. Which is probably just as well because Mr Barley is now pointing out his latest creation to Edie – a Boris Johnson gnome wearing a bikini and having a swim in the bird bath. A goldfinch sits on the edge looking traumatised by the scantily clad interloper in his regular bathing spot. In the flowerbeds, at the edges of Mr Barley's slug maze are a selection of rapidly deteriorating slugs in various stages of explosion that I can only hope the children didn't see.

As Cheryl and the endless stream of kids wave goodbye and go off clutching their flyers and a stack of laminated leaves to tie onto bushes and branches, I go over to say hello to Edie and her granddaughter, earning myself a hug from both of them and

170

Cynthia too. *Everyone* is so friendly here. I've never known anything like it.

'Dad says he'll pop down later,' I tell Cynthia, thoroughly enjoying the way her face lights up almost as much as Dad's did at the mention of her.

Edie and her granddaughter follow me down the now much wider and less treacherous path towards the tree. Baaabra Streisand lifts her head from Alys's lap and regards us with interest.

'Oh my God, a sheep! Can I stroke her?' the granddaughter asks.

I go to advise against it due to her bloodthirsty tendencies, but Baaabra seems to understand and hefts herself up and trots over inquisitively. The granddaughter drops to her knees and starts stroking her neck and tickling her chin.

'See?' Ryan calls over. 'She's only scared of you if you're scared of her.'

I turn around and poke my tongue out at him, making him laugh.

Now the kids have cleared out, it's quiet at the top end of the strawberry patch again, and he's already picked up a shovel and gone back to digging out rogue bramble bushes, moving full steam ahead with the plan of reopening the strawberry patch.

'It's a grand idea,' Alys says, making me wonder if I said that out loud.

She's looking pointedly between me and him, clearly having seen every second of that little exchange.

I direct Edie around the trunk, telling her to be careful of the roots that spider out from the base and the loose chain that's draped around it.

The granddaughter has now got Baaabra's head on her shoulder while she tickles her under the chin and the sheep looks like she's about to fall asleep standing up. 'Grandma, can we have a pet sheep?'

Edie laughs. 'No, but how about we bring your mum back and visit this one? She seems to like you.'

'She likes everyone other than Fliss,' Alys adds helpfully. 'Maybe she's pre-emptively jealous of losing her owner to another woman.'

I choke on thin air. This place is hazardous for throat health. 'I assure you, *that's* not going to happen.'

'Animals can sense these things, you know,' Alys continues. 'It's been her and Ryan for years now, and look at how much he likes you.'

I follow the direction she points in and look across to Ryan, who's leaning on his shovel and watching us with a smile on his face.

He lifts a hand and grins when he sees me looking, and then quickly looks away.

I don't realise I'm still watching him until she clicks her fingers to get my attention back. 'He's lonely, Fliss. You're the first woman he's let in for donkey's years. Well, of the non *Ovis aries* variety. Baaabra Streisand can sense it, I'm telling you.'

'We're just friends,' I say assuredly, even though the words make me flush warm all over. 'It isn't like that between us. It never was.'

Baaabra Streisand chooses that moment to attempt to eat one of the granddaughter's plaited bunches and the girl squeals in delight as she pulls it out of her mouth and waves it in the sheep's face, teasing her like she's dangling a toy mouse in front of a cat.

I'm once again grateful to the sheep for her excellent timing as it distracts the attention from anything to do with me and Ryan.

The granddaughter stands up and Baaabra trots happily behind her new friend. Edie has brought photos of her shop taken over the years, and I search out the daisy carving again and both she and the granddaughter *and* the sheep pose and let me snap pictures for the website, as they point at the carving and hold up the aged photos in front of the tree.

I keep glancing up at Ryan and meeting his eyes across the distance, smiling every time until one of us looks away.

'Eager to get hot and sweaty with him?' Edie says, ensuring I choke again.

'There's a lot of weed removal to be done if we want to reopen the strawberry patch,' I say when I've recovered, deliberately ignoring the implication.

'I can't wait to come strawberry picking here,' her granddaughter says. 'Are you really going to reopen?'

'As soon as we can. We're hoping by the weekend. We need to get the rest of the ground cleared and a bit of sun on the berries, and we should be good to go.'

'We'll leave you to it,' Edie says. 'But let me know when opening day is and we'll be here. Nothing better than a freshly picked strawberry.'

Before they go, Alys ropes us all into a game of "Guess the Gadget", and Edie's granddaughter wins by correctly guessing the image in question is a heated ice cream scoop and cheers like she's won the lottery when Alys's friend messages back to grudgingly give her the point.

Maybe "Guess the Gadget" has the potential to catch on after all.

Alys assures us that she's quite happy to stay chained to the tree with Baaabra, so I escort Edie and her granddaughter back to the entrance, and the sheep follows until she reaches the end of her lead, and the granddaughter runs back to give her another cuddle, and she bleats forlornly as she watches them leave, then she goes to sit by Alys but turns her back to show her annoyance at not being able to keep her new friend.

Ffion goes to sit with Alys to keep her company. Tonya is at one of the picnic tables near the care home sorting colouring-in leaves, laminated leaves, and flyers into some sort of order that only she understands; Godfrey is recovering from his new-found fame by reading his newspaper and sipping a cup of tea; Mr

Barley is doing … something atrocious to a gnome version of Nigel Farage; and Ryan is leaning on his shovel, his forehead glistening in the *good* way under the morning sunlight.

I pick up a garden fork and go over. 'Busy morning, right?'

'Oh, that?' He waves a hand in the direction of the gate. 'Just a standard day at the office.'

It takes me a while to realise he's joking and then I overcompensate by laughing way too hard.

'Seriously, Fee. It fills me with hope. *Everyone* we just saw – kids and teachers, residents, Edie – they're *all* so excited about the possibilities of this place. They all said they're going to come here to pick strawberries when it reopens.'

'A bit of rain yesterday and the sun today and these berries are ripening. Look at that one.' I point out a glossy red berry not far from our feet. 'We're going to have a glut by the weekend at this rate. Do you honestly think we'll be able to open in time?'

'Yes.'

'That simple?'

'We make a good enough team to do anything.' He grins and I have to lean on my fork to make sure no one can tell how shaky my knees are. 'All we have to do is clear out the last of these brambles today, and then lay weed-suppressant fabric down so they don't regrow, and it gives people a stable surface to walk on.'

'Did someone say something about the first strawberry?' Godfrey is behind us even though I've been so swept up in Ryan's pale blue-grey eyes that I didn't hear him move. I'm also fairly certain that those things in their ears masquerading as hearing aids are actually some kind of radio-controlled signal amplifier that ensures they never miss a word spoken between me and Ryan.

'What a moment!' Tonya shouts, jumping up from the table fast enough to send her neat piles scattering again. 'We need to record it for posterity. Someone special should eat it and we'll take photos and put them on social media.'

'Godfrey?' I suggest. 'That could be a nice "circle of life" moment? The ex-owner eating the first strawberry from the newly restored patch ...'

'No.' Tonya sweeps both hands out to the sides. 'You two!'

I glance at Ryan and he raises an eyebrow. 'Us?'

'You two are the brains behind this operation. It's only right. Here, I can't bend that far – you pick it and give it to me, and I'll go and give it a nice wash while I collect my camera.'

Ryan meets my eyes doubtfully, but Tonya is a difficult woman to argue with. I bend down to do her bidding, plucking the ripe berry and dutifully handing it to her. She thrusts it into the air in victory.

'Why don't we all do it? I'm sure we can find a few other ripe ones.' I look around the carpet of strawberry plants in hope, but she's already retreating up the garden towards Seaview Heights.

'No, no, just one will do,' she calls back. 'A strawberry is meant to be shared!'

Godfrey goes to talk to Mr Barley, leaving me and Ryan alone.

'Ever get the feeling they've been waiting and planning for this moment?'

'Very much so.' I nod in agreement. 'Although I think Baaabra Streisand's already eaten the first ripe strawberry, but it seems cruel to spoil her fun.'

'Judging by what I've had to clear up, I think Baaabra Streisand's eaten several ripe *and* unripe strawberries.'

It makes me laugh out loud but he goes red and looks away. 'I'm still an expert on ruining the moment and know just the sophisticated and refined topics to make women swoon, obviously.'

I still can't stop laughing because he's hilarious, no matter what topics he's talking about.

Tonya comes back with a camera around her neck and a piece of tissue paper cradled in both her hands. She's also got a trail of people following her like some Pied Piper jiggery-pokery is going on. Nurses from the care home and some of the other residents. I spot Steffan lurking behind the hedge as the rest of them come into the garden.

'Here to witness such a special moment,' Tonya trills. She's holding the tissue-wrapped strawberry like it's made of paper-thin glass.

In the background, there's the tell-tale beep of someone's phone recording video. With a bit of luck, it'll be angled wrongly to face the ground or the corner of a flowerbed or something. I don't fancy being on video. Again.

My dad appears in the gateway, and Cynthia makes a noise and rushes over to him so fast that she forgets all about the Zimmer frame and leaves it rocking in her wake.

'Has some sort of alert gone out or something?' I say to Ryan.

He shakes his head, looking bewildered. 'I guess it's a good sign if this many people are so interested in the first strawberry ...'

'Here, now, take it gently.' Tonya approaches us using much the same tone you'd use when training a puppy. 'Someone take a picture of me handing it over!' She barks at the group and several camera flashes go off again as she holds out the strawberry on a bed of tissue paper. It's been washed and sliced in half.

'I'm not photo-ready,' Ryan protests, pushing a hand through his hair self-consciously.

'I haven't been photo-ready since 1992.'

It makes us both giggle and a camera flash goes off.

'At least we're non-photo-ready together?' I offer with a shrug, and he meets my eyes and smiles that soft understanding smile that I always felt I was the only one who got to see.

We both reach out to take our halves of the strawberry at the same time and our fingers brush. It shouldn't be weird, not after I stroked his hair and got so close to him last night, but the touch of his fingertips still makes something spark inside me, and when I look up at him, he's looking down at his hand like he's feeling it too.

I pull my hand away quickly and can't help noticing that Tonya hasn't taken her eyes off our fingers either.

I wave the strawberry half around in front of me, and Ryan holds his half up too. 'All this for half a strawberry.'

'Wait, wait, let me get the perfect frame.' Tonya moves backwards like a movie director lining up a shot. 'Ryan, inch a bit to the right. Fliss, you step forwar— No, not that much! Now turn to face each other ...'

We do as she says and all the while she's making "hmm, hmm" noises and holding her camera up to look through the viewfinder.

'Yes, that's good. We've got the sun off to one side and the edge of the tree in the frame. Now link arms like you were taking a sip of champagne at your wedding ...'

I snort. 'Seriously?'

'Of course.' She looks like she doesn't understand the problem. 'Quickly, before the sun moves and I have to reposition you. There will only ever be one "first strawberry" – we must get this right.'

'No one would ever know if it was the seventh or eighth strawberry.'

She puts a hand on her hip and frowns at me. 'Some of us believe in honesty, Felicity. Now, are you helping or hindering?' She claps her hands together and makes a shooing motion.

Ryan's biting his lip to stop himself laughing, and failing fast. 'Careful now or she'll put you in detention.'

It makes me laugh again as he holds his arm up, strawberry held by the stem between thumb and forefinger, tanned forearms flexing in a way that makes me blush for no reason, and I slide my arm through his so they hook around each other's inner elbow and aim the strawberry halves towards our own mouths.

His skin is warm against mine and I can feel every tiny flex of solid muscle that makes me feel a lot hotter than the sun beaming down on us.

'Hold position!' Tonya yells, and a load of shutter clicks go off from the gathered residents.

'Do you ever find yourself in weird positions and wonder how you got there?' I whisper.

His eyes crinkle up as he laughs, and I know we've both got the overwhelming urge to ram the strawberry up each other's noses. 'I can't think of anyone better to be doing this with.'

It makes me go flushy all over and I'm sure my cheeks are so red that they're going to struggle to tell them apart from the strawberry.

He untangles his arm to knock his strawberry half against mine. 'Cheers.'

'Happy strawberry patch reopening,' I say, wondering what exactly people are supposed to say in these situations.

'I'm just celebrating having my partner in crime back.' He gives me that look again, the one that makes me feel like the only person in the universe as he winds his arm through mine again.

'And, action!' Tonya yells before I have a chance to get more overheated.

Ryan squeezes my arm using only his muscle power and it catapults me back to the present with the gathered crowd and Tonya doing a countdown.

On one, we both take a bite out of our respective strawberry halves, and I close my eyes as the sweetness bursts across my tongue.

'Mmm,' Ryan whispers. 'I'm not sure it's worth all the fuss, but it's good.'

'Let's *not* use that as a marketing slogan.'

He laughs and opens his eyes. 'Good, but not worth a fuss. Story of my life.'

I blink at him curiously. I want to know everything about his life. I know this isn't what he had planned, but I also get the feeling he's happy here. We spent a lot of time talking about places we wanted to go and things we wanted to see. Before, he was raring to get away, but he seems different now. Settled, secure in his own skin, which is something he never was before, and something I've never felt either. That sense of being happy where you are, a feeling of home … I left here to go looking for it, but never found it. It seems like Ryan found it without ever leaving.

Even though the gathered residents have started filtering away, I realise we've still got our arms linked and untangle them quickly. When I step back, I stumble over a strawberry plant and his hand closes around my arm and keeps me upright, pulling me against him until I crash into his left side and his arm comes up around my shoulders, holding me there.

'Aww, I've always said strawberries were a romantic fruit,' Tonya says, amid the noise of another shutter click.

'What would you consider an *un*-romantic fruit?' Ryan asks without taking his arm from around my shoulders.

She thinks about it for a long moment, and instead of letting me go, his hand drifts up and down my arm.

'Well, pineapples have a bit of a prick, don't they?'

I meet Ryan's eyes and we both burst into giggles.

Tonya looks annoyed at our immaturity. 'They *have* prickly bits, and you have to cut them off when you cut through that tough old skin.'

'I reckon quite a few people around here have prickly bits,' Ryan says in my ear, making me howl with laughter.

He always had radar for saying the funniest things at the *worst* possible moments. His laughter is shaking through me too and his head is pressed against mine. 'What are we even talking about?' he says against my ear.

'I don't know.'

'I think you two have been out in the sun too long,' Tonya says. 'Do you need to go and sit in the shade?'

I look up and meet his eyes and the sparkle of laughter in them makes that familiar feeling of butterflies flash through my body.

'I think that would be a very good idea,' he murmurs, wetting his lips like he has some kind of innuendo in mind.

I've totally lost track of this conversation, and I extract myself from Ryan's arm, trying to work out how just one arm can enclose me in such a tight hug. His arms are incredible.

I manage to step away without falling over anything this time, pick up the garden fork and put some space between us. 'I'll start over here and we'll meet in the middle. There's no time to lose if we want to open by Saturday.'

Which is not exactly a lie, but I've been getting far too close to Ryan again, too many touches, too many hugs, and it can't continue. I'm not staying here for much longer, and that's without the whole aspect of not having told him what I really do for a living and having been lying to everyone since the moment I got here. He thinks we're friends, but a friend would've told him the truth by now.

'Excuse me?' It's that afternoon when an elderly man appears at the gate. 'Is this where the sycamore tree protest is?'

It reminds me that we need to redo all the signs. Mr Barley found some pieces of plywood and is in the process of painting them up to put out on the road to advertise the strawberry patch reopening this weekend. Ryan's started laying down the weed-proof fabric between plants and is trying to map out some sort of path for visitors to follow, because the random popping up of plants is the opposite of how they used to be in neat rows, and we've had to cut through all the runners so they don't trip anyone up.

I stand up and lean on the fork I'm still using to twist out the last of the blackberry roots. 'It is. How can we help?'

'Only that tree helped me once, and I had a flyer through my door this morning saying what was happening to it, and I'd like to do my bit in return. What can I do?'

'It helped you?' I ask.

Ryan has left the roll of weed-proof fabric and is making his way up from the other end of the strawberry patch. He stands next to me and goes to shake the man's hand but glances down at his muddy ones and thinks better of it.

'I'm Ellis,' the elderly gent says. 'When I heard you were looking for stories about it, I wanted to share mine. That tree saved my life.'

Ryan's eyes meet mine and we both shuffle closer to hear his story.

'I was a sailor in the Royal Navy. It was a few years after the war when we had an accident. We were somewhere in the Bristol Channel, and we collided with something under the water, hard enough to crush the fuel tanks. There was an explosion. I was thrown from the ship, dazed and concussed. I came round floating in the water, not knowing where I was. I'd lost my hearing in the blast so everything was muffled, there was blood in my eyes and I could barely see anything. I knew drowning was a real danger if I expended my energy in struggling against the tide, so I floated on my back, but I didn't know where I was or which way I was going, I could've been heading into a busy shipping lane or a riptide for all I knew, and I kept looking around for a landmark or something, and out of nowhere, the sycamore appeared on the horizon. I was who knows how many miles out that way.' He points out to the sea beyond. 'I'd seen it many times before in passing, knew it was on the coast of Wales, so I kept my eyes on it, knowing if I kept going towards it, I'd reach land.'

'And you did?'

He points towards the cliff to our left. 'By the time I got near there, the coastguard were combing the beaches for survivors. They said I was lucky to be alive, but I don't think I would be if it wasn't for the tree. I'd got all turned around in the accident. If that tree *hadn't* have been on the horizon, I'd have headed further out to sea, and that could only have ended one way.'

'There's an anchor carved on the tree.' Ryan holds a hand out towards it. 'With the initials "E.M" and the words "January 1949 ~ Thank you." That wasn't you, was it?'

'Gosh, is that still there?' He looks at the tree in wonder, blinking watery eyes in the afternoon sunlight. 'Yes, it was me. It *was* my anchor. I was in hospital for months, and when they finally let me out, I wanted to pay tribute to it in some way – to let it know what it had done for me.'

I don't know what it is about hearing these tree stories, but I've got a lump in my throat and if he says much more, I'm going to burst into tears again. I look over at Ryan and he meets my eyes and gives me a tiny smile, and I have absolutely no doubt that he feels the same.

'Would you like to see it again?' Ryan offers to escort Ellis down there.

'I would. I wondered if it would fade. Apparently they say only the carvings of the truest love stories stay, and mine wasn't exactly a love story.'

'A life story,' Ryan says, his eyes on mine. 'The most important kind there is.'

'I'd like to stay and help, if there's anything I can do,' Ellis says as he goes to grip Ryan's outstretched arm.

'Tonya will sort you out with something.' I point out the pink-haired lady who's currently talking on the phone with a notebook in one hand doing such serious negotiating that I feel quite sorry for whoever's on the other end.

Ellis thanks us both and walks with Ryan down to the tree. Baaabra Streisand, who is still sulking about not being able to snaffle any more strawberries, gets up from her dog basket like it's an imposition on her time, but she simply *must* investigate whether he has any food about his person.

Once thoroughly investigated, Ellis strokes the sheep's head as Ryan points out the carving, and then shows him up to the picnic table to keep Mr Barley on track with the signs he's painting.

He walks back down to where I'm pretending to still be digging out blackberry roots and not watching his every move. His hands are still covered in rapidly drying mud, but he nudges me with his elbow. 'Told you there was a story behind that anchor.'

I can see the emotion in his eyes, and the urge to give him a hug is too strong. 'C'mere, you.'

'I'm all muddy.'

'So am I.' I let my fork drop and hold my hands out in front of me. 'No touching, I promise.'

He steps into my arms and ducks so my head fits on his shoulder. His arms come up around me and his elbows press into my back, holding his dirty hands away from my pale yellow T-shirt, and he somehow manages to bend double enough for his head to drop onto my shoulder too.

'Thanks, Fee.' He breathes the words against my neck.

'I didn't do anything.' I'm not a hundred per cent sure that the words come out because I'm lost in a flood of his warm body, tight hug, and cologne, but his arms tighten around me so I assume he's heard something.

'None of this would be happening without you.' His lips press into my neck as he speaks, brushing against my skin, and I let my elbows press into his back too, warm through his vest top, and it's a good job my hands are dirty or I'd not be able to stop myself sliding them over his muscular shoulders.

His lips find my neck again and his arms get even tighter when my knees go weak, and I can feel his smile against my skin, doing nothing to improve the situation.

Getting headbutted by a sheep is one thing, but Ryan Sullivan's lips on my neck was definitely *not* on my agenda during this trip.

# Chapter 12

It's a couple of days later, and between us, Ryan and I are laying
the fabric down on the paths between plants, and so far there's
been a lot of shouting of the Chuckle Brothers infamous quote
when moving something long, a lot of giggling, and probably
not enough weed fabric laying. The Seaview Heights residents
are all occupied. Ellis has come back again and has taken over
sign-making from Mr Barley and is painting signs that advertise
the strawberry patch, Alys is making up words you can have in
Scrabble on a game with her friend through her phone after
correctly identifying a garlic mincer this morning, and Mr Barley
has moved on from garden gnomes and is now making a Boris
Johnson scarecrow to keep the birds away.

'I don't know why he insists on them always being naked,'
Tonya muses in the middle of setting up for the arrival of her
grandson to film the campaign video. 'We had an argument this
morning over it being inappropriate with children visiting the
patch, and he reluctantly agreed to put lingerie on it. I don't
understand why. Have you *ever* seen Boris Johnson in lingerie?'

'I'm glad I've got cataracts,' Morys says.

'The gnomes were bad enough, but now he's thinking of having
the whole political party as scarecrows too.'

'Not much different from the actual government then.' Ryan gives me a wink.

'Oh no, now he's making a sign for the scarecrow telling the birds to do something unspeakable with their own beaks!' Tonya rushes off towards his workstation, waving her fist and yelling, 'For heaven's sake, there could be *children* here!'

My phone beeps with a message and I let go of my half of the weed-proof fabric roll to look at it.

'Oh my God, Ry, listen to this,' I say as I read the message. 'The mum of that boy from Cheryl's class has sent me an email. It wasn't just that he was conceived here. They'd been trying for a baby for over two years, and they'd had tests and seen specialists, but no doctor could pinpoint the problem. One day they were walking their dog along the coastal path and they made a wish on a sycamore seed for a child, and then she says they both got a tingling feeling at the back of their necks and *knew* that they should, y'know, do the deed there and then.'

'It's the dog I feel sorry for. I bet he didn't know where to look.'

In what could have been a dignified and emotional moment, I let out an ugly snort of laughter, and Ryan grins at me. He was always abnormally proud of making me laugh at inopportune moments.

I'm trying to frown at him but it isn't helping. 'And it worked. She did a test a couple of weeks later and it was positive.'

He raises an eyebrow. 'It's a nice story, but it's just coincidence. The tree didn't *give* them a baby.'

'I know. It might be a special old tree, but no tree can do *that*. They believe it did – that's what matters. People believe in magic when they see this tree. That's something everyone needs in this difficult world. That childlike wonder … That belief that when you throw a sycamore seed from the clifftop, in the long seconds it takes to spiral down, you *believe* a wish is going to come true – something that we're all too old to believe in anymore.'

'I'm not too old to believe in magic!' Cynthia shouts from where she's taken over arranging our marketing materials into organised piles.

A little while later, a fifty-something couple come into the strawberry patch holding hands. 'We met through the tree. Can we share our story?'

Tonya is immediately on hand with a notebook and pen. Ryan and I are still fiddling around with weed-proof fabric and setting out paths. We've reached quite near to the entrance by now so we listen too.

'When I was nineteen, I was being a big show-off and I fell out of the tree and broke my arm,' the man says. 'We met in the fracture clinic at the hospital.'

'And I was eighteen,' the woman continues. 'My younger sister wanted to make a wish but there were no sycamore seeds on the ground so I climbed up to get her one, and when I jumped back out, I misjudged it and broke my ankle.'

I hold my finger out towards Ryan, jokingly scolding him. 'This is why I keep telling you to be careful.'

He closes his hand around my pointing finger and folds it down gently. 'You always did take better care of me than I took of myself.'

Instead of letting go like I expected, he lets our joined hands swing between us, jiggling mine around like he's trying to get my attention even though he's already got it. He doesn't seem to want anything. He's just sort of playing with our joined hands, and even though we're both dirty from the digging and definitely shouldn't be holding hands, I don't attempt to extract my fingers.

'While I was sitting in the waiting room at the hospital, this one—' the woman juts her thumb towards her husband '—gorgeous lad with a broken arm that he was, sat down next to me, and started talking. And we both realised we'd had almost the exact same accident. Such a coincidence.'

'We had a good chat in the waiting room, but that was it, we were called to our separate appointments. I'd been hoping to catch her on the way out, but she was in a wheelchair because of the ankle and her parents had wheeled her away before I came out – they thought I might be a bad influence, what with our penchant for falling out of trees. It had felt like serendipity that we'd both fallen out of the same tree, and I couldn't stop thinking about her.'

'I couldn't stop thinking about him either. I was feeling sorry for myself and he'd made me laugh and forget about the ankle for a while. I'd been trying to delay leaving because I was hoping to catch him again too, but my parents were having none of it and rushed out of there.'

'And then, like fate was playing a hand itself, when we went back two weeks later for our follow-up appointments while the injuries were still healing, lo and behold, there she was again.'

'My uncle had taken me to the appointment instead of my parents that time, and he was quite happy to wait while we had a coffee in the hospital cafeteria.'

'We discovered we only lived ten minutes apart, swapped phone numbers and chatted every night. I used the excuse of checking up on her injury.' The man still has a proud smile, even so many years later. 'Her parents couldn't argue with that.'

'We got married four years later, on the beach down there with the tree watching over us,' she says.

'The night before our wedding, obviously it's tradition not to see each other, but we both snuck out and met here. We threw a sycamore seed from the cliff and shouted our wish to the sea. A long and happy marriage.'

'So far so good,' the wife adds. 'Thirty years and counting.'

'We put our names on the trunk that night too.'

They're both looking at each other adoringly. Alys and Cynthia have gathered around like walking heart-eyes emojis, Tonya's furiously scribbling their story down in her notebook, and Ffion's making a heart shape with her two thumbs.

I glance up at Ryan. He's watching, but he looks sceptical. Before, we talked about anything and everything, but we never really spoke about love or relationships. Whenever the topic bobbed near the surface, I'd avoid it like I'd avoid an angry wasp on a summer's day in case the mere mention of the word "love" would somehow clue him in that I was head over heels for him.

'That's sweet.' I nod towards the couple who are now filling Tonya in on the ins and outs of their wedding day, complete with photos that the whole group are oohing and aahing over. Even some of the blokes have come over to have a look, although Mr Barley is busy making a child-friendly scarecrow sign telling birds to get lost … in definitely *un*-censored terms. He hasn't *quite* worked out the difference between swearwords and non-swearwords yet, and he's in for an almighty row when Tonya catches him.

'Yeah. I guess some people are lucky in love.'

'Aren't you?' I don't even want to know, but I can't stop myself asking.

He lets out a sarcastic burst of laughter. 'I was lucky in a few things, like the campsite taking off the way it did, but love …' His eyes are on mine and I feel like I can't breathe. His fingers tighten around the hand he's still holding. 'No.'

We look at each other in silence for a long moment.

'You?' he croaks out. His voice is rough and low so as not to disturb the chatter of the group.

I know we've already established we're both single now, but we haven't mentioned how we got there. Like before, I'm still convinced that the mere mention of the "l" word will tip him off that I had a massive crush on him – not that kissing him didn't do that anyway – and to be honest, I'm not sure how much I'm over the crush. Looking at him *still* does things to me. 'No. Unlucky in everything. I've never been in love.'

'Oh. Right.' He lets go of my hand and steps away quickly, like he can sense the crush as I always thought he would. 'No, me neither, obviously.'

Why is that obvious? He's thirty-eight and gorgeous, funny, and kind, with absolutely no clue of *how* gorgeous, funny, and kind he is. Even after nearly two weeks of adjusting to the shock of him still being single, I *still* can't believe that someone hasn't snapped him up by now.

'But you still believe in magical trees and wishes coming true?' He raises a dark eyebrow.

'I can be old and cynical and jaded when it comes to relationships, but no one's ever too old for a bit of tree magic. That's like saying you're too old to read Enid Blyton or enjoy Disney films or laugh at Mr Bean.'

'Well, while I still love all those things, I think I missed my chance when it comes to love.'

'Me too.' I look over at him and can't help the way my mouth curves into a half-smile at the sight of his half-smile. That's exactly how I feel about him. That *we* missed *our* chance. Especially with what he said the other day about not being good enough … That maybe if I'd been braver, told him how I felt sooner, if I hadn't waited until the night before I left … because I was *so* certain he felt the same, that *he'd* tell *me* how he felt as soon as we were no longer boss and employee, that he wouldn't let me leave Wales without telling me …

'Fresh Welsh cakes!' Ffion shouts, walking down the garden with a batch of freshly made Welsh cakes on a tray, followed by a couple of nurses bringing out trays containing bowls of clotted cream, jam, and sugar, and a teapot and set of cups.

Ryan and I stand back as the group descends on the baked goods, dragging along the fracture clinic couple, Ellis, and my dad, who's come down to see Cynthia with the excuse of bringing my gardening gloves. He's now examining the hedgerows with Morys and discussing what would be best to do with them.

'He's enjoying himself.' Ryan's gaze follows mine.

'Yeah. He loves gardening. I knew something like this would be right up his street, but he needed a push to get out and about. I think he was feeling like he didn't have anything to offer anyone, and coming here, and Cynthia being *so* pleased to see him and everyone asking for his gardening advice has given him a confidence boost.'

'I wish I'd known. I could've done something. Asked for his advice or his help with maintaining the campsite borders or something.'

We're both watching the feeding frenzy but I look back over my shoulder at him. 'You always were too nice for your own good.'

He's blushing when he answers, steadfastly ignoring the compliment. 'Well, if he needs anything again, let me know, all right? When you've gone—' He cuts off the sentence abruptly and I watch his Adam's apple dip as he swallows. 'We're not going to lose touch this time, are we? Swap numbers and that. I don't want to lose you again … lose *touch* with you again.'

'You could always add me on social media …' I try a sneaky attempt at getting to the bottom of why he's not on Twitter or Facebook.

'I don't *do* social media,' he says instantly.

'What about your business? *Everyone* has to be on social media these days.'

'Exactly why I'm not on it. I like being awkward and doing the opposite of what everyone else does.' He opens his hands and does a bow. 'My assistant handles all that for the campsite. I take photos when I walk Baaabra Streisand and he puts them on the internet to show things to do around the area. It's only on there at all because he gave me the same lecture when he started working for me.'

I go to question him further, but … 'Did you say you *walk* your sheep?'

'She needs her exercise too. She's on a lead all day, so she needs a break from that, and with the campsite full, I don't have an empty field I can put her in. Sheep appreciate a change of scenery. Just don't say "walkies" too loudly or all hell will break loose.'

I know he can see the cogs in my mind turning and he holds a finger out and beckons me closer as I put two and two together, because I've been here every day for a couple of weeks now and I've not once seen him walk his sheep.

'Does that mean you leave the tree unattended?' I whisper to him, being careful that no one's in earshot, even with their hearing aid signal boosters tuned in.

His breath moves the hair by my ear when he speaks. 'Only very late at night when Steffan has gone home and I'm certain no one's going to check. And I always leave my lamp on in case anyone happens to glance down.'

I love that he trusts me enough to tell me that, like no time has passed between us. This is exactly the sort of thing Harrison would be proud of me for – earning his trust and getting his secrets, another possible "in" to securing the land, but the idea of it makes me feel ill. I look up into Ryan's genuine, trustful eyes, and I can't imagine ever betraying him.

Which makes me *brilliant* at my job, and I start wondering how long I'm going to have left before I have to do something about this. Harrison isn't going to let this go on indefinitely without expecting something in return, and he's following the campaign, so he's going to see the strawberry patch is reopening and that I'm doing the opposite of what I'm supposed to be doing.

I'm so lost in thought that I don't realise Tonya is trying to get our attention until she lets out a shrill whistle to attract it, inadvertently piercing the eardrums of everyone within a ten-mile radius. We go across when she beckons us over to the group where the tray of Welsh cakes looks like it's been decimated by a shoal of starving piranhas.

'Fliss, you can make jam, can't you?'

'Jam?' My voice goes so squeaky that it sounds like I've been sucking helium out of balloons. Who the heck *makes* jam? Outside of trying to impress Paul Hollywood on *The Great British Bake Off*, that is. You buy it in a jar with "Hartleys" written on the front like any normal person. 'Of course,' I say brightly. 'What chef wouldn't know how to make jam?'

Oh God, it can't be *that* difficult, can it?

'We thought we could set up a little sideline for opening day and have a table outside with tea and Welsh cakes. The nurses are going to make them fresh from the kitchen – they've just agreed.' She indicates towards the two blue-uniformed nurses sitting with them.

'I think "agreed" is a bit strong a word,' one of them says.

'As I'm sure you know with this lot,' the other one says with a grin to me and Ryan. 'Either you agree or they agree for you.'

'There's nowhere nearby to get food,' Alys continues. 'For opening day, we thought it would be a novelty if we could offer Welsh cakes and cream and sugar with strawberry jam made from the strawberries grown right here. Our Welsh version of a cream tea. Maybe in the future, we could make jam and sell jars if it proves popular.'

'Sounds great. Yay.' I do a little clap. Inside, I'm feeling very much *not*-yay. How on earth do you make jam? Would they notice if I scooped some out of a supermarket-bought jar and said I'd made it?

In the crowd, my dad does a thumbs up, which I take to mean he *can* and *will* make jam on my behalf. I also catch Ryan's eyes flicking from me to him. I'm about to create a distraction, but thankfully Tonya has arranged a flyer swap with another local event planner, and the girl chooses that moment to walk in carrying a stack of flyers. She hands one out to each of us while Tonya grabs a stack of ours and dashes across waving them around.

'Sandcastle building competition.' I read aloud from the flyer she's just given me. 'Is this really *still* going?'

I'm consistently surprised by how Lemmon Cove seems to have avoided the trappings of time passing and stayed exactly as it was when I left. This annual sandcastle building competition has been going since the Seventies. It was still going when I left, but it was never popular enough to have any sort of advertising materials then.

'It's a *huge* deal now,' Cynthia says proudly.

'I'm *over*booked at the campsite next weekend with how many tourists are coming,' Ryan adds. 'The strawberry patch will be open by then, so it should have a good impact for us. This is the main access route to the beach, so a *heck* of a lot of people will be walking by. There's actually a route down from the campsite but I'm going to block it off so they'll all be forced to come this way.'

'I admire your sneaky, underhanded tactics.'

He grins like it's the best compliment he could ever get.

'It's a real thing for sand artists now,' Alys says, going back to the flyer in her hand, while Tonya swaps our stack for the sand-castle competition stack and sends the girl on her way. 'There's a £500 prize and your creation gets in all the local papers, and national news websites cover it.'

'We should enter.'

'This is not just kids slopping sand into a bucket and upturning it anymore, Fliss,' Ffion says. 'The people who enter these days are real sculptors. Artists. They travel around the world entering competitions like this. It's serious business.'

'It could be fun. And if there's that much local interest then it could be great for our cause, even if we don't win. It says here the entry fee is only a tenner – I'll pay that.' I gesture to Ryan. 'You're good with your hands. You and whoever's the best designer do it together.'

'Ah, just one problem,' Alys says. 'There's only two of us who are young and fit enough to make it down to the beach.'

'And I'm not doing it on my own. You work with food, you

must be able to, y'know, sculpt things.' Ryan looks at me expectantly and mashes his hands together.

'I assure you, no one has ever done *that* to food,' I say with a raised eyebrow, but the wider his smile gets, the more I smile back, even though I hate that he has absolutely no doubt that I *am* a chef. I thought I would've been caught out by now.

'Go on,' Morys says. 'We'll manage here while you're down on the beach next Saturday. Someone will take over on tree duty, and the rest of us will man the strawberry patch. You've got nothing to lose.'

I look at Ryan and shrug. 'I'm in if you are.'

'It's a date.'

'Yeah, the—'

'And not the twenty-third of August this time.' He winks at me. 'A real date, yeah?'

I'm caught off-guard at his casual suggestion. Me and Ryan on a date. What could possibly go wrong?

# Chapter 13

'Why don't you go and see him?' Cheryl says without me saying a word. It's only ten p.m. but she's getting ready for bed because she gets up early for summer school and I've always been a night owl. Sharing a room is not ideal.

I'm standing at the bedroom window, watching a hedgehog pottering around in next door's garden, and I turn around to look at her. 'The hedgehog?'

She laughs, knowing full well I'm winding her up and the "him" in question isn't wildlife-related.

'Because I made the mistake of getting too close to Ryan Sullivan before. It didn't end well that time, and I'm not going to give history a chance to repeat itself. There's nothing between us.'

'Then someone needs to tell *him* that. I was there when you walked into the strawberry patch the other day and he literally illuminated when he saw you. He excused himself mid-conversation and *sprinted* across to you.'

'He's being polite.'

'He's just invited you on a date!'

'It's not a date.' I say it so firmly that I'm trying to convince myself more than her. 'It's just for the strawberry patch. The publicity.'

She rolls her eyes. 'Fliss, what happened between you two?'

I've never told her. I've never told anyone. The only people who know are me and Ryan. 'Something that's never going to get a chance to happen again.' I sigh. 'I shouldn't *be* spending more time with him. I should be … leaving.'

'Is that still on the cards then?'

I look over my shoulder at her. 'I have to go back. I have a job, a flat, a …' I was going to say "life" but I don't have much of a life in London at all. It's certainly not something to miss.

'I know, but you seem so happy here. And Dad's been so much happier since you arrived.'

'That's Cynthia, not me.'

'Yeah, but you've got him involved in the strawberry patch. I didn't know how to push him out of his comfort zone, but you did. I think he feels "whole" with both of us here. It's the closest we ever get to Mum now. When all of three of us are together. He's been talking about clearing out the spare room so you'd have your own space, and it's been nice having you around. I didn't realise how much I miss my big sister when you're away.'

I can't stop myself going over and giving her a hug. It's been nice to be here too. It's been a long while since I shared a house with my family and I had visions of it being the stuff of nightmares, but it's been warm and homely and it feels like I've never been away.

The thoughts are making tears threaten to fill my eyes again, so I extract myself from the hug. 'Maybe I will go and see him …'

'The hedgehog?'

She laughs when I hit her with a pillow.

After I say goodbye to Dad, who's busy doing a video call with Cynthia even though her camera is pointing at the floor and his is showcasing a particularly interesting spot of the ceiling, so maybe being equally inept at technology is a sign of romantic compatibility. The hedgehog in question scurries across the path when I step out onto the pavement and it makes me smile. I can't remember the last time I saw a hedgehog.

'It's just me, Ry,' I call out quietly when I reach the strawberry patch.

He turns his industrial-sized torch towards me, illuminating the path between strawberry plants as I head towards the tree. 'You disappear for fifteen years and now I get to see you both day and night? Can we flip it and have the next fifteen years like this?'

I ignore him. They're just words. They don't mean anything. They *can't* mean anything.

Baaabra Streisand is sleeping beside the tree trunk, and I push myself up on tiptoes to see what Ryan's doing.

He's sitting cross-legged in the tree using a little knife to do … something … to a strawberry. 'What are you up to?'

'Aw, you've caught me red-handed. I was trying to carve strawberries into roses and present you with a bouquet of them tomorrow.'

'That's romantic.' The words are out before I can stop them.

'Yes, it is.' He meets my eyes and holds my gaze unwaveringly.

My legs feel so unsteady that I have to drop down off my tiptoes, and after a few moments, he shakes himself and looks away.

'Godfrey showed me how to do it. He used to make them for Henrietta.' He puts down the one he's working on and picks up another, and leans forward so I can see what he's doing. 'If you carve four thin strips here, you can peel them back to look like petals.' He does that around the widest part of the strawberry and then moves up to the narrower part and does the same in between the "petals" below so they overlap. 'And then you do it again at the narrow part, and then criss-cross the tip, and voila.' He hands me the mutilated fruit that really does look like a rose, his fingers hovering over mine as I take it carefully because it's so delicate.

197

I can't help smiling at the idea of a guy who would put in the effort to do that. The last time someone bought me flowers, they were mostly dead from the supermarket clearance bucket and still had the "reduced to 10p" sticker on them, *and* I later discovered were out of guilt for cheating on me. 'Beautiful.'

'The benefits of befriending a man who sold strawberries for forty years. I was going to do a whole load and put them on skewers and wrap them in pretty paper like a real bouquet, but now you've caught me, I'll have to think of something else.'

'You don't have to do anything romantic for me …' I trail off, automatically pushing myself up on tiptoes again as he leans further down.

His fingers are still around mine where mine are around the strawberry and they tighten so much, the fruit is in real danger of being crushed.

'Fee …' His eyes close and my name comes out as a breath, his hand coming up to brush my arm, trailing up and across my shoulder. He leans so close that our foreheads are millimetres away from touching, and …

He overbalances and has to grab a branch to stop himself falling headfirst out of the tree.

'No. No, of course not.' He yanks his hand away and scrambles backwards, and I step away, my heart pounding and my breath coming in such short, sharp pants that I could've just ran a marathon. Except not, obviously, because me and running don't mix.

'Sorry if I overstepped the mark earlier with the whole date thing. The words were out of my mouth before I could stop them. As is tradition whenever I'm around you.'

'Of course. I get it, Ry, you didn't mean it like that.'

He looks confused. 'I meant it like *that*, I just didn't mean to ask you in front of everyone.'

In that moment, something snaps inside of me. 'All right, I've had enough. What are you playing at? All the touches, the hugs, the hand-holding, and now you're asking me on a date too? You're doing exactly what you did before. No one can correctly interpret these mixed messages. I got it wrong before and I'm *not* going to get it wrong again!'

He looks taken aback by my sudden outburst, and I take a step back in surprise because I didn't realise I was going to say that.

'Oh, come on, Fee. Seriously? Don't you know how I feel about you?'

'No!' I snap. 'No, Ryan, I don't. I showed you how I felt fifteen years ago and you clearly didn't return it then—'

'You think I didn't feel the same.' He says it more to himself than to me, shaking his head. It's not really a question at all. 'There were two reasons I didn't kiss you back, and believe me, that wasn't one of them.'

I take a deep breath and steel myself to ask something I should've asked years ago. 'Then what was?'

'There was someone else.'

'What?' It comes out sharper and louder than I intended it to, but I've spent years imagining potential answers to that question and *that* was not one of the possible responses.

'That came out wrong,' he says quickly. 'Not someone else in *that* way. It was to do with my father's business. There was this girl. My father had gone into business with her father … I was supposed to marry her.'

While I'm still trying to get my head around that, he scrambles out of the tree and reappears from behind the trunk. 'It was to cement the ties of the business. There was an assumption on my shoulders that she and I would get married and continue running their business together, and then pass it on for generations to come.'

I thought I was shocked into silence, but I take a step away from him when he comes closer. 'You were seeing someone else at that time?'

'No! God, no. Nothing like that. I barely knew her. We'd played together a few times when we were children and that's it. My father had always made comments about it, but I'd taken them jokingly; I'd never thought it was something they'd actually expect us to go through with, but when he had that heart attack, it changed things. He had to hand the business over to me sooner than he'd planned. Her dad had invested a large sum of money into the company, and working with me wasn't what he'd signed up for. He didn't like how young I was. Everyone knew I didn't have my father's business head. They thought that marrying his sensible, business-minded daughter would "sort me out" and make me into an adult. And I was obviously never, ever going to do that, but my dad was *so* ill, and the guilt was piling up on me. I couldn't tell him, Fee, not then.'

'You make it sound like you were supposed to have an arranged marriage!'

'You know who my father was. He was a *huge* name around here, and there was an expectation on me to carry on the business. He wanted me to do that *with* his business partner's daughter, and what I wanted didn't matter.'

'You didn't tell me,' I say as he takes another step towards me. 'We were so close, Ry. We told each other everything. Or so I thought …'

'I thought you'd hate me. I was scared it would look like I was leading you on, but all I wanted was you, Fee.'

I can't take all of this in. I know that what he's just said should register in a monumental way, but it's like I'm floating above, hearing it but not really present.

'It wasn't that big a deal before, not until my father realised I was head over heels for you and that didn't fit with his plans. The pressure from him amped up. And then if I'd tried to explain it to you, I thought I'd lose you as a friend. And then that night under the tree … My heart soared when you kissed me and then sank because there was this thing I hadn't told you about. It felt like I was betraying you *and* his expectation of me. I wasn't "free" to be in love with you, Fee.'

'That's why you "couldn't do this *now*"?'

He nods and reaches his hand out. 'I thought I could deal with it without you ever having to know. It hadn't mattered before, but when I met you ... This vague, jokey thing suddenly *did* matter. I thought I'd tell him when he was stronger, but he never *got* stronger. When you said you were leaving ... I couldn't hold you back. I reasoned that it would give me a chance to sort the situation out. I thought I'd deal with it while you were away and then when you came back I'd be able to explain everything, but the years went by and you never *came* back, and ... I couldn't just randomly call you years later and go: "Hey, you know that situation I couldn't tell you about all those years ago? Guess what, I finally handled it. Marry me now, yes?" You'd have had a life by then. I thought you'd have met someone, and you'd be happy and I couldn't blaze in and ruin that.'

Something about his outstretched hand is impossible to ignore, and I slide mine into it and give his fingers a squeeze.

I often feel so jaded and cynical that nothing shocks me anymore, but this certainly has. I had no idea Ryan had this going on in his life. I knew about his father, and I knew how much Ryan didn't fit in with the expectations on him, but this is the first time I've realised there was a reason he didn't kiss me back that night. 'What happened? *Did* you sort it out?'

'Eventually. It only took me five years and an engagement.'

'What?' I yank my hand out of his. 'You actually went through with it?'

'No. I stopped it before it went that far. You don't understand how ill my father got, Fee. It was the only thing that made him happy. I honestly thought refusing would kill him.' He shoves a hand through his hair and sighs, his eyes lingering on mine before he eventually looks away and walks around the tree, going to stand by the barrier and look out at the sea.

201

I'm lost with how I should feel. I'm hurt that Ryan had this thing in his life that I didn't know about. It changes the friendship I always thought we had. 'You should have told me. You didn't have to deal with that alone. I could have helped.'

I avoid Baaabra's snoring form and walk around the tree to lean on the barrier next to Ryan.

'Then I'd have had to tell you how I felt about you. And that was the second reason …' He lifts his head and looks me directly in the eyes. 'You deserved better than me.'

The sentence takes the wind right out of my sails. 'What?'

'This is a prime example of why. I wasn't brave enough to stand up to my father. You deserved someone stronger than me, someone who didn't have all the family baggage that I had. Someone who would put you first. And at that time, I *couldn't* do that. And believe me, I've regretted it for every moment of my life since then because you left thinking I didn't feel the same, and that wasn't true, but I reasoned with myself that it was for the best, because you deserved a chance to go out and live your dreams and see the world, and if I'd kissed you back and explained everything, it might've made you stay, and that wasn't what you wanted.'

'What about you, Ry? *You* wanted to travel. You wanted to see the world. You wanted to live in a bustling city, and go on holiday to New York, and drive around France in a campervan, and walk on the beach in Bali, and eat dinner at the top of the Tokyo Tower—'

'Exactly. And I knew I never would. When we talked about where we wanted to go, showed each other photos of all these amazing destinations, they were possibilities for you. They were only pipe dreams for me. I knew I'd be stuck here. I was destined to take over the family business, to live here in Lemmon Cove, nowhere else. I couldn't hold you back. When my father had that heart attack, it changed everything. I was barely in my twenties, and it catapulted me to the head of his company – something I

202

hadn't intended to become until much later in my life, not until after I'd had a chance to *live* it. I've never once regretted taking over Sullivan's Seeds because it led to meeting you, but it happening so young, so unexpectedly … It changed all of my plans for the future. Of all people, *you* know how much I was out of my depth.'

'But that was your own lack of confidence. That was *not* how *I* saw you. Yeah, you'd been thrust into a business you knew nothing about, but you faced the challenge head-on. You learnt. You were innovative and ambitious. You breathed life into a stuffy old company. You made every day better. When it really mattered, you had a backbone of steel. The gruff old farmers who'd been growing for your father for years and were set in their ways … They were *awful* to you, and you took everything good-naturedly, but when it came down to it, you stood up to them kindly and firmly and left them with no doubt that they would be doing things your way from then on.'

'And then you had to make me a cup of tea to calm down because I was shaking so much.'

I grin at the memory. 'But you did it anyway. You were exceptional, Ryan. I wished I could be more like you.'

The sarcastic, disbelieving laugh he lets out cuts through me like a physical pain. Maybe it was more about his lack of confidence than he let on. On the surface, Ryan was funny and buoyant, but I was the only person who saw when he was hesitant and unsure, who understood that he rambled to cover nerves, sang stupid Nineties songs as a distraction or did stupid dances to wake himself up when he was knackered after being up working until all hours or unable to sleep for worrying about his father's health.

'You must think I'm stupid for never leaving. Even after I lost the business, I had to stay here and pick up the pieces. It went under because of me. I was too young, too inexperienced; I made bad business decisions and it caught up with me.'

'The cucurbitacin poisoning was no one's fault. No one knows how that happens or how to prevent it.'

He shakes his head. 'That's just one thing, Fee. One failure in a long line of failures I was responsible for. Wrong investments, bad suppliers, unreliable buyers. I couldn't wreck the family business and then swan off into to the sunset. My family had no income. It was my responsibility to fix the mess I'd made. The one thing I couldn't fix was us – the mess I'd made of losing you.'

'You could've got in touch. No matter how many years had gone by. I thought I'd read you so wrongly. I was so sure we were more than friends.'

'I'm sorry. I'm so sorry, Fee. I was trying to do what I thought was right in the wrong way.' He drops his head down onto his arms. 'God, of *course* we were more than friends. I could barely keep my hands off you. How many times daily did I find an excuse for a hug? I dragged you to every business meeting possible because I hated being away from you. You were the highlight of every single day. I nearly kissed you so many times.'

'*I* nearly kissed *you* so many times! And that one night, it was a now-or-never moment, and I thought I'd regret it forever if I let it pass ...' I say to the sea instead of looking at him.

He doesn't lift his head and his words are muffled through his arms. 'You deserved someone who could give you the world, and I couldn't.'

'How could you ever think that?' I know I shouldn't touch him, but he's right there, his head is still bowed onto his arms, and my fingers reach out and stroke through his dark hair. 'You were the best thing in my life. You made every single day better just by existing. You might not have had confidence in yourself, but I thought you were the best thing in the world.'

He shudders as my nails brush through his hair and I go to pull my hand away, but his shoots out and grabs it as he lifts his head and turns to look at me. 'You were going off on this big adventure. You were excited. You'd been talking about it for weeks.

A flat in London. All the places this fancy new job would send you. The shops you'd go to, the things you'd buy with your new salary that was a hell of a lot higher than I could afford at Sullivan's.'

'Yeah, I wanted an adventure, but it came at a price – the cost of leaving you. All I *really* wanted was for you to tell me you felt the same. That would've been the best adventure I could've asked for. I left because I thought you were going to leave, and I was so scared of being left behind and seeing *you* go. It would've broken my heart, so I broke my own heart to protect myself.'

'I'm sorry, Fee.' His lips move against my skin as he keeps holding my hand against his mouth, his stubble scratching with every movement. 'We should have had this conversation many, many years ago.'

He glances up at me, almost to gauge my reaction because he looks unsure about whether I'm going to wallop him or not, and then he pushes himself upright and uses his hold on my hand to tug me closer.

My other hand is gripping the top of the metal barrier fence, my knuckles white, and his grip is so tight that my fingers zip with pins and needles when he finally releases my hand.

'Can I do something I should've done fifteen years ago?' His voice is a breathy whisper, and I nod almost imperceptibly because I can sense what's coming seconds before he surges forward and kisses me. A kiss that's a million times different from the last time we were here.

I can't help the whimper when his mouth finally touches mine.

A shiver of electricity goes through me. *This* is what I always imagined kissing Ryan would be like.

It's both hot and heavy and soft and gentle. A kiss that's been trying to burst forth for many, many years. My hands are in his hair, on his neck, clawing into his shoulders. He's cupping my face with one hand, his other splayed out on my lower back, supporting me, even though I'm leaning heavier and heavier against him until eventually he sinks down to his knees, dragging me with him because I can't tear my mouth away from his yet, not until we tumble over onto the grass. He lands with a huff and I let out a squeak. His arms tighten around me like a vice, holding me safely against him, and then pulling me tighter and tighter, splaying his hands out wider, like he can't touch enough of me, until I can push myself up on one elbow and look down at him. I brush my fingers through his hair, stroke his face, and he pushes himself up until he can fit his lips against mine again, and I lose track of time as we lie there, snogging in the grass.

When I'm breathless and panting and can't think straight, he says, 'That was worth waiting for.'

And it makes me laugh so hard that I might actually be hysterical, even though he's absolutely right – it *was* worth waiting for. 'Next time, can we wait about fifteen seconds instead of fifteen years?'

'Fifteen seconds is too long.' He surges up to kiss me again, and then lets out a long breath and drops his head back against the grass and runs a hand over his face, looking dazed, possibly oxygen-deprived, and like he can't get his head around this turn of events.

I'm not sure I can either.

Maybe our wishing tree really does answer wishes.

And I'm so happy that I can almost forget there's still something I haven't told him.

# Chapter 14

That Saturday is opening day. It's eight o'clock in the morning when I leave the house with three jars of jam Dad made last night, and although he tried to show me how to do it myself, the thought of all that fiddling with thermometers and straining and sugar boiling points was enough to bring me out in a cold sweat.

Even though the sun rose hours ago, the grassy verges are covered in early-morning dew drops, the first sign that autumn won't be long in coming, and I get that familiar sinking feeling when I think of what the next few weeks will bring. Whether we save the tree or not ... whether the strawberry patch is a success or not ... I cannot stay here. I *have* to go back to London and somehow explain this whole mess to Harrison and hope he lets me keep my job. And when did I start saying "back to London" instead of "home"? I shouldn't be thinking like this. London is home. Lemmon Cove hasn't been for a long, long while. And yet the thought of not breathing sea air and scaring off flocks of sparrows every morning in favour of cramming myself onto a sweaty tube and breathing in pollution and exhaust fumes makes the stone in my stomach grow even bigger. And then there's Ryan. Every time I think about leaving Ry, it puts me instantly on the edge of tears and I push the thoughts down, like if I just don't think about it, it will never happen.

I'm dodging cars parked on pavements even at this time of day and the Seaview Heights car park is also packed, and I have to squeeze between cars to get in. They couldn't all be here for strawberries, could they?

There are so many people that it feels like I'm already late. Tonya and Ffion are sitting at a table on the care home driveway, inviting visitors to their cake stall. Someone's obviously spent half the night baking, because there's a huge cake stand full of Welsh cakes, a pile of dainty china cups and saucers and a teapot with jugs of milk and sugar, and a big bowl of clotted cream.

'Ooh, you are clever.' Tonya grabs a jar of jam from my hand before I've fully removed it from my bag, unscrews the lid and plunges a spoon in, smacking her lips together as she tastes it. 'I wish I could do that. Will you give me the recipe and full instructions before you leave?'

'Oh, I was a bit rusty, my dad is really the—' I stutter.

'Fabulous!' She shoos me out of the way to serve a customer wanting a cup of tea and two Welsh cakes, and that familiar guilt bristles at me again. They all think I'm something I'm not, and that I slaved over a hot stove for most of the night in the kitchen, when all I really did was peer over my dad's shoulder and try to take in what he was saying.

They're not charging for the food, but there's a donation box on the table and the man puts a couple of pound coins in and nods his thanks.

'Now go and see your boy,' Ffion says when the man leaves. 'He's got a real spring in his step this morning and I think we all know why.'

'Ry's not mine,' I say, even though the words make me feel flushed and fluttery. 'The spring in his step will be from all the sugar flying about from those Welsh cakes.'

Tonya fixes me with a knowing look. 'The fact you knew who I was talking about says it all.'

'Well, you were unlikely to be talking about Godfrey.' I give her a wink. 'Although you could've meant Mr Barley or that mankini-wearing Jeremy Corbyn gnome that's ... sticking out of the hedge?' I squint towards it.

'Picking blackberries, apparently,' Ffion says. 'We've given up on trying to stop Mr Barley now as long as they're not naked or doing something that would scar innocent children for life.'

The care home owner, Steffan, is skulking around at the top of the driveway, pacing back and forth in front of the entrance to the white brick building. I watch as he does a circle of the building and returns, and I get the feeling he's trying to keep his eyes on everything at once, and is maybe a bit overwhelmed by it all.

He catches me looking, and I give him a nod, and when he returns it, I try a wave that ends up coming out more like a salute. Maybe we should have got him involved in this. Everyone has treated him as an enemy because he's selling the land, but he's obviously having second thoughts, or I wouldn't be here.

I see Ryan straight away when I walk into the strawberry patch, the temporary metal gates thrown aside to welcome visitors. He's near the two trestle tables that have been set up as a checkout area and are currently manned by Godfrey and Mr Barley. He's putting together make-your-own punnets ready for customers to grab and fill and then pay £2.50 for as they leave. There are already a few people putting strawberries into the recyclable handled boxes, taking their pick from the hundreds of plants.

Ryan grins when he sees me, and that familiar warmth floods in again. There's something so nice about feeling like people are pleased to see you. It doesn't happen in London. The people at work are about as indifferent to me as they are to the staff water dispenser in the corner, but here, since the moment Cheryl greeted me in the train station car park, I've felt wanted and welcome.

He's wearing a plain blue T-shirt today, which arguably does more for his biceps than his usual tank top look does. The sleeves are positively straining around muscular arms, and he's got on black three-quarter-length cargo trousers with his feet shoved into trainers instead of hiking boots, and I can't tear my eyes away from his solid calf muscles that look like he spends half his life mountain climbing. He's the kind of guy who could make socks and sandals look sexy. Although I hope he never tries it, just in case.

'Gosh, I'm so awful at this, but you'll know. What is it?' I jump when Alys shoves her phone in my face, so focused on Ryan's legs that I hadn't noticed her approaching.

'I sent her a picture of my tomato slicer last night and she got it straight away. I can't let her win this one too. You're my "Guess the Gadget" expert – any ideas?'

I look at the photo onscreen and recognise it immediately because my mum had one. 'It's a strawberry huller. It's your friend's way of showing support on opening day.'

As I watch her walk away happily to text her friend, I feel guilty again. Any guessing of gadgets has been pure coincidence, fluke, and luck, but even that somehow ties into me being a chef. Everything is tainted by this lie, even the most innocent of things that should be fun.

'Good morning,' Ryan says cheerily. I'm gravitating towards him even without knowing where I was going. He leans down to give me a one-armed hug, and I can't stop my hand sliding up his warm arm and giving him a squeeze back. The familiar scent of his saltwater and bamboo-esque cologne surrounds me and when I go to pull back, he holds on for a moment longer, his stubble grazing when his lips press against my forehead.

Neither of us have mentioned the other night again since, although there have been a few stolen kisses behind the tree trunk when the residents aren't looking, but there's a cloud hanging over us. I'm holding back because of the lie, and I know Ryan's holding back because my life isn't here anymore. And I can't get the idea of him being supposed to marry someone else out of my head. It was a long time ago and it shouldn't still bother me, but the fact he could keep something like that a secret puts a totally different slant on the no-secrets friendship I thought we had, and I've spent so many years thinking he didn't kiss me back that day for one reason, I still haven't quite processed that it was something else entirely.

'Hi.' I can't get the grin off my face even after he pulls away. 'It's not nine o'clock yet. Where are all these people coming from?'

'Seaview Heights started to get some calls last night – people enquiring about parking, payment options, opening times, that sort of thing. Tonya did some digging and discovered that one of the major tourist websites has chosen it as their "pick of the week" for things to do in South Wales, and it's gathered the right kind of attention.' He taps the table and I notice the stack of newspapers on one end.

He picks one up and holds it in front of him, accidentally making the cardboard punnet he'd just folded together pop apart. 'This morning's paper.'

'Front-page news!' I squeal so loudly that several hearing aids go on the blink. 'This is *amazing!*'

It's the most widely circulated newspaper in South Wales, and covering the entire front page is one of Ryan's photos of the tree at dusk with the sunset sinking into the ocean behind it, and the headline splashed across it reads – *Centuries-old strawberry patch reopening amidst stricken seaside sycamore.*

I scrabble to turn to page 4 for the full story, my fingers clumsy with excitement. 'Oh God, Ry.' I feel my face fall. 'It's us.'

There on page 4 and 5 is a whole double-page spread, led by a huge photo of me and Ryan, our arms linked as we took a bite of the first strawberry the other day, and surrounding it are smaller photos of us laughing, digging, laying the weed fabric, and trying to wrestle a gnome from Baaabra Streisand's mouth. No one is allowed to eat Tony Blair.

211

On the opposite page, there's a half-size photo of us hugging. I didn't even realise Tonya had taken a photo, but it must've been after the strawberry tasting when Ryan hugged me because there he is with his arms around me, my head on his chest, his chin resting on my forehead. Both of us have our eyes closed and look totally enrapt with each other. The framing is perfect – a beautiful sunburst on the left and the strawberry patch spread out behind us. It was the morning after rain and Tonya has managed to capture the glistening of the red fruits and the raindrops on pretty white flowers reflecting from the sun and looking like they're sparkling. The picture is so … joyful. It would make me want to visit if I wasn't already here.

Underneath it is a picture I took of all the residents standing in front of the tree with Baaabra. The sun is dappled through the branches and shining down on the group, and both pictures together are so magical that you can almost see fairies dancing through them.

'You look so happy,' Godfrey says. I hadn't realised he was listening.

'So in love with each—' Mr Barley grunts when Godfrey stamps on his foot under the table they're sharing, having forgotten that there's nothing covering the table and their legs are clearly visible.

'With life itself,' Mr Barley corrects himself.

I don't even recognise myself in these photos. My usually sweaty skin looks glowing, and my grown-out hair looks neat and shiny because the camera is kind to split ends, and the blue bits look professionally blended with my dark hair and exactly the kind of metallic shade it looked on the box. Usually I look like someone dyed a bus blue.

All of this *is* fantastic, and I *should* be ecstatic, even though I'm an introvert and the idea of photos of me being in a paper that thousands of people read makes butterflies swish around inside and not the good kind of butterflies.

However, it won't be fantastic if Harrison is one of those people.

'Have you checked the petition?' Ryan's eyes are dancing. 'The paper only went out at seven o'clock this morning and there are already ten thousand more signatures than there were last night. Our website has crashed three times with the amount of traffic, and Tonya's had so many emails that she's paying her grandson to be her personal assistant for the week. He's got at least three enquiries from national newspapers and a TV camera crew are on their way here.'

'Oh my God,' I say. He thinks I'm so overjoyed I can barely find words, and I *am* for the sake of the tree and the people here, but there's going to be no hiding a TV crew from Harrison. Or national newspaper coverage. And then what? I lose my job. I have rent and bills to pay in London, and Harrison is a *big* name in business; he's bound to blacklist me with other companies. I didn't spend the past four years as his assistant only to throw it all away, but how am I ever going to convince him that this is all part of a cunning plan to undermine the protest?

I sigh, attracting attention from Ryan, Godfrey, and Mr Barley because I should be happy, not sighing.

The article is beautiful as well. The headline reads "*No more wishes at the magical seaside sycamore tree?*" and it gives a perfect rundown of the tree – the carvings and the stories behind them, the strawberry patch and Henrietta's wish to see it as it used to be, and the plight of the care home residents losing their garden space to a hotel. It finishes with links to our website, Tonya's Twitter account, and the petition, and there's an appeal for readers to share their stories if they've ever visited the seaside sycamore tree.

Godfrey's signing copies. He's such a celebrity that he might start charging for his autograph soon. Even Baaabra Streisand has been relocated to a gatepost at the upper end of the land, so she doesn't get disturbed by people looking at the carvings.

There's a steady stream of customers all morning. Other residents come out to support their friends, the staff get involved, and Steffan skulks around, pacing from the driveway to the rear of the building and back again, peering over the hedge every time he passes.

There are so many strawberries on plants, and with the sun out, they seem to be ripening in front of our eyes. The tree is a huge hit with visitors, and there are many disappointed children because it's still summer and the huge bunches of sycamore seeds dangling high above aren't ready to fall yet.

By lunchtime, Ryan and I, Tonya, and Godfrey have done countless interviews, both in person and over the phone. We're going to be on the local news tonight and a special interest program on Monday night. The biggest UK-wide newspapers have already published stories about us on their websites, and the number of signatures on the petition is going up every second. Tonya's grandson keeps shouting out random numbers like 18,137 and 20,989. It's a gorgeous day and there are plenty of people on their way down to the beach who come in to pick a punnet of fresh strawberries to go with their picnics.

Tonya's phone hasn't stopped ringing, Ryan's assistant at the campsite keeps putting calls through to his mobile, and I'm in the middle of telling a little girl about how I used to pick strawberries here when I was her age when my phone starts buzzing and Harrison's name flashes up. Even though I was expecting it at any moment, it still makes me jump.

Of course, I'd forgotten to put it on silent, and the loud ringing and buzzing has attracted everyone's attention, including Ryan's. The idea of talking to Harrison in front of the people I'm betraying is detestable, but now I can't even quietly ignore him because that's going to make them even more suspicious.

'Go on, Fliss,' Godfrey says helpfully. 'I can manage here.'

I reluctantly put the phone to my ear and say his name so

brightly that my voice has probably just registered on the National Grid.

Nothing.

'Harrison? Hello?'

I pull the phone away from my ear but the screen still shows the call is connected.

'Are you there?'

Silence.

I can't talk to him here anyway. Apart from being overheard saying something a chef wouldn't say, there's so much din from strawberry pickers and people visiting the tree that I can't hear myself think.

'I'm going to …' I say to Godfrey, waving the phone around and gesturing towards the gate.

Like he can sense my unease, Ryan's watching me from across the patch. 'Okay?' he mouths.

I give him a thumbs up and quickly hurry out of the gate, feeling very much *not*-okay. 'Harrison? Are you there?'

I put a finger in the other ear to try to block out the noise around me. I can hear the office sounds behind him so I know he's there, but he's silent. Like he's too appalled with me to even speak. This can only be a bad thing, and I brace myself for the yelling that will inevitably follow.

'Well, this looks like quite a love story.' He surprises me by talking quietly instead of yelling, although the yelling would be preferable to the menacing tone in his voice.

He's obviously read the article. I am recognisable then. I was hoping I might've got away with it.

'A love story? *Noooo. Noo-oo.*' No one needs to put that much emphasis on a simple "no". I couldn't make it sound any *more* like a love story if I'd tried.

I go up the coastal path and huddle in a corner of the hedge between the pathway and the car park, trying to find somewhere quiet. 'I can't really talk right now.'

215

He laughs a mocking laugh. 'Oh, I assure you, Felicity, you *can* find time to talk now.'

'I'm doing my job,' I hiss into the phone. 'I'm doing what you told me to.'

'You're hugging some guy on a strawberry patch! Sharing food with him!'

Ah, there's the yelling.

'A strawberry patch that did not exist until you got there. And this is the same guy from the sheep video, isn't it? Is this the campsite-owning Tree Idiot?'

'Er … no? That's someone els—'

'It says here "Local campsite owner, Ryan Sullivan!"'

Something about Harrison knowing Ryan's name makes the hair at the back of my neck stand on end. 'Oh. Oh! *That* guy! Yes, that's him.'

'Right. And?'

'And?' I tuck my hair back and look around to make sure I'm not being overheard.

'Are you buying him off with freshly picked strawberries? Trying to seduce him? What's your angle on this? Because you *look* smitten.'

'Looks can be deceiving,' I mutter. 'I'm *trying* to get to know people. To gain their trust. Get right to the heart of this protest, like you told me to.' I grit my teeth as I say it. I'm doing *nothing* he told me to. 'No one's going to let me in on their plans unless I prove myself to be trustworthy.'

He does a chortle that makes me go cold all over despite the summer sun. You know something's gone horribly wrong in your life when even one of the most devious, underhanded businessmen in Britain laughs at the notion of you being trustworthy.

'Have you had a chance to chat to the care home owner yet? I sent him a second set of copies of the paperwork last week – in case he'd misplaced the first lot seeing as it's taking him so long to sign – and he's *still* dithering about it. Give him a kick up the backside when you see him, will you?'

'He's … around.' I peer over the hedge again and spot Steffan skulking around the car park. He catches me looking and I duck down behind the hedge again fast.

'Without him getting a wiggle on, we'll lose the hotel company and all their future business if I don't deliver on this pronto.'

'Isn't there somewhere else they can plonk their hotel? This place is special, it doesn't deserve …' I trail off because I hear him suck air in through his teeth.

'Special, is it?' The menacing tone is back too.

'Well, not to *me*,' I stutter. One day I'll start thinking before I speak. Today is not that day. 'To the locals. They won't give up without a fight. The more of them I meet, the more it doesn't seem worth it.' Maybe this is the way out without upsetting either party. If I could persuade Harrison that it's not worth the hassle, he'd never have to know that I'm not doing my job, and no one in Lemmon Cove would ever find out I'm not a chef.

'Felicity, you'd make a truly terrible businesswoman.'

Then again, maybe not.

'You don't get this far into a transaction and then decide to walk away. How will we ever recoup the costs we've already funnelled into this?'

Ffion walks past and gives me a curious glance.

'Maybe by not offering things you don't have in the first place,' I snap into the phone, ashamed of being caught red-handed, so to speak. I give her a nod and a smile, but inside, I'm shrivelling up like a lettuce leaf on a sunny windowsill.

I turn further into the hedge, trying to block out the noise of traffic and the slamming of car doors from the car park.

'Felicity, this is a *disaster*. It's going from bad to worse. That petition is gaining far too many signatures, and now the newspapers have got a hold of the stories. I sent you there to prevent this very thing.'

'I'm trying, okay?'

'Really? Because so far, it seems like you're *trying* to save the place. If you cost us this client, your job *will* go with them. Do you understand that?'

*If you lose this client, it will be because you sold them land before you owned it.* 'Yes, Harrison,' I say meekly, annoyed at myself for not telling him where to shove his client. The more time I spend here, the more I despise my company and everything they stand for.

'Have you tried blackmail? I'll do some digging on this Ryan Sullivan chap, see what we can dredge up. That might help.'

'No!'

I can hear the raised eyebrow over the phoneline. 'Who is he, Felicity? What does he want?'

'Nothing. He's just a guy. He loves this place and he doesn't want the landscape ruined by a hotel.'

'Of course he doesn't. He owns a flaming campsite, for God's sake. That's like those towns where you have a McDonald's and a Burger King next door to each other. A constant competition. From what I understand, his campsite is currently the *only* place to stay in the area. A hotel would drastically decrease his visitor numbers. If you think this is about *anything* other than business, you're more naive than I thought.'

I want to tell him he's wrong. Ryan's not like that. But the cynical part of me wonders how much of a point he's got. A hotel opening across the way *will* have a detrimental effect on Ryan's business. There's no denying that.

'So what've you got on him? In the three weeks you've been there, you must've got something. It certainly looks like you've got close enough …'

His tone leaves me without a shadow of a doubt that I have to give him something. I look to the sky for inspiration. 'He lost his last business because he accidentally poisoned someone with squash.'

'Excellent.' I can imagine Harrison steepling his fingers like Mr Burns. 'That will be useful information. Is it public knowledge?'

'Yes. Er, I think,' I say, distracted by doing another check for eavesdroppers.

Harrison tuts. 'Then how am I supposed to blackmail him with it? It's no use if the public already know. That would've been perfect too. We could've run a story about him serving poisonous food; that would've soon finished his little establishment off. What else?'

'You would do that?' I say in horror. 'Put out a completely fake story and destroy someone's livelihood?'

'Well, I can't now, can I? Because you haven't found me any decent information.'

'Ryan's not like you.' I push myself up on tiptoes and peer over the hedge. He's introducing a little boy to the Donald Trump scarecrow, with its straw hair and face made of orange peel. 'He's worked incredibly hard to get to where he is. He's dedicated and innovative, and smart, and he really cares about people.'

'A people pleaser, good.' I can hear the biro scratching across paper as he writes it down.

'That's not what I said. He's dynamic, and ambitious, and fun. He hates social media and his business has gone from strength to strength, and he wants to expand into glamping holidays and self-contained chalets. This tree and the strawberry patch are more important than money to him.'

'What's important to *me* is that when I send my staff to do a job, I get results. Weeks later and all you've done since you got there is made the situation worse and stirred up the protest as opposed to quelling it. If there's something I should know …'

'The phone signal's really poor here.' I scratch my nail across the speaker a couple of times. 'I think I'm losing you. Don't worry, everything's under contro—' I hang up before he can yell again.

It wasn't a clever thing to do and he'll know it had nothing to do with the signal, but I was zero-point-three seconds away from doing something stupid like telling him exactly where he can shove his job. I'm getting caught up in all this and it isn't reality. Everyone else here is fine. They live here. When the protest is over, win or lose, their lives will carry on. My job, my livelihood, and my ability to pay my bills all rest on Harrison not firing me. I can't jack in my job and stay. I look over the hedge at Ryan again. No matter how much I wish I could.

'Are you the one?'

I scream at the unexpected voice behind me as Steffan melts out of the hedge between me and the car park.

'What?' I snap at him, my heart hammering from the shock. I step far enough away to put a bit of distance between us and turn to face him with my hands on my hips, trying not to show how petrified I am that he overheard something he shouldn't have.

'Are you the one? You know, *the one*?' He gives me a conspiratorial wink and thumbs his nose.

It's a good thing I realise what he means or I might think he was proposing. But my stomach turns over at the thought of him knowing I am, indeed, the "undercover man" Harrison has told him about. 'I don't know what you're talking about.'

'You saluted me earlier.'

'Just being friendly.' I can't bring myself to tell him the truth. I don't trust him as far as I could throw him with a starfish's strength. And I don't want him to think he's got an ally. 'If you think there's anyone who's not who they say they are, you're wrong.' I hope I sound more confident than I feel, because I see an opportunity. If I can propagate some seeds of doubt in Harrison's word, maybe it'll make him think twice about signing the paperwork.

He doesn't elaborate and I don't say any more because it's a fine line between seeds of doubt and accidentally letting on that I am "the one".

'You're their leader, right?'

'No. Ryan's the one in charge. I'm just a visitor.'

'You visit every day.'

And am *extremely* pleased to know I'm being monitored. 'I love it here. This place is special.'

'I had to open the relief car park before nine a.m. today,' he says after a while. 'And Ryan's opened up the campsite's parking area too, and people are still queuing to get in.'

I'm not sure what he wants or why he's telling me this, but I can sense his unease and doubt, and my mind comes back to what I thought earlier – maybe we should be working with him, not against him. 'You have a good business here. Of course it won't always be this busy, but over time, maintaining this place, keeping the strawberry patch open and saving the tree … You'd get more money than some soulless hotel has offered you for it.' It's plainly a lie. I don't know how much the hotel has offered, but there are probably more zeroes in it than a few strawberry plants could earn in a century.

He raises a disbelieving eyebrow.

'More importantly, you'd get the goodwill of the people. Look at this protest. Look at the petition. There are thousands upon thousands of signatures now and it's going up every minute, and with the number of newspaper, internet, and TV interviews we've done this morning, it's only going to get more attention. People worldwide are commenting on the stories about the carvings we're posting online. People are making plans to come and visit. You'd hurt so many people by selling it, but you'd make so many people happy if you decided to keep it.'

I think he's going to dismiss me, but he thinks about it for a few moments. 'It's worthless. It might be great at the moment, but when those berries are picked and all those weeds start to regrow, I'll be in the same position I was before, except I'll have lost the trust and respect of the companies I'm working with.'

'But you could do something with it. You could replant the strawberry patch as it was – we're working with what we've got

221

this year, but if proper beds are dug and paths are laid down, there'd be room for so many more plants. Over the course of a few years, it would bring you back *more* revenue, and regularly, rather than a measly one-off chunk.' Undoubtedly very, *very* big chunk, but still.

'We tried that. It couldn't be maintained.' He shrugs. 'Who'd do it?'

'I would.' I fold my arms. 'Ryan would. I can't volunteer any of the residents because I don't know their physical limitations, but everyone out there has been doing everything they can to save it – they'd do what they could to maintain it too.'

'It's seasonal.'

'So is everything. We can work around that. Put up polytunnels for early crops and open in the spring. Open up access to the tree and it would extend through the autumn until the sycamore seeds have fallen. In the winter, we could interplant other crops – low-growing flowers like daffodils and snowdrops. You could sell bunches of them as a drive-by … Even open as a pick-your-own daffodil plot. One of the people I've spoken to runs a third-generation florist shop down the coast. We could look into supplying them – I'm sure they'd be open to discussion. You have this huge amount of land and you're throwing it away, and destroying something really important in the process.' I stop myself because I'm getting choked up thinking about losing the tree, and I have to take a deep breath and bite the inside of my lip to stop myself crying.

I can feel his eyes burning into me and instead of instinctively turning away like I usually would, I try to muster the strength and turn the same look back at him. And I realise something.

He looks tired. He looks normal. Not like some evil money-hungry businessman, but like a man who's probably in over his head like the rest of us. He inherited Seaview Heights from a business partner. It probably wasn't his first choice of career, and maybe he has no idea what he's doing either, and now he's stuck between

Harrison's persuasion tactics and doing what's right by his residents. His dark hair is peppered with grey streaks, and there are patches of grey at his temples. The dark circles under his eyes suggest he's been losing sleep over this, and although I'd guess he's only in his late fifties, his stressed face makes him look older.

'Are you a gardener?' he asks.

'I used to be. I worked with Ryan.' I watch as he considers this information. 'How about you?'

'Insurance claims handler. Well, I *was*. Seaview Heights was a passion project for my business partner – and best friend of thirty years – and when he died, he left it in my hands. I didn't want to let him down.'

We look at each other for a few long moments.

'None of us really know what to do for the best,' I start softly. 'We're all out of our depth here. But surely the one thing we can all agree on is that this is *not* the place for a hotel. When this day is over, we're going to bring you all the earnings today, and judging by how busy we've been, it'll be a fair amount. If this is only about financial motivation for you, then at least let that money be an indication of what we could do here. If you sign that paperwork, you'll be taking so much away from the area and taking the most important thing away from your residents – hope.'

His eyes narrow and I realise I've mentioned paperwork I'm not supposed to know about. 'I'd best be getting back,' I say in a rush. 'Look how busy we are. They need all hands on deck.'

'It was nice to talk to you,' he calls after me.

I wish the ground would swallow me up. I hope he thinks I was just assuming about the paperwork because thinking before I speak is not one of my strong points.

Ryan's serving a family of five with a punnet of strawberries each when I get back onto the patch. 'Everything okay?' he asks as they leave.

'*Fine.*' I put so much emphasis on it that he can plainly see straight through me.

'I just had a chat with Steffan,' I say before he has a chance to question anything. 'Suggested polytunnels and growing other plants to maximise profit. If we could grow winter flowers, I thought Edie might be on board with using some in her shop's bouquets …'

'Oh! Supplying the shop!' Ryan taps the table excitedly, making Alys and Cynthia who are on checkout duty look up from the customers they're serving. 'You know how the local greengrocer used to buy soft fruit from Sullivan's Seeds because people love produce that's grown ten minutes down the road?'

I nod.

'I have an idea, and you're my girl.' He uses his finger to do the "come hither" gesture. 'It'll be like stepping back in time to when we worked together. We all know things were better back then. The music was definitely better.'

I roll my eyes. Trust him to think of that. 'It didn't exactly end well the first time, did it?'

'It ended with Cliff Richard doing "The Millennium Prayer".' He makes a vomiting noise. 'No music decade deserved to be seen out with that.'

His ability to make me laugh at inappropriate moments definitely hasn't changed. 'Firstly, everyone knows Cliff peaked in 1988 with "Mistletoe and Wine", and secondly, I wasn't talking about the music.'

He grins like he knows exactly what I was talking about. 'You know how I always used to drag you along to meet suppliers and potential buyers in case I rambled and said something I couldn't recover from?'

I nod again, the memories making me grin.

'When we're less busy here, what if we go and talk to the owner of the little shop in Lemmon Cove? If he'd be interested in selling strawberries that were grown here, we could get the promise of a contract in place for next year. It would be a guaranteed income for Steffan. We could block off a part of the strawberry patch and use a greenhouse to ensure an early crop.' His eyes are dancing as the idea comes alive. 'What do you think, Fee?'

I wonder why it matters what I think. 'If anyone can do it, it's you. You were incredible at talking bulk purchasers into buying our products.'

'Mainly because I rambled so much, they'd agree to anything to make me shut up.'

I laugh. He's not exactly wrong, but it was always one of the most endearing things about him.

'Will you come? I can't do it without you.'

I cock my head to the side, intrigued by his lack of confidence. 'You never needed me to believe in you, Ry.'

'Yes, I did. My whole world fell apart without y—'

He's cut off by the shriek of a child as they find a Boris Johnson gnome holding a butter knife in one hand and a decapitated slug in the other, swiftly followed by the yell of Tonya as she rushes off to give Mr Barley a bollocking and another lecture on child-appropriate gnomes.

He meets my eyes and the laughter we've both been trying to hold back bursts out.

'We're still a team, right?' His eyes are crinkling at the corners and every time I think the laughter has stopped, I start giggling again.

'Right.'

'Well, until you go home. Then I'll have to get used to life without you again.' He's suddenly serious as he looks down and then looks back up at me. 'I'm not sure how easy that'll be.'

It's a good thing we're standing near the checkout tables because I need to hold on to one for support. My voice chokes when I go to say something, and all I can do is look up and give him a nod.

It's not going to be easy for me either. In fact, right now, going home seems like the worst plan I've ever had.

# Chapter 15

I think it's a joke when I get to the strawberry patch the following Saturday morning. Ryan's waiting for me at the gate with a sack full of beach buckets and tools over his shoulder and a loop of rope running through the handles of more colourful plastic shovels and spades than I've ever seen before. It looks like he's raided the contents of the Lemmon Cove surf shop and gone to a few others on the way back for good measure.

'Are you serious?'

'We don't joke about the sandcastle competition in Lemmon Cove, Fee.' He puts a stern hand on his hip, but when I reach him, he slides a palm around my waist and bends to press his lips to my cheek, and I'm surrounded by his crisp green cologne, like a mix of fresh cut grass and new leaves emerging in spring. 'We need to get down there to secure the best spot. People are claiming the best ones already.'

'It's not even nine a.m. yet!'

His hand closes around mine. 'Exactly. Don't want to be late!'

I wave to the residents as he tugs me past the strawberry patch. Ffion is on tree duty, sitting in the deckchair with the chain draped across her, reading parts of her romance novel aloud to Baaabra Streisand. The sheep looks more interested in the sweets

Godfrey is eating. The strawberry patch is open early to accommodate all the extra visitors, and there's already a queue at the punnet table, being manned by Alys and Mr Barley.

'Good luck!' they all chorus as Ryan hurries us onwards.

The coastal path is busier than I can ever remember seeing it. There are families and groups of friends heading downwards, all carrying buckets and spades and various sandcastle-building paraphernalia, some of which I can't even identify.

The hedges rise on either side as the path slopes further, and we have to wait as the path bottlenecks to a little wooden gate, and then turns sandy, with grass and brambles on either side and a picnic area full of wooden tables and benches, and then it turns into the narrow climb down a rocky path that crosses diagonally across the cliffside before turning steeply downwards towards dunes and the open beach.

Ryan's grip on my hand tightens like he's trying to reassure me. The path is only wide enough for one of us at a time, and he goes first, walking sideways so he can keep a check on me, so familiar with the walk that he barely even looks where he's going.

I used to run up and down this path with ease, like one of those sure-footed goats you see on sheer mountainsides in David Attenborough documentaries, and I suddenly want nothing more than to do that again. If I lived here, I'd go down to the beach every day, get fit again. Feel alive again. I've felt like my lungs have expanded since I've been here, free of the traffic pollution in London.

The beach is already packed. There are banners up advertising the local surf shop who sponsors the competition. Someone's hauled a food and refreshments van across from the next beach while the tide is out, and there's a podium set up for the three judges who assign us one of the seven-by-seven metre square plots the beach has been divided into, and give us a list of rules that I look over as Ryan fills in our entry form, and gives our team the name Seaside Sycamore Champions.

It really is serious business now. Three hours' building time, a maximum of six people per team, a strict list of permitted tools and a ban on sand additives, and the only embellishments permitted are ones found on the beach today. Last time I was here for the annual Lemmon Cove sandcastle competition, it was a few kids with buckets and spades.

'We're this way. See? You need to be early to snatch the ideal spots.' Ryan takes my hand again and starts walking to one of the huge squares drawn out in the sand.

He's wearing black three-quarter-length trousers that look like they were purpose-made to show off muscular calves, and a navy T-shirt with a surfboard on it. Sand has blown into his dark hair already, and when he stops at our assigned square, I reach up and brush it out, and for just a moment, his eyes close and I can forget we're on a crowded beach.

'Ooo-ooo,' Tonya coos from above, and we jump apart to see her, Cynthia, and Alys waving from the clifftop under the tree. Mr Barley is holding Baaabra up on her hind legs and waving her hoof in our direction.

We wave back and give each other a guilty look, like they've caught us doing something that would make the gnomes blush, even though it was perfectly innocent.

The other teams already in place are planning their builds with military precision. There are charts and everything. One bloke has got papers spread out on the sand in front of him and is using a pointer to direct his teammates. When he catches me looking, he steps in front of his papers to block my view like I might try to steal his plans.

'So, what are we doing?' I go to speak to Ry, but when I turn around, he's on his knees in the sand, plotting out our square.

'Right, we need a moat around the edge here.' He uses a finger to draw an imaginary line, because no actual construction work is allowed to start yet. 'And then the building goes here, and we need the strawberry patch here, and the tree right at the end here.'

'How often have you done this?' I can't hide how impressed I am. I haven't even thought about building a sandcastle since I was still in primary school.

'Every year.' He laughs when I look at him in disbelief, his ice blue eyes twinkling up at me. 'On behalf of the campsite, my assistant and I usually form a team and recreate the campsite in sand. A few tents, a couple of campervans, I did a real campfire one year but I used a bit too much kindling and they disqualified me for putting the safety of the other contestants at risk.' He uses his hands to mime an explosion.

I can't help laughing at how serious he is.

'We came runner-up once, but my dream is to win. I want that trophy outside the main entrance to the campsite.'

'Oh, how times have changed. Once upon a time, you wanted the world, Ry. Now you want to win a sandcastle competition.'

He finally looks up and meets my eyes. 'I want to win a sandcastle competition with *you*, Fee. I want to put that winner's certificate up and remember our victory together every time I walk into my office.'

My knees go weak and I tell myself it's just delayed response to the climb down, nothing more. 'And if we don't win?'

'Not winning is not an option.'

'We just walked past a bloke building an alligator out of sand! I think not winning is very much an option. Someone over there is practising sculpting wheels for a car!'

He ignores me. 'The strawberries will go here. Oversized, of course. I was hoping they'd allow red powder paint and real leaves, but we'll work with what we've got. Can you find some branches to represent the tree?'

There's a row of stones at the top of the beach that are always covered with debris left by the tide, and I leave Ryan still figuring out the best place to put a moat, despite the fact that Seaview Heights doesn't have a moat, and head up there, joining a few other partners doing the same thing.

'A mermaid.' One woman smiles at me with a shell in her hand.

'Tree,' I say, picking up a few twigs.

'Don't you just love Lemmon Cove?'

I give her a tight smile, and it takes me until I'm halfway back down the beach with a handful of twigs and some driftwood to stop and look around. The squares are filling up and when I glance back up the cliffside, there's a steady stream of people making their way down.

Yes. Yes, I do.

This place is wonderfully, charmingly weird. I used to think it was a bad thing. My younger self was embarrassed by the quirkiness of Lemmon Cove, but now I think everyone needs this kind of enchanting chaos in their lives. Harrison and my colleagues in London will never understand what it's like to feel part of a community like this. They will never know the joy of seeing people take sandcastles so seriously.

It's ten o'clock when the klaxon sounds to start building, and Ry and I leap into action. He starts digging out the moat, while I start scraping sand into a bucket and upturning it into the area he's marked out for the care home, but most of it misses and falls into the moat so he has to dig it out again. I don't seem to have lost the knack I had years ago of knowing which tool Ryan needs before he has a chance to ask for it, and there's much passing of spades and sculpting tools, most of which look like they belong on a cake-baking show and Alys will almost certainly want a photo of for "Guess the Gadget".

We are a team of well-organised, master sandcastle builders who are clearly going to win.

A couple of hours later, my confidence is somewhat waning.

Ryan's carving out windows from a block of sand that in no way resembles Seaview Heights, and I've got my hands around a vaguely boob-shaped strawberry that bears absolutely no likeness to the fruit at all. Any fruit, that is, not just strawberries. To be honest, they look like some kind of amoeba you'd expect scientists to find in a horror movie about alien life forms on Mars.

'Ry, do you ever get the feeling this isn't going very well?'

'No, it's going great.' He sits back on his knees and surveys the mess in front of him. 'That part where half the building has fallen into the moat is *exactly* what I had planned, and that flood from where you threw the bucket of seawater into anywhere *but* the moat is just what we were going for. I'd say we're right on target.'

I'm biting my fist in an attempt to contain my giggles. 'I thought you said you do this every year!'

'I …' He pauses mid-sentence with his mouth open and his hands gesticulate as he tries to explain. 'By "me" I meant "my company", and by "do" I meant … supervise while my assistant does it because he's good at this sort of thing, and I'm … not.' He looks down at the sloppy sand with an expression of resignation. 'As you can tell.'

The giggles get the better of me and I end up howling with laughter.

The tree looks like someone's melted a reindeer. The twigs sticking out of the sand-trunk have a hint of "broken antler" about them, like someone's put a chocolate reindeer in the oven.

I look around at the competition, who all seem to be faring much better than us. 'Oh, look, that guy's doing Mount Rushmore but with cats. Someone's built the Pyramids in actual size.'

'Actual size in a seven-by-seven metre square?'

'You know what I mean. And now he's sculpting Cleopatra to go with them.'

I meet Ryan's eyes and we both burst into giggles again.

'Go on, Seaside Sycamore Champions, you can do it!' Tonya yells down from the clifftop.

'Well, we're not giving up. We have half an hour left to save this thing. We can still win.'

I look around at the truly magnificent pieces of sand art

231

surrounding us. 'If there's one thing I always admired about you, it was your eternal optimism.'

A few squares over, there are three toddlers being encouraged by their parents to make a starfish. It looks like it's recently been run over by a bus, and one of them is sitting in it, and it's still better than ours. 'Your eternal, utterly misplaced optimism.'

When the end klaxon goes, we stand back and look at our masterpiece.

The other teams all cheer and high-five and congratulate each other, taking a moment to look at all the other awe-inspiring pieces of work around them.

A child comes to look at ours and starts laughing.

Ryan drops his arm around my shoulder. 'It is a disaster.'

I look up and narrow my eyes at him. 'So, not winning then?'

'I am truly impressed that we managed to create something so spectacularly awful.'

'Still, at least we were brave enough to enter. It's the taking part that counts, right?'

Dad and Cheryl have joined the gang standing beneath the sycamore tree now. They're all still cheering us on, despite this disaster.

'We'll be brave enough to enter again next year.' Ry drops his head to lean against mine. 'And we'll need to practise a *lot* beforehand.'

'Next year,' I agree with a determined nod. The thought of not being here next year makes my skin go cold despite the blazing sun. It's the stupidest thing, but I suddenly can't imagine not being here next year, not getting to do this again.

If I was brave, I'd tell him the truth about my job, I'd trust that he'd understand that no matter what it started off as, it changed the moment I saw him. If I was brave, I'd tell Harrison exactly where to stick his job. I wish I was brave enough to stay.

Although I'm not sure 365 days until next year will be enough time to practise our truly diabolical skills when they announce the winners.

'We didn't come last!' Ryan cheers.

'We came second to last! After a guy who seems to have based his design on a decomposing pigeon!'

'Hurrah!' Ryan cheers. He's so excited that I can't stop myself hugging him, except he goes to hug me at the exact same moment, and he ends up half-picking me up with one of my legs hooked across his arm and sort of shaking me a bit, and the awkward position makes us laugh even harder.

'Oh my God, Ry,' I say into his shoulder, where I'm clinging on for dear life.

He goes to spin us around, but his foot slips into the moat with a splosh and he stumbles, and we both crash down right on top of the sand version of Seaview Heights.

His whole body is shaking with laughter as the sand disperses underneath him, spraying us both and seeping into what's left of the moat with a few sorrowful glugs, and I'm laughing so hard that I can barely hold my head up and my forehead drops onto his shoulder. I can't remember the last time I laughed so much or had fun like this.

'To be fair, I think we did it a favour,' he says as earnestly as he can muster when he's laughing too much to fully catch his breath.

'Not quite champions, eh?'

'I don't know, I would consider any day that ends with you lying on top of me to be a "win".'

If I wasn't melting from the sun and the exertion anyway, I would definitely have melted at that.

I lift my head. 'Ry ...'

The atmosphere snaps the moment I meet his eyes, and before I realise what's happening, his lips are on mine.

It's nothing more than a peck, but my eyes close for a brief few seconds, and everything drifts away apart from the press of his lips against mine. There's no crowded beach, no sand making things unnecessarily gritty, and no wolf-whistles and cat-calls from elderly residents on the clifftop above. There's just me and Ryan, our foreheads pressing together, breathing against each other's mouths.

And then he groans and drops his head back, splattering more sand in every direction. 'I've got a sand-strawberry the size of a turtle in my back and no idea how I'm going to get up again, and I may well have broken at least one coccyx.'

'How many do you have?' I ask, giggling as I push myself back onto my knees and up to my feet and hold a hand down to pull him up. He reaches out and slots his fingers around mine, but instead of pulling himself upright, he leans up on his elbows and looks over his shoulder at the sandcastle teams celebrating their wins. A woman wearing a dinosaur costume has sculpted an actual dinosaur and is now sitting astride it.

'And you wonder why you ever wanted to leave Lemmon Cove ...'

I follow his gaze, and when I look back down and meet his eyes, his mouth tips into a half-smile that looks much more serious than his jokey tone sounds.

Covered in sand, my chest feeling tight from laughing so hard, and with Ryan's hand in mine, that's a question I cannot answer. The only thing I know above all things is that I don't want to do it again.

I don't want to go back to London.

# Chapter 16

I have to tell him. This can't carry on. I feel sick as I head back towards the strawberry patch that night. I can't stop thinking about him after today. The beach, that kiss, the feeling of having something I don't want to lose. Whatever is happening between me and Ryan deserves a chance, and without me being honest about my job, it isn't going to get one.

He will understand why I couldn't say anything before. It won't change things. And he's kept things from me too. He doesn't have any moral high ground to stand on when he was essentially betrothed to someone else and I never knew. Of all people, he will *know* that some things can't always be shared at the ideal moment. I keep repeating it in my head, but it doesn't alter how much I believe it.

Ryan's at the upper end of the strawberry patch, tidying up after the tourists of earlier. He grins when he sees me, but instead of a traditional greeting, he starts singing the inimitable first bars of "Saturday Night" by Whigfield.

I laugh quietly so as not to wake the residents. 'You never fail to impress with your ability to find a Nineties song for every occasion.'

From the beam on his face, this is surely the best compliment I could ever give him.

'So I even get to see you on Saturday nights now?' He comes closer and we do an awkward half-hug, half-kiss thing. We have both plainly forgotten how you greet a fellow human.

'Today was fun. I …' I decide to be honest. 'I didn't want it to end, thought I'd come back and see if you needed any help.'

His smile gets even wider. 'You must have a sixth sense because I do. The residents were knackered so I sent them inside earlier and promised I'd do the clean-up. Tourists, good. Torn bits of cardboard punnet and squashed strawberries everywhere, not so good.'

He carries on humming "Saturday Night" and I start collecting up debris because it gives me an excuse to avoid the conversation a bit longer. Every time I think of saying, "Ryan, I need to tell you something …" a wave of nausea washes over me, and each time I go to open my mouth, my lips and tongue feel like they're no longer working in sync.

'Can you help me with this?' He's got a roll of duct tape and is poking at a piece of torn weed fabric with the toe of his shoe.

When I go over to him, he crouches down and shows me the tear. 'If you hold this part, I'll stick.' He pulls the tape off the roll and leans over, his hands brushing against mine as he sticks down the parts I'm holding. 'I can't wait to get some proper wooden paths laid in this place.'

I appreciate his confidence that it'll ever come to that. The fabric paths are temporary and the plants are in temporary positions. All of this was only ever meant to be temporary, and I can't think about the implications of it being permanent.

We're both crouched and I look up and meet his eyes and something crackles between us. The dimples right at the corners of his mouth dip as he smiles.

*Come on, Fliss. Just blurt it out. You can tidy the words up later.*

*They just need to be out there. You can't explain anything if you haven't said it yet.*

It's the perfect moment. I swallow and run my tongue across my teeth, trying to persuade my lips to form the words.

And then I overbalance and have to ram my hand down onto the ground to keep myself upright.

The moment is gone.

'Ry,' I start, quieter than an inaudible mouse, but he's already stood up so he doesn't hear me.

I'll put it off for a bit longer. It's fine. Another moment will come along in a minute and I won't miss it next time.

He yawns loudly and stretches until something in his shoulder makes a cricking noise, and while he's distracted, I pick up a dropped strawberry and hold it out on my palm towards Baaabra Streisand, who removes it from my hand with her teeth surprisingly delicately. When it's swiftly devoured, she headbutts my leg looking for more.

'Your sheep's trying to kill me again,' I say, but I smile as I reach down and pat her head. We've reached an understanding lately. She doesn't try to headbutt me over any more cliffs, and I sneak her the odd strawberry when Ryan's not looking.

'My sheep's not getting her usual amount of exercise chained up by the gate all day. Usually she does circles round the tree but she can't with so many people visiting. Seeing as you were surprised the other day, do you want to go for a ...' He holds a finger up in a "wait for it" gesture, puts on a shrill voice and turns to Baaabra. 'Walkies?'

Baaabra practically bounces. If she was a dog, she'd be wagging her tail and turning in circles of excitement. Even her lips have pulled back and it makes it look like she's smiling.

'You're going to walk your sheep?' I look up at the care home. The curtains of every window are shut, but lights are still glowing from inside. 'Now?'

'It's late enough to leave the tree. And I think Steffan's wavering.

He came to talk to me about long-term sharing my car park yesterday – he wouldn't have done that unless he was seriously considering keeping the strawberry patch open. I suspect he liked that box of cash from opening day, and that agreement we got from the Lemmon Cove shop owner for fifty punnets a week starting next spring.' Ryan unhooks the chain from around him and disentangles Baaabra Streisand's lead to slip the handle over his wrist, and picks up the torch. He holds his other hand out to me. 'C'mon. Just down to the beach for a sheep-walk.'

'That sounds like a ewe-phemism.'

He laughs as Baaabra Streisand rushes ahead of him, yanking us both through the open strawberry patch gate.

We head downwards in silence, our joined hands swinging between us. I thought the walk down might be harder for the second time in one day, but with my hand in Ryan's, I can forget everything until we're nearly at the bottom.

'Ahh, the easy part.'

His hand falls out of mine as we reach the wide-open sand dunes at the end of the narrow path, a steep incline down to the beach. He lets out a whoop and dashes off and I follow.

It's physically impossible not to half-run, half-slip, and half-slide down a sand dune, and I end up doing a combination of all three and somehow managing not to break any bones. Ryan reaches the bottom long before I do and turns around with open arms, waiting for me to barrel straight into them, like he always used to.

His arms wrap around me and stop the momentum of running headfirst down such a steep hill, encircling me tightly and rocking us both from one foot to the other as he buries his face in my hair.

I will *hate* this dune when we have to walk back up it, but for now, I like it very much.

'Always hoped I'd get to do that again one day,' he says into my hair.

Why does he have to keep saying the perfect thing? The right thing? The thing that makes those butterflies take off again?

Instead of letting go, his arms tighten and he turns his head to the side, tilting us back with one foot so we're looking up at the tree above us, a shadow against the night sky, and I know we're both thinking the same thing.

'What if we fail?' he whispers.

'We won't – because of you.'

'Because of *you*, Fee. I was getting nowhere until you came along. Just a guy chained to a tree. With a sheep.' He squeezes me and I remember saying something similar to him a few weeks ago. 'You brought the place back to life. Like you always did at Sullivan's Seeds. I always used to say the plants were sad on your days off and only perked up when you were in.'

It once again makes my knees feel weak. 'We should string some fairy lights around the tree. Especially in the winter when all its leaves have dropped and it's a skeleton of branches. It would still be a destination then. Somewhere people wanted to visit. Late night picnics at the strawberry patch could be another thing to look into, or picnics on the beach … The perfect date on a moonlit winter night. It would look pretty decorated for Christmas too. Multicoloured lights, sprigs of holly and mistletoe, those oversized baubles hanging from its bare branches …'

It makes us both realise I won't still be here in the winter, and the sadness pervades. His arms drop from around me, and his hand trails down my arm, across my T-shirt sleeve until his fingers slot between mine.

I swallow hard. 'Ryan, I …'

'Yeah, I know.' He squeezes my hand gently. 'Your life isn't here anymore.'

'It's not that. I want …' I *love* it here. I want to stay, but how can I? I want to talk about it with him, see if he thinks there'd be a future for us if I moved back, but it can't begin with him thinking my life is so different to what it is.

239

I don't know how to end that sentence, and he doesn't push me for an answer.

We turn around to follow Baaabra Streisand as she trots across the sand. She keeps picking up a shell, tossing it away, and then running after it, and I can't help laughing. Whoever knew sheep made such good pets?

The beach is empty tonight in contrast to how busy it was this morning. It's pitch black apart from the light of a small crescent moon, and the tide is out, making the sand seem endless as we walk towards the cliff in the distance with a castle ruin on it. The retreating tide has washed away the footprints of the day, and apart from the set of hoof prints we're following, it's like we're the only people who have ever been here.

'You ever wonder how many break-ups it's been responsible for?' His voice is no more than a whisper but it sounds loud in the silence of the night, and it takes me a moment to realise he's talking about the tree.

'With the carvings fading legend,' he continues. 'How many people visited and seen their carving has faded and took it to mean their other half wouldn't be true or whatever nonsense they used to spout in Victorian times, and not just that it wasn't deep enough or it'd been battered by the weather or carved over by someone else. The Tree of Inadvertent Break-Ups.'

'Aw, that's so cynical.' I glance up at him but he looks away this time. 'You used to believe in magic and sycamore wishes more than anyone. What happened?'

He does a long shrug, lifting my arm too as he moves his shoulder. 'Stopped believing in happy endings, I guess.'

'Seriously, Ry,' I say slowly because I'm not sure I want to know. I should have asked him straight away, but it didn't seem like the right moment to push him on it, and the thought of him hiding this secret when I thought we shared everything makes me feel uneasy. 'What happened with the woman you told me about the other day?'

'I went along with what my father wanted. I ended up engaged to her.'

He mentioned something about it the other day, but to hear him actually say it so straightforwardly … I stop in shock and the movement yanks my hand out of his.

'That wasn't meant to sound like I jumped straight into bed with her. It was years after you left, Fee. I missed you like hell for a couple of years, I was low and lonely and my father's constant pressure got the better of me. I gave up on you ever coming back. I stopped fighting. Without you, I didn't have anything to fight *for.*'

'Ryan …' It makes the guilt spike again. The day I kissed him was such a huge misunderstanding for both of us. It could've been so different. If I'd hung around to hear his explanation, if he'd explained things to me earlier, if either of us had had the confidence to let each other see how we really felt years before …

'I know you didn't expect to hear that the other day, but the least I can do is explain. We were together for about five years in the end, but my heart wasn't in it. The relationship moved on without me. Both our families were involved, and it was assumed we were on the path towards marriage and children. I proposed because she was expecting me to propose and I didn't want to let her, or the families, down. I felt like I *should* marry her rather than I wanted to. Don't get me wrong, the first few years were great. We got on well enough that I actually thought I was lucky, but it faded, and we were trapped together more than anything else. I knew what love felt like, and that wasn't it.'

A shiver goes down my spine and I glance behind me because it genuinely makes me feel like I'm being watched. There's no wind tonight, the air is completely still, but the tree rustles above us. We look at each other and he slowly raises an eyebrow until we both burst into nervous laughter.

'So what happened?' I ask when the tree is silent.

'People around here will be quick to tell you that I'm cruel and cold and heartless because I broke it off two months before the wedding, but she was buried in wedding plans and I was waking up at night in a cold sweat at the idea of making that commitment when neither of us were happy. It became all about the wedding for her. More and more guests, more and more money we didn't have on outrageous things, more outlandish ways to impress people and go one better than all the weddings we'd been to over the years. I'd always thought Bridezilla was a myth until then. And I hate all that stuff, I wanted a small private wedding with only our families there, and she was all ice sculptures and glass carriages and inviting people she hadn't been in touch with since primary school, and I realised that she didn't know me at all or care in the slightest about how I was feeling. It might've seemed harsh, but it was always going to be kinder to break it off beforehand than go into a loveless marriage.'

'That didn't go down well, then?'

He grunts. 'Her father pulled out of the business and left my dad with almost nothing, and that turned into the beginning of the end for his business empire. He didn't speak to me for a while afterwards. I'm not sure he ever truly forgave me or understood why I couldn't go through with it. She was furious about losing the Big Day, but not so much about losing me. She planned the wedding to impress her friends, not because she wanted to marry *me*. The groom was interchangeable.'

Even though he doesn't sound overly bothered by the whole thing, there's a wobble to the last sentence.

'One thing you've *never* been, Ry, is interchangeable.' I take his hand again and give it a squeeze and he knocks his shoulder into mine as we walk along.

'See?' he murmurs. 'This is why I've been single since then. The half-hearted relationships have never been worth it. I want something that makes me feel alive. Something that lights up my life and makes me feel like I can do anything. Some*one* who believes in me and makes me feel like I'm the king of the world. And nothing's ever come close to the girl I let go ...'

I choke.

He tugs me to a halt. 'Fee, I know things are weir— Ow!'

I've been so absorbed in Ryan talking that neither of us have noticed Baaabra Streisand coming back until she kicks a clump of wet sand at his leg.

'There's no way she's full sheep. She's some sort of half-dog crossbreed, right?'

He's laughing as he bends to brush sand off his leg without letting go of my hand.

Whatever he was going to say, the moment is gone as he picks up a shell by his foot and tosses it and the sheep runs after it.

'How about you?' He swings our hands wider as we follow her. 'Why has no one married my Fee yet?'

I wonder if that "my" doesn't have something to do with it. 'Lurched from one disappointing relationship to another, trying to fill a void with dull spark-free relationships that usually end in cheating, lying, and occasionally, stealing money from my bank account. That was a fun one.'

He bursts out laughing. 'I'm sorry. I don't mean to laugh, but seriously? *Who* does that?'

'A man who was quickly relegated to "ex".' I can't help giggling too, even though it was far from funny at the time. Everything seems better with Ryan listening. 'I've kind of given up in recent years. There are only so many disappointing relationships you can put yourself through before you wonder if it's worth it, and the older I get, the more it feels like I'm looking for something that doesn't exist.'

I meet his eyes in the darkness and I *know* we're both thinking the same. It did exist, once. But we lost each other, and maybe it's too late now.

He looks away, but his grip on my hand tightens. 'Do you ever regret leaving?'

I think about it for a while. The answer is both yes and no, and somehow I think Ryan will understand that. 'You can regret leaving people without regretting leaving the place. I had to leave here. I had to know what else was out there. If I'd have stayed, I'd have spent the rest of my life wondering "what if".'

'And what's it like out there?'

I screw up one eye and use my free hand to do a "meh" gesture. 'It's not so great actually.'

He laughs. 'I'm sure the rest of the British Isles would be *thrilled* with that portrayal. Have you considered writing adverts for tourism boards?'

It makes me laugh out loud again, but he's not going to distract me with humour. 'How about you? Do you ever regret staying?'

He's quiet for a while too. 'I think you can regret aspects of staying without regretting the act of staying itself. I didn't have a lot of choice, but on the other hand, I'll never regret doing what was right for my family, but I'm also sorry for the things I never got to do and the people I've lost along the way ... the people who had to go when I couldn't.'

The tone in his voice makes it obvious he's talking about me. I close my eyes and keep my head fixed straight ahead. My breath is shallow and fast, and I close my eyes and force myself to concentrate on breathing.

The tree rustles above us again, making us both turn back to look at it as the noise cuts through the silence of the darkness.

Another moment for telling him is lost. Ryan goes to run a hand through his hair and accidentally clonks himself on the forehead with the torch he's forgotten he's holding.

It makes me laugh, and even in the night, I can see how red his cheeks go.

'Sorry, I must sound like such a backwoods, small-town country bumpkin to you now. I bet you can't wait to get back to your glamorous London life.'

I snort so hard that even Baaabra Streisand looks round at

244

me. 'Believe me, there is *nothing* glamorous about it. And no. I wish I could stay.' It's the first time I've said it out loud and he stops walking immediately.

'Aren't you happy there?'

It's such a simple question, and I don't realise I'm going to cry until I go to answer him with a flippant "of course" and a sob comes out instead.

His arms are around me in an instant, pulling me tight against his chest and squeezing hard. Knowing exactly what I need without a word being said, like he always did, and just the act of someone caring makes me cry harder. It's been a long time since I felt like I mattered to someone.

'It's complicated, Ry,' I stammer out eventually. It's the perfect opportunity to tell him the truth, to tell him about Harrison and Landoperty Developments and trust that he'd understand it was only a job until I got here and remembered how much I loved this place, but at the same time, why would anyone believe that? I've outright lied to his face hundreds of times since I came back. *That* is something he won't forgive me for, and I can't bring myself to take that risk while his arms are around me and the crescent moon winks from behind a cloud.

'If you're not happy there, know that there is *always* a place for you here.' His hand strokes through my hair, his fingers twirling in the strands, a gesture of comfort that makes me feel more loved than I have any right to feel.

'Oh God, will you stop it? I've done nothing but cry since I got here and you're making it worse.' I push myself out of his arms and wipe my eyes with the back of my hand, annoyed at myself for not just coming out with it.

I've ruined things with Ryan once, and the fear of losing him again is overpowering. Kissing him was the biggest risk I've ever taken, and from that, I realised that taking risks doesn't pay off. It changed me. It changed how I approached things. It knocked my confidence and made me doubt everything I thought I knew, and this brings it all back in spades. I *think* he'll understand why I told the lie I did, but the idea that he might not is too much of a risk to face.

I force myself to turn away and carry on walking. Baaabra Streisand is a silhouette in the distance now, clearly not hanging about to wait for us two slowcoaches.

'How about you?' I say when he catches up with my increased pace. 'Are you happy?'

'I thought I was. But seeing you again has made me realise that I've never been happy without you in my life.'

'Oh my God, Ry.' Why does he keep coming out with these things that make me trip over my own feet?

He grabs my hand and pulls me to him, sliding his arm around my waist, his other hand coming up to stroke through my hair, and I close my eyes and let out a breath.

'You coming back here has been the best thing that's happened to me. I should never have let you go. I should have kept in touch. I didn't think you'd want me to …'

'I didn't think *you'd* want to. I thought you'd forget about me. I wasn't that impor—'

'My world stopped turning without you. That first Christmas after you left, I kept driving past your house because I thought you'd be home and I might get to "accidentally" run into you and be all casual and nonchalant, but it never happened. I couldn't even bring myself to look you up online because I didn't want to find out you were married. I've spent fifteen years convincing myself that we'd have another chance someday, and I didn't know what I'd do if I found out you were happily married with a brood of children and a gorgeous husband, off somewhere living your dream life. It was better if you existed only in my memory.'

'Why are you saying this now?'

'Because the tree has given me a second chance. That tree has brought you back into my life. I don't know how much time you get off in a restaurant, but it can't be that much so I know you're going to leave again soon, and I don't want it to end the same way, because this time, I don't think you want to go.'

'Ryan, there's something I need to tell—'

We're suddenly headbutted apart by a sheep crashing straight through the middle of us.

'Argh! That sheep!' I'm struggling to stay upright from the momentum as Baaabra Streisand stands there staring at us. I meet Ryan's eyes and we both burst into hysterics.

By the time I stop giggling, Ryan's sobered up and his eyes are on me. 'The universe's way of trying to tell us something?'

'Clearly,' I agree. Maybe I'm not meant to tell him. Maybe this is all a mistake and I shouldn't even be contemplating staying here and his sheep really does have perfect timing after all.

When I look at him again, he's got a mischievous glint in his eyes. 'Is it warm in here or is it me?'

I raise an eyebrow. 'We're outside.'

Even so, he starts flapping his T-shirt from the bottom like he's overheated. 'Wanna go for a swim?'

'It's nearly midnight!'

'Exactly. It's boiling tonight. This is Wales – you have to make the most of the rare times it's warm enough to go in the sea. Go on. I've always wanted to go night-time skinny-dipping and I never have. And I bet you never have either.'

'For very good reason! You're completely mad!'

He grins like it's a compliment. 'Something to remember us by when you're back in your block of flats and your boiling hot restaurant kitchen.'

That sets my nerves wrangling for an altogether different reason than stripping off in front of Ryan, but his wide smile and the glint in his eyes is impossible to ignore. 'I'm not taking my clothes off in front of you!' Unlike his curved muscular body, I'm not skinny enough to be made for skinny-dipping.

'Underwear-dipping then.' He rips his shirt over his head with one swift move, and honestly, it's a good job it *is* dark because

247

even in this low light I can see the outline of his abs, and if we were in full daylight I might not be able to stop myself licking them.

He takes his phone out of his pocket and drops it on top of his T-shirt on the sand, and notices me watching. 'No one's going to steal it. There's not a soul around. You've been living in London for too long, Fee.'

That I can definitely agree with.

I watch the ripple of muscles as he toes first one shoe and then the other off, and then he steps back, leaving the three-quarter-length trousers on. He flashes a grin at me and takes off running down the beach towards the low tide, giving me privacy to strip off, and although it's tempting to just go and paddle at the shore, it *is* warm tonight, and I have enough regrets when it comes to Ryan that I don't want to add "not moonlight swimming with him" to the list.

I slip my trainers off and put my phone next to his, wondering if it's more likely to be stolen or eaten by Baaabra Streisand, who has come to stand next to me in some display of feminine solidarity as I reluctantly strip my T-shirt off too. Whoever thought I'd be bonding with a sheep, topless, on a moonlit night?

I'm wearing a scaffolding-like sports bra that's going *nowhere*, but I use my top to cover our phones in case any would-be thieves wander by, and then feel guilty for being so cynical.

Somewhere down the beach, Ryan shouts as he enters the water.

Baaabra is still standing there, looking between me and the phones, and I wave my hand for her to follow me, surprised when she does. Maybe she's hoping this'll lead to her chance to drown me as we start running down the beach together, feet sinking in the wet sand where the tide hasn't long gone out.

'Oh my God, that's *freezing*,' I shout as I crash into the ocean.

Ryan holds his nose and sinks under the water and surfaces again with a splash, wet hair across his forehead as he pushes it back and shakes seawater out of it, and I squeal when it splashes me. I pluck up the courage to duck under the surface too … I've come this far, I may as well go all the way now.

When I come back up, blinking sea salt out of stinging eyes, I splash him too and he laughs and dives towards me. He swims around me, a wide expanse of tanned skin and muscled back that my hand automatically reaches out and trails down as he comes up next to me.

My hand falls away as he stands up to full height, using both hands to swipe seawater away from his face. He comes nearer and I'm certain he's going to lower his lips to mine, but an annoyed "baa" draws our attention to the shore.

The tide's reached its lowest point and is on the turn again now, and Baaabra Streisand is on the edge of the shallowest waves, looking down disdainfully when her hooves get wet every time it creeps further up the beach.

Ryan reaches out and lifts my hand again, pulling it to him on the surface of the water. 'Do you miss it? If I ever left here, it'd be the worst part for me. I'd miss living by the sea. Not many people get to live in places like this, and it's easy to forget how privileged we are sometimes.'

I let my other hand drift across the calm surface of the waves. I haven't been in the sea since the summer I left. I used to swim here every day and I'd never realised how much I miss it.

'It's funny how fifteen years ago, I couldn't wait to get away. And now …' I look towards the tree on the clifftop and then back at him. 'I wish I didn't have to.'

He steps closer and uses the grip on my hand to tug me against him, our bodies pressing together with very little clothing on the upper half. And wet, dragging bottoms on the other half, which I'm certain are going to let out a stream of embarrassing air bubbles at any second.

'Fee, can I say something?' His thumb brushes across my hip where his hand is splayed out, so hot that even in the cool water,

I'm convinced there will be a pyrography-style burn mark on my skin when he releases his fingers.

I nod, too lost for words to do much else.

He pulls me impossibly closer and his chin comes to rest on my forehead, his other hand tangling in my wet hair and cupping my head as he holds me against his chest.

His heartbeat sounds louder, amplified by the water, so loud that it almost drowns out the quiet words he whispers against my forehead.

'I stopped believing in wishes because the last time I made a wish on that tree, it was fourteen years ago. I'd been missing you like mad for a year. The wish was that you'd come back into my life when the time was right. I'd given up on it until the moment you walked in. Since that day, I've trusted in the sycamore tree. I don't know if the time is right now, but if you're not happy where you are, change it. Fee ...' He pulls back and waits until our eyes meet. 'I couldn't ask you to stay before, but if it's what you really, *really* want now ...'

I know he's serious because he can say that *without* making a Spice Girls reference.

'You deserve to know how happy that would make me, and *you* deserve to *be* happy, wherever that is.'

My entire body breaks into goose bumps and I can feel every single fine hair on my arms rising, and it's probably a good thing we're in water because it's keeping me buoyant when every muscle in my body has forgotten how to work.

His fingers get even tighter on my hip as the soft stubble on his chin drifts down until his lips are on my cheek.

It's not even my cheek, not really, more the side of my face beside my ear, but his lips press there gently, making me feel even more wobbly than I did already from the constant lap of the waves. His lips press harder, his breath ghosting across my skin, making the goose bumps rise again and a shiver goes through me.

'Ryan ...' I whisper his name for no reason, nothing more than a plea in the night. My fingers have got a vice grip on his arm, there are definitely going to be five white marks where my nails have been digging in, and the nape of my neck gets a tingly feeling.

'I know,' he whispers, and it feels like he has to persuade himself to push away.

His fingers have stuck in my hip and it takes long moments to unfold them.

I *have* to tell him, but he looks dazed, probably as dazed as I feel, and I don't think I can form coherent words. Instead of splashing me again like I thought he might to ease the tension, he flops onto his back and his legs pop out of the water. I watch him for a moment, unsure if he's going to say anything else or if I should say something, although I have no idea what, and I'm desperately trying to think of words – the right words to make this sound not as bad as it is, and I can feel panic clawing up my chest because I *still* can't think of how to say it, and my breathing is getting faster and shallower, and I force myself to stop thinking and take deep breaths. I do the same as Ry and turn onto my back, floating on the surface, looking up at the tree on the cliff behind us.

It's the most exposed I've ever felt with a man, and not just because I'm only wearing a bra. Because, like always, it feels like Ryan can see everything that's inside of me, and I'm certain he's going to know about the job lie because that's the sort of thing Ryan would see through.

He reaches out and catches my hand, tugging me closer and we just sort of drift in comfortable silence, never letting go of each other.

I know one thing above all else – I don't want this to end.

# Chapter 17

'Henrietta's coming!' Godfrey shouts as soon as I get to the strawberry patch the next morning.

He's sat on one of the benches, and there's a pile of rose-carved strawberries beside him. I'm guessing they're Ryan's work because Godfrey's hands are shaky as he pushes them onto skewers and stands them into a vase that's sitting beside him, wrapped in pink-and-gold-spotted tissue paper and tied with a pink ribbon.

Ryan's up near the gate on the phone, and I wave to him, but instead of waving back or smiling, he turns away.

It makes something go cold inside me, but I try not to read too much into it. The blinding sun is behind me so maybe he just didn't see me in the glare. I step over the chain still attached to Ryan's waist and go to stand by Godfrey.

He looks up with a watery grin. 'We told her nursing home about her wish and restoring the strawberry patch, and asked them to look out for a day when she might be up to the journey, and they phoned this morning to say she's having a good day and they've got a free ambulance to bring her over. Ryan carved these for me with his dexterous young hands, mine aren't up to it these days.'

'How many are you making?' I ask.

'Until the vase is full or until she arrives, whichever comes first.'

I wave to Tonya who's on a video call with her grandson discussing something about flyers, and Alys comes over with her phone. She leans across the back of the bench and holds it out so we can both see it. 'What's this?'

It's a photo of a lot of sieves hanging up in the homeware department of a shop.

'A moon lander! A pirate ship!' Godfrey throws out random guesses to wind her up.

'It's a mass-sieve problem,' Alys announces proudly. 'I thought of it myself and *she* didn't get it.'

I laugh out loud, mainly at how proud she sounds of such an excellent pun, but a feeling prickles at the back of my neck, and I look across the garden at Ryan, still on the phone, his eyes on me.

I smile but he doesn't return it. Something's wrong. No matter how many years have passed, I still know Ryan well enough to know that.

Alys helps herself to a un-rosed strawberry and wanders away.

'Count yourself lucky,' Godfrey says. 'She showed us a photo of a cow and a potato the other day and it was a cow-ch potato.'

It shouldn't be funny but it makes me burst out laughing again.

Ryan's stalking back across the garden now, his lips pinched tightly together, a frown line creasing his forehead. Maybe it's something to do with Henrietta's visit and he's got to break the bad news to Godfrey?

'Good morning!' I say brightly.

'Yeah, morning,' he mutters. He looks at me for a long moment and my skin tingles in the worst way possible. I have a *terrible* feeling about this.

'Fliss, can we ...' Ryan trails off at the noise of a heavy vehicle pulling in and I push myself up on tiptoes to see over the hedge

253

to the car park and the nursing home ambulance arriving. 'Henrietta's here.'

Godfrey lets out a squeal and almost topples over in his haste to get up.

'Here, let me help.' Ryan looks between me and Godfrey, but the elderly man has already tottered halfway across the garden and looks like he could fall over at any moment. Ryan looks momentarily perplexed by what to do with the chain, and then unclips it and shoves it at me while Godfrey moves at an impressive and unsteady-looking speed. 'One of the nurses brought him a tub of edible glitter, can you start glittering the edges of the petals and I'll be right back?'

'Of course.' I wrap the chain around myself with a determined click and sit on the bench. I wiggle my fingers towards Baaabra Streisand, who's tied to the gatepost in her usual place, safely out of reach of strawberry pickers, although whether it's for her sake or theirs is anyone's guess.

And I try not to think about that "Fliss". Ryan has never, ever called me anything but Fee. It started the first time I met him at Sullivan's Seeds when he went to call me Fiona, realised mid-name, and styled it out to Feeee-licity.

There are at least twenty stems of strawberries carved into roses in the crystal vase, and I undo the tub of edible gold glitter and use the little brush provided to start dabbing it onto the edges of the petals.

The strawberry patch isn't open yet so it's quiet for Henrietta, and eventually, after a bit of commotion in the car park and deciding the coastal path is too steep and negotiating the gateways from the driveway to the garden, a nurse from the nursing home pushes Henrietta's wheelchair in.

The little old lady is tiny and so shrunken that she looks lost in the chair, a shadow of the woman I remember running the strawberry patch when I was young, but her toothy smile is so bright that nothing else matters.

Godfrey walks beside her, clasping her hand, and Ryan's sort of hovering behind him, making sure the path is clear for them and that Baaabra doesn't try to eat anyone on the way past.

The nurse stops the wheelchair and lets Henrietta take it all in for a while. Godfrey kneels beside her and points out the different areas for each type of strawberry and tells her a bit about how we're planning to make it even better next year. She clasps his hand between both of hers, and eventually Ryan helps him to his feet and the nurse pushes her onwards. Everyone else is standing back, offering her a wave when her gaze falls on them, but not wanting to overwhelm her.

She halts the nurse when he goes to wheel her past "their" bench, and Ryan helps Godfrey sit there while her chair is stopped in front of it. I've just about finished glittering the strawberries when he sends me a questioning look, I nod in confirmation and he beckons me over. I pick up the bouquet and take them to put on the bench beside Godfrey so he can give them to her.

She smiles at me, but she's only got eyes for him.

There are tears all round when he settles the bouquet on her lap and she remembers sitting on that same bench in their younger years and eating the rose-shaped strawberries he carved for her with a glass of wine as they watched the sun go down, and they both cry and embrace each other.

I can feel my lip wobbling as I look across them and meet Ryan's eyes. He looks away. And then I have to dive out the way and pull the chain with me when she points to the sycamore tree and they set off towards it.

Ryan looks like he's miles away, staring into space like he hasn't even noticed them go.

I gather the chain and go to stand next to him. 'Everything okay?'

He looks startled, like he hadn't seen me move either. 'Fine. Thanks for doing that. I appreciate it.'

It's so clipped and curt, nothing like his usual warm and easygoing manner.

'It's fine. It's an honour to help. They're such a lovely couple. They deserve every moment of happiness they can snatch now.'

He looks at me for a long moment before he decides to speak again. 'I've never seen anyone look as happy as she did when she realised where she was, apart from Godfrey when he realised she *knew* where she was.'

Maybe it's all okay and I'm just imagining things. Maybe this visit has taken a lot to organise and he's just stressed out.

'The tree granted a wish.' I step a bit closer to him.

He takes a step away. '*We* granted a wish. It was your idea. Your drive. Your belief in magic.'

'Yours too.'

'Fee ...' he starts, and then stops and shakes his head.

'What's wrong?'

'This isn't the time. Not with Henrietta here. I don't want to ruin their moment.'

Maybe it's the tree. Maybe something's happened with the campaign. Maybe Steffan's signed that paperwork after all. And it's kind of nice that Ryan doesn't want to dampen a special moment by sharing bad news.

All of this feels extraordinary. Truly magical. Like something bigger than us. Something otherworldly and ethereal, like the tree itself. It should be a huge publicity moment, but it feels private and special. Tonya's taken a couple of photos, but only from a distance so as not to disturb Henrietta, and I get the feeling they're more for Godfrey himself than for any kind of publicity. This is a private moment between two people who are still desperately in love.

We watch as Godfrey points out the carving of the strawberry in the tree trunk that they did on the day they took over the patch and see Henrietta nod in recognition. The nurse wheels her chair right up to the metal barrier around the cliff edge, and she pushes herself up on shaking arms to get a better view.

In the distance, we hear her talk to Godfrey about something she remembers, and he tells her about the last time she visited and her wish to see the strawberry patch as it used to be, and she looks around again, smiling.

She asks to make a wish again, but it's too early in the year for the sycamore seeds to fall, and she starts getting upset when Godfrey tries to explain.

'Wait, wait, wait, maybe we can find you a special one, Henrietta.' Ryan takes off without a word, jogging towards them. 'Can you give me a moment?'

She nods, clearly not immune to Ryan's calming presence. I follow him down towards the tree as he climbs into it with well-practised ease and looks around for the lowest hanging clump of green winged seeds. He has to shuffle out on a branch, cling onto it with his knees and reach up to grab at the clump, and at the last moment, even though there is otherwise no wind today, a breeze whistles through and blows the bunch of seeds directly into his outstretched hand.

A wink from the tree again.

Henrietta and Godfrey are watching him in awe, and the nurse is watching him like he's a lunatic, but he gets back down with ease and crouches in front of Henrietta's chair as he gives her the sycamore seed. 'That must be a very special wish. I think the tree wanted you to have it.'

Her eyes well up as much as mine do and she pats his hand as she takes it from him, a thank you croaked with emotion. He stands back to give her space, but doesn't come anywhere near me.

Henrietta is turning the sycamore seed over and over in her hand, looking at it like it's the most important thing in the world. She pushes herself onto her feet and steps up to the edge, clinging onto both the barrier and her husband's arm, her limbs shaking as she holds the hand with the sycamore seed in it over the edge and opens her fingers, letting it drop.

In the autumn, the dried out brown seeds would twizzle and

twirl and dance down towards the sea, but it's too early in the year and the seeds are still green and wet, and it plummets limply to the sand below, but it makes her happy anyway.

'I wish to be young again!' She shouts at the top of her shaky voice, making a couple of dog walkers look up from the beach below.

'For as long as your carving exists on that tree, you always will be,' I say.

She overbalances and Godfrey and the nurse hold her up and help her back into her wheelchair.

I reach out and touch the tree. 'All of these people are timeless. Some of these carvings have been here for centuries, but to anyone seeing them now, it could've been yesterday, or last week, or last year. Every name in this tree is immortal in their own way.'

Henrietta reaches towards me, scrunching her fingers together like she wants me to come closer, and she curls gnarled, arthritic fingers around my wrist when I crouch down beside her chair.

'I got everything I could ask for out of life,' she whispers with a shaky voice. 'Someone who loved me as much as I loved him, and a job that never once felt like work. I went to bed every evening with a smile on my face and woke up every morning still smiling. What more can anyone ask for?'

It, of course, makes me cry again.

'The most important thing in anyone's life should be the people they share it with,' Godfrey adds.

Henrietta seems to lose the thread of the conversation and goes back to staring out towards the sea, so I push myself up and go to stand next to Ryan, the chain jangling with every movement. He turns away again.

'What's wrong with you?' I whisper out of the corner of my mouth.

'Nothing, Fliss.'

That "Fliss" again. It makes coldness drip down my spine. I stare at him but he won't look me in the eyes. 'Ryan ...'

'Now is *not* the time, okay? Let Henrietta and Godfrey enjoy their moment without ruining it.'

I feel like a schoolgirl being chastised by a headmaster in front of the whole class as I step away and try to focus on the two in front of me, instead of giving in to the tears that his sharp tone makes prickle at my eyes.

Henrietta seems lost in time and the nurse and Godfrey share a look and mutually decide it's time to go. They take the scenic route around the strawberry patch to get back, Henrietta letting her arm dangle down and touch strawberry leaves as they pass.

Steffan is lurking by the gate and I raise a hand in greeting. Better not salute him this time in case it's misinterpreted again. He nods at me and gives me a smile, and after stopping to chat with Henrietta and Godfrey, he disappears back inside.

'He likes you.' I didn't realise Ryan was watching the exchange until he speaks.

I think he suspects I'm his "undercover man", but I can't say that aloud. 'I wouldn't read too much into it.'

'Wouldn't you?' He raises an eyebrow and I have a horrible, sinking feeling. Ryan is *never* like this.

'What's that supposed to mean? Ry, you've been off with me all morning – what's wrong?'

'Nothing.' He turns and stalks off up the path, and I start to follow, but before he gets halfway up, he turns back around. 'Actually, Fee, there *is* something. Where do you work?'

His voice wavers, but his face is stony and I instantly know he knows.

I swallow hard. 'Why?'

My voice comes out unsteady even though I'm trying to sound non-committal and vague, like I can somehow still wriggle my way out of this. There's no telling for sure that *that's* what he's talking about.

'Riscaldar,' Tonya answers for me. Ryan's voice has risen enough to attract the attention of the remaining residents and I hadn't even noticed them shuffling closer.

'No,' Ryan says, slowly, like he's turning it over in his own head. 'No, I don't think you do.'

He knows. A wave of nausea crashes through me. It's not like I didn't know this day was coming, but I didn't want him to find out from someone else. I've tried to tell him so many times, but being with him, tentatively dating him, stealing kisses when no one's looking, and the whirling emotions of wanting to stay here and not go back to London, to maybe make a real go of things with Ryan ... It's made me take leave of my senses, and I was so scared of doing something to mess that up that I've bitten my tongue every time I've gone to blurt it out.

There's no *not* facing it now though. 'Can we talk in private?' I nod towards the tree and go to start walking towards it, but he shakes his head.

'No. I think everyone deserves to hear this ... Or is it just me you've been lying to and everyone else knows the truth?'

The group of residents are curious. They're gathering closer, intrigued by what's going on. Despite the numerous hearing aids that are regularly on the blink, none of them have misheard this, and I see them exchanging looks, intrigued by the anger on Ryan's face and the tone in his voice.

'I've tried to tell you. I *meant* to tell you. I know it looks bad, but it's *not* what you're thinking.'

The noise he makes was probably meant to be a laugh but it definitely doesn't sound like one.

'What do you know?' I ask.

'Why? So you can carefully gauge how much of your story has been exposed and what lies you need to feed us next to maintain the illusion?' Ryan's voice is spiky, hard, cold. I've never heard such venom in it.

'I didn't mean that.' I glance at the residents, who all look away. 'I meant how. Who told you?'

'I took a phone call this morning from Landoperty Developments, once again trying to bribe me to call off the protest. A guy named Harrison this time, offering me vast amounts of money for the expansion of my business into holiday chalets and luxury glamping tents, if I would back off and let Steffan sell up …'

'What did he say? He could be angry, throwing around lies …' Even as the words come out of my mouth, I'm exasperated at myself for not admitting it straight out. Ryan's always hated being lied to. Even at Sullivan's Seeds when trainees would turn up late and be full of outlandish excuses – he'd tell them to just admit they'd overslept and be done with it.

'Funnily enough, he didn't *say* anything. He didn't need to. I worked it out for myself.'

'How?' I'm confused. I was certain that it must be Harrison dropping me in it out of spite. He saw the pictures in the paper. He knew there was something between me and Ryan. He'd be petty enough to want to throw a spanner in the works, and not one of Alys's puns this time.

'Because I trusted you. When I told you I wanted to expand into holiday lets … That was the first time I'd ever said it out loud. Because I didn't think I could do it, but with you here, believing in me, it gave me the courage to think, "You know what, maybe I can." You are the only person I've ever told. For him to know that, there's only one way he could've found out.'

'I might've mentioned it to someone el—'

'For God's sake, Felicity.' His use of my full name cuts through like a knife. Ryan hasn't called me that since the day we met. 'You've been here for weeks now – *no one* gets that amount of time off work. And there is *no way* that someone who was as bad in the kitchen as you were could possibly change enough to be working in a five-star celeb-filled restaurant. I knew it was unlikely, but I trusted you. I thought I knew you. Wrong again.'

261

'Ryan ...' I can barely get any words out, and my chest is so tight with panic that I feel like I'm going to choke.

'Go on then.' Ryan crosses his arms, uncrosses them again, and then recrosses them in the opposite direction. 'Explain this to me, because as far as I can see, there's only one explanation.'

'It's not what you think.'

'No?' The group of residents is growing, and he looks at them and then back at me. 'Because what I think is that you work for Landoperty Developments and when I said I was expecting some chap in a business suit to turn up and offer me wads of money, they were smarter than me. They knew I'd be expecting that, and that it'd be easy to refuse. What they actually did was send the one person I'd never suspect. I think they sent you as an inside man – to infiltrate the protest and get the inside scoop on our plans, and specifically what you could bribe us with in exchange for abandoning the protest. I can't see any other reason for you being here. Am I wrong?'

The quake in his voice makes my heart break. He's not just asking – he's *begging* me to tell him he's wrong. If there was ever a time for complete honesty, *this* is it.

'That's how it started, but it changed the moment I saw you. I had no idea you'd be here.'

'And if it was someone other than me, that makes it okay, does it?'

'I didn't mean it like that,' I say, all too aware that I'm digging myself in deeper. 'I meant that meeting you again changed everything. I didn't agree with what I was sent here to do, but I had no choice. I couldn't afford to lose my job. As soon as I got here and realised what was happening, I couldn't go through with it. I tried to get taken off the project because of you and my history here, but Harrison was having none of it. All the time I've been here, I've done the opposite of what I was supposed to be doing. You *know* that. It's my boss I've been lying to, not you.'

'Oh, apart from that thing where you told us all you worked

in a restaurant.' He waves a nonchalant hand around. 'You even went so far as to point out *which* restaurant—'

'I was put on the spot! I didn't mean for anyone to look it up.' I glance at Tonya, who's gone so pale that even her pink hair seems to have faded in the last five minutes. 'I thought I'd be walking into a bunch of strangers who wouldn't know me or care why I was ther—'

'A bunch of helpless old biddies ripe for taking advantage of, you mean?'

'No!' I sigh because it's been a long time since anyone thought quite this badly of me, and it somehow hurts more because it's Ryan – the one person I've always thought the world of. 'I know what this looks like, but you have to realise that I've been helping. I've been doing everything I can to save this place, just like you have. I *love* this place, Ry. I'd forgotten how much until I set foot here again. From that moment on, I couldn't do the job I was sent here to do. For weeks, I've been trying to hide from Harrison because I was supporting the protest and *not* trying to stop it like he wanted. I've been searching for excuses to stay here because I don't want to go.'

He scoffs and turns away, shoving a hand through his hair so angrily that I'm surprised he doesn't yank a few handfuls out.

'We've done this between us, all of us. I've been just as committed as everyone else.' I gesture to the group of residents. Even Godfrey has come back from seeing off Henrietta, and instead of going to his usual bench, he comes down the garden to see what all the fuss is about.

'Fliss has done so much …' Tonya ventures, and I give her a smile because the last thing I expected was for any of them to stick up for me.

'And she's very good at "Guess the Gadget",' Alys adds. If this wasn't a serious situation, I'd laugh. Of all things to be proud of, I'm not sure I'll be adding "Guess the Gadget" to my CV anytime soon.

Ryan's been fidgeting on his feet where he stands, but he stops and looks me directly in the eyes for the first time in this conversation. 'None of that changes the fact that you came here to destroy the strawberry patch – to assist in culling this tree.'

'I didn't know it was here, Ry.'

'I find that difficult to believe.'

'No, I really am that inept. I stumbled into a meeting and didn't know what it was about until I overheard mention of Lemmon Cove and blurted out that I was from here. Harrison had no idea if it was on the old strawberry patch or if there was a tree or not because he doesn't care about things like that. I assumed it was somewhere different because I couldn't even entertain the prospect of them killing the seaside sycamore. I didn't know until Cheryl picked me up from the train station.'

'Okay, *if* that's true – why didn't you tell me?'

It's a simple question that deserves a simple answer, and there *should* be a simple answer but whenever I try to vocalise it, it sounds worse.

'When it's just been me and you,' he continues. 'When I've asked you direct questions about your job. When we've talked about what we've been up to over the years. When I've asked you for recipes, wondered about how you got into the restaurant business … If you *really* had a change of heart, why didn't you tell me the truth?'

'Because of this! Because I was so scared of you reacting like this. Because I know what it sounds like and I didn't want to lose you.'

'Or could it have been because you were biding your time and getting to know us all, getting under our skin so you could underhandedly work out the best way to bribe us? I know how heartless, soulless companies like yours work.'

'Then why would I have tried so hard? Why would I have done anything I've done?'

'So we fell for it? So we didn't suspect you? The point is, I don't know. Because I don't know *you* at all, do I? My mistake was thinking you're the same person I was in love with fifteen years ago, and you're not.'

'Neither are you,' I snap at him. 'You own a campsite across the path – are you seriously trying to say that this wasn't business-motivated for you? That a luxury hotel popping up here wouldn't have had a detrimental effect on *your* business?'

'Do you really think that?' he asks.

'Well, it's okay for you to stand there and hurl insults at me, but it's not okay for me to question your motivations? You want to expand and you've got the perfect piece of land to do it. You *told* me you'd made an offer on this place for your chalets and it got rejected.'

A gasp goes through the group of residents.

Ryan does such a scornful laugh that it should be studied for new and previously unknown types of sarcasm. 'I never told you that because it's not true. I made an offer on this patch because I thought it was the only way to save it. *If* it had been accepted, I wouldn't have been able to afford to expand as well – I would've used the money earmarked for my expansion to save it. But just so you know, when and if I expand into glamping and holiday lets, it'll be in that space over there.' He points across the coastal path to a patch of greenery way out behind the campsite. 'I'm currently in negotiations with the owner about the price. He's sticking his boot in and trying to get more money because there are no other options for land nearby so he's got me over a barrel.'

'Oh, right.' I swallow hard. 'I didn't know that, did I?'

'No, you assumed I'm as corrupt as you are.'

It hits me like a brick has just dropped onto my toes. Is he right? Do I think the worst of people because I *am* the worst type of person? I'm just as bad as Harrison and his cronies.

I don't realise I'm crying until Godfrey nudges a handkerchief into my hand.

'Why don't we all have a nice cup of tea?' Alys suggests.

'No, thank you.' Ryan gestures towards me. 'I've met enough people like Felicity in my lifetime, the kind who will step on anyone to get to where they want to go.' He does that laugh again. 'The funny part is that when things have been bad for me, when I've been hurt and taken advantage of, *you* are the one person I've always thought of to remind myself there's good in the world.'

Ryan never loses his temper. He never did. Nothing ever riled him. We never argued because we always saw eye to eye and agreed on the important things. I know I've hurt him, but I've never been on the receiving end of his anger before, and it hurts more than any physical injury ever has before.

'This is exactly why I didn't tell you. I knew you'd react like this.'

'I'm not reacting to the job – I'm reacting to the fact you lied about it. I've spent the last few weeks thinking you live a completely different life to the one you do. There's this huge pretence between us … And I can't get over that.'

'So, that's it? Fifteen years of being in love with you, and you with me, and it all ends here because you won't give me the benefit of the doubt?' It'll be a miracle if he can translate what I've said through the tears.

'Do you know when I'd have given you the benefit of the doubt? At any point in the last four weeks. If you'd have told me yourself rather than feeding my secrets back to your boss.'

'I don't even remember telling him. It must've slipped out. He caught me off-guard the other day, the patch was busy, and I was trying to tell him what a good person you were. The opposite of him.'

'And the opposite of *anyone* who works for him.'

We stare at each other. Ryan is closed off and angry, and I get the feeling I could defend myself until the sycamore is in leaf bud next spring and it wouldn't make any difference. He will never trust me again and who can blame him?

'Now, I live here, and you don't. So why don't you swan off

back to your fancy London life and all your corrupt friends and leave us alone?'

'Ryan ...' Godfrey says warningly.

He shrugs and goes to walk away. 'Okay, I'll go.'

'No, you're right.' I look at the residents gratefully. I want to go and hug them, but I'm not sure hugs from me would be the most welcome thing at the moment. They must hate me as much as Ryan does. 'This is your place, not mine. I only wanted to stay because of you. Without you, there's no point.'

I turn to the residents. A few of them have got sneers on their faces, Ffion has walked away, Morys looks like he's contemplating how much damage a walking stick can really do, and Tonya's hovering, looking unsure of how to help. 'Thank you for everything. Thank you for making the world a better place. Whether you believe me or not, my time here has changed my lif—' I can't finish the sentence without sobbing, which is quite fitting really, considering how much this place has brought me to tears in the past few weeks.

I turn and walk away on stiff legs, clutching Godfrey's handkerchief to my face.

I should've known it was too good to last and I wouldn't be able to get out of it without hurting both of us.

# Chapter 18

I can't leave it there. That's the one thing I know above all else. When I walked away yesterday, I was intending to pack and go straight back to London, but it felt so wrong that I never even pulled my bag out from under Cheryl's bed. My biggest regret is leaving Lemmon Cove before with things left unsaid, and I can't let history repeat itself.

Ryan was right – I *should* have told them straight away. I should have been honest from the very start. I didn't deserve the trust I had from the residents, who let me in and embraced me as one of their own from the first moment.

So I've been up half the night, teaching myself to make cakes, and then I was up for the other half of the night anyway, tossing and turning and going over and over in my mind how I can possibly make this right.

It doesn't change the sense of trepidation as I walk towards the strawberry patch the next morning, wondering if I'll be barred at the gate and threatened with grievous bodily harm by Zimmer frame, and if there'll be gnomes made in my likeness with voodoo pins stuck in them.

I know they aren't going to want to see me, but I have baked goods and I'm not afraid to use them. I didn't even ask for my dad's assistance because this is my mess and I have to be the one to dig myself out of it. And it only took three batches to get right. I will never be above bribery when it comes to baked goods.

I hesitate at the gate to the coastal path and briefly rethink my tactics. They must hate my guts. Walking in with a basket full of cakes is an insult, isn't it? A few cupcakes don't make up for the weeks of deceit. I can hear the residents chattering from behind the hedgerow and force myself to go in. I have enough regrets without adding this to them as well.

From the joy of Henrietta's visit in the morning to the devastation of my lies being revealed in the afternoon, yesterday was one of the worst days of my life, beaten only by the day I kissed Ryan so many years ago, and I can't just walk away and let them think I didn't care, or that Ryan was in any way right about what he said yesterday.

The chatter stops instantly when I appear in the open gateway. The board game men are back at the chess on a flowerbed wall and one stops and slowly lifts the other one's knight in my direction, and in slow motion, each head turns towards me.

Including Ryan's, who's standing in the middle of the group discussing something with Mr Barley.

'Fliss!' Tonya squeaks loudly, ensuring the dolphin population also know of my arrival.

'I came to apologise,' I say in a rush. 'I brought cakes. I know I'm not a chef, and I know I shouldn't have told you I was, but—'

'You think we can be bought off with fancy cakes, do you?' Morys says.

Well, I *had* been hoping ... I shake my head. 'There's nothing fancy about them. They're just plain vanilla fairy cakes with icing and a ... well, it was going to be a cherry on top, but a strawberry seemed more fitting, so ... enjoy.'

'Lovely, Fliss, thank you.' Cynthia removes the basket from my hand and puts it on the bench beside Godfrey.

The atmosphere is tense and awkward. None of them know

what to say to me, and look torn between accepting the cakes and throwing me out. Possibly both.

'I suppose your dad made those,' Ryan mutters.

'No. I did.'

'So you think cooking a batch of cakes means you become the chef you've pretended to be?'

'It wasn't meant like that. Ry. Can we—'

'One of you will have to mind the tree.' He addresses the residents as he unclips the chain from around his waist and drops it on the ground. 'I can see a campervan over there that looks like it might be stuck, and quite frankly, digging it out with a teaspoon is preferable to staying to listen to this carefully concocted tale, and then maybe I'll book myself in for a nice root canal instead.'

'Ry, please, don't go,' I call after him.

Despite their hesitations, the residents have descended on the basket of cakes, but I stand watching as Ryan crosses the coastal path, uses one hand to vault over a low gate on the other side, and jogs up towards the campsite.

At a loss for what else to do, I gather up the chain like Rapunzel's hair and carry it back towards the tree, but it feels like I'd be overstepping a mark to attach it to myself now. I don't know what to do. I can't just insert myself into the middle of the group of residents and make conversation like nothing happened, and none of them look in the mood for whatever stumbling explanations I can try to give, so I end up standing in the middle of the strawberry patch, clutching the piles of chain in my arms.

'Didn't expect to see you again,' Tonya ventures, holding a cake and breaking pieces off to feed into her mouth.

'Are you the only one talking to me?' I ask as she approaches.

'For now.' She pops another bit of cake into her mouth. 'But wait 'til the sugar rush kicks in. They'll come round.'

I laugh despite how uneasy I feel. 'It wasn't supposed to end like this. It wasn't supposed to *be* like this. The tree wasn't

270

supposed to be here. *Ryan* wasn't supposed to be here. I wasn't supposed to get into this much of a tangle.' I jiggle the metal, meaning it figuratively and literally, and the heavy chain chooses that moment to slide from my arms and land straight on my toes.

There has got to be some karma in that.

'I always said he was waiting for someone,' she says while I shake my throbbing foot.

I look towards where the residents are gathered near one of the flowerbeds. Godfrey is sitting by himself on his bench, his eyes closed and his face turned towards the sun, one leg crossed over the other, his foot tapping to an unheard rhythm.

'Godfrey?' I ask. This confusion happens way too often.

'No, silly. *Him*.' She sweeps her hand towards the campsite, where Ryan has now got his head under the bonnet of the stuck campervan.

'So it wasn't just an excuse to get away from me,' I say more to myself than anyone else.

'Ryan can fix anything.' She gives me a meaningful look. 'The only thing he can't do is tell a girl when he's in love with her.'

She must be talking about his ex. He said people hadn't been happy with him about it. 'He wasn't in love with her. That's *why* he broke it—'

'Oh, not *her*, you daft thing. Honestly, you're as *twp* as he is. I mean you, Fee.'

It's the first time anyone other than Ryan has called me Fee, and it makes my stomach drop as butterfly wings simultaneously burst into life in my belly. I do something that's a half-laugh half-scoff and couldn't really be considered a noise at all.

'And you,' she continues. 'Like Baaabra Streisand's human counterpart, I know a "Woman in Love" when I see one. We've all seen the carving, you know …'

'What carving?' I look over my shoulder towards the tree, like it might provide the answer.

271

'I've always wondered if the "Ry" in it was him, but we never knew who the Fee was, not until you walked in anyway.' She wags a finger at me. 'That love heart isn't for nothing.'

'It's still there.' My eyes inexplicably well up again when I realise what she's talking about. If they've seen it, it must still exist. 'Does Ryan know?'

'He's never mentioned it, but I've seen him looking sometimes.'

'I thought it had faded – another sign we were never meant to be. I keep looking but I can't find it.' I'm aware that I'm giving her exactly the gossip she's fishing for, but I can't seem to stop myself talking. 'Do you know where it is?'

'Of course, this way!' She marches off towards the tree, pink curls bobbing behind her and I have to hurry to catch up.

'Right about …' She squints at the tree when we reach it, examining it like an artist deciding which colour to paint next, probably in much the same way as Michelangelo painting the Sistine Chapel in the 1500s. 'Here!' She suddenly squeals and a nearby seagull squawks in fright.

Her finger is pointing towards the tree like E.T. trying to phone home, and at first I don't see what she's pointing at, but then all at once, the carving Ryan did on the day I left is right there.

I reach out and run my fingers over it. The faded heart shape containing the words Ry + Fee etched into the wood forever, long-standing proof of *why* I risked that kiss.

'It's really there.' I half-thought I'd imagined it. Maybe I'd got caught up in the emotions of it being my last day and he'd just carved a circle or something, and since I came back, I've been one hundred per cent convinced that the fact I couldn't find it was a sign we were never meant to be.

It's in exactly the place I thought it would be, but higher up. I've misremembered it as being lower, but it's there. It's been there all along. Nestled between a carving of a carousel horse and an Edelweiss flower.

'Maybe the tree waited until you were ready to show you,'

272

Tonya says, doing nothing to allay my fears about her mind-reading abilities.

The thought makes the hairs on the back of my neck stand on end, but I force out a fake laugh. 'More like I was looking in the wrong place.'

'It's never too late to fix something that was broken. The tree brought you back here for a reason. You and Ryan have given a lot of us a second chance with the strawberry patch – why shouldn't it give you a second chance too?'

'Because he'll never forgive me? You heard the venom in his voice just now. He hates me.'

'He could never hate you, Fliss. He's hurt and shocked. People react in the heat of the moment when they find out things like that. He needs some time to process things. Apology cakes might not work for a while, but you should keep bringing them in; we'll be sure they don't go to waste.'

It makes me laugh again, but it's not a real laugh. An actor with a cue card up reading "laugh now" would come across less wooden. 'I think I'm going to have to go home.' I say it to the tree so I don't have to look her in the eyes.

'Come back tomorrow, won't you?'

'No, I mean to London. Maybe I can still salvage my job out of this mess.'

'Oh, Fliss.' She pulls me down and forcibly hugs me. 'You're not happy there. You don't even like your job – why would you *want* to salvage it?'

'Because I'm an adult and I have responsibilities.'

'The only responsibility you have is to make yourself happy. If you stay, there is *always* a chance to fix things with Ryan. If you leave now, there *never* will be.'

The tree rustles above us like it's whispering an agreement.

I'm about to burst into tears again when my phone rings, and I can't hide the groan at the name onscreen when I pull it out of my pocket. I'm going to use talking to Tonya as an excuse to avoid him for a bit longer, but she must clock the look on my face because she gestures towards the punnet table where the first few customers are starting to filter in. 'I'd best get back anyway before Mr Barley does something unspeakable to that Jacob Rees-Mogg scarecrow. He's having far too much fun sticking that pole in.' With that, she's gone, and my phone is still ringing in my hand.

'Harr—' I say as I reluctantly answer it, but he interrupts before I can get the full word out.

'Ah, Felicity—'

'I quit.' I don't realise I'm going to say it until the words burst out before I can think about them. I can't take my eyes off the carving. It's still here after so many years. What if Tonya's right? I didn't want to come back here, and maybe the fact that mere weeks later, I don't want to leave does mean something. Even if it's nothing to do with Ryan. Being back here makes me feel more alive than I have in years. Spending time with my dad and sister makes me wonder why I've stayed away for so long.

'Oh, that's useful,' Harrison says. 'Because I was phoning to sack you. Saves me the trouble. We'll mark your date of departure down as the day you left the office, so don't expect me to pay you for the sabotage you've done on my time.'

'I haven't—'

'I've just had a *very* interesting chat with Steffan, Felicity. He's burnt the paperwork I sent him and apparently the land is no longer for sale.'

I squeal in delight, which will certainly tip Harrison off about what I've been doing here. Several residents turn to look at me and I duck further behind the tree because I can't share the news while still on the phone to Harrison.

'He says he was talked out of it by a woman with blue hair,' Harrison continues. 'I wonder who that could possibly be ...'

'Talked out of it is a bit too strong. I only suggested how he could make better use of it. I didn't ...' I stop myself because I'm still lying and there's no need for it now. 'You know what? Yes, I did try my absolute hardest to talk him out of it. What your hotel company is trying to do to these residents is unthinkable. This place is *beautiful*. There's a tree here that's simply magic.' My fingers are still tracing the outline of the heart shape. 'So many people love this tree. This patch of land is special. It's something that money can't buy – something that can't be sold and bought as an object. It has a personality. It has a family.' I look at the residents who are doing all they can to run a strawberry patch despite being mostly octogenarians who probably had no plans to go back to work anytime soon. The number of people we've met who've shared their stories of the tree, knowing that those are just a handful of the people it's touched over the course of its life.

And then there's Ryan. I push myself up to see over the hedge, where he's now attempting to tow the broken-down campervan out with his own truck. Someone who would literally chain themselves to a tree in an attempt to save it. Someone who hasn't been home all summer, who hasn't slept in a bed for weeks, and judging by the activity over on the campsite, was more than likely needed there but made saving the tree a priority instead, because making the world a better place was a priority to him. Nothing changes that, no matter what he thinks of me now.

'What you do is wrong. What *we* do is wrong. We have never, ever made any place better.' I realise that's true as I say it, and I'm as guilty as he is. 'I don't want to work for a company who would even consider cutting down a three-hundred-year-old tree that's touched countless lives, and that's without even taking into account the residents who live here.' I think of what Ryan said about his father's time living here. 'For some of these people, the brightest thing they have in their lives is waking up every morning and seeing this incredible view. Property companies should care about that. Money is not the most important thing in the world.'

'Well, I'm glad you think that because *this* property company no longer requires your services. We're business-people, Felicity. We have no room for sentimentality. I hope you know how much you've thrown away.'

'I don't care.' The branches of the sycamore rustle above me, and when I glance up, I'm almost positive they're bending down towards me, the arboreal version of encouragement.

'Well, then.' He sounds taken aback. To be fair, it is the most forthright thing I've said to Harrison since I joined Landoperty Developments. 'I'll be sure to inform all my friends in the industry of your insolence, should you try to get a job with any of them.'

I expected as much, but it still stings a bit, and makes my already sweaty palms produce so much extra moisture that the phone is in danger of sliding out of my hands. I still have a flat in London. Am I really giving that up? Am I really intending to stay here? I know Dad and Cher won't mind for now, but without a job, and with whatever penalties I'll owe my landlord for quitting without notice, however much it will cost to go back up and collect my stuff ... I try to stop the racing thoughts and quieten the little voice in my head that's screaming about not thinking things through.

'I hope some crummy old tree was worth it,' Harrison says down the line.

'It was,' I say confidently, stamping out my own doubts for a moment. 'It's about so much more than the tree. It's the people here, the village, my family, the whole landscape.'

The line goes dead mid-sentence. I stare at the blank phone screen in my hand. That's it. Four years of my life, over. I expected more, somehow. More yelling. More anger. More acknowledgement of how flipping hard I've worked these past few years, of how much overtime I've done, how many ridiculous errands I've completed on his whim-of-the-day.

He doesn't care. People like him never will. They see nothing but monetary gain. People, lives, nature ... none of it will ever matter to a company like that, but it does matter to me. I don't want to be the person Ryan thinks I am.

I sink down on the grass and lean against the trunk, and the branches wave above me. It doesn't feel as bad as I thought it would. For years, I've struggled and strived to do my best in fear of Harrison firing me, terrified of this very moment, but sitting here with my back against the tree, its solid strength holding me up … It *was* worth it. There will be other jobs for other people at other companies less morally bankrupt than Landoperty Developments. There will never be another seaside sycamore tree.

'Felicity!' Steffan is marching down the patch towards me, attracting the attention of all the residents who are watching him curiously. 'I want to talk to you.'

I scramble to my feet because that doesn't sound good, but he stops halfway down and looks around. 'Actually, I would like to talk to all of you. You all deserve to hear this.'

The residents gather around as I walk up from the tree.

'I've decided not to sell.'

The residents cheer so loudly, but my eyes are still on the campsite and I see Ryan turn to look at the commotion.

'Everything you said the other day is right,' Steffan continues, nodding to me. 'That's why I've decided to keep the strawberry patch, and I want you to run it.'

'Me?' I can't hide how taken aback I am. I did *not* see that coming.

'You used to be a gardener, and you obviously still know your stuff. Everything you said the other day made more sense to me than anything has in months.' He leans a bit closer like he's telling me a secret. 'I think we both know you're not going to get your old job back, but no matter, I want you to come and work here.'

I never even admitted he was right about who I was. It makes a shiver creep across my skin. There really is no one I *haven't* lied to.

'Head gardener,' Steffan continues. 'Full time, all year round.

You can manage everything to do with the strawberry patch in the summer, take charge of the tree visitors in autumn, and do maintenance and preparation during the rest of the year. It has to be you. Everything here changed when you arrived. I can't think of anyone better to turn this place into something truly spectacular.'

'What made you change your mind?' I say so nervously that I trip over the words and ask him what made him mind his change by mistake. The idea of getting to stay here is tainted by the idea of Ryan never forgiving me and when I look down at my hands, they're shaking.

'I've been thinking about it for a while. Dithering, reconsidering, questioning, flip-flopping back and forth. Admittedly I didn't expect the residents to react to the sale the way they did, nor did I expect how pushy Landoperty Developments would be, and I certainly didn't think our little overgrown garden area could mean anything to the general public, or that anything could ever come from it other than a bramble farm. But seeing Henrietta yesterday was the final straw. How happy it made her to come here because of what you and Ryan did. I took over this place to honour a lifelong friend, and he would shove me off the cliff himself if he knew I'd thought of selling it. I've known Godfrey and Henrietta for years; she lived here before her illness took hold. They used to sit by the window in the dining room and hold hands for hours, just looking at the view. Seeing the joy it brought her yesterday made me realise how preposterous it would be for any resident to look out and see the brick walls of a hotel.'

I don't think it had much to do with me, but it still makes me blush with pride. I don't know what I thought the outcome of all this was going to be, but we've all been so focused on saving the tree that I never stopped to imagine what it would feel like if it actually happened.

'I can see what this place means to all of you,' Steffan is saying.

278

'Talking to you the other day, Felicity, invigorated me in a way I haven't felt since before my best friend died. I've been trying to keep things ticking over since then, but you've made me realise that I can do better. I can strive to make it the best it can be rather than keep treading water. Your passion for this place is inspirational, and that's exactly what we need. People who can see the best in things, rather than money-grabbing old fuddy-duddies like me.' He looks around at the group. 'And I assure you I've been called much worse than that, and I undoubtedly deserved it.' He turns back to me. 'I hope you don't think I'm being presumptuous, and of course you can refuse the job, but I could tell how much you loved this place from our conversation the other day, and I can't think of anyone I'd trust more in the role.'

Trust. Not exactly my strong point recently.

'Take your time to think about it, of course, and come to see me in my office tomorrow.' He points towards Seaview Heights. 'We'll get a contract drawn up and discuss the details.'

This can't be real. It's what I've wanted for weeks – the chance to stay *and* to save the tree and strawberry patch, but mainly to fix things with Ryan, and somehow that seems more important than anything else at the moment.

'Well done, Fliss!' Morys claps me on the shoulder when Steffan leaves.

'We knew you could do it,' Alys says.

'Good job!' Ffion pumps my hand up and down.

'You're all being very friendly,' I say as they crowd around me with hugs and cheek pinches and congratulations. 'You're forgiving me?'

'You did what you came here to do.'

'I assure you, I've done the opposite of what I came here to do.'

'No, you haven't,' Cynthia says. 'Your intentions changed from the moment you trod in that sheep poo when you first arrived.'

I laugh at the unwanted reminder. I'm not sure the sheep poo was *solely* responsible for my change of heart.

'We know that. Ryan will know that too.' Tonya gives a stern nod.

I look over at the campsite. Ryan is standing by the freed campervan with his assistant talking to him, but his eyes are on us. He must've guessed what's going on from the celebrations. Ffion's singing "Oh, What a Beautiful Morning" and Alys has climbed into a flowerbed and is kicking her shoes off as she dances.

'Are you going to go and tell him?' Tonya asks when she sees me looking.

I try a half-smile in his direction and he turns away.

'I don't think he ever wants to see me again.' I can't keep the sadness out of my voice, because I don't know what else I can do. Ryan hates me, and the idea of working across the path from him every day is … not as good as I expected.

# Chapter 19

'Fliss, you can't leave,' Cheryl says as we're sitting at the dining table with Dad the next morning, and I'm picking at a bowl of cereal after another sleepless night.

'I can't take that job.'

'You've already told them you will,' Dad says.

'I didn't agree to anything; the residents just assumed I would. I'm supposed to have a meeting with Steffan this afternoon, but …' I trail off.

Running the strawberry patch would've been a dream come true, but Ryan and whatever was happening between us was my main reason for staying. Spending time with him again, reigniting whatever was there before – that was the exciting part.

And now, how can I even think about it? To accept Steffan's job offer and run the strawberry patch across the path from Ryan. I'd see him *every* day. A few days ago, that seemed like the answer to every wish I've ever made. Today it seems like torture.

'You're happy here. Ryan will come round.' Cheryl obviously has more confidence in him than I do.

'If he ever speaks to me again, he will be barely tolerating me. I know Ryan – he doesn't forget things like that. He won't forgive me.' I don't realise I'm crying again until Dad reaches over and squeezes my shoulder.

'You can't *really* be considering going back to London ...'

'I still have a flat there. I can get another job ...' I mumble, but my heart isn't in it. The thought of returning to the city fills me with dread. I can no longer imagine stepping out of my door every morning and *not* taking a deep lungful of salty sea air, and I have *no* idea how I've lived hundreds of miles away from my family for so long, but every time I close my eyes, I see the look on Ryan's face when I walked into the strawberry patch yesterday and how he jogged out so fast that even a brisk walk wasn't speedy enough to get away from me.

I clonk my head down onto the table. 'I've loved him for so long. I thought the universe had finally clicked into place and given us a second chance. I messed it up with him before. I ran away rather than staying and facing him—'

'And what would you be doing if you left now?' Dad reaches across to squeeze my shoulder again. 'Fliss, take it from someone who's been running away from life for years. This isn't the answer.'

'Dad's right. You can't go, Fliss. You'll regret it for another fifteen years if you do.'

She's probably right, except for the fact I'm going to regret it for a *lot* longer than fifteen years. I'm not sure I'll *ever* forgive myself for this.

'Even if you don't take *that* job, you could find something else locally,' Cheryl continues. 'Is Ryan really the only reason for you to stay?'

'What about us?' Dad says. 'It's been wonderful to have you home again.'

'You've found Cynthia again now. And now Tonya knows how good you are with plants, she'll be after you for all sorts of gardening advice. She's already threatened to set up a Seaside Sycamore gardening tips blog.'

'It's not about any of that, it's about you pushing me out of my comfort zone. Making me realise it's not too late for another chance at life.' Dad presses each finger into the wooden table and twists each one in a circle. 'I always thought my happiness died with your mother. You girls know I've been struggling for years, wondering what right I had to carry on enjoying life when she was gone, but watching you dive back in and get your hands dirty, overcome all that awkwardness and reconnect with people you hadn't even realised how much you've missed … It made me realise that I've been shut away from Lemmon Cove too. I've lived here in name only, but you forcing me to come and help has reminded me there's a whole community out there to turn to for support, and that I can help them too. Made me realise I'm not quite as ready for the knacker's yard as I thought I was. It's been nice to reconnect, and to know there are people out there who care, who aren't obligated to look out for me because they're my daughters …' He gives me and Cheryl a pointed look.

'Dad's going to give my summer school class a lesson in topiary next week,' Cheryl says. 'And the school garden needs serious work, I'm going to ask the head if he can come in and help the children give it a makeover when we start back in September.'

'That's fantastic.'

'Kerr family hug!' Cheryl says – something we haven't done for many, many years.

We do the traditional groan, and then get up for a group hug in the middle of the kitchen, and the feeling of being warm and loved with my family makes something unfurl inside me, and I can't imagine not coming back here for another few months.

'What about *you*, Fliss?' Dad's arm tightens around my back. 'None of this has anything to do with Ryan. You've loved being back here and you don't want to go. Why would you even consider it?'

'Because I've messed this up so badly—'

The hug is cut off by my phone ringing and I'm surprised to see Godfrey's name flashing on the screen.

283

'Hello?' I answer it cautiously.

'Fliss, thank heavens!' Godfrey's voice is harsh and panicked. 'You need to get down here quick! There's been an accident!'

I don't think I've ever run so fast in my life. It usually takes ten minutes to walk to the strawberry patch from home, but I make it in under five. Godfrey is standing on the roadside, and he yells my name when he sees me dashing towards him. He must be waiting for the ambulance to direct them in.

'What's wrong? What's happened?' I shout without slowing down. He didn't get as far as telling me who was hurt or what had happened on the phone.

'It's Tonya! She's had a fall. I think her hip's broken. People of our age don't recover from things like this!'

I barrel across the car park and crash through the gate to the coastal path, where Cynthia is tottering on her Zimmer frame outside the entrance to the strawberry patch. 'Oh, Fliss, what a relief!'

'Has someone called the paramedics?' I shout as I run towards her.

'Not yet! We can't find a phone!'

'But Godfrey just called …' I skid to a halt in front of the open gateway, metal panels back up on either side, narrowing the entrance like it was at first. I can see Tonya lying on the ground, surrounded by Alys, Ffion, and Mr Barley. I feel sick enough at the thought of Tonya being hurt, but the sight of Ryan kneeling beside her too makes the nausea double. Of course he's there. It wouldn't be an emergency without him.

'Quick! You go to her and I'll call the ambulance! Give me your phone!'

'If no one's called an ambulance, what's he …' I don't have time to question what Godfrey's doing out on the road. I scramble my phone out of my pocket and shove it at her as I go in, only slowing down as I approach the group gathered around the poor woman lying on the ground. She's on her back, one arm gingerly cradling her hip without actually touching it, and someone's put a folded up jacket under her head.

'Cynthia's calling an ambulance,' I say as I kneel down beside Alys. Ryan's on the opposite side of Tonya's prone position and I stay as far away from him as possible.

'My phone's missing.' Ryan doesn't look up. 'Tonya's is smashed, Alys's hasn't got a signal, the battery's dead on Mr Barley's, and everyone else's is back in their rooms.'

'Hello, Fliss dear,' Tonya says feebly, sounding frail and wobbly. She's one of the fittest among them, and it's shocking to see her looking so shaken and weakened.

At least she's conscious, that's something. The hand that's not cradling her broken hip is hanging limply in mid-air, like she's tried to raise it and given up halfway through, and she's letting out a series of long moans.

'Has anyone moved her?' I ask the others, avoiding looking at Ryan while I try to remember what I've seen people on TV do in an emergency. 'Has she hit her head?'

'I don't know. I didn't see what happened.' Ryan speaks to the strawberry plant next to him, avoiding my gaze too.

'Why has no one called an ambulance yet? Where are the staff? You could've shouted for the nurses in the time it's taken me to get here!'

'What?' Ryan looks up at me, confused eyes meeting mine and then looking away again sharply. 'This happened seconds ago. No one's had time to call an ambulance.'

'Godfrey called me nearly ten minutes ago!'

'What?' Ryan's eyes meet mine again.

Alys and Mr Barley exchange a look, and I watch as another look I don't understand passes between the three of them and down to Tonya.

'Action!' Ffion suddenly shouts.

In the blink of an eye, Mr Barley has yanked Tonya to her feet

285

and all four of them are stampeding towards the exit like those lizards you see scampering across desert sands to outrun a snake. Alys runs in zigzags to evade capture.

'What the hell?' Ryan says, sitting back on his knees like the sonic boom of their sudden movement has knocked him backwards.

'Tonya!' I shout after them. 'Aren't you hurt?'

The four of them pile out of the gate and Mr Barley slams another metal panel into place. Alys slings a heavy silver chain around it, which Ffion padlocks and whips the key out with a flourish before Ryan's even got to his feet.

I look up at him in bewilderment and he reaches out a hand to pull me up. I've slipped my hand into his before I've realised I'm not meant to be doing that, even though he lets go the second I'm on my feet, and we both start walking towards the entrance.

'Of course I'm not hurt,' Tonya calls as we approach the gate where the residents are now gathered around outside, looking pleased with themselves. 'But I'd make an excellent actress, don't you think? I might apply to some casting agencies this afternoon. I'll google them.' She whips her definitely *not* broken phone from a pocket by her definitely *not* broken hip.

I glance at Ryan and he gives me a bewildered shrug.

'And I've got your phone.' Cynthia waves it around in front of her.

'And I pilfered Ryan's earlier,' Alys announces proudly while patting the pocket of her tunic.

Ryan and I share another bewildered look. 'What are you doing?' We ask in unison.

'You can't call for help, and neither of you are leaving until you've talked this out. You love him. He loves you. The pair of you have been blummin' miserable without each other. Fliss, we know you're thinking about not taking the job, but you're not going to miss the meeting with Steffan today. You're one of us now. We're not going to let you go, and you're not going to give up the joy you've found here and go back to a place that makes you unhappy. Ryan, she's the love of your life. Over the years, you've spoken to all of us about your "one that got away" and we all now realise that's Fliss.' Tonya looks proud of herself and does a bow as she finishes.

'One little white lie doesn't eradicate all the good things between you,' Godfrey takes over. 'Take it from an old man who's lost the love of his life to a cruel and unforgiving illness and would give anything for another day with the woman she was. Some things are worth fighting over – this is not one of them.' He turns to me. 'None of us have any doubt that your intentions were good, Fliss. Not even Ryan – he's just too stubborn to admit it.'

'So you're stuck.' Alys claps her hands together cheerfully. 'We'll provide you with food and refreshments if this goes on too long, but you're not coming out until you've made up.'

'*Kissed* and made up,' Ffion interjects. 'Quite a lot of kissing would be perfectly acceptable.'

'You can't do that. We'll go out the other way ...' I trail off as I turn to the other entrance from the care home driveway. The solid wooden gate that's always open is closed, and I have no doubt there's a padlock on the other side of it. Even Baaabra Streisand is gone from her post.

On cue, Morys walks into view on the coastal path, Baaabra trotting in front of him on her lead like a well-behaved dog.

'And we've got your sheep and you're not having her back until you sort yourselves out.' Tonya folds her arms. 'Go on now. There's no point in arguing with us; we're well organised. The staff are in on it so you won't get any help from them either.'

'No wonder no one came running at the supposed "fall",' I mutter.

'Just remember that customers are waiting, and every moment you're in there, the strawberry patch is losing valuable trade,' Godfrey says.

'So hop to it,' Morys calls over, standing at the grassy verge while Baaabra Streisand potters around. 'Or I'll let your sheep eat whatever she wants and you'll have to deal with the aftermath.'

'Have you people ever heard of The Boy Who Cried Wolf?' Ryan calls after them as they all start to stroll away to give us some privacy, although I get the impression they aren't going to go far.

The communal batch of hearing aids must choose that moment to stop working because no one replies.

'They're holding my sheep hostage.' Ryan pushes a hand through his hair and sinks down on the nearest bench.

'There's a sentence I didn't expect to hear today when I woke up this morning.'

He looks up at me, and the moment our eyes meet, we both burst out laughing and something eases in my chest for the first time since I saw Ryan on the phone the other day.

'I can't believe they did that.' He shakes his head fondly.

'I'm not sure if we should be horrified at their deviousness or give them points for ingenuity,' I say. 'Did they really fake all that?'

'I guess they think we're worth it,' he says.

'That's L'Oréal,' I mutter. 'Maybe they've got confused by the TV adverts again.'

He's leaning forward with his elbows on his knees and he pushes a hand through his hair again even though it didn't need pushing back. 'Oh God, Fee, I'm so sorry. I've been taken advantage of by companies like the one you work for and it skyrocketed me back to how stupid I've felt in those moments. In my younger days, I was completely out of my depth and I got stepped on by a lot of hard-nosed business types who only care about the bottom line. The thought of you being like that …' He waves his hands around his head like his brain is exploding. Or like he's doing the Steps dance move to "Tragedy". 'Before the phone call was

288

over, my barbed wire walls had shot up. Alarms were ringing inside my head and I couldn't think of anything else.'

'I don't work for them anymore. I know you don't believe me and I don't blame you, but being here has shown me a different side to what they do, and seeing things from your perspective … what you said about making the world better … I've realised I don't want to be part of a firm that makes the world worse.'

'I didn't mean to be so hard on you. I haven't slept for a couple of nights because I was lying there having flashbacks of all the horrible things I said, and no matter what, you didn't deserve that. When I got back yesterday and they told me about Steffan deciding not to sell because of you …'

'It wasn't because of me, it was because of all of us.'

'Yeah, but you saw a way to bring Steffan in, to talk to him, to involve him. I'd counted him out as an enemy, but *you* saw past that. You found a better way, just like you always used to.'

'It wasn't just me,' I repeat, even though my face has heated up.

'I felt like such an idiot when Tonya told me what he'd said and about the job offer and … I'm so sorry for how wrong I got it. She knew you were wavering about taking the job, and I realised you might leave *because* of me. I was trying to psych myself up to come over when the "fall" happened.' He does the air quotes and it makes me smile.

'Dad and Cheryl were trying to persuade me not to go when Godfrey phoned.' I wring my hands together. 'I didn't mean for any of this to happen the way it did. I know I lied to you, but it wasn't meant to go this far. That first day when I walked in, I hadn't planned anything, and you were there, this guy I've been trying to avoid for fifteen years, and—'

'Is that why you've never been back? Because you were trying to avoid me?'

'No. Yes. I don't know. Seeing you again was both my best dream and my worst nightmare. And that day I walked in and you were there, in exactly the place I last saw you, in the place I made the most embarrassing mistake of my life, and I wanted to be cool and sophisticated but I nearly got impaled by a walking stick and trod in sheep poo right in front of you. And I don't think you realise it, but you're *gorgeous* and it's intimidating, and I didn't want to be this stupid, pathetic girl who still had a crush on you all these years later.'

As if any conversation with Ryan would be complete without Nineties music, he sings a line of "You're Gorgeous" by Babybird. 'But I think that about you. *You're* gorgeous. *I* thought *you'd* think *I* was stupid for still being head over heels in love with you. You're beautiful and sophisticated and successful – and I've never lived anywhere outside of here.'

'But you have a home here. It's only in the past few weeks that I've realised how important that is. You have people who love you; you're a huge part of a community who rallies round when you need them.' I wave a hand towards the blocked gate where some of the residents are still loitering.

'A community who would stage an accident to prevent me making another huge mistake?'

'I'm sorry, Ryan. I didn't mean to lie to you. I was overwhelmed and intimidated and embarrassed and you asked me what I did, and I wanted to be more refined than the foot currently in sheep poo indicated. I couldn't outright say I'd been sent by Landoperty Developments to stop the protest. One of the staff brought out a tray of cakes and I thought of cooking, and then you asked me about it and I thought of a random restaurant. It was a throwaway comment, but then Tonya looked it up and you all seemed impressed and started asking questions about it, and it spiralled out of control, and then I didn't know *how* to tell you the truth, and the more time we spent together, the more I realised what it would look like and how you'd react if you found out.' It's been a long time since I took a breath and I have to suck in air by the time I stop myself.

290

'I get that. And I know I proved your point. And I didn't tell you about the holiday lets to catch you out or anything. I just wanted you to think the best of me – that I was ambitious like the guys you must meet in the city. I've been negotiating about that field for ages. I was ready to give up, but you genuinely did make me feel like I could do it. Seeing how much you've put into the strawberry patch has been inspiring.'

'Seeing how much you love it, how far you're willing to go, has been inspiring to me.'

'Oh, Fee.' He sinks back against the bench and clonks his head back onto the backrest with a long sigh, and I realise how deep the dark shadows under his eyes are, and have to fight that familiar urge to smooth the crow's feet around his eyes out with my fingers.

He opens his eyes and blinks in the sunlight, lifting his head and looking straight at me. 'I'm sorry for my reaction the other day, and I'm sorry for my reaction fifteen years ago. I should have been more adult on both occasions.'

I shake my head, but he speaks again before I can correct him. 'I'm not sure I deserve another chance, but can we start over? Not fifteen years ago, not the other day – right now?'

Tears have sprung to my eyes and I have to bite my lip to stop it wobbling.

He gets to his feet and reaches me in one long stride. 'I made the mistake of letting you go before, I'm not going to do it again.' He holds his hand out and his fingers close around mine when I slip them into it, and he tugs me to him, his other arm sliding around my back as he lowers his lips to mine.

It's nothing more than a peck this time, gentle, cautious, like he's waiting for me to shove him away, but it still makes everything in the world fade out, apart from my heart pounding and the hot flush that flashes through me. His hand tightens on my hip and I press back, returning the kiss, letting him know it's okay, and just as it starts to heat up, he stops.

His forehead drops against mine. 'I have no doubt we're being watched right now, and last time we got too close, Tonya put it on YouTube. I don't know about you, but I don't want *this* on the internet because it would end up on sites far racier than YouTube. How about we ...' He pulls away and jiggles the hand he's still holding, tugging me with him as he heads towards the tree.

I follow gladly, still trying to get my head around the unexpected twists and turns life can throw at you. I never thought I'd be mid-kiss with Ryan Sullivan on the seaside strawberry patch again. When he looks over at me, he seems ecstatic and like he couldn't get the smile off his face if he wanted to.

'They're right, you know. You are my "one that got away". They've caught me at sad and lonely moments and I've told them about you. About how you made my life better, how much I was in love with you, how much I regretted letting you go ...' He squeezes my hand tighter as he glances up at the tree. 'And I will always believe the tree brought you back for a reason, and I'm not going to ruin it this time.'

My eyes close in anticipation and his hand slides into my hair and he pushes me back against the tree trunk, cradling my head right above the carving of our names as he pulls my lips to his. There's nothing soft or gentle about it this time as his whole body presses against mine, and we're grasping at each other, pulling each other closer. I didn't think we were holding back when we kissed the other day, but we were compared to this. It feels like the first time again. An apology for everything that's happened between us and a declaration of love at the same time, and it's a good thing the solid trunk of the tree is at my back because I doubt I'd still be upright without it.

His soft stubble is making my jaw tingle, and I'm not sure if I can hear the wind blowing or just the rush of blood in my own head as every atom in me centres on our lips. Each point where his body touches mine is a burning hot pressure point, and I'm clutching him closer, one hand scrunched in his hair, the other at the back of his neck, my fingernails leaving indentations in his skin.

I can't kiss him hard enough, deeply enough, just *enough*. Every time we need to gasp for air, instead of pulling away, we dive back into the kiss, holding on to each other like we're drowning in it. No kiss will ever be long enough to make up for lost time.

He's panting and I'm gasping for air when we finally do pull back and he leans his forehead against mine, bracing the other hand against the tree because he's definitely holding both of us upright.

'Now *that's* something I should've done fifteen years ago.' He breathes the words against my lips.

I let out a burst of laughter. 'I think we might've been too young to fully appreciate a kiss like *that*.'

He pulls back until he can meet my eyes, his thumb stroking gently across my jaw. 'We were too young for a lot of things, including admitting our feelings, but I'm not going to make the same mistake again. I love you, Fee. Just as much now as I did fifteen years ago. This time, I'm not asking you to stay – I'm *begging* you to. You make me feel like we can tackle anything as long as we're together. The world has been a better place since you came back, and I don't want to let that go again.' He holds his hands out and I slip mine into them and he squeezes them tight. 'I'm in a better position now. I can leave the campsite in good hands and go on trips. I want to go places with you. Visit some of the destinations we always said we would, but always, always come home together in the end.'

I'm perilously close to tears again as I let one hand trail up his arm and slide my fingers into his hair and then trace them down his neck and across his chest, until the magnet pulling me to him is too strong and I pull his head down until I can kiss him again.

'I've never stopped loving you, Ry,' I murmur against his

mouth. 'Every relationship has failed because they weren't you. I can't think of anything better than staying here with you.'

Judging by the whoops and cheers from the direction of the care home, the residents must be watching from the windows, because by the time we emerge from the cover of the branches, the gates are open, Baaabra Streisand's back in her place, and the first few families have come in to pick their own strawberries.

Even though the sea breeze isn't particularly strong, the branches above us are rustling and waving around, and I look at Ryan and I know we're both having the same thought – the tree is cheering us on.

He pulls me in for a hug, his hands clutching into my top like he can't possibly pull me any closer but he's trying anyway. 'Welcome home, Fee,' he murmurs in my ear.

Home. I like the sound of that.

# Chapter 20

'And the winner of the Tree of the Year competition is …'

It's a couple of weeks later and the Tree of the Year ceremony is online, so we're all gathered around Tonya's phone while the internet buffers slower than a dial-up modem, and we wait for the man on the screen to make his announcement after a pause that any talent show TV presenter would be proud of.

The tips of the sycamore have started to turn yellow as September creeps in, and it won't be long before the tree is once again open for wishes as the sycamore seeds start to fall. The strawberry patch is still open and we've put up polytunnels to protect the plants from the first frosts of autumn, and customers are still coming.

'The seaside sycamore tree!' The tinny, juddering voice shouts through the speaker and Alys squeals so loudly that she makes Tonya jump and drop the phone.

'I knew we could do it,' she says as she fishes the phone out of a strawberry plant.

'Congratulations, Seaside Sycamore Tree, you will receive a grant towards the conservation efforts, and we have many delighted listeners who are already booking their trips to Wales,' the man onscreen says.

Ryan throws his arms around me and picks me up, spinning us around, and my hands slide into his hair and stroke his face when he puts me down again. He leans down to press a respectful kiss to my cheek, considering the number of residents gathered round and customers who have stopped to hear the announcement.

Steffan, Godfrey, Mr Barley, Morys, Alys, and Ffion are also here, along with my dad, who's standing to one side with his arm around Cynthia. Cheryl's clapping, and most of the nurses are outside, enjoying the early autumn sunshine with the residents.

There is so much hugging that I lose track of who I've hugged and end up hugging both Alys and Tonya at least four times, until Dad extracts me from the group by clapping a hand on my shoulder and pulling me over to Cheryl.

'I want to show you girls something.' He beckons for us to follow him down to the tree. Cynthia comes with us, and when Ryan looks at me questioningly, I grab his hand and pull him along too.

Dad searches the trunk for a few moments, but seems to know exactly what he's looking for. He rubs his fingers over the indentation in the bark and then steps back so Cheryl and I can see it too.

It's the carving of Mum and Dad's names that they did on their wedding night. One that's been here all this time and we never knew, never noticed it amongst all the other carvings of lives gone by.

He stands in the middle with his arms around mine and Cheryl's shoulders, holding Cynthia's hand against Cheryl's arm, and Ryan's holding mine on my other side.

'I probably should have showed you girls this long ago, but it's always felt too painful to face. The people we love are every-where, even when they're gone. To me, your mother will always be a part of this tree. I've avoided it for a long time, but there's so much love here today that it seemed like the perfect moment. I'm relieved that it will stand here for a long time to come.

I'm crying again. So is Cheryl. So is Dad. There are hugs all round as they walk back up to the strawberry patch, and Ryan and I stay by the tree.

'We did it,' he whispers, squeezing the hand he's still holding. 'We make a good team.'

He leans down to press his lips to mine, his hand sliding into my hair and tilting my head to meet him, keeping it soft and gentle and not long enough with the number of people who are still celebrating nearby.

Eventually, he tugs me over to lean on the barrier and look out at the perfect sea view, and seconds later, one of the branches above us rustles, and a brown sycamore seed glides from the tree and lands on the grass behind us.

My eyes go wide. 'I guess the tree agrees.'

'I've always said it knew we were trying to save it,' he whispers, like speaking normally would break whatever magic exists in this canopy under the branches.

I look up at his laughing, crinkled eyes and wonder if there's something to be said for trees granting wishes after all.

He bends over to pick up the seed and holds it out to me. 'Go on, this one is most definitely meant for you.'

My fingers brush his warm palm as I take it and turn it over in my hand, and eventually, I hold it out to him and nod for him to take half and we break it apart like a wishbone.

Half a wish each seems fitting somehow.

'I wish for the success of the strawberry patch,' I shout into the universe and we both throw the seeds over the cliff and watch as the two halves twirl downwards. The tide is at its highest point so the sea is lapping at the cliff edge and the helicopter seeds land perfectly in the water below.

I let out a whoop and he laughs, grabbing my hands and pulling me to him. 'This one's guaranteed to come true. I think the tree owes us a little magic, don't you?'

'Maybe it's us who owe the tree a little magic,' I whisper against his chest where he's pulled me to him, and his arms tighten as I move so I can look up at the branches shifting above us.

Maybe the magic of any tree is in the life that's passed underneath it while it stands there unmoving for generations, and maybe *that* is the kind of magic that makes wishes come true.

I look over the edge and see the sycamore seed bobbing on the water's surface below. Or maybe sometimes it's pure magic and sycamore wishes made at a seaside strawberry patch really do come true, even if you have to wait a while.

# Acknowledgements

Mum, this line is always the same because I'm *always* eternally grateful for your constant patience, support, encouragement, and for always believing in me. Thank you for always being there for me – I don't know what I'd do without you. Love you lots!

The biggest thank you to an amazing author and one of my very best friends, Marie Landry. This book simply wouldn't exist without you. Thank you for the constant encouragement, gifs, cheerleading and handholding, and for always making me laugh and giving me something to smile about every single day! Caru chi!

A huge thank you to Jayne Lloyd for being a wonderful friend through difficult times, who also gets full credit for inventing 'Guess the Gadget' and an extra big thank you for allowing my characters to play it! Thank you, Jayne!

Thank you, Charlotte McFall, for always being a tireless cheerleader and one of the best friends I've ever had.

An extra special thank you to Bev for always writing lovely letters, always taking the time to ask about my writing, and for always being so encouraging and supportive and kind!

Bill, Toby, Cathie – thank you for always being supportive and enthusiastic!

The lovely and talented fellow HQ authors – I don't know what I'd do without all of you!

All the lovely authors and bloggers I know online. You've all been so supportive since the very first book, and I want to mention you all by name, but I know I'll forget someone and I don't want to leave anyone out, so to everyone I chat to on Twitter or Facebook – thank you.

And an extra big thank you to the Socially Distanced Book Club on Facebook too. This lovely group has adopted me this year and been nothing but supportive, loyal, and wonderful cheerleaders for all my books. They've made me giggle late into the night and run for cover whenever sequels are mentioned! Thank you, ladies!

The little writing group that doesn't have a name – Sharon Sant, Sharon Atkinson, Dan Thompson, Jack Croxall, Holly Martin, Jane Yates. I can always turn to you guys!

Thank you to all the team at HQ and especially my fabulous editor, Belinda Toor, for always knowing exactly what each book needs!

And finally, a massive thank you to *you* for reading!

**Keep reading for an excerpt from**
*The Little Bookshop of Love Stories …*

# Chapter 1

It is a truth universally acknowledged that today is the Mondayest Monday ever.

I've been fired. Again.

I trudge home through the afternoon drizzle that's so well timed it's like it waited for me to leave work. I'd left my umbrella behind and was in such disgrace that I wasn't bold enough to go back in and get it. My boss was one angry step away from fire spurting out of his ears. I think the sight of me again would've tipped him over the edge.

The job had been going well too. I'd been there almost a year, and apart from a few warnings about my clumsiness and the odd wage deduction for breakages, being a waitress at a dog-friendly pub within walking distance of my flat wasn't too bad.

That was before this afternoon.

A family out for a walk had come in for an afternoon meal, and as I carried the tray of desserts to their table, the little boy dropped his monkey directly into my path. I stumbled over the plastic toy, instantly decapitating it with my shoe, and the tray slipped in my hands, and like a moment from a cartoon where an unseen crowd in the background do a slow-motion gasp of horror, the child's ice-cream sundae flipped over, doing such an impressive mid-air somersault that if gymnastics judges had been watching, it would've scored a perfect ten. The ice-cream bowl was deposited upside down on the head of its chosen victim like some missile-based hat.

As the child burst into screaming tears – unsure if caused by ice cream on head debacle, murdered monkey toy, or a fair mix of both – the ice-cream bowl continued its pursuit for gymnastic glory by cartwheeling from the child's head to the floor, at which point the family dog leapt from beneath the table and devoured it. As the dad yelled, the mum cried, and the child wailed while ice cream dripped slowly down his neck, the dog clattered the empty metal bowl around the floor, careening into tables, doors, and other diners, dodging any attempt to intercept him with a speed Mo Farah would envy.

When the bowl was eventually wrestled from the dog with only a few teeth marks to show for its adventure, the family were offered their meal on the house and a complimentary voucher, while they bundled their ice-cream-covered child and now some-what pukey-looking dog into their car to rush it to the vet's, lest it had consumed an errant chocolate chip lurking in the ice cream. We watched in horror as they squealed a three-point-turn, the mum in the back seat, trying to haul the dog away from licking the ice-cream-covered child. The dog got so annoyed that he barfed in her lap to show his appreciation. This created a domino effect of vomiting as the child then turned to puke out of the window, and the dad hit the brakes, causing the mum to lean forward and throw up all over the front seat.

And all before they'd even left the car park.

The upshot is that I was on my final warning for clumsiness so I lost my job, and I'm now responsible for the cost of the family's meal, their dry cleaning, car cleaning, the vet's bills, and the vouchers they took despite swearing they wouldn't come back even if every other restaurant in the country was situated in a stagnant swamp and run by zombies. I also got to spend my last half an hour of the job shovelling vomit out of the car park.

Really, it could've happened to anyone. And at least it gave the other diners some amusement as they ate. I did appreciate the little old woman who patted my arm as I collected my things from behind the bar and said, 'Your luck has to change sometime.'

I wouldn't bet on it. Bad luck seems to have been with me my entire life. Everyone has 'one of *those* days' occasionally, but I seem to have them every day. It's a rare event worth marking on the calendar when something *doesn't* go catastrophically wrong.

At least my flatmate's out. I'm grateful for the small mercies as I let myself into the cramped two-bedroom space I share with a twenty-two-year-old student whose only hobbies seem to be eating my food, sleeping during daylight hours, and humping a string of scantily clad girls who could do so much better. Him not being here to mock me for losing yet *another* job is the only bit of luck I'm going to have today.

I shrug my damp jacket off and shiver, cold and wet through to my skin from the persistent drizzle that somehow makes you even wetter than heavy rain. I need to go and change, but first – chocolate. I go into the kitchen, open the cupboard that's supposed to be mine, only to find he's eaten my last chocolate bar. I was saving that Wispa for an emergency and it's gone. My fingers curl like claws and I shake them at the ceiling. 'Argh!' I shout to myself, grateful for the empty house.

I start belting out 'Chandelier' in an attempt to cheer myself up as I open the fridge and peer inside, on the hunt for any morsel of food he *hasn't* eaten, thoroughly enjoying the uninhibited singsong despite the fact I have a voice that would make honking geese jealous and can't hit any of the high notes. It doesn't stop me trying though.

It doesn't make any food magically appear in the fridge either.

I'm just hitting the last and highest 'chandelier' in the chorus – the one capable of shattering glass chandeliers even when sung by someone who can actually sing – when I close the fridge door and let out a scream of shock, because my flatmate is not out. He's standing behind the fridge door, laughing silently, with his harem of gorgeous twenty-something women gathered around him looking like they've just stepped out of *Love Island*.

'Is your mum drunk?' I overhear one of them say as they walk away sniggering.

I'm not drunk. I'm also not his mum. I'm nowhere near old enough to have birthed that food-stealing Lynx addict. I might have to agree with her on the singing though. And start doing my hair more often.

My hair elastic chooses that moment to snap, pinging the back of my head and causing my wet hair to drop around my shoulders. No doubt I've walked home looking like I've been lying on my back at the bottom of a bottle of gin too. I should possibly start checking my hair before being seen in public. I sigh and gather it up in one hand, pulling my long hair out from where it's already got tangled around my shoulders, pick up my bag and coat from where I dumped them and trudge upstairs, thinking about facing the drizzle again to go to the shop and get some food in. And some alcohol. Definitely some alcohol.

I unlock my bedroom door and go in, closing it behind me and wanting nothing more than to collapse on the bed and pretend this day didn't happen. I dump my stuff and go to flop on the inviting duvet, but I catch my foot on a power lead and trip over, the movement yanking my laptop, which is plugged into it. I yelp and try to catch it as it starts to fall from the bedside table. I leap forward and thank every lucky star in the universe when it lands on the pillow and I manage to get hold of it before it crashes to the floor.

Maybe I was due some luck today after all. My flatmate hammers on the wall from his room next door at the sound of my yelp, telling me to keep it down.

I roll my eyes and set the laptop back on the bedside table, push its lead in right underneath the bed so no one can trip on it and switch it on to make sure it's not damaged.

I've just lost my job, I cannot afford a computer repair bill as well, and I'm going to need it to start job-hunting tomorrow.

I get changed out of my work clothes while it starts up and sigh in relief from across the room in the middle of pulling on my baggy old jogging bottoms when my usual desktop picture of Belle's library from *Beauty and the Beast* appears on the screen.

I finally flop down on the bed and reach up to open my Facebook groups and see if anyone's got any good book recommendations today. Reading about books is the only way to improve this day. I quickly check my emails first and almost laugh at the one with a subject line declaring, 'You're the winner!'

More spam, no doubt. Despite having a surname that begins with 'Win', I've never won anything in my life. That's why I have to refresh my email screen a few times and rub my eyes to make sure I haven't already fallen asleep and this is just a dream.

*Dear Miss Winstone,*

*Robert Paige here. We've just held the prize draw for the bookshop and I'm delighted to inform you that yours was the ticket that came out of the hat. Congratulations! You have won Once Upon A Page! Please get in touch at your earliest convenience and we'll arrange a visit so I can officially show you around your new property and agree on a transfer date.*

*Kind regards,*

*Robert Paige*

*PS: I'm really glad it was you, Hallie. I think you'll be good for this place!*

I take my glasses off and clean the lenses with the bottom of my T-shirt but when I put them back on, the email is still there. And another one hasn't turned up that says, 'Hah! As if!' I know Robert

Paige quite well. He's not one for joking around, and it's the beginning of May so he's missed April Fool's Day by a good month.

I let out a squeal and then clamp my hand over my mouth expecting my flatmate to start banging on the wall again, but his music comes on loudly – 'Let's Get It On' by Marvin Gaye, how imaginative – and the headboard starts banging against the wall as one of the two scantily clad girls he was with starts moaning. Have they really got nothing better to do on a Monday afternoon? The light fixture rattles and plaster falls from the ceiling as the banging increases in speed, and I use the opportunity to flop back onto the bed and muffle my scream in the duvet as I roll around in excitement, and clearly overestimate how wide the single bed is, because I roll right off the edge and land on the floor with the duvet wrapped in a knot around me.

Ouch. My still-damp hair has fallen over my face and I pull it back, spitting out blonde strands as I check my computer screen again to make sure it's not all a dream because that would've been certain to wake me up.

The email is still there.

This is actually for real. I've actually won a bookshop. And not just any bookshop – my favourite bookshop in the world. Well, of the ones I've been to, anyway. And by 'the world' I mean the little area of the Cotswolds between where I grew up and where I live now. I haven't ventured much further than that, except on the pages of books. The world is endlessly big when you have books.

How can this be happening? Owning a bookshop has always been my dream, but people as unlucky as me don't get dream jobs. I've always wanted to work with books, but the opportunities are few and far between around here, and the one time there was a job advertised for a bookshop manager, even though I thought the long three-bus daily commute would've been worth it, two of the buses were late on the day of the interview, and by the time I eventually made it, soaked through from the rain and with a broken heel – torn between hobbling in barefoot or limping in one-heeled, they refused to see me because of my poor time-keeping.

I've lost every job I've ever had anyway. What's the point in trying to work with something I love? Reading should just be a hobby, and I should pursue a sensible career in … whichever job I manage to keep the longest without getting fired.

I'd bought the ticket on a cold and damp January afternoon on the way back to the bus stop after visiting my mum and sister – always a good excuse to go into Once Upon A Page and have time for a browse.

Robert Paige was behind the counter as always, sitting in his chair crocheting blankets to send to war-ravaged children in Bosnia, an unusual hobby for an eighty-year-old man, which just made him all the more eccentric and engaging, like the time I'd gone in one day and found him with multicoloured streaks of long fake hair attached to his wiry white locks and sparkly rainbow nails because he'd let a child in the shop give him a makeover.

On this particular afternoon four months ago, he dropped a bombshell – he was retiring. He'd been the bookseller at Once Upon A Page for as long as I could remember, from when I was two years old and my mum took me there to buy the latest picture books, to when I was a pre-teen desperate for the newest Judy Blume, to now – when I still spend too much of my paltry wages on books. He was a permanent fixture in that shop – the kind of friendly old face who makes you feel welcome, who knows something about everything, and would always, always be there. I could never imagine seeing someone else behind the counter.

And then he dropped an even bigger bombshell. He wasn't selling Once Upon A Page – he was giving it away to someone who wanted to take over running it. And to make it fair, in the months leading up to his retirement, he was selling tickets for a prize draw to choose the winner.

At £30 a ticket, and a strict one-per-customer rule, it wasn't cheap. The amount of books I could've bought for that … I couldn't really afford it, and I thought it was absolutely pointless because the only thing I've ever won in my life is head lice from a boy in primary school, but I don't think that counts. Robert's excitement about his plan was even more infectious than the head lice, and it was impossible not to get swept away on the daydream of somehow being the winner. How amazing would it be to own a bookshop? To get to live and breathe books every day? To get paid for stroking books, arranging books, talking about books, recommending books, and thrusting books into the hands of unsuspecting strangers?

I read book blogs online and am a member of countless Facebook groups, but to actually get to do it in real life, to step out from behind the computer screen and share my love of books with real people? It would be amazing.

I'd dutifully bought my compulsory-purchase-with-ticket book – a cookbook for Mum because I still live in hope that she might actually follow a recipe one day – and handed over money that really should've gone towards the electricity bill, and for a few nights afterwards, I'd gone to sleep dreaming about being a bookseller, about that gorgeous little shop being mine, about me sitting behind that polished mahogany counter, handing out free bookmarks and crocheting blankets for Bosnian children. Well, maybe not the crochet part. Last time I picked up a crochet hook, I got fired from my job at the haberdashery shop for nearly having a customer's eye out.

And then I never thought about it again. Every time I've been in since, Robert's been sitting there with his crochet hook and yarn, and he hasn't mentioned another thing about retiring. I thought he must've changed his mind. And let's face it, I would never win, no matter what. Luck is never on my side.

Until now. I haul myself back up off the floor and perch on the edge of the bed, leaning forward for another look at the email, still convinced it can't be real.

Maybe this is why I've never had any luck in my life. Maybe it was all being saved up for this moment. Maybe fate or the universe or whatever powers that be decided I would have the worst luck in the world, just so on this ordinary day in May, I could win a bookshop, and a new chapter of my life could start.

Once Upon A Page is in the tiny Cotswolds village of Buntingorden, about forty-five minutes away from the rabbit-hutch-sized box someone's had the nerve to call a two-bedroom flat that I currently share with an apparently irresistible twenty-something who barely grunts at me if we happen to be forced to pass in the hallway, smells like mouldy cheese, and never apologises for eating my food, even when I scrawl 'Hallie' all over the packaging, feeling like a college kid sharing a house for the first time, not the mature, adult woman I supposedly am. Waitressing doesn't pay well enough to have grown out of flat-shares by now.

I say a cheery goodbye to the driver as I jump off the bus and skip down Buntingorden High Street the next morning. Skip. I'm thirty-five. I'm not sure what's worse – still living in a flat-share or skipping in public. I've been here many times before because my sister lives in the Cotswold Hills just beyond. There's no traffic through the street, so the bus stop is at the upper end and I walk the rest of the way because it gives me an excuse to go past the bookshop every time I visit her.

The high street looks like it belongs in an award for prettiest high streets in the UK. The honey-coloured stone buildings are tall and the street is narrow as it winds towards the green hills beyond. The cobbled road is smooth under my feet, and the endless fronts of independent shops lined up before me are bright and colourful, with flags bearing logos flapping above their doors, and gingham-patterned bunting in an array of colours crisscrossing overhead all the way along the street. Old-fashioned Victorian streetlamps with modern-day bulbs dot the path, holding up baskets with pretty flowers spilling out. Near the top of the street is the town square, where there's a Gothic fountain burbling away, surrounded by a hexagon of steps, plenty of benches, and concrete planters full of more flowers with bees buzzing around them. Once Upon A Page is directly opposite this little nature idyll in the middle of the otherwise bustling street.

I stand outside the shop window that displays a selection of books for children and adults, surrounded by garlands of artificial green leaves and spring flowers. Robert's goldfish is swimming in a bowl at one shaded side. I breathe it all in for a moment. The smell of coffee from the sandwich deli down the street mixes with the mingled floral scent of the hanging baskets and the indescribable mix of fragrances coming from the candle shop next door. There are bowls of water outside every shop for thirsty dogs, and signs on most doors saying 'dogs welcome'. I'm surprised the street hasn't been used in a movie yet. It exudes a romantic, welcoming, closed-in feeling, like nothing bad could ever happen here.

Once Upon A Page is attached to the only empty shop on the street and the two buildings are connected by a set of steps leading up to a roof terrace that's been closed off for as long as I can remember. The boarded-up windows of the shop next door are out of place on this quaint little road and I turn away from them as I go in the warm blue door with a little bell above it that jingles every time it's opened.

'Hallie!' Robert Paige gets to his feet and sets his half-finished crochet blanket on the counter in front of him as he hobbles over to give me a hug and a kiss on both cheeks. 'Congratulations. I'm so glad it was you. This place can only be run by someone who *adores* books, and I can't think of anyone more deserving.'

It still doesn't seem real. Even as I look around the cosy shop, with its plush grey carpet, miles of wooden shelves full of lovely books, and breathe in the scent of worn leather from the sofa and chairs gathered around a low table in the reading area, and the delicious papery, sweet and musky smell of thousands of books that permeates the air, I still can't believe it. Working in a bookshop is what I've dreamed about my entire life.

'Now, of course it comes with the flat too, and the roof terrace, but the railings up there need reinforcement before you can open it to the public again ...' Robert is saying.

'What?'

'The flat above the shop. It's a teeny little thing but it's served me well. I moved in a few years ago when the commute got too much for me. It's yours now, but you'll have to give me a couple of weeks to arrange for my belongings to be moved out.'

I squeal so loudly that the three customers who are browsing look up from their books in fright, probably thinking I'm here to test the smoke alarms and have started an early fire drill.

A flat too! I didn't even know there *was* a flat above this shop. I hadn't really thought about it. There's an upper floor to the shop, and I assumed the second upstairs window you can see from outside was a storage room. But a flat I can actually live in? Alone? Without a twenty-something lad who thinks a vat of Lynx is an appropriate substitution for showering regularly? It's like all my dreams are coming true at once. I could win the lottery *twice* and it wouldn't be this amazing.

A customer goes to the counter with a pile of books, and Robert pats my hand and quickly hobbles back to serve her, and I watch for a moment as he gets into a deep conversation about the books she's chosen. He seems to know something about each one as he taps the prices into the till and then loads them one by one into a 'Once Upon A Page' branded paper bag. No matter how much I love books, I can't imagine ever being as knowledge-able as he is.

My excitement about taking over this place is tinged with

sadness because I'm going to miss him being here. He's like a grandfather to everyone. A friendly, non-judgemental face, which is a welcome sight on the way home from visiting Nicole, her husband Bobby, and our mum, who lives in an annex in their garden. Robert is a purveyor of books featuring single heroines like me who are happy being single and don't need a man in their lives and no one thinks any the worse of them for it. Books with heroines whose mothers are always trying to set them up with inappropriate men. Books with heroines whose dating escapades are enough to put anyone off for life. Books about women who can be single and childless in their thirties and still be happy and fulfilled in other ways, no matter how much my mum believes otherwise and is eternally determined to see me married off, like some Jane Austen novel where I'll be considered a spinster and it'll bring shame upon the family if all daughters aren't married before the age of twenty. I'm not sure my mum has realised we don't live in the 1800s anymore.

I try not to think about the minimum-wage job and crappy flat. I *am* fulfilled. I'm fulfilled by my overflowing bookshelves and my Kindle, bought through the necessity of not having space for any more books in my tiny room of the flat, and not being willing to leave them in the communal living room where Mr Lynx could get at them. He'd probably use them to swat flies or something else unthinkably awful, if he didn't try to eat them. He seems to eat everything else that belongs to me.

I let Robert get on with serving as I go for a wander around the shop, feeling a bit like I'm floating above it, dancing on a cloud, going 'wheeeeeeeeee'. This is really going to be mine. I don't have to add 'fired from pub waitressing job' to my CV and start the demoralising misery of job-hunting again. I can give notice to our landlord. I'm actually going to have my dream job. This is even a step above chocolate taster for Cadbury's or quality control for McVitie's.

I let my fingers trail along the spines tucked into every shelf.

Old clothbound hardcovers, new paperbacks, and non-fiction coffee-table books on every subject you can imagine. After the open area at the front, with the counter and the reading area, and the tables to display new arrivals and picks of the week, there are endless aisles of wooden shelving that run up and down to the back of the shop. Shelf after shelf of floor-to-ceiling dark-coloured cherry wood with visible knots, each one holding hundreds of books, so crowded that books are piled in front and on top of the spines facing outwards. The highest places are accessed by *Beauty and the Beast*-style sliding wooden ladders attached to the front of the shelves on runners. I refrain from re-creating the scene where Belle slides along when she returns her book in the opening scene of the old Disney movie. It would not be the first time I've wanted to, and also not the first time I've given it a try when no one's looking.

Once Upon A Page is the sort of shop you could easily lose a day in. You can get lost in the rows of tall shelving, picking up anything that looks vaguely interesting, and before you know it, it's five o'clock and Robert's ringing the bell for closing time, and you've accidentally missed the last bus home, but you emerge with a hotchpotch mix including a book of poetry when you didn't think you liked poetry, a romance novel, a book about the French Revolution, a classic that you should have read but haven't, a travel book about a destination you'll never visit, and a children's book you remember reading when you were younger.

Upstairs is solely dedicated to the children's area. Robert has always been a huge supporter of getting children into reading, and while he's still nattering away with the woman he's serving, I go up and have a look around. It's changed since I was last up here. It's a long, narrow area, with white plastic bookshelves lining the walls, not as tall as the ones downstairs and more spaced out, with room for all manner of picture books to be displayed with their colourful covers facing outwards. There's a set of tiny chairs and tables, on which are a stack of printed colouring-in pages and a selection of coloured pens and pencils, and at one end of the floor, there's a polka dot rug with a load of brightly coloured beanbags around it, all in front of a huge Peter Pan mural covering one wall.

I feel the first little flitter of worry about what I'm getting myself into here. I don't know the first thing about children or children's books, and I have to remind myself that Robert is an eighty-year-old man and is probably not the target audience either, but he manages, probably because of everything he's learnt since he started running this shop, and I can do that too. I can learn. To work in a place like this, to *own* a place like this is all I've ever wanted. Any amount of work I have to put in is worth it.

When I go back down the wooden stairs at the right-hand side of the shop, all customers have gone and Robert is waiting for me. 'Would you like to see the flat? If you'd rather stay where you are, you can rent it out for a little extra income. There's access around the back as well as through here.'

I almost laugh at the idea of *not* living in it as I follow him between shelves and through a little office at the back. It's sparse for an office, with a desk and chair, a computer that looks like it was technologically outdated in the Eighties, a few filing cabinets along one wall, and a cupboard under the stairs that's obviously for storage because the door's open and there are folded tables and display stands spilling out. He points me through a door that leads to a narrow staircase and hands me a bunch of keys on a key ring. 'Pop up and have a look around so you know what you're dealing with. I fear it may be smaller than you imagine.'

'It could be a toad's armpit and it would still be better than where I'm living now.'

He hovers in the office doorway to keep an eye on the shop while I go up and let myself in the cream door at the top. The flat inside is an odd shape, long but narrow, warring for space with the children's area on the other side of the dividing wall. The front door leads to a small kitchen and living area in one.

A door divides that from a bedroom that is barely big enough for the single bed and wardrobe it currently holds, and squeezed in at one side is a bathroom.

The bedroom window looks out on the high street, and I rest my elbows on the sill and pull the net curtains aside. The fountain burbles away in the town square opposite, and I watch a young boy hopping up and down the steps while his mother talks into her phone. I remember sitting there reading on my way back from the library when I was young and so eager to get started on the books I'd taken out that I couldn't even wait as far as getting home.

The sun is shining down, making the water glint with the reflection as the noise of the street filters up, muffled by the thick triple-glazed window. Back across the flat, there's another window that overlooks the green bank of the river that flows past Buntingorden, and a back door that leads down a fire escape and out into a tiny patch of unmaintained garden and then onto the river footpath.

It might be small, but it's *amazing*. It's *so* much better than where I'm living now, and I'm still convinced I'm going to wake up in a minute because how can this be real? The unluckiest person in the Cotswolds has somehow won a bookshop *and* a flat, all in one day. My usual types of days are the ones where you lose your job, flood your flat, and walk in on your boyfriend snogging someone else all in the same afternoon. I've had more than one day like that. More than one boyfriend like that too.

When I'm done, Robert is still standing in the office doorway and looking like he's been on his feet for too long. From the bottom, he directs me around the flat's kitchen to make two cups of tea, and when I take them downstairs, he's sitting on one of the leather sofas in the reading area. It's almost in the centre of the shop, down a bit from the counter and surrounded on three sides by bookshelves. You often see students sitting there to study and people poring over books and furiously scribbling notes.

Robert spreads paperwork across the table in front of him as I put the two mugs down and one wobbles in my hand, nearly spilling its contents right across the important-looking documents. I breathe a sigh of relief once the mugs are safely out of my hands. That would *not* have been a good start to this adventure.

'This isn't just a big joke, is it?' I ask as he lifts his tea with a shaky hand and sips it.

He laughs. 'I'm not a joker, Hallie. You've been coming in here long enough to know that. The shop and flat above it are yours. It comes with only one condition – that when you are done with this place, whether it's in two months' time if you decide bookselling is not for you, two years when you meet a nice young man and want to settle elsewhere, or in many decades when you've given this shop all you have to give, you will find someone to pass it on to.

'Once Upon A Page must never be sold. Its legacy is in the love for it. *That* is why it's thrived for so long. Ownership is passed from one person to the next, like I'm passing it on to you now. I took over forty years ago from a very dear friend of mine. He had taken over from his father, who had run it for a number of decades, and I believe it had been passed to him from a distant cousin. The chain goes all the way back until it was founded in the 1870s. Each owner has taken over only because they love books and want to share that.

'There have been hard times, but the shop has always survived. From hardship comes greater strength. The roof terrace was the result of a bomb during the war, and the innovative owner at the time chose to make the best of a bad situation rather than give in to despair. He took out the rest of the fallen roof, reinforced the floor, and built a set of steps up to it.

'Once Upon A Page's legacy is in the love of the written word, and you must agree to that condition before we sign any of this paperwork. This is not a property to "flip" or sell to the highest bidder – and believe me, there are high bidders who are *desperate* to get their hands on it – but when you decide to give it up, you must do as I have done and give it away freely. It doesn't matter who you choose; it can be a family member, a friend, a customer, or a stranger, as long as you know they will love it as much as you do, and will agree to being part of the same legacy – to give it away when their time is done.'

I nod. This is a dream job – the *last* thing I want to do is sell it. And it's unthinkable to talk about giving it up already. I can't imagine ever wanting to give it up. This is a gift, something that will change my life, certainly not something to make a quick profit from. 'How did you know everyone who entered the prize draw would be genuine?'

'I didn't. I just had to trust my instincts. I carefully observed who I offered tickets to. When money-grabbers came in enquiring because they'd heard it was up for grabs on some mysterious grapevine, I sent them packing. I firmly believe this shop is special, and that it has a little hand in its ownership. I didn't think it would steer me wrong.'

'You don't have family to leave it to?' I ask gently. I've never asked him about his family before.

'I'm alone in the world, although I believe that anyone who loves books is never truly alone, and that's always been enough for me. I would've loved a family, but it was never meant to be. I lost the love of my life years ago, but don't you worry about me. I have many good friends all over the country and all across the world, both real and fictional. My head is alive with a million characters who have stayed with me over the years, and now it's time for me to fulfil my final two dreams – to let Once Upon A Page live on with someone who loves it like I do, and to retire to the beach in Cornwall. I've wangled myself a flat at an assisted living facility on the southern coast, mere steps from the door to the sand. It's all I've ever wanted for my autumn years.'

His words make me tear up, and I pick up my tea and turn

319

away for a moment to compose myself under the guise of taking a sip. Pure joy gives way to a little nudge of fear. What if I let him down? Beyond a few Saturday shifts in the now-closed local library when I was sixteen, I don't know anything about book-selling, and even less about owning a business. Is passion for reading really enough? It feels like it is at the moment, but I can't begin to imagine how much learning I've got ahead of me.

Like he can read my mind, he pats my shoulder with an age-spotted hand. 'I was in engineering when I took over. I'd never even considered working in retail. I learnt as I went, and it wasn't always a smooth curve, but the rewards are worth it. Seeing customers happy when they finally come across a book they've been searching for. People asking for recommendations and then coming back to tell you how much they've enjoyed something you've recommended. Seeing children's faces light up as they get lost in the magic of a story. It's not always easy – the hours can be long, the constant carrying and stacking of books is physically hard work, and you'll often have slow weeks when you feel guilty for taking even minimum wage for yourself. But this shop has stood here for a century and a half. I can't imagine a world without it. I've always found it worth any hardship that has come my way.'

I kind of appreciate that he doesn't make it out to be all flowers and rose petals. I *know* he's always worked extremely hard in this shop. It seems like he's dedicated half his life to it. I only hope I can be worthy of the gift he's giving me.

'I'm not going to lie to you, Hallie,' he continues. 'The shop isn't in the best financial position. There have been a few ... shall we say, lean years? I've feared closure more than once, but Once Upon A Page has always managed to bounce back, and I believe it will again, but it needs someone new at the helm, someone to reinvigorate it.'

Reinvigorate it? Me? I do the opposite of invigorating things. There are straw-stuffed scarecrows standing in fields that are

320

better at invigorating things than me. 'How bad?' I swallow hard.

'You need customers. Lots of them. Something to pull people in. This is a busy little street and plenty of folks walk past, but I mostly rely on my few regular and loyal customers. Without something to breathe life back into this shop ... I think we'll be lucky to see Once Upon A Page still open by the end of the year.'

Flipping heck. I knew the shop had been quiet when I'd come in lately, but I'd always blamed it on the time of day because my hours can be quite odd around my shifts at the pub.

'But if I thought that would faze you, I don't think your ticket would've come out of that hat.'

I gulp. It does faze me. He's not just giving me a bookshop – he's giving me a bookshop I have to *save*. Or lose in a matter of months, thereby wiping out a legacy that goes back 150 years.

'There's still time to back out, Hallie ...' he offers gently, holding out a pen.

I take it and twist it in my hands, turning it over and over between my palms. 'No.' I push down my fears. This is the most amazing thing that's ever happened to me. It's inconceivable to think of walking away because it'll be a challenge. Maybe a challenge is what I need. My life needs reinvigorating too. Maybe me and the bookshop can reinvigorate each other. 'I love this place. No matter what it takes, it's not going under on my watch.'

'I knew you'd say that.' He signs some of the papers and hands them to me, getting up to go and fiddle with something at the counter and giving me time to scan through the documents. Title deeds and Land Registry transfer of ownership forms. I try to read them but most of the words go right over my head, and I sign the dotted lines he's pointed out anyway.

'Congratulations.' He sits back down and clinks his mug against mine in a toast. 'You're the new owner of Once Upon A Page. How does it feel?'

'Like I could do with a few books on how to run an ailing bookshop?'

He laughs as the bell above the door jingles the arrival of a customer. Buntingorden is always active. We're in a designated Area of Outstanding Natural Beauty, and tourists love the quaint charm of the high street. People come for holidays in the hills of the surrounding area, the scenery is beautiful, there are plenty of rivers and lakes that make popular holiday spots, and the walks are endless and loved by locals and tourists alike.

The customer comes over and asks if Robert's got a book I've never heard of, and he thinks for a moment and then directs him to aisle seven and tells him to look on the third shelf along at the bottom, and I can't help but be impressed that he could know that without looking it up on whatever stock system he uses.

He must notice because he laughs again. 'When you've worked here for over forty years, you'll know the place like a well-read book too … I'll leave you the basic instructions, but I don't want to tell you what to do. This is your bookshop now. I want you to put your stamp on it and do things your way. It's survived for so many years because new people do fresh things and keep it up to date. Your generation understand what people want better than this old fogey does. You can do whatever you want to make sure it stays here for centuries more.'

It makes me feel a bit teary again as he sorts out the paperwork, keeps what he has to file with his solicitor and gives me the relevant documents that I need. I get the feeling he's been preparing for this day for a long time.

He disappears into the shelves and hobbles back with a book from the Nineties about how to succeed in retail and gives it to me as a present because it's the closest thing he's got to 'How To Run A Bookshop', a fictional book that I really wish existed.

He hands it to me with an aged grin. 'I hope the old place brings you as much happiness as it's brought me, Hallie. I have a sneaking suspicion it will.'

It makes me feel more excited than I've ever been before and more nervous too. Everything in my life has always gone wrong and I can't help worrying that this is destined to be the same. It's more than I ever dreamed of and I don't know how I can ever be worthy of continuing the sprinkling of magic this shop brings to our little corner of the world.

# Letter to the reader

Dear reader,

Thank you so much for choosing *The Wishing Tree Beside the Shore*. I hope you enjoyed reading Fee and Ryan's story as much as I enjoyed writing it, and hopefully you loved getting to escape to the seaside strawberry patch this summer!

I've always wanted to set a book in Wales, particularly around the South Wales Gower coastline, incorporating the beautiful beaches that I grew up visiting, and it was lovely to finally be able to do that! Obviously Lemmon Cove is fictional, but you'll have to let me know if you catch any nods to real places!

If you enjoyed this story, please consider leaving a rating or review on Amazon. It only has to be a line or two, and it makes such a difference to helping other readers decide to pick up the book, and it would mean so much to me to know what you think! Did it make you smile, laugh, or cry? Did the residents' antics make you giggle? Do you think you'd be any good at 'Guess the Gadget'? I don't think I would! What would you wish for if you could visit the seaside sycamore tree in the autumn and throw a helicopter seed from the cliff?

Thank you again for reading. If you want to get in touch, you can find me on Twitter – usually when I should be writing – @be_the_spark. I would love to hear from you!

Hope to see you again soon in a future book!

Lots of love,

Jaimie

Dear Reader,

We hope you enjoyed reading this book. If you did, we'd be so appreciative if you left a review. It really helps us and the author to bring more books like this to you.

Here at HQ Digital we are dedicated to publishing fiction that will keep you turning the pages into the early hours. Don't want to miss a thing? To find out more about our books, promotions, discover exclusive content and enter competitions you can keep in touch in the following ways:

JOIN OUR COMMUNITY:
Sign up to our new email newsletter:
http://smarturl.it/SignUpHQ
Read our new blog www.hqstories.co.uk
🐦 : https://twitter.com/HQStories
📘 : www.facebook.com/HQStories

BUDDING WRITER?
We're also looking for authors to join the HQ Digital family!
Find out more here:
https://www.hqstories.co.uk/want-to-write-for-us/
Thanks for reading, from the HQ Digital team

ONE PLACE. MANY STORIES

ONE PLACE. MANY STORIES

**If you enjoyed *The Wishing Tree Beside the Shore*, then why not try another delightfully uplifting romance from HQ Digital?**

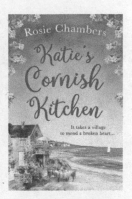

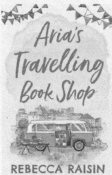

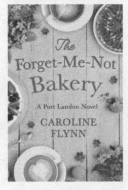